STEPHEN EARLY

ETERNALS OF SHALISTAR

THE SCOURGE OF BAELOR

Eternals of Shalistar: The Scourge of Baelor

Copyright © 2022 by Stephen Early

This is a self-publication
created through blood, sweat and tears.

Published in Fort Worth, TX

Library of Congress Control Number: 2021921414

ISBN: 978-1-7379411-5-6 (pbk)

0 0 0 0 0 0 1

Cover art, map design, and graphics by Adam Potter
apotterdesigns.com

Visit us at EternalsofShalistar.com

Books by Stephen Early
ETERNALS OF SHALISTAR

Book One
THE ENEMY OF MAGIC

Book Two
THE SCOURGE OF BAELOR

For Lorelei

PRONUNCIATION
OF NAMES

Aleph | awe-lef

Daeric | day-ric

Anlace | an-luss

Jeru | jay-roo

Esgar | ez-gar

Iska | ees-ka

Baelor | bay-lore

Agus Tull | agg-us, tull

Lucien | loosh-un

Remus | ree-muss

Rufus | roo-fuss

Viveka | viv-icka

Nephilim | nef-ill-em

Artour | are-tore

Balafas | bal-ah-fas

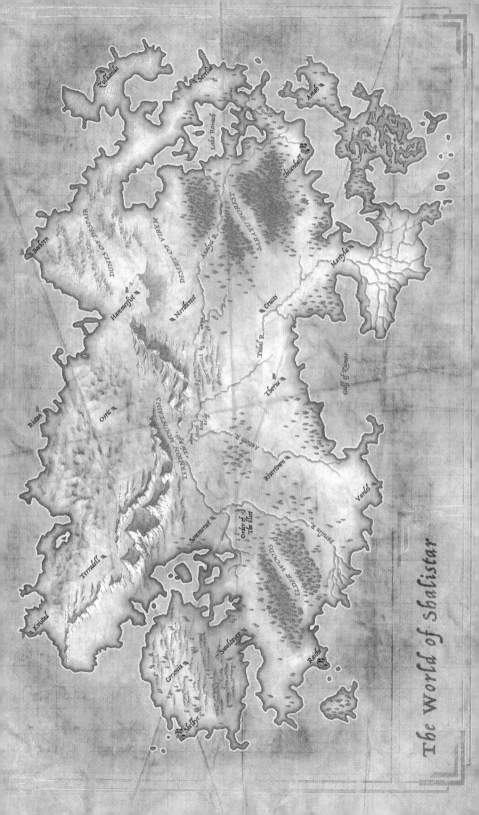

The World of Shalistar

ETERNALS OF SHALISTAR

THE STORY SO FAR...

The world of Shalistar has reached the climax of its final age. Magic and sorcery, the forbidden arts, have taken root in the hearts of the inhabitants. This wickedness is embodied in the form of "The Messenger," a cruel being who offers power and prestige. Those who accept the gift are granted unnatural abilities, but find themselves slaves to Baelor, the unmerciful master of "The Messengers." Born within this world of darkness is a group of warriors who follow the will of Aleph, the creator of Shalistar. Through His guidance, they have kept the darkness at bay for thousands of years.

At the end of the age, the Order of the Elect uncovers a conspiracy to execute the royal family. Under the influence of Lucien, the chief messenger of Baelor, the evil magistrate has seduced many within the world to desire the gifts of Baelor. The citizens of Shalistar now have a choice. If they bow their knee and surrender to Baelor, their lives will be spared. Those who do not will be swiftly executed. Under the cover of night, Aleph helps Anlace and Daeric to find a remnant of people and help them escape to The Rift. Among these is the last survivor of the royal family, who goes by the name of Esgar.

While on their journey north, Father Anlace opens his most precious journal and begins retelling the past. The tragic backstory reveals the fate of Princess Iska and a plan to keep Daeric, the chosen vessel of Aleph, from the clutches of Lucien and his magic-wielding clerics. As the darkness spreads across the land, children are being sent to schools dedicated to the instruction of sorcery. Anlace reveals the enemy's deception, and a vicious battle is fought within the throne room. Roderick, a young cleric, and follower of

Baelor, takes the life of Michael, Daeric's father. Desperately trying to save Iska, Anlace makes a deal with Balafas and unknowingly seals her fate. The unfortunate death of Iska plunges Anlace into a state of mourning, which lasts for many years.

After their arrival at the Rift, Jeru joins them. The guardian announces that a large army is close by, and Anlace is selected to lead Aleph's chosen people as their general. Meanwhile, another directive is given for Daeric to climb to the top of Shaddyia and walk through the doors of Aleph's temple.

A handful of brave individuals, including Esgar, step forth to accompany him. The expedition is intense, but Aleph's intervention enables them to escape sickness, frostbite, and starvation. Only Daeric and Esgar make the final ascent up the steep rock face, to the summit of Shaddyia.

Before they can walk through Aleph's temple, they are confronted by Lucien, who takes a moment to offer them a deal. On the verge of accepting this offer, Aleph transports Daeric within his mind to several key moments in the past and reveals the truth about who he really is.

With the help of Jeru, Daeric resists Lucien's offer. In the wake of his defeat, the guardians quickly take the chief messenger captive and "clip" his wings as a sign of his defeat. Without another word, they kick Lucien off the summit of Shaddyia. With the opposition removed, Daeric and Esgar walk up the temple steps hand in hand. As their quest ends, they open the door of the temple and step through into the great beyond.

PART I

⊂ 2 ⊃

CHAPTER

1

The sun rose in the east, blanketing the Rift in a golden light, as I walked the ramparts of the Ternion Gate. Unease lingered in the atmosphere following the expedition's departure two days earlier. I missed Daeric and wished he were here by my side, but I knew that was an impossibility, so I banished my troubling thoughts and focused on the report being delivered.

"Anlace, the enemy has crossed the North Road Bridge," announced Merwin. "I am sure they have already seen Lionel and Daeric's handiwork and are headed this way."

"Have the groups been assembled?" I asked.

"Yes. As you commanded, we have broken up our force into three battalions. Father Marec and Father Seth will be departing shortly for the shores of the river. They are down in the camp, about to leave."

"And the women and children?"

"They are heading into the fortress now," Merwin finished.

Suddenly, I heard the screech of gears as the portcullis lifted at the south entrance. All the women and children walked through into the safety of the stone keep. The children shouted and ran around the immense courtyard.

Their mothers were not so enthusiastic and tried in vain to call them back to their side.

Several of my brothers saw the situation and assisted the frantic women. Gareth and Mark called out to the misbehaving children in an authoritative voice that immediately got their attention. After several stern words to the little ones, the excitement ceased, and the two brothers continued leading the large group through a door on the left side of the courtyard.

After all the women and children made it inside and the commotion ceased, I went back to the report with Merwin walking at my side. We took the better part of an hour, moving along the ramparts of the fortress, inspecting the walls, and encouraging the few men stationed there.

After the rounds were made, we descended the ramparts and walked back to the camp to see the other leaders off. Merwin continued to speak to me about the hope he kept for Daeric and his expedition to succeed. Hearing my son's name brought a sliver of pain to my heart. I didn't want to have this conversation with Merwin, but I didn't want to be rude. I knew he needed a moment to speak what was on his heart, so I listened and embraced the pain I was feeling.

"I had a dream, Anlace. In that dream, I saw Daeric returning down the mountain, and he was holding the hand of an illuminated being," Merwin stated proudly.

"Do you feel like the dream symbolized Daeric's victory?" I returned.

"Yes. He was holding what I could only assume to be Aleph's hand. That must stand for victory, right?"

"I hope so, my friend. You and I have been together for

a while now, and this is what we have fought for. We can only pray that Aleph's plans be accomplished through us and Daeric."

At the campsite, many men were busying themselves breaking down tents and preparing for our departure. I slowly walked through what was left of the camp, looking at all that remained of our group—five hundred men, and only a handful were well-trained warriors. The rest of them were common folk who never held a sword. As I strolled by, I couldn't help but think to myself, "How many of these men will never set their tents back up again? How many of the women will lose their spouse in battle?"

"Father Anlace!" A loud booming voice resounded, interrupting my thoughts. I turned around to see the large form of my friend and guardian, Jeru. "Might I have a word?" He politely gestured for me to join him. We dismissed ourselves from Merwin, and once we were out of my brother's earshot, Jeru continued.

"Take courage, my friend. Aleph has seen the enemy and sits upon his throne at the top of that mountain." Jeru pointed towards the peak of Shaddyia. "As Daeric draws near the end of his quest, he will meet the adversary, Lucien." I looked into the eyes of the faithful guardian. "Don't worry. Daeric will see the truth of who Lucien really is, and he will resist him."

"Will you help him?" I asked hopefully.

"Yes," said Jeru. "But I cannot go if this army is in the leadership of a general who lets fear be his master." I bowed my head, hearing the rebuke. Jeru gently placed his hand on my shoulder. "Aleph needs you strong this day. Many will fall, but you cannot let that stop you from what he has called you to do. No matter the outcome today, Aleph is in control and will have victory in the end."

Hearing the guardian's words brought courage. Warmth filled my entire being and strength entered my limbs. I stood up tall, placing my hand on Jeru's massive arm. "You can go to my son, now," I said. "Thank you for ministering strength to me. You have always been a good friend."

"The honor is all mine," Jeru said as he retreated several steps away from me. "I will take my leave now. Lead these people in battle, and no matter what happens, Aleph is with you. Your victory has already been won." Before I could respond, the guardian launched himself into the air. We followed his ascent with our eyes and saw his body transform into beams of light. I followed colorful streaks of red, blue, and green until they were lost in the golden rays of the beautiful sunrise. Merwin rejoined us, and we continued moving through the camp, performing our duties in preparation for the battle ahead.

The next morning, I was startled awake by the sound of a loud horn. I heard commotion all around me. Without any hesitation, I put on whatever I could for modesty's sake and peeked out the flap of my tent.

Bodies were rushing past me in a blur. Joining the fray, I followed the rest of the people to the edge of camp. I could see a large battalion of soldiers dressed in black emerging from the cover of trees on the other side of the Antioch River. Merwin handed me a spyglass to look through. As I placed the long metal object up to my eye and looked through the glass, my field of view was instantly magnified. I watched anxiously as the enemy came into clear view.

Many infantries appeared, with a smattering of clerics in their midst. I saw one of them cross his hands in front of his chest. Suddenly, his dark body lifted into the air. He stayed there for a moment, then spoke a magical word and came back down to the ground. I moved the eyepiece slowly and gently up and down the line of trees, scanning the battalion carefully, taking a few minutes to count all the clerics. There were a total of eighty-three.

With the number tallied, I lowered the spyglass and made my way over to where Marec and Seth were standing. They were directing several of their brothers and giving them orders for the upcoming battle. When they saw me, they nodded their heads, dismissed the brothers, and gestured that I should join them.

"Father Anlace," Seth nodded, greeting me with a smile.

"Good morning, gentlemen," I returned. "Were you able to destroy the bridge?"

"We did. My men were working on it into the early morning. With the bridge taken down, it should slow their crossing of the river—at least for now," Marec explained.

"It was a peaceful night," Seth grunted. "Until all the explosions and then the blasted horns."

"Yes," Marec answered. "They are trying to bring fear to our camp by flaunting their numbers."

"True. However, I remember someone recently saying that numbers don't win a battle," I replied with a smile. "I don't see

Lucien or any other messengers in their ranks," I reported.

"Neither did we. It is peculiar to say the least," Seth spoke.

"However, we cannot be caught off guard. I am sure they are nearby and will make their presence known soon enough." We spent the rest of the morning discussing our strategy and how to minimize casualties at all costs. We prepared our troops with words of encouragement, but the tension in our camp was at its peak. When the enemy finally attacked, fear had already done its work.

They waited until the dead of night. A line of black-cloaked troops begun crafting a bridge to replace the one we destroyed. Several of our refugees reached their breaking point and decided to take the battle into their own hands.

With a cry of despair, they came out from the safety of the large rocks that kept us concealed. I heard Marec shout a warning to them, calling them back to the line. But alas, they were fear-stricken and could not hear any commands. We watched in astonishment as the insane group held bows and unleashed a volley of arrows at the enemy soldiers who were cutting logs across the water.

A war cry sounded from a nervous refugee, and the enemy looked up in confusion. When they saw who was threatening them, they began laughing. I heard a loud, thunderous voice split the darkness.

"Allow me to show you what true power looks like!" I heard the cleric shout from across the river. He stood upon a rock above the waters. Before any of us could calculate what was happening, we saw a ball of flame shoot out of his right hand. The flame was then immediately followed by another from his left. The refugees saw their mistake, only too late. The balls of flame hit next to them and exploded, launching their flaming bodies through the air and into the flowing river.

Ten more clerics joined the first and began shooting fire, ice, and electric current toward us in unison. The impressive display of sorcery kept us tightly hidden behind the rocks and trees. Several spells found their mark. I looked down the line and saw refugees ignite in flame. Another pair screamed as they were impaled by ice spears. Trees smoked as the electric currents hit them, rendering them useless as hiding places. The danger increased as the clerics continued launching destruction spells. There was nowhere to go.

"Everyone, behind the large rocks! Get out from behind the trees!" Seth shouted down the line. I saw refugees desperately running towards us as destruction spells landed at their foot heels. The few who made it out alive were shortly huddled behind the safety of the large boulders, breathing deeply.

We could hear the clerics congratulating each other from across the river and laughing at our misfortune. In desperation, we remained completely pinned in this location. There was nothing we could do. The clerics were put on watch, and if any of us stepped one foot out from behind the boulders, they would launch destruction spells at us. Fear was taking hold of our group, with complaining and grumbling from the troops.

"Where are the guardians? Have they abandoned us? Are we expendable?" The barrage of complaints continued throughout the ranks.

"What are we supposed to do now?" I asked aloud, looking over at Seth and Marec. They both shook their heads, not giving any answers. They were in the same dark place I was. In frustration, I turned my face skyward.

"Where are you?!" I cried out desperately to Aleph.

"Right here with you." The still soft voice of my creator responded immediately from within me, startling me in the process.

"They are winning," I responded to Aleph.

"No, they are not."

"What are we supposed to do? We can't move. If we do, they will take us out."

"Wait for me. I am sending you help from above," Aleph encouraged me.

"Are you sending guardians?"

"No," Aleph replied. *"Help is coming in an unexpected way."*

"How long do we have to wait?" I questioned Aleph. "They will finish their bridge soon enough, and then their infantry will be upon us."

"Be watchful, wait until morning, and then tell your men to fall back to the fortress. I will make my presence known shortly."

"Please hurry. I'm not sure how long we can hold out from this position," I pleaded with my creator.

"When you hear the scream of the messenger, look to the sky. My wrath will be swift," Aleph commanded me.

"I don't understand…"

"Look to the sky." His voice trailed off with these final words, leaving me to my own thoughts.

◇

The rest of the battalion was tightly huddled against the rock, on top of each other. Periodically, a magical explosion of fire, ice or electricity would hit to the sides or behind us. But for now, we were safe. So, we stayed put, using each other for support. After several hours of stillness, the sounds of construction began again. The voices around me began to groan.

"Silence!" I shouted. "Enough of that. Aleph is with us. Be patient!" The groaning ceased immediately, and all was quiet again. Then, from the mouth of Seth, came a beautifully simple song to Aleph. He sang the words repeatedly. Hearing it made courage rise within me. Shortly later, I heard Marec's voice. Within another minute, all of us were singing the song from our hiding spot. It was a beautiful moment.

As our voices lifted high, the sun began to rise in the east, and with it came an unnaturally thick blanket of fog. As the queer weather spread throughout the valley, I heard the enemy across the river shouting curses and complaining at not being able to see anything. My mind raced with thoughts as our song continued. I heard a shout from across the river insisting, "They're over here!" and then another responding. "No, imbecile! They're over there."

I told the men to keep singing as I pulled myself up over the rock. I lifted my head slightly over the safety of cover and saw that the fog was thickest over the waters of the river, completely blinding our side from view. Aleph provided us with the camouflage we needed to escape! I watched as explosions of destruction spells erupted far down the line. Aleph was taking the sound of our voices and throwing it into various locations. They couldn't see us and were blindly casting spells in all directions. I ordered the men to keep singing as I moved quietly behind the rocks.

I went down the line, instructing everyone. "Don't stop singing!" I spoke softly. "Nod your heads if you understand me. I want you to break cover and retreat to the fortress at my signal. Aleph has made provision with camouflage. Don't be afraid! He has heard us and is here to rescue us. Now, follow me to the fortress. We are going to continue singing but stay low. Let your steps be silent and your voices be loud."

Under the cover of fog, I was the first to come out from the safety of the rocks. I stayed low, at a crouch, moving slowly back towards the camp. I continued belting out my song as I went along. Glancing behind me, I saw the rest of the battalion following in kind. It was almost comical, and I stifled a laugh at the foolishness of the scene. I saw my men hunkered to the ground, moving slowly, and singing at the top of their voices.

The enemy was baffled. They continued to fire magical attacks at us from across the river. But with Aleph's assistance, they were confused at our location, and the explosions occurred away from us. I even saw several explosions erupt where we were huddled together only minutes before. It was too late now. We already moved from that position.

Before we knew it, our song ended, and we were all safely back at our broken-down camp in front of the Ternion Gate. I knew the enemy would only be stalled for a brief period. Soon they would finish the bridge and cross over the Antioch River to meet us. Hastily, we grabbed all the supplies we could and continued towards the safety of the fortress.

CHAPTER
2

I spent the rest of the day pacing the walls of the Ternion Gate. Everywhere I looked, I saw fear in the eyes of the people. A gloom from Baelor was released, keeping my soldiers and the refugees in a state of panic. Even after the miraculous escape from the river, the people were still gripped by fear. I could sympathize with them because only a day before my mind was locked in battle with the enemy. I was succumbing to the deceptions as well.

To prepare for what lay ahead, I disguised my unruly emotions. I took my time, going from one person to the next, encouraging them and giving them hopeful news. I decided not to mention any specifics of what Aleph spoke to me while we were pinned down at the river. I didn't quite understand it myself, and there was no need to speak in mysteries.

I walked the wall, occasionally receiving a report from Merwin. He was stationed close to the river, watching the progress of the enemy from the shadows. As I prayed for several refugees, he politely approached and bowed humbly to the group.

"Sir. If I may?" he asked, gesturing for me to join him privately. Once we were out of earshot, he gave me his report.

"The enemy is close to completing the bridge. They have over a hundred skilled soldiers working to finish. They are not leaving anything to chance and are guarded by twenty clerics."

"Then there can be no surprise attack," I answered.

"No, sir. They are watching the river closely. The fog has lifted, and they have a clear view all the way to the camp."

"Has everything been broken down? Are we all safely behind the walls?"

"Yes sir."

"How long do you think we have?"

"A day at the most. However, I believe they will finish by tomorrow morning," Merwin said with a tremor in his voice, bowing his head.

"It's going to be okay. Aleph is not taken off guard by the enemy's plans."

"I know, but…"

"We must be strong, Merwin. These people are weak and running out of hope. They need to see confidence in us." Merwin looked up at me with a glimmer in his eyes. "Don't worry. I'm reminding myself as well, my friend."

Merwin smiled at my final comment. "Aleph knew you would make such a grand leader. That's why He chose you so long ago. I will admit, when Lady Iska rescued you from Balafas, I had my doubts. It was jealousy because I wanted the position for myself. But once again, you have shown your strength, and I could not have been more mistaken."

"You are a fine warrior, Merwin, and a devoted friend. I

have no doubt that Aleph has a path for you to walk that will lead you to a place of authority and leadership over many people. But first, let's get through this nightmare that is in front of us."

"Yes sir. What do you need me to do?"

"Get back to the river and stay hidden. Come back as soon as they begin to cross. We need to be prepared for their arrival. The walls will hold them for some time, but they will be relentless until they find a way into the fortress." I thought a moment about sharing Aleph's words but decided to keep them to myself. I dismissed him, and he whirled around quickly, moving swiftly down the ramparts to the stairwell, his white cloak flapping behind him.

The rest of the day was uneventful as we sat upon the wall, watching the horizon, waiting for the war cry of the enemy. I continued to walk back and forth, refusing to sit. A young man handed me a bowl of stew and asked if I would join him and his family for dinner. Knowing my place, I refused gracefully. I needed to keep my eyes and legs moving, so I ate my supper and continued my duties.

When my bowl was empty, I directed several brothers to divide the families of women and children into various parts of the inner keep and designated several leaders to watch the door they were placed behind. With the task complete, I took a seat against a pile of hay and closed my eyes. Within the darkness, my thoughts drifted to Daeric and Esgar. Where were they this evening, I wondered. Did they make it to the summit? As I pondered these questions, I heard a soft whisper from Aleph inside me.

"They are safe." As the words were spoken, I could see a picture in my mind: a small cave carved into the face of the mountain and a fire warmly lighting up the inside. There against the back of the cave was a table with plates, silverware, and a carafe of water. The plates held the remains of a dinner eaten shortly before. Beside the table, huddled in a warm fur blanket, were Daeric and Esgar. They looked dreamily into the fire and were smiling. Seeing the image filled my heart with warmth. Again, Aleph's voice spoke to me.

"They are with me." I felt tears on the brink of overflowing, and I softly replied to the creator my thanks. He showed me my son, and I was overwhelmed with gratitude. *"You need to rest."* The voice continued calmly. *"Tomorrow will be full of trials, and I need you to have strength."*

I looked up and down the ramparts. My brothers obeyed my commands, and only those who were assigned watch were left on the wall. I would take a moment of rest until Merwin came back with an updated report. Weariness of the day and the stress of my position came flooding in like a tidal wave. Before I knew it, I was fast asleep.

"Anlace, wake up! They're here!" I heard Lionel shouting at me from an unknown direction. I opened my eyes, looking into the face of my gray-bearded, elder brother. I slept through the entire night. Lionel took my hand and helped me into a standing position, gesturing for me to look over the wall.

I peeked over the stone and saw thousands of black-cloaked soldiers only two hundred yards from the southern gate of the keep. They were marching into the green space in front of the walls. The sight of such evil before me took my breath away. Without the cover of trees, I could clearly see the expanse of the group. The colossal army was ready for war.

The multitude was broken into four sections. Each one contained infantry, magic wielding clerics, a small unit of riders, and several commanders in the rear and to the sides. Each of the clerics were strategically positioned next to a larger soldier carrying a massive shield. I concluded that this was their protection from any arrow storm and that the large soldiers would give their lives to protect the clerics.

I looked over at Lionel, who wore a cool smile on his face. "What do you think?" I asked my most trusted brother.

"This will be a long day," he replied, adjusting his long-wizened hair into a knot that rested firmly on top of his head.

"For us or them?" Lionel turned his head to me and laughed.

"These cursed individuals before us are going to regret the day they decided to come here and pick a fight with us! Aleph curse them all!" With this dramatic declaration, Lionel turned on his heel, whipping his brown cloak behind him. He moved back down the high wall, encouraging people as he went.

Moments later, I was joined by Marec and Seth. We stood watching the immense army, and for the next hour or so discussed our strategy for defense of the keep. As my brothers shared their thoughts, I found my mind going back to Merwin. Why didn't he return? Was he okay?

We were loudly interrupted as several destruction spells exploded into the walls of the keep. There was a short tremor, and then stillness. I was encouraged by the fact that the walls were high, and it would take more than fire and ice spears to bring them down.

Suddenly, a loud horn blasted from the ranks of the enemy. My brothers and I looked over the wall to see several riders separating from the black army, traveling with a bundle on one horse. I could hear the bow strings being pulled from my men on the wall and shouted for them to hold their fire. As they came nearer, I looked in horror to see the crumpled body and fiery red hair of my dear brother, Merwin, slung over the saddle of the horse.

Seth and Marec recognized it as well, and the same look came on their faces. I made a move and was restrained by my two elderly brothers at my side. "No, Anlace! It's too late for him!" I was stunned as I watched the scene unfold before me.

The riders stopped about a hundred yards from the southern gate. They quickly unseated themselves from their horses and grabbed the body of my friend, pulling him from the horse. I heard a scream as he hit the ground and realized he was alive!

"Let him go, you cowards!" I screamed from the top of the wall. The riders looked up at me and laughed to each other. Then they mounted their horses and rode back into the protection of their army.

I watched as Merwin struggled to stand, but he collapsed onto the ground, crying out from the pain. I noticed a long arrow protruding from his right leg. I looked over pleadingly at Marec and Seth. "We have to go get him!"

"You know we cannot! If we raise the southern gate, they will flood the keep."

"He is our brother, Seth! We cannot leave him!"

"That's what they are waiting for, Anlace. It's a trap," Seth replied. "They are luring us out. The second a white cloak comes out from the safety of these walls; the arrows will fly."

"You don't know that! Aleph has protected us from the rain of arrows before," I replied.

"I'm sorry, Anlace. Merwin knew the risk when he took the assignment," Marec stated calmly. I couldn't believe what I was hearing from my fellow leaders. They were going to leave him to die!

Suddenly, I heard a loud, commanding voice from the ranks of the enemy. "Hear me now, traitors behind the wall!" The three of us looked over and saw a commander on horse next to Merwin. He held an amplifying device to his mouth. "The royal magistrate has sent us here for one purpose. We desire a peaceful transfer. We know you are harboring the daughter of our late King Remus. She is needed back in Raithe to stand trial."

"So, you can murder her like the rest of her family?!" I shouted boldly.

"Not so! The magistrate has a place for her. She will not be harmed. I have my orders, and they will be upheld."

"You can take your orders back to Balafas and go to hell! You will get nothing!"

The commander got off his horse and moved over to Merwin, grabbing him, and forcing him to a standing position. As my brother struggled to stand, the commander lashed out with his mailed fist and pounded Merwin's injured leg. I heard him scream again, and my temper flared. "Let him go, coward!" I screamed from the top of the wall.

"Gladly. Give me the princess, and it will all be over." I looked over to Seth and Marec, who stared blankly at me. They didn't know the identity of Esgar yet and were puzzled at the exchange.

"Anlace! Don't do it!" cried Merwin from below. "Give them nothing!"

"Quiet, dog!" shouted the commander. "This is your last chance!" The commander moved himself behind Merwin and pulled his sword from its sheath. "If you defy me, then he dies!"

"Don't do it!" cried Merwin.

"What is your response?" shouted the commander. I grabbed the hilt of my sword and raised it, commanding an attack, when suddenly a loud noise erupted from the peak of Shaddyia, followed by a blinding explosion of light. A loud commotion ensued as all heads turned toward the source of brilliance, shielding their eyes from the radiance. I looked down below and saw the entire army doing the same.

My heart skipped a beat, and I thought of Daeric and Esgar. Was the explosion signaling their victory? Did they make it to the top of the mountain? Was Jeru assisting them? I turned my focus back to the enemy at hand and saw they were still reeling from the tremor of light. I felt Aleph's presence, and with it came courage. I looked down again and shouted to the commander.

"It's too late! She's gone, and all the plans of your true master, Baelor, have failed!"

The commander winced at the mention of the name Baelor. "I serve the magistrate..."

"You serve none other than the Eternal named Baelor!" I felt as if my voice was not my own. "You have surrendered to his control and have been judged this day! I pronounce that you and the magistrate's army have fallen short! You will now receive the wrath of our true creator!"

As Aleph's powerful words were spoken through me, I felt a shaking all around. It was hard to stand, and all of us on the wall were bracing ourselves to stay on our feet. I forced myself to a standing position and witnessed violent shaking from within the black army. They were desperately trying to hold their position but stumbling over each other. The commander was knocked off his feet as well. I saw him crawling towards his horse and climbing over the saddle. He kicked the horse, and the four-legged animal galloped back into the massive black army with great difficulty.

Merwin remained alone a hundred yards from the front gate, tucked in a fetal position and shaken to his core. His eyes were closed, and he was praying to Aleph. Following my brother's example, I breathed the words. "Aleph, come quickly!"

As if in response, there was a loud, ear-piercing screech that erupted from the skies above. Everyone clapped their hands over their ears as the sound went through each of us. Then I remembered my creator's words to me. *"When you hear the scream of the messenger, look to the sky. My wrath will be swift."* As the scream came closer, I followed Aleph's instructions and raised my head towards the sky. Then I saw it.

It looked like a large, falling black cloud coming closer to us. As the cloud came nearer, I could see the outline of a grotesque black form. It looked like a bird or a raptor with no wings. Its claws were slashing and grasping skyward, desperately trying to grab onto anything to stop its descent. The being came closer, and shouts arose from the army below.

"It's going to crush us! Find some cover!" Bodies began running around, but I stayed locked in my position, staring upward as the monster descended.

"Aleph's wrath is not for us," I calmly said to myself.

The creature, as if hearing my words, turned and fell swiftly, with its clipped wings facing skyward. In that moment, time slowed, and my vision magnified. I could see far above me the amplified head of the beast; its beak like a raptor, and its eyes glowing red. Suddenly, recognition fired in my mind. It was Lucien! This was its true form; the beast was unmasked, and its wings were clipped. I locked eyes with the pitiful creature as it fell, looking at me in desperation. I felt a pang of sorrow and pity for the fallen messenger.

I could tell it was not interested in my pity, nor did it care a bit for my empathy. In response, it screeched one last time. The sound brought me back from the waking vision. I turned my gaze from the falling creature to the army outside the southern gate. They were still reeling from the tremors. Suddenly, as Lucien fell, its shadow appeared in the middle of the massive army. The men looked up at the immense creature and tried to scramble away. But there was nowhere to run.

The chief messenger crashed into the middle of the black army with a loud explosion that seemed to come from underground. A large ring of shadow expanded, until it covered every part of the army. The shaking became violent as the ground underneath each soldier cracked and opened. I watched in horror as the openings expanded into each other. Without any solid ground to stand upon, the soldiers and clerics fell helplessly into the depths of Shalistar. The screams of thousands echoed throughout the Rift until all was silent.

As the shadow passed, all that remained was a pile of lifeless bodies, crushed under the weight of Lucien's grotesque form. The chief messenger was trapped within an island of ground that stood in the center of an endless black void. The island went deep into the depths of darkness. Its root, lost from view, was known only by Aleph Himself.

We were in shock. Only moments before, we were standing before a massive army, about to wage a battle we could never win. But now, the army was gone, and all that remained was the monstrous form of the adversary. I looked a hundred yards from the creature and saw my brother slowly sitting up. Aleph spared him the wrath brought upon the army. I shouted my thanks and commanded my men to bring him inside the keep.

Turning around, I looked at the faces of the people. The hopeless nightmare ended, and we were safe from any harm. Aleph once again saved us! All at once, we shouted praises together. The roar of our applause echoed through the entire valley. As if in response, we saw blinding streams of light streak across the sky and land right in the center of the keep. I smiled as the light dissipated, and the form of my friend and guardian, Jeru, came into view.

CHAPTER
3

The night was filled with raucous celebration. Everyone was ready for a triumphant feast. We filled the courtyard with tables and food, dancing through the night to every known instrument. It was a perfect evening, full of joy and laughter. I sat calmly at a table right in the middle of the festivities, recording in my journal every detail I could remember about the battle we won.

I hadn't been able to write down my thoughts since we crossed the North Road Bridge and being able to sit down and use my pen was a blessing. I was able to pour all my emotions and pent-up frustrations onto the page. It was a place where all the bitterness towards Aleph, Seth, and Marec could be written out and reasoned within my mind. It was my safe place, and the place I loved most to meet with my creator.

As my pen moved over the last sentence, I saw two of my brothers carry Merwin out and sit him gently beside me. My heart filled with warmth at seeing my friend alive and well, resting at my side.

"You are a sight for sore eyes!" I exclaimed, patting him on the shoulder.

"You know me. I'm not one to miss a party!" Merwin replied. We sat there for the next few moments in silence. Merwin was enjoying the cool air as the dancing and music continued all around us. I felt awkward, and the guilt inside me needed to be known.

"Merwin...I'm sorry..." I stated.

"You have nothing to apologize for," he responded before I could continue. "It was all my fault. I didn't listen to Aleph and got too close to the camp. I made too much noise and was shot by an arrow. You can bet I'll never make that mistake again."

"You could have been killed."

"But I wasn't. Aleph spared me, and I am grateful. There are no regrets here, my friend—except for the fact that I have been sitting here for five minutes and I have yet to be offered a beer."

I playfully punched Merwin in the shoulder and stood up. "It's good to have you back." I shouted to several of my brothers to see if they could find Merwin a beer and then moved to a table in the corner where Jeru, Seth, and Marec sat. They all smiled as I approached.

"Father Anlace!" Jeru's voice boomed. "It is so good of you to join us!"

I sat down with the three of them. "So, what are you discussing?"

"We were about to ask Jeru what the next step is in Aleph's plan," Seth responded. "Aleph has gathered us here, and Daeric has completed his mission. Now what?"

Jeru leaned forward wiping a bit of beverage from his bushy

black beard. "What do you think, Anlace? What has Aleph shown you about what is to come?" Jeru asked the question with a smile on his face, like he already knew the answer but was enjoying the entertainment of my response.

"I've been thinking about this all day, and I have several questions." I started listing them off one by one. "First... what do we do about Lucien? He is beginning to stir and will awaken soon. Two... what is the ring of darkness around Lucien's prison? Three...what is this defeat going to mean for the rest of the world? And four...where do we go from here?"

After I finished my list of questions, all eyes at the table rested on Jeru. He sat back, relishing the moment. "Three of these questions I will answer, but the fourth is up to you. Firstly, Lucien is not to be harmed. He will awaken soon and find his way back to Raithe. Second, the darkness is an opening into the eternal void. The ring will be closed soon enough. But first..." Jeru paused for a moment and silently asked Aleph if he could reveal the next part. We all leaned forward in anticipation. After a moment of contemplation, Jeru continued.

"The fissure cannot be closed by human hands. When you leave here and are far enough away, Lucien will call them forth."

"Who?"

"The destroyers of the age," Jeru sadly responded. "The Nephilim."

Marec looked as if he was punched in the gut. "But they were banished..." Seth and I were confused. But it looked like Marec knew what Jeru was speaking about.

"Who are the Nephilim?" I asked curiously.

"As you already know, centuries before King Rian received his crown, there was a rebellion in which a third of the guardians were swayed by the poisonous words of Baelor and surrendered their existence to him. This was unnatural. When we were written, Aleph gave us a strict code of conduct that we were to adhere to. He did not give us authority to have a choice. So, by choosing Baelor, they cursed themselves by going outside of what they were given authority to do.

"Sometime later, Aleph began to write His masterpiece and created humans. Unlike us, He gave you all the authority to have free will and choose. Those of us who kept the code and did not rebel were given the assignment to serve you. And so, we did, and it was an absolute joy! Aleph, in His perfect wisdom, created humans with so many different lives and personalities. He wrote different talents into each one of you. He began writing a masterful story, indeed!

"The days and years would go by in the blink of an eye. Thousands of individual stories were being written within his masterpiece, and we were on the frontlines, allowed to be a part of it all! The guardians would share stories from all over the world, and some humans became famous among us. We would even gather as groups to watch your lives. It was entertaining, to say the least. But we were not allowed to make our presence known unless Aleph specifically willed it. It was forbidden to interact with humans without orders in hand, and those orders could only come from Aleph, Himself."

Jeru looked around and leaned in, gesturing us to do the same. He continued in a hushed voice. "There was in our ranks a small group who became obsessed with the lives of humans. They would abandon their orders and be found in parts of the world they were not supposed to be in. The flames of their desire were stoked by the words of Baelor, which resulted in their demise."

"What did they do?" I asked.

"They would meet with humans and share forbidden knowledge of Aleph. I am speaking of deep mysteries. Guardians know this knowledge, but we are not allowed to share these mysteries with just anyone. They are kept hidden from the view of the world until Aleph allows the mysteries to be revealed. You gentlemen have been allowed access but have only received a sliver of the knowledge of Aleph's mysteries."

These guardians I speak of, however, opened vast amounts of knowledge about the creator, and it caused a series of events that led to a catastrophic ending. Aleph nearly destroyed the entire world and started over. However, his hand stayed, and the story continued."

Jeru resumed telling us about the judgment of the fallen guardians. "Not even Baelor and his messengers dare to cross the boundary of revealing the mysteries of Aleph. These guardians committed the most unspeakable act of treachery and were to be dealt with immediately. Aleph called all His guardians to the Rift. I remember it as if it were yesterday." Jeru's face clouded over with a look of fear as he remembered the details. "Even Baelor and his messengers were there that day. Aleph made sure nobody would ever forget the events that transpired."

"Today, I am grieved. I poured my heart and life into a story of creation. I have given my creation the authority to think and make choices on their own, allowing them an opportunity to go through their lives asking questions that will lead them to me. The greatest reward they can have in this life is to find me, and when they find me, they will want to know more about me! At that time, they will ask questions of me. They will ask questions about me. At that time, I will answer them. Because they have searched for me, I will open all my vast knowledge to them and will share with them the mysteries I have kept secret from everyone else! As the author of their story, I ALONE HAVE THAT RIGHT!

"These traitors you see before you have robbed me of that right. You have been given the gift from your beginning to see all my mysteries; however, you have not been given the authority to share those mysteries with anyone unless I have given you the words and assignment to do so. This day will never be forgotten. I have already gone ahead in time and silenced any of this knowledge from going forth, but this treachery in our ranks must be dealt with immediately.

"As I place my hands on the eyes of these traitors, they will be blinded and will forever stumble in darkness. They will become the Nephilim, the fallen ones. My mysteries will no longer be seen by them. All memory of my glory will be removed from them. They will forever be without knowledge. They will be dumb, always questioning but never receiving answers. You are henceforth banished to the eternal void until the end of the age, where you will emerge for a brief period. At that time, Baelor's rage will fill you, and you will be a part of the final act, destroying the world that I have created."

◇

Jeru leaned back in his chair as he finished. We could see how difficult it was for him to revisit that day. After several moments of silence, Marec asked a question.

"The Nephilim are returning?"

"Yes. They will be the Scourge of Baelor—his instrument of wrath upon those who have been protected by Aleph."

"What will they destroy?" Marec countered.

"Baelor will undoubtedly try to harness their power to further his cause. I'm sure his sorcery will be at work in them too. His rage will be in them as well, which makes these creatures extremely dangerous. With his messengers at hand, along with a large army of soldiers..."

"And clerics," added Seth.

"Yes. This world is at its tipping point. The battle we won here was only the catalyst to usher in the final act. Lucien's fall opened the gateway to darkness, and out of the void will come the fallen ones. The stage has finally been set," Jeru said, staring into eternity, listening to some unheard commands.

"What do we do?" I asked desperately.

"You must leave here." Jeru responded from somewhere far away. Then suddenly he was back and staring at us. "You must go in the morning. Lucien will awaken soon. Upon his arising, he will summon the Nephilim and return to Raithe. His wings are clipped, but he is still a dangerous foe and will not forget the insult I have given him. He will want revenge."

"Where do we go?" I asked again.

"Each of you must take your own path. It will be for you to

decide," he said, speaking to Seth and Marec. The guardian turned his gaze to me. "As for you, your path is Hammerfist. When you get there, stay hidden. The enemy controls the city and has for some time. Aleph will lead you there."

Jeru stood up and looked down at us. "It is time for me to depart. I have been called to assist with other tasks."

"Wait a second." I halted Jeru with my hand. "What about Daeric and Esgar?"

"They are with Aleph and will return at the right time. Put their care out of your mind. You have other assignments that you must deal with."

"Thank you, Jeru. For everything!" I said, wrapping my arms around the guardian. Seth and Marec did the same.

"Aww. You humans always give the best hugs!" Jeru said with a beaming smile. After the embrace ended, he stood up straight again. The party around us stopped, and all eyes were on the guardian. "It will be a while until we meet again face to face. I will miss you all, and I bless each one of you in the light and favor of Aleph." With those final words, Jeru bowed and launched himself skyward, once again becoming a streak of brilliant light as he flew across the sky.

CHAPTER
4

I was sleeping peacefully for the first time in a week. There was nothing in the world I cared to know about and was not in a hurry to have visitors come into my room. All I wanted was to continue my blessed slumber for several more hours.

"Anlace, they have returned!" I heard the urgent broadcast fading into my mind from the other side of my dreams. It wasn't Aleph, but a human voice. I stirred slightly as a hand touched my shoulder. I grunted and rolled over, uninterested.

The voice, insistent on disturbing me, cried out again. "Sir, the expedition! They have returned from Shaddyia!" I recognized the voice this time to be Halsey, my fellow brother. But the words were not coherent to my mind, just yet. I rolled over once again and buried my head in the soft pillow, trying desperately to return to my dreams.

A sudden crash startled me awake. I abruptly sat up and looked groggily at the intruders standing in front of me. "Thank you," I heard Halsey say to Lionel. "I've been trying to wake him up for several minutes."

"Young bucks like him have to be dragged out of bed!" Lionel barked. "He's lucky I didn't have a bucket of water on me, or he would have been drenched." I knew my body was still trying to catch up from lack of sleep and not accepting of the sudden wakefulness. I turned my head toward the older brother near the door and smiled faintly.

"Try it, old man. I'll be on you before you can blink." I stepped out of the soft bed, and my feet were treated to an incredibly cold floor. I walked over to a wooden dresser that held a bowl of water. Cupping my hand in the bowl, I drew out a generous amount and brought it to my lips, drinking in the cool liquid. After hydrating myself, I took a long stretch and turned around to face the other brothers in the room.

"The expedition has returned!" Halsey reported excitedly.

"Are Daeric and Esgar with them?" I asked hopefully but knew the answer before he responded.

"No, sir. They are not."

"When did they get here?"

"Just now. I came to wake you as soon as I saw them. I figured you would want to greet them yourself."

"Your thoughts are correct, my friend." I said with a smile. "I apologize for my mood. It's been a while since I got a good night's sleep."

"You have nothing to apologize for, sir. We all deserve rest, especially you."

"Thank you. Please tell the team I will be with them momentarily." I concluded.

Halsey bowed and left through the door, almost knocking Lionel over in the process. The elder grunted and moved over to the other side of the bed. Deciding he didn't like the current state I left it in, he went to work, moving the pillows and arranging the covers until they showed no wrinkles and were tightly tucked into the frame.

"I never took you for a maid," I teased my friend.

"How long have we lived together, Anlace? Twenty years? Not one time did you come into my room at the sanctuary. If you did, you would have seen how neatly I kept it."

"You're right." I was shocked at the revelation. "It's funny. Now that you mention it, I never entered anyone's room. Isn't that strange?" I reached for my tunic, which was folded neatly on the dresser. "But I know that is not the reason for this intrusion. What news do you have?"

"Lucien has awakened." Lionel said, shifting his stance. The report overtook me, and a shiver of cold entered the room.

"How long?" I asked quickly.

"An hour."

"Are there any refugees outside the fortress?"

"Yes. The late-night festivities caused several people to indulge quite heavily. They somehow snuck past our watch to get a look at our adversary and the void."

"Did you stop them?!"

"We did. But not before the beast awoke and breathed curses on them. They were shaken by it," Lionel replied.

"Undoubtedly! Hopefully, it has taught them a lesson they won't soon forget. Now, what about Lucien?"

"So far, he is not a threat. Any magical spells he has tried have no effect. He tried casting fireballs at the troops who come near, but the spells do not move beyond the dark circle. Aleph has an unseen shield around the void, which is good for us. All he can do is hurl insults and curses at us from his prison." As Lionel concluded his report, a thought, or a strange picture, entered my mind.

"You say his magical attacks have no power?" I asked.

"Yes, sir. It seems that way." After several moments of contemplation, I decided.

"After I have met with the expedition and debriefed them, I would like the entire community gathered at the south gate. Leave no man, woman, or child in their beds. Every one of us needs to be assembled."

"Will do, sir. Now get ready and start your day," Lionel replied with a bow and left through the bedroom door.

After I was dressed, I left the "borrowed" room in haste. It was located on the right side of the fortress, amid a long corridor that held other similar rooms and a common area. This was where nobility stayed whenever they were passing through. I requested meager accommodations, but the people were insistent that I have the softest bed. Not willing to offend, I graciously accepted the offer.

With a good night's sleep and a spring in my step, I was ready for the day. I opened the door to the courtyard and stepped through. I could see my orders being obeyed as men, women, and children were being gathered. I walked through the courtyard, nodding to the people as they greeted me good morning. When I was about halfway across, Geoffrey joined me.

"Where are they?" I asked him anxiously.

"They are in the common quarters, resting their feet and warming themselves. Right this way," he said, with a gesture of his hand.

We covered the rest of the distance, all along receiving many thanks from the refugees for our bravery and leadership. I stopped before opening the door and asked Geoffrey one last question. "Do they look traumatized by recent events?"

"No sir. Not to my awareness," he replied.

"I don't want to put too much on them too soon. They have been through quite a bit."

"You are very considerate, but they are okay. Come now, see for yourself," Geoffrey concluded.

Without another word, we stepped into the common quarters. I noticed a large pile of equipment that was dropped near the door. The contents were cold and frozen. A large pile of water was forming under the equipment as the snow was melting. One look at the rough pile told me this group survived a frozen hell and needed a warm room in which to thaw out.

The group didn't see or hear us enter the large room, so I was able to investigate the situation without interruption. I looked to the right and saw Samuel, sitting on a sofa with his head resting gently against a large pillow. Several other people were with him, lounging on the other pieces of furniture. They all looked worn out. Artour was sitting with ten others at a large table in the center of the room. The volunteers were talking together quietly while Artour was moving his pen excitedly over the pages of a small journal. Undoubtedly, he was recording the events of the expedition in detail.

To the left of the room, a large fireplace was brilliantly lit, creating a warm and pleasant atmosphere. The rest of the group was huddled close to the flames. In the middle, sitting cross legged, were Loretta and Groth. They were holding out their hands and warming themselves. I was pleased to see all my friends in one place, unharmed. There were, however, slightly fewer volunteers than when the journey began. I said a silent prayer to Aleph for His protection upon those missing and asked that He would see them safely returned. I was about to take a step further into the room when I heard an unmistakable voice call out from the left side.

"Well, don't you stand there looking so puddle glum! Get over here and give me a hug!" Loretta saw me and bounced over to where we stood. I looked at Geoffrey with a smile and stepped toward the fun-loving woman with short dark hair and a beaming smile. She met me with an embrace that almost lifted me off the ground.

"You sure do have quite a bit of strength in you!" I exclaimed as my feet came to rest back on the floor. "I would not believe it to look at you."

"It's okay, sir. All the people in my family are small," Loretta began to explain. "But we sure do eat healthy. My mother always made me eat all my veggies and clear my plate. Plus, I keep a steady regimen of herbs each day that boost the immune system and create a lot of energy. I could get you on the same schedule. It works wonders!"

I let out a chuckle. "Perhaps so. I could always use a shift in my diet."

Loretta continued speaking. "Aleph knows, Groth sure won't do it. I've tried to get him to eat his veggies for our entire marriage. You could sooner push an alligator over a cliff!"

"Are you saying something about me?" The loud, booming voice of Loretta's husband rang out, and moments later we were joined by the tall muscular man with thinning blonde hair.

"Just telling them about your terrible eating habits," Loretta said with her arms crossed.

"And what is that supposed to mean?" Groth countered.

"That you continually decide to live on an all-protein diet."

"Sorry, my love. Life is too short to eat veggies!"

Loretta looked my way and shrugged. "You see what I mean?" I realized at that moment every eye in the room was focused on the three of us and were waiting in sheer anticipation of what was going to happen next. An awkward silence followed as I thought about my next words. Suddenly, another voice resounded from the other side.

"Enough bickering, you two!" Samuel cried out as he leapt over the sofa and threw himself into my arms. "It's good to see you, Anlace!"

"It is good to see you too, Samuel. I am glad you are safe." I then turned my attention to all the rest of the people in the room. "I am happy that you all are safe, and I thank you for your bravery! You helped Daeric and Esgar finish their mission, bringing us a victory." There was mutual agreement and commotion from all gathered and after we exchanged greetings, I asked them to sit down so I could hear about their journey into the heights of Shaddyia.

Artour took the next half hour laying out the quest. He described how Aleph provided food for them every day from the brown bag in Daeric's backpack and how the meal was different every time they opened it up. Artour allowed me a moment to ask questions before he continued. He then told me how Loretta was sick and in critical condition until Aleph breathed over the camp and healed her.

His story became animated and dramatic as he described how the group became separated after Groth almost fell to his death in an icy crevasse. He retold how the strength and courage of the group rescued Groth from the abyss. Finally, he spoke about the trip back down and how the wind was at their backs, carrying them in half the amount of time, down the mountain and to the Rift. When all was described in full detail, Artour sat back with a look of satisfaction.

I gave everyone my thanks once again and began to debrief them on the Battle of the Rift and the glorious outcome. It took me longer than I'd thought it would, and my story was met with every kind of emotion and reaction. Faces of shock and awe stared back at me. I concluded by telling them how Jeru gave us instructions to leave the Rift and how we needed to go quickly away from here. I allowed several questions from the group and commanded everyone to meet at the south gate. There was something extremely specific that I felt like Aleph wanted us to do.

A brief time later, I stood atop the wall above the southern gate, gazing out over the crowd. Everyone was assembled and waiting eagerly for me to speak. I was facing the enemy, who was imprisoned on an island anchored over a void of endless darkness. The crowd was staring up at me in anticipation.

Until this moment, I didn't know what I was going to say. I saw an image of us walking around the perimeter of the black void. Other than that, I wasn't sure what was going to happen. But as I stood there in front of the community, my heart was flooded with words. Taking a deep breath, I opened my mouth and spoke.

"We have won a mighty victory. The army commissioned to see to our destruction has tested the hand of Aleph and fallen short of his glory. That army has been destroyed!" The crowd roared their applause to the creator. After several moments, I raised a hand, and all went silent.

"Until now, I was unsure of how to proceed. But now I speak to each of you in authority and confidence. Your bravery has been recorded in the annals of time! With great courage, you have followed Aleph to the Rift and stayed strong, even in the face of overwhelming opposition. Aleph thanks you for your obedience. Each of you has a path to walk upon. Our remnant will now be dispersed throughout the entire world. You are to go where He leads you and be the light within this world of darkness." The crowd began to softly murmur as I continued.

"The enemy imprisoned before you is named Lucien. It is the chief messenger of Baelor. After we have left the Rift, Aleph will release this foul creature from its prison. When Lucien returns to Raithe, this world will undergo a period of destruction beyond imagination." The crowd began to groan at the mention of calamity. I raised my hand once again, and the crowd was quiet. "Our assignment is to bring hope to those who have none. The people will be lost and desperate, seeking for answers. Lucien's messengers will be everywhere, offering Baelor's gift as the solution to their misery. We are to stand amid this darkness and let the light of Aleph shine bright!

"We will all leave together through this gate. Simply ask Aleph where He wants you to go, and when He responds, head in that direction. Don't worry about provisions. He will provide everything you need as you make your way toward your destination. But before we go, Aleph has asked that every one of us walk around the perimeter of the dark void and look upon the true form of your nemesis.

"Take note of several things. First, its wings are clipped. Aleph has punished this beast for its pride. It will now move slowly throughout this world, having to rely more than ever on humans to conduct its plans.

"It is also important for you to see the hideous image of its true form. This enemy has been revealed to you. Even though it will don a human disguise upon its return to Raithe, within your mind, you will see the enemy for who it really is. With this revelation in mind, you will go and free others who are trapped within the deception of the enemy.

"Finally, notice the prison it is in. Unless Aleph wills it, Lucien cannot step beyond the boundaries of this island. It is completely at the mercy of our creator. This prison is only a glimpse of its future. In the end, it will be much worse, and Lucien knows that. Its goal is to gather many to its master until the final hour. This enemy has already been defeated, as you can clearly see. It is now time for you to take this knowledge with you into the world. There are many trapped within the sorcery of Baelor and it's time to set them free!" As I concluded my speech, the roar of the crowd reached its apex.

I spent the next hour witnessing the entire community

walking slowly around the perimeter of the black void. Men, women, and children marched together, singing songs of praise to Aleph, and gazing at the true form of Lucien within its prison. As songs blasted forth, the abomination covered its ears with its grotesque claws but was unable to keep the beautiful sounds from being heard.

The beast tried to throw itself into the void to drown out the noise but hit an invisible barrier every time it came close to the edge. The people continued to sing and walk around the void. Suddenly, an explosion of fire and ice hit the invisible barrier. In desperation, Lucien tried to hurl destruction spells at the people but was unable to do so. As the spells failed, the people cheered and sang louder. They all continued to circle the enemy several more times. All one could hear for miles was a beautiful chorus being sung by the community and mixed in with it was the inharmonious sounds of screeching and agony that came from Lucien as he was reminded of his inferiority.

By the end of the day, the fortress was empty. I was alone on the wall watching the last of the community leave the open expanse of the Rift. All that could be heard were the animals and birds as they hunted for their evening supper. I looked out and saw the enemy curled up in a fetal position, completely worn out from the events of the day. It looked miserable and pathetic, and I couldn't help but feel a bit of compassion for the beast.

"Am I right to feel this way?" I asked Aleph.

"*Of course, you are,*" he replied from within.

"Even towards the enemy?"

"My love is for ALL creation. Including my enemies."

I looked around at the empty courtyard below me. "It looks like it's just you and I left," I said as I began walking down the stairs.

"I wouldn't necessarily say that," Aleph returned.

"What do you mean?"

"I have made special arrangements. It is dangerous to go alone."

"But I'm not alone. I have you."

"Correct, but it would also benefit you to have companions for your journey to Hammerfist. Human interaction never hurt anyone."

"But everyone is gone," I replied.

"Don't worry. They are on their way back. Get a good night's rest. You will leave in the morning."

With that, I went back to my borrowed room and closed the door. It was a long day for me, and I was exhausted, looking forward to another night of rest in a soft, warm bed. Before I could muster another thought, I drifted off into a deep, deep sleep.

"Anlace!" A voice spoke to me from somewhere on the other side of my dreams.

"Get up, young buck! Before I douse you with water!" Another voice called to me, this one gruff and impatient.

"Get up, sleepy head! I'm making sausage and eggs! Everyone's favorite." Still another voice rang out, this time joyful and quick of speech.

"Sir, you've been asleep long enough. I think it's the right time we got on the road!" I began to come out of the dream I was in. The room slowly came into view, as I saw several figures standing at the foot of the bed.

"There you are sleepy head! It's about time!" Loretta exclaimed.

"Another second more and it would have been the water bucket for you," barked Lionel.

"Sir, the sun is up, and the day has started. We must get on the road if we are going to make it to Northcrest," Merwin reported.

Suddenly, the door opened to the sound of an internal debate. The large man who entered was covered in dried mud. "I knew I should have fastened the reins tighter," exclaimed Groth. "I've been putting harnesses on horses since the dawn of time! I should have known better."

The brute looked down at me still in bed. "Oh, good, you're awake!" At that final comment, I laid myself back into the soft mattress of the bed and sighed a deep breath.

"So, this is what you had in mind?" I silently asked my creator. "This is certainly going to be an interesting adventure."

CHAPTER
5

The weather was perfect for traveling. With clear skies and the warmth of the sun shining brightly, we were all anxious to get on the road and begin our journey. The trees of the valley moved softly as the wind blew through the leaves, swaying the branches back and forth, as though they were dancing in ethereal harmony. Small animals came out of hiding to catch breakfast in the tall grass. I decided a final inspection would be in order and began making a list of all we packed.

Provisions were loaded onto two carts. There was plenty of meat, cheese, fruit, grains, and some veggies. Tucked securely up against the back of one cart was a medium-sized chest that I didn't recognize. I reached in and opened it to find a collection of different jars and bottles full of grains and powders of all kinds. A potent aroma filled my nostrils as I scanned the bottles. I could only imagine how many different results could be realized with the contents of this chest. There was a response to my thoughts as Loretta swiftly jumped into the front seat of the cart.

"This is all I could muster in a night," Loretta stated as she stared back at me. "Spices to make any dish taste delectable and special powders to create some pretty amazing explosions!"

"I don't doubt it. I witnessed the aftermath of your "creations" at the North Road Bridge," I returned sarcastically. "Did you happen to pack anything for sores and wounds?"

"Yes, but I don't keep those locked up, silly bear! Those vials I always keep on me," she said, patting a unique leather utility belt that was buckled around her waist. Along the left side were a line of colorful vials that were attached to the belt.

"These herbs and powders are incredibly special and quite rare. We took several trips all the way to the cliffs of Vardel to find these ingredients. Groth isn't as adventurous as I am. He had a tough time going into all those caves." She leaned forward and whispered, "Groth is afraid of dark caves! They give him the jitters!"

"What's that you're saying?" boomed the large man's voice.

"Nothing, darling!" returned Loretta, feigning innocence. She looked back at me and winked. "He did it because he loves me and knows that I love my herbs."

I smiled as Loretta finished her short tale. I was hugely impressed at the companions Aleph had given me for this journey. I let the thought of their skills and how they would come into play, entertain my mind as I finished taking stock of our supplies. As I came to the cart I would be driving, I opened the compartment under the bench and noticed something that took me by surprise. Sitting in the compartment were six bundles, neatly wrapped in parchment. I was curious and opened one of the packages to see what was inside.

They looked like simple, old brown cloaks, but upon further inspection, I noticed they were in fact white cloaks, camouflaged by an old brown fabric. The plain, dirty brown material was sewn over the white cloak, hiding them from plain sight. I smiled as I moved my fingers over the expert stitching. Just as before when Lionel and Daeric infiltrated the enemy camp, Aleph provided us again with a way to keep ourselves protected from magic. This would also allow us to keep hidden our identity as members of the order.

I made a final inventory of all the supplies in my journal and called everyone together. Our carts were outside the gate, facing southeast. Merwin was resting in the back of my cart within a soft bed of hay and blankets. His wound was healing quickly, thanks to one of Loretta's special balms.

In the other cart, the vibrant married couple began bickering about who was going to steer. Overhearing the argument, Lionel let out a grunt and quickly moved his horse over to our side, away from the two. Together, we stared out into the beautiful green valley towards the fork where the great river separated, creating the Analyd River, which flowed southeast. Suddenly, there was a screech, and we all turned back towards the void and the creature trapped in its prison.

"What do we do about that?" Loretta asked, nervously.

"Nothing. It is in Aleph's hands now. After we are safely away, Lucien will be released—along with the Nephilim." The weight of my words overwhelmed me. I looked over at Lionel and sensed he was feeling the same way.

"Never in my life did I ever think I would hear those words," said Lionel, shaking his head.

"We better be off then. I want to be far away from here when they come out of that void!" Groth countered. We all agreed, and without another word, the caravan moved southeast, toward the river.

We made swift progress that morning, stopping only for a quick lunch and then continuing east. As we came out of the valley and into the rolling plains of the Flint Hills, the temperature began to rise, leaving the chill in the air behind us. I took in the beautiful scenery, adoring the vibrant green grass that dressed the endless hills all around us. As the cool wind blew over the rises and crests, the tall grass bowed with a soft whisper. I closed my eyes and imagined the land communicating to its creator in a mysterious way.

The tranquil sounds were suddenly interrupted by frustrated commentary from the cart in front of me. The larger man was complaining about the way Loretta was steering the horses. I turned around and tapped Merwin on the shoulder as I pointed to the two of them. We gave a chuckle, shaking our heads.

Truth be told, I enjoyed watching the couple as they commenced their daily routine. Their arguing was constant, but it was all in playful fun. They knew each other well and had a hard line on what made the other tick. I was envious of the love they shared. What they possessed was precious and valuable. Seeing them argue reminded me of Iska. Would we have been any different? Would our conversation about mundane things have driven each other crazy? Would she have known me as well as Loretta knew Groth?

I let my thoughts drift and continued to scan the horizon. Within the midst of the Flint Hills, I noticed something peculiar. The long, tall trees that populated the area were placed there by the creator eons ago with a unique characteristic:

Aleph planted the trees two by two. As I stared up and down the rolling green mounds, sure enough, every tree I saw had another right by its side. Would Aleph's creative mystery ever cease? Aleph wanted each tree to have a friend, and so upon creating this part of the world, He made it happen. Not one, but two trees were planted at a time, side by side. It was the trivial things like this that overwhelmed me with Aleph's goodness.

Later that afternoon, we stopped abruptly at the top of a hill. In the green valley below, we spotted a small group of travelers taking a break, sitting in a circle. I quickly got my party's attention, asking them their thoughts on the situation. Groth took the spyglass from me to get a better look at the group below us.

"I see five of them," he reported. "Four men and a woman. Their cloaks are worn and dirty, and they're wearing common clothes. They've had an exhausting day, from the looks of it, and are resting. I don't see any provisions nearby." The large man looked over at the rest of us.

"What do you think?" I asked, looking at Lionel.

"Could be trouble," he stated, keeping his eye on the group below.

"It's tough out there right now, as we all know," Merwin added. "Maybe they were traveling to the Rift?"

I held my hand to my mouth and shouted boldly down to the bottom of the hill. "Hello there!" A dark haired member from the group stood up and waved a hand above his head, acknowledging our presence. I looked over to the rest of my companions and nodded to them. "We're going to see what they need. Be on alert, regardless."

As one, we made our way down the large rolling hill to the bottom of the valley, where the group was huddled together. As we came closer, the details of their situation became apparent. Their packs were torn, and clothing was hanging out of the ripped sacks. Their faces and tunics were dirty, and they appeared tired.

We approached slowly until we were twenty yards from the group. I got off the seat of the cart and hopped into the tall green grass. Lionel cantered up beside me on his horse. I held up a hand, signaling him to stay put. The elder brother turned his horse slightly, not taking his eyes off the group. I walked slowly up to the camp with my hands held out. My new camouflaged cloak whipped in the wind over the top of the tall blades of grass as I approached. A well-built man holding a hammer stood up and took a step towards me.

"That's far enough!" he shouted, pointing the blunt object at me.

"We mean you no harm," I returned politely.

"How do we know you are not one of the magistrate's soldiers?" The spokesman of the group asked.

"That is a valid question. You look like you have been through a lot, and I empathize with you." I turned and gestured to my companions. "We have come from the Rift, where we fought a battle against the magistrate's army. By the hand of Aleph, we have been spared and are on our way to Northcrest."

"Are you, now? I would caution you to take your friends and go the other way. All you will find there is the enemy," the foreman stated.

"Is that where you came from?"

"Yes. We barely escaped with our lives. The messengers came out of nowhere." The man bowed his head and stifled the rest of his words.

"It's okay. We understand. You don't have to say anything further." The foreman slowly looked up.

"Can you help us?" he finally asked, pitifully.

"Of course. We have food and can mend your wounds, if needed. We will be on our way in the morning at first light. You may join us if you wish. However, I would counsel you not to go to the Rift."

"Why is that?" the foreman asked, curiously.

"Let us dine together, and we will give you the answers you seek," I stated evasively.

"No. You will tell us now." The foreman insisted, holding his hand up.

I looked back to my companions, and each of them nodded their heads, gesturing for me to continue. I crossed to the foreman until I was only several feet in front of him. I could see the muscles in his face twitching nervously, making his thin black mustache quiver slightly.

"Something has happened at the Rift…" I spent the next few minutes explaining everything to him. I spoke about the adversary Lucien and how he fell from the sky. Then I mentioned how the Nephilim would be summoned. The foreman took it surprisingly well. After several more minutes of contemplation with his companions, the leader came back to us.

"We will dine together this evening—that is, if you have

ample provisions. In the morning we will change our course, going south. You and your companions can join us if you wish."

"We cannot. Aleph has given us a task that lies in the direction of Northcrest. Come sunrise, we will part ways." I concluded.

After we worked out the plan, my friends and I joined the supervisor and his party in the valley of tall green grass. The leader's name was Cal, and he was a smith from Northcrest, which explained the hammer he carried. The rest of his companions were completely silent throughout the entire meal. One member of their party was noticeably young, not much older than Daeric and Esgar, and kept entirely to herself. We provided a simple pheasant dish with red potatoes. Loretta donated some spice, and before long we all supped hungrily.

As we ate, Cal informed us of what happened. The story was the same as we heard it from other people all over Shalistar. The Night of Shadows came to Northcrest and consumed the city. Messengers harvested the people, forcing them to choose Baelor. Those who did not were swiftly eliminated. Cal escaped and found his companions on the outskirts of the city. To increase their chances of survival, the companions joined Cal and made their way towards the Rift. I looked over at the other four sitting nearby. They were withdrawn, not wanting to speak of the events. Understanding, I let them keep their silence.

As Cal finished his story, I glanced over at one of the companions, the younger girl named Viveka. She was staring into the flames of the fire. I could see the slight movement of her lips, as she was speaking under her breath. I looked next to her and saw the same actions being performed by her silent companions. Only a trained eye could see it, but all four of Cal's companions were murmuring or praying some unknown words under their breath as they sat before us. I looked over to Lionel, who was picking a piece of the bird from his teeth. The elder looked back at me and winked, letting me know he was aware of what I saw. I sat back and stretched out my legs, feigning relaxation. This was an interesting turn of events.

After supper settled and we were all about to go to sleep, I sat down next to Lionel. He moved to the outskirts of the camp, with the cowl of his cloak drawn over his head. His eyes looked intensely over the entire group of strangers. In his hands was a smooth piece of stone, which he moved up and down his blade. Having been on missions with Lionel before, I understood that expression well. I leaned in close to my friend, keeping our conversation secret from the rest of the group. "You want to keep the first watch?" I asked the elder.

"Those were my thoughts, exactly." He whispered the next words into my ear. "We are in danger, Anlace."

"Why so?"

"Have any of them looked you in the eyes, except Cal?" he asked, nodding towards the strangers.

"No. They haven't."

"Exactly my point."

"They could be praying."

"That is true. But not to Aleph," he stated, turning to look at me.

"Are you sure?"

"Positive."

"Who do you think they are?"

"Clerics, if I had to guess." Hearing the thoughts of my friend spoken aloud made me shiver. Lionel was on point, and I could tell his gift of discernment was in full operation.

"How do you want to handle this?"

"Carefully. We don't want to arouse suspicion." The elder brother stood to his feet and began to stretch his hands above his head. "I will draw them out. Force them to reveal themselves."

"Do you think Cal is one of them?"

"No. Cal is innocent. Baelor has used him to position his minions."

"Do you think there are more of them around?"

"I don't think so. This is a scouting party of some kind, or even an assassin's coven. One thing is for sure. They were waiting for us. I will feign sleep, and when they make their move, you will know it."

"I am sure I will. Can you manage them?"

"I will have the element of surprise on my side. But I will need some help. The cloak will protect me, yes. But I will need your assistance to finish the job."

"You will have it. I trust you, my friend. Your gift of discernment has never been wrong."

I finished our conversation and moved over to the other side of camp. Groth, and Loretta were already stretched out for the night, resting peacefully. Seeing them like that caused a stab of pain within me. Would it have been like that for Iska and me? Would we have been the type of couple who fell asleep in each other's arms, or would we stick to our sides of the bed? It was a silly thought, especially for the moment; however, these thoughts haunted me for the past eighteen years.

Knowing this was not beneficial to the current situation, I stored the pain deep in my heart and returned my focus to the mission at hand. I went over to the cart, opened the compartment under the seat, and took two bundles from within. I unsheathed a dagger at my side and cut the paper from the unopened packages. Merwin stared at me from the back of the cart.

"Do I have to ask?" he questioned softly.

"I'm preparing for the worst," I answered as I passed him.

"The worst, what?" he responded.

With the ugly brown cloaks in my arms, I crossed over to where Groth and Loretta lay. Not wanting to stir them, I gently laid a cloak over each of their resting bodies, like a warm blanket, to keep the chill in the air from invading their spaces as they slept. Leaning in closely, I whispered into Groth's ear.

"If you are still awake, don't respond. Just listen. If there is trouble, put these around you immediately. They will protect you both from the power of magic." Groth and Loretta both opened one eye and winked, acknowledging they heard me. I smiled and continued. "I apologize for the crudity of this ceremony. As you can imagine, the order has been in disarray as of late." I leaned in closer and whispered as softly as I could. "As Master of the Order of the Elect, I commission you both as members and bestow upon you the symbol of authority." Groth and Loretta smiled as I placed my hands on them. "I bless you both in Aleph's light."

After speaking these words, I got up and was met with glances from the quiet strangers. I could see their faces in the light of the campfire. They were searching me for an answer.

"Evening prayers with the kids," I said, pointing to Groth and Loretta. The strangers looked at each other and shrugged. "You all don't talk much, do you?" I asked, prodding the strangers, who responded by nervously shuffling their feet in the grass. "Good night," I concluded and laid myself down, bending tall blades of grass as I collapsed into the ground.

"*Anlace, awaken!*" I heard Aleph cry out to me from my slumber and opened one of my eyes. Within my peripheral vision, I could see the four strangers sitting across from me. Within the firelight, they were chanting softly under their breath with their arms crossed in front of them. My heartbeat rapidly as the realization of my error struck me with full force. Lionel was right. We were in danger. From the looks of it we had taken company with a group of clerics!

Before I could move an inch, a scream echoed into the night, as one of the clerics fell forward grasping his chest. The other three sprang up, whipping around. Lionel was revealed behind them, holding a bloodied blade in his hand. With only seconds to respond, I jumped up, drew my blade, and shouted. Two of the clerics turned my way. One of them kept his focus on Lionel. By this time, I was joined by Loretta and Groth. Merwin was still mending and stayed put within the back of the cart. Cal was roused from his sleep as well and standing in the middle of the camp, looking in both directions from fear as he realized the truth of the situation.

The female cleric named Viveka took a step toward us and spoke an unknown word. Suddenly, from her fingertips came a flicker of flame. The cleric next to her raised both his hands and followed her lead. He spoke an arcane word, and I could see a thin line of electric current wrap around his hand. Through a sideways glance, I spotted Groth, and Loretta with dirty brown cloaks around them. I silently thanked Aleph for His protection and stepped forward to address the clerics.

"Sheath your spell now, and nobody else will be harmed." The female cleric looked down at the dead body of her companion that Lionel dispatched only moments before. She looked back at me with a snarl on her face.

"Shut your mouth! You are nothing but Aleph's lap dog!"

"You don't have to do this!" I tried reasoning again.

"I said be quiet, villain!"

"We are not the enemy. We are here to serve the people of Shalistar."

"Wrong again, slave! You are here to serve me! We are the chosen of Baelor, bestowed with his gifts! We are the power and future of this world. The Shift has come and all that was secret has been revealed to the world!"

"You have been deceived, young one," I said, taking another step closer. "Your master has been defeated and in a cowardly fashion is unleashing an ancient power so devastating and unholy…you cannot imagine the destruction that will come in its wake!"

"The world will tremble under the power of Baelor's might!" the second cleric cried out.

"They're too far gone for reasoning, Anlace! Let's end this now!" Lionel shouted, his blade above his head.

"This is your last chance!" I exclaimed to the leader. "Sheath your spells, or we will end you!" The female leader turned to her companions and nodded. They spoke a word, and the spells were released. Fire and lightning hit me all at once. I could feel the heat of the flames as they burned through the camouflaged cloak. The electric currents wrapped themselves around me but did not penetrate the protective barrier that the cloak provided me. All I could feel was a tickling sensation.

The clerics looked at each other desperately and hurled more spells. I heard a scream from behind them, signaling that Lionel took out the other cleric. The two facing me threw spells out of desperation, but seeing that I was protected, they changed strategies. The female stepped forward and cried out, "Burn in hell, lap dogs!" She then turned her spell toward the tall grass outside the cleared camp area. It landed in the thickness of the green and erupted into a ball of flame. The grass immediately caught fire. She grabbed her companion, spoke another word, and vanished before our eyes.

I saw the green fields light up in flames and spread quickly. We didn't have much time. The horses were struggling and neighing in panic as the flames drew closer. "Everyone, to the cart, now!" I wasn't sure whether the cloaks would protect us or not from the spreading fire but didn't want to chance it.

We all ran hastily toward the carts. Lionel mounted his horse before any of us reached him. Groth helped Loretta up and mounted quickly after. Cal jumped into the back of the cart and took his seat up front.

I was the last one into the cart. The heat from the flames was agonizing, but the smoke was worse. I accidentally breathed in and began coughing hysterically. My eyes were full of tears as I stumbled into the cart. I took a seat, and Cal began slapping me on the back as hard as he could. The action took me by surprise at first, but then I realized the outer brown cloak was caught up in flames, and he was trying to beat them out.

In desperation, I ripped the cloak off and held it outside the cart. Cal took the reins and pulled hard, expertly shouting a command to the horses. Without any hesitation, the large animals charged forward, knocking us off balance and desperately holding onto the sides to stay seated. As we made our escape, I whipped the cloak through the air, hoping to stop the spread of the flames. After several attempts, the fire was out. I looked behind me as we sped up the hill and saw a blazing inferno spreading quickly in all directions. Another moment within the valley would have led to our demise.

We came to the top of the hill, and I took a gasping, deep breath of air. I bent over as a spasm of coughing overcame me. I spent the next few moments hacking out the foul smoke from my lungs. Cal gave me an encouraging pat on the back as I struggled to find air.

Eventually, I evened out. I was thankful to take a breath and leaned back. My head was throbbing from all the coughing, and I felt weak, as though I were going to pass out. When we were safely away from the blazing fires caused by the destruction spell, we stopped. Cal encouraged me to lie down in the back of the cart, taking full control of the reins.

I rested back and held the cloak in my hands. The silky white fabric was now clearly revealed. The flames scorched large sections of the ugly brown that concealed it—no more camouflage for me. I took the last moments of the evening to tear the remaining brown fabric from the guardian's cloak until all that remained was pure white. As I held the cloak to myself, I closed my eyes and thanked Aleph for the protection He had given me.

I curled up and laid my head down upon my arm. My lungs were burning from the smoke, and it was hard to breathe without coughing. I used the rest of my time that day to analyze all that happened.

Today was a narrow escape. Two of the clerics we encountered used a teleportation spell, which told me they were going back to give news to their commander that we were alive. I shook my head in frustration. Was I blind? I couldn't see the deception! Without Lionel and his discerning eye, we would have perished. After one last fit of coughing, I thanked Aleph for my faithful elder and finally slipped into a restless time of sleep.

CHAPTER

6

My eyes opened to see the sky above me spinning in multiple colors. The beautiful face of my darling, Iska was looking down at me. Her dark, emerald, green eyes stared into mine and a worried look spread across her face. I returned her gaze with a smile and reached out to touch her. Iska gently took my hand and shook her head.

"No, Anlace. You must lie still. You are not well." I noticed the voice was not of my love, but sounded like Loretta, my faithful companion.

"But please…Iska." I pleaded. "It's been so long."

Iska looked worriedly to her side. "It's been two days, and he's not getting better." Cal came into view, looking down at me in curiosity.

"He's obviously in the thrall of a magic spell. He breathed in a lot of smoke from those unnatural flames. Keep speaking to him, Loretta. We should give him some time before we move on."

"But…the sounds…" she cried, turning her head, and looking fearfully behind her.

"I know. They're getting closer. But we need to have Anlace

coherent."

"When do you think that will happen? I'm not entirely comfortable playing the role of Iska, whoever she is. Groth gave me a dirty look earlier."

"Iska... Please hold me." I begged, reaching out towards my love. Iska looked at Cal and after a moment, shrugged her shoulders. She leaned down and put her arms around me, letting me lie against her. I took a deep breath and was suddenly met with a spasm of coughing. My lungs burned as I wheezed. With every gasp of air, a wave of nausea came over me.

The gentle touch from my love was little comfort to the raging fire in my chest or the stabbing pain in my head. It was hard to keep a muddled thought for more than a second. I could hear other voices as well, more distant, talking about me as though I weren't aware. "He thinks she is Iska."

"I know that Merwin." Lionel replied gruffly. "This is a nasty spell he's caught in. He's seeing more hallucinations than a deviant on mushrooms."

"What do we do? Those noises are not getting any further away. I don't particularly care to meet the owner of them."

"Neither do I," Lionel grunted. "Neither do I." The world around me began to fade slowly away until all the voices were nothing but garbled gibberish.

Within a dream, I saw a picture of a battlefield. As far as the eye could see were piles of rubble. I walked past each of these destroyed buildings and monuments, feeling a deep pain in my heart. On and on, as far as the eye could see were mountains of destroyed cities. "What is this?" I asked aloud. My voice echoed throughout my dream. "What are you showing me?"

Suddenly, a brilliant flash knocked me off my feet. I covered my eyes from the light. Then I heard a voice. *"They have built for themselves cities of costly stone and hoarded within their wall's treasures of vanity. Their pride and arrogance led them to the destroyer. Seeking temporary riches, they have given themselves over to wickedness. Their outcome will be a pile of rubble."* The light flashed once again, and I slowly opened my eyes.

The mountains of ruin were still there, placed throughout the entire landscape. However, there was something new. Upon the top of each pile was an ornate golden throne. Curiously, I examined the top of the closest mound. I felt a surge of energy flow through me and climbed to the top of the rubble. As I neared the golden throne, I could see a crown resting on its seat. A moment of confusion ensued as I reached out and took the metallic object in my hand. Beautifully crafted jewels hemmed the crown on all sides.

"Sit, Anlace," the voice softly whispered. I turned around, facing the battlefield from the top of the ruinous mountain. As I placed myself onto the throne, the first thing I noticed was how uncomfortable it felt under me. Holding the crown in my hands, I ran my fingers over the jewels. They were finely cut, and the edges were sharp.

"Why are you showing me this?" I asked the voice.

"I want you to see the place I have for you at this time," the voice returned.

"What about the other thrones?" I asked, pointing to the piles around me.

"*They will be inhabited as well. This world will now be destroyed, one stone, one tree, one life at a time. But you and my chosen will stand within the destruction and wait for me. This place of waiting will be full of danger, and the enemy will see you clearly. But this position is a place of victory and will be for my glory.*"

"I don't understand."

"*I don't expect you to Anlace. Not yet. You have not seen what the destroyer looks like. Only through this terrifying process will you fully understand.*"

"What process?" There was silence, a deep foreboding silence. "Tell me!"

The world began to dim all around me. "No…please. I need to know!" The piles of rubble faded. "You can't leave me with this!" The dark battlefield all around me began to dim. "Please, Aleph…I need to know." I softly cried as the world around me completely vanished.

Abruptly, the dream was over, and I sat up painfully. My hand covered my eyes, trying to stave off the vibration coursing through my head. The longest night of revelry in the king's army couldn't hold a candle to the pain I felt buried deep in my skull. Keeping my eyes open was a treatment of agony. I compromised with the pain by squinting.

I could feel sweat flowing from every pore in my body as the fever exited, leaving me shivering from head to toe with the chills. My throat was insanely sore, and it hurt to even speak. The sound that came out was a raspy whisper.

The skies above me churned slowly in circles, making

me dizzy. I reached for the bucket one of my companions thankfully left beside me and heaved. All that came up was a tiny bit of dark yellow and green bile that tasted bitter and foul. Mixed in the goo were streaks of red—blood from my bleeding lungs. After several minutes of dry heaving, I groaned and laid back down inside the cart. Merwin scooted over at the sound of my pain and wrapped a large wool blanket over me.

"Your fever is breaking, sir. That's a good thing," my brother stated as he dabbed my head with a wet cloth.

Suddenly, from out of nowhere, I felt the ground under us begin to shake, and what followed was a roar that echoed throughout the entire world. It sounded like it came from under the earth. Within the roar, I heard a deafening rattle. The sound was altogether unsettling.

"What is that?!" I gasped.

"We don't know," Merwin said, looking toward the horizon behind us. "The sound has been heard periodically since the night we escaped the clerics."

"Where are we?" I asked, straining to look around.

"At the edge of the Flint Hills, close to the river. Loretta thought it would be best to stay near the water."

"We need to get to Northcrest," I commanded through chattering teeth.

"Not with you in this state, sir," Merwin returned.

I reached up and grabbed Merwin by the collar and pulled him close, letting him know I was serious. "There is not much time. That sound…the Nephilim." As I spoke that word, Merwin tensed within my grip. Suddenly, memories of the dream replayed themselves, and I gasped. "We must get to safety. We need to get behind the walls of Northcrest!"

The single action depleted me of all my strength. My grip lessened, and I collapsed back into the floor of the cart. Merwin grabbed me and helped set me down gently. He looked at me with concern. His soft red hair was disheveled, and bags of worry were under his eyes. I felt bad for my companions and was angry at myself for not seeing the deception sooner. The clerics could have destroyed us. If it weren't for Lionel, we would all be dead.

"It's all right, sir. You need to rest." He pulled the blanket back up to my chin and tucked the corners under my sides. I lay there, shaking uncontrollably, until all went dark.

I opened my eyes to see the brilliant blue sky all around me. The sound of the river was off in the distance. My orders were being followed because I could feel the wheels of the cart moving us along. I strained to sit up and get a look at our surroundings. As I did so, all the blood rushed into my head, and my world began to spin once again. I heard a ringing in my head and felt the dull throb of pain there as well. Would the effects of this magic spell ever cease?

I looked groggily around me, fighting the nausea. The trees were growing thinly all around us, which told me we were heading northeast, about to cross the Analyd River. From behind me, I could still smell the smoke in the air. How much of the Flint Hills was scorched by the fires of sorcery?

To the north was the shelf of the Ternion Mountains stretching majestically far beyond my vision. The white-capped peaks were sparkling within the morning light.

Around me, the tall grass of the valley was exchanged for short, dry shrubs. The weather was turning dry, making my throat parched, so I reached for the canteen next to me and tipped it up, taking in a generous amount of cool water. As the liquid went down my throat, I collapsed back into the cart. I haven't tasted anything so refreshing in a long time.

I sat in the back, taking in the scenery change all around me. I was on edge, listening to the occasional other-worldly roar at our backs. Every time I heard the cry, my heart would stop, and I would turn to search out the ancient enemy that was endlessly pursuing us. Then I heard Cal shout.

"Northcrest is ahead!" I turned northeast to see the first glimpse of the city. It was an old habitation that sat on top of the hill. It stretched along the horizon for several miles. The sandstone ramparts were high and foreboding, with several watchtowers spread evenly along its base. Within the walls sat the town. I could see large spires rising above the clearance of the outer walls, creating an impressive skyline. The color of sandstone graced all the buildings in the city and against the desert backdrop, created a mystical picture.

Northcrest was not a city I ever been to in all my travels and adventures with Aleph. I was excited to be in a new place, but I quickly put the emotions far away. The enemy made its move and eliminated all opposition from this once mighty stronghold. We were in a dangerous place with no friends to help us. We needed to be shrewd to remain hidden. Our immediate need was shelter. Aleph obviously wanted us here, but for what exact purpose, I was not sure.

We stopped our carts at a safe enough distance from the city and discussed the situation. I was weak, but with the help of Lionel, I sat on the edge of the cart and addressed my companions.

"I apologize for my inability these past couple of days. I'm not used to being an invalid." The companions gave me their support and accepted my apology gracefully. "As you can all guess, the ancient enemy has been released from the void. The Nephilim are coming this way. We are not safe out in the open. The only chance we have at survival is to get behind the walls of the city. If we keep moving on, they will destroy us. Filled with Baelor's rage, they have no doubt been given the assignment to do so. Lucien will not let this insult go unpunished."

"How do you want to handle this?" Lionel asked.

"I'm open to suggestions." I replied.

"All the inhabitants of this city are under the control of Baelor. They have surrendered to him, and it seems impossible," Merwin stated sourly.

"I agree. But we are on Aleph's path, and He has a way for us to enter," I countered.

"Perhaps I may be of assistance?" Cal spoke softly to himself. We all turned to look at our new companion. He was lightly tapping a rock with his hammer. It looked to me like this action was a nervous twitch or a way for him to fidget. I could relate. I created several ways of doing that myself. However, when our new companion saw us staring at him, he stopped his tapping and spoke. "The Nephilim…are they dangerous?"

"Yes. A danger we cannot even imagine. We are not safe in

the open," I explained.

"So how is being behind the walls of a large city with tall buildings going to be any better?" Cal asked inquisitively. We all took a moment to try and produce an answer. After several beats of silence, he continued. "Exactly my point. If these beings destroy this city, you can bet we are going to be in as much danger inside the walls as we are outside of them."

"So, what are you suggesting?" Lionel asked abruptly.

"I have been a citizen of Northcrest for many years and know it very well. I have been on many errands, delivering swords and shields all over the city, including the prison."

"What about it?"

"The prison in this city is unique. The only one like it in all Shalistar. It's underground. The entrance is secluded on the eastern side. If the monsters are coming to bring destruction upon the city, I would surmise the safest place for us would be underground."

"So, you want us to turn ourselves in at the front gate? That's your plan?" Merwin asked.

"Yes," Cal responded and bowed his head. "I know it's not as thought-out as you would have liked it to be."

"Maybe so. But I think you have received Aleph's wisdom in this circumstance," I agreed.

"You can't be serious," Lionel huffed, turning away sharply.

"Is this the only way?" Loretta asked fearfully.

"I think so. The best chance we have at survival is to be as far underground as possible, when the Nephilim arrive," I concluded.

"I've never been to prison before," Groth said, voicing his thoughts aloud.

"Neither have I, sweetheart." Loretta said as she put her arm around her massive husband. "This will be a milestone in our marriage, for sure!"

Suddenly the ground under us reverberated violently. Small rocks lifted into the air and danced above the surface until the rumbling stopped. The silence in the air was split by the sound of a loud roar. Within the monster's cry was a repetitive rattling. The nightmare was close. We were running out of time.

We stored the cart and horses by a cluster of large rocks, taking what we needed, or thought might come in handy should we ever escape. Walking side by side, we approached the front gate of the city. Questions and doubts pounded my mind as we came closer. We were undertaking a huge risk, and all the pieces needed to fall perfectly into place for the plan to work. Perhaps we should have discussed other options?

My busy mind was interrupted as I heard a shout from the top of the ramparts. "Whoa, there! Don't you all look like a tattered group? Commander Zant said I should be on the lookout for trouble the likes of you! Who are you, and where did you come from?" I glanced sideways at the solid face of Lionel and nodded. He and I took a step forward, separating us from the rest of the group.

"We are members of the Order of the Elect and have come from the Rift." I could hear a murmur begin to spread from the group of guards, no doubt regarding my white cloak. I didn't feel the need to mask our disguise, so I ignored them and continued. "We are here to warn you of danger. You have no doubt felt the tremors?"

"You mean the rock splitters?"

"Yes. Exactly those."

"Been having those for days now. What of 'em?"

"The tremors come from a terrifying source of power; a monster headed this way. Please tell Commander Zant that we surrender and would like an audience with him after we are processed and placed in prison."

"A monster, you say?" the guard shouted down at us. "What kind of monster? What does it look like?"

"We don't know. Please, sir. There is not much time…" The guard left his post on the wall, leaving us staring up at his silent subordinates. After a minute or so, the gate opened into the city, and standing behind the entrance was the same guard I was speaking to along with several of his comrades. He approached Lionel and me confidently, with his hand on the hilt of his sword. He stopped several feet short in front of us and turned to look at his fellow soldiers.

"Look at this rabble. They say a monster they've never seen is headed this way and is a danger to us. Are they crazy?" The soldier came up close until he was only inches from my face. "No…they are hiding something. Commander told us to be on the watch for folk like you. You 'order folk' are crafty. What are you hiding?"

"There is no deception on our part. We only wish to surrender and speak with your Commander."

"Commander ain't here. But that's all right. You all can wait for him to get back. I got a nice cozy cell for you underground!" He gestured toward his assisting guard. "These gentlemen will relieve you of your weapons."

The guards made a move toward Lionel, and he grunted, taking a step back. I placed a calm hand on his shoulder. "Do what they say," I told my elderly friend. Lionel looked over at me. For a second, I thought he was going to disobey. Begrudgingly, he removed his weapons and placed them on the ground.

Soon we were stripped of our belongings, except for the dirty brown cloaks upon the backs of my companions and the long wooden branch Merwin crafted into a walking stick. When the guard attempted to relieve him of it, he gripped it tightly and shook his head. "It's my leg. One of your men injured me days ago, and I'm healing. I need it to walk." The guard took the staff from Merwin and looked it over as thoroughly as he could before handing it back. He then knelt and examined Merwin's injury. He stood up, nodding his approval. Without any further hesitation, our group of six was ushered towards the massive front gate.

The iron portcullis screeched as it came down behind us. My companions and I found ourselves within the confines of Northcrest, the enemy city. This unexpected turn of events put me on edge, and I prayed under my breath for Aleph to show me the path.

Before we could take another step, the ground quaked violently as a terrifying roar erupted. The guards remained frozen in fear, looking at each other nervously. Their leader stepped in and gathered them together, encouraging them weakly. No amount of black golden armor could hide the look on the leader's face—he was afraid, and he had every right to be. What he didn't know is that the Nephilim were close, and they were eternally tasked with the job of destroying this world, one city at a time. Northcrest was about to become a pile of rubble amid the battlefield, and there was nothing we could do to stop it.

CHAPTER
7

The tall sandstone buildings loomed high above us as we hurried to the east side of the city. The soldiers continued to shoot quick, nervous glances behind them as the ground vibrated. We passed shops and taverns of all shapes and sizes. I noticed Loretta hungrily eying a trade shop with a cart out front full of herbs. My elder brother looked at me in frustration and a realization hit me. Lionel had a plan I should have listened to. Everything moved forward so quickly, I didn't have a chance to think about it. He was not happy with me and I decided I would speak to him about it if we shared the same cell.

The people in the city moved about quickly. They obviously felt the tremors and heard the agonizing roars. They fluttered around fearfully, preparing however they could for the looming disaster. The sight of our military escort brought out the hecklers, who threw spoiled food and rocks at us as we passed them.

I looked into their angry eyes and saw the prison that confined them. Fear was now their master. They bent the knee to Baelor's messenger and received the gift. Any purpose or desire for a dream unfulfilled was removed. All I could see was emptiness, like looking down the hollow shaft of a water well. They served a master who was unmerciful, and they knew with every fiber of their being that death would have been a better choice. But now it was too late, and they were angry. They needed someone to lash out at to justify the emotions overtaking them. Conveniently for them, we happened to be walking by at that moment. Seeing the enemy of Baelor in front of them, they couldn't resist, and took whatever they could to throw at us. We maintained our focus on the mission and went forth with the tide, which soon led us to the outskirts of the city.

Right around lunchtime, we entered the military compound to see rows of men and women amid training. Several clerics were moving within them and shouting instructions to the bewildered group.

"Baelor has revealed all the mysteries! As clerics, it is the gift we receive," the hooded man directed. "The magic flows freely from the void. Simply surrender to the power that is flowing through you and imagine in your mind the spark of a flame." The cleric flicked his thumb and index finger, and there appeared a sliver of fire.

As he was about to demonstrate the spell on a target in the corner, another violent quake threw the cleric off balance, followed by the unnerving roar of the ancient adversary. It sounded as though the noise was right outside the gates of the city. I looked westward but could not see anything past the large stone buildings all around me. A nervous conversation broke out from within the ranks of students. The clerics shouted for them to stand firm and not be afraid.

As we were escorted past the clerics, I searched for the face of the young woman who attacked us days before, the one named Viveka. She was nowhere in their midst. We stopped before a door leading into a small building on the right side of the compound, furthest away from any towering structures. The door opened, and out came a large, dirty-looking soldier with a massive belly. The leftovers of lunch stained his brown beard, and he licked his fingers as he spoke.

"How many?"

"Six. They have requested a word with Commander Zant."

"He's out. Should be back soon. He went to Hammerfist to oversee a transfer from Amah."

"Yes sir. These prisoners need to be detained until his return."

"Very well. Have they bowed their knee?"

"No sir. They are the Order of the Elect." The face of the fat warden brightened at the mention of our identity.

"Are you sure? A capture like that could boast a large reward."

"Not entirely. That is the prisoner's testimony. Why they would surrender that information is beyond me. However, I have brought them to you. Will they be processed?"

"Yes. Have their weapons been removed?"

"They have, and without any altercation, I might add. They came willingly and peacefully."

"Hmm, good. I will take them from here," the warden replied greedily. "You six, please follow me." We followed our escort through the threshold into the small office. Along the walls were chests filled with all kinds of belongings, from prisoners who came before us. "Would you please remove your cloaks and hang them there?" the warden politely asked, pointing to several hooks along the wall. "Don't worry, they will be safe until you are released." He said this last statement without any emotion. He obviously said these words many times before, and it was now a part of his daily life.

On the other side of the door, I could faintly hear steps and hurried dialogue. I could make out a few words: "We are under attack! The west gate is overrun!" I looked at my companions and saw the troubled looks on their faces as well. They heard the same words as I. The warden on the other hand was bent over his desk and hungrily eating a piece of cake, oblivious to anything around him.

We quickly removed our cloaks, hanging them up. We then lined up next to the warden's desk. He grabbed a large turkey leg from his lunch plate before stepping over to an iron door along the back wall of the office. The door was completely solid, forbidding any kind of entry other than with the key that was fashioned for it. The iron door squeaked open, revealing a long staircase illuminated by small sconces along the side. The staircase went down into the underground. I strained to see the end of the descent, but all that was revealed was a blanket of darkness far below.

"This way," the disgusting fat man said as he took a large bite from the turkey leg. "This way to your cell."

Loretta moved in front of me so she could have a quick word with the warden. I listened as she tried to give him several dietary tips on the way down, but the gluttonous man would hear none of it. He continued to chomp away as we descended the stairs into darkness. Finally, we came to the bottom of the steps and a large wooden door with a window cut into it. The window was outfitted with iron bars.

The warden struggled to pull out the ring of keys from his bulbous waist. He was having a tough time gripping the key ring and the turkey leg at the same time and lost his grip. The key ring fell and hit the hard floor with a loud clang.

"Oh my…" the warden exclaimed, bending down.

"Please, don't you trouble yourself, sir." Loretta exclaimed and quickly skipped over to where he was. Effortlessly she leaned over. In one fell swoop, the key ring was in her hand, presenting it to the warden. "You know, a steady exercising regimen would do wonders for you sir," she stated, patting his belly.

The warden puffed his tremendous gut out and grunted. Grabbing the key from Loretta, he whipped around, facing the door. He took a moment to lick his fingers sloppily before trying several of the keys in the lock. The only light was a sconce on the wall—it was a wonder he could see anything at all in this dreadful abyss. However, after several attempts, the obese mass put the correct key in the door and turned the knob. I cringed as it opened with a loud squeak.

Before crossing the threshold, I looked back up the staircase that led to the courtyard of the military compound. I made a guess that we must be a couple hundred feet underground. When the destruction started, we might be safe.

We walked down a long hall of cells, all of them empty, a result from the Night of Shadows. The prisoners themselves were visited by the messengers and made a choice. Unfortunately, most of the prisoners surrendered to Baelor, in exchange for their freedom. The ones who refused, were executed quickly. The warden ushered us into a larger cell further down the hall. As Lionel passed by, I saw my brother lean in and connect with the warden's shoulder. The impact made the turkey leg fall from his grip, landing with a thud on the floor.

The warden's face was aghast, realizing his precious food was now covered in dirt and dust. "Clumsy old fool! Watch where you are going, dog!"

Lionel turned quickly and bucked up, ready to pounce on the warden. I wrapped my arms around the chest of my dear elder and whispered in his ear. "This is not the plan, Lionel. Relax, my friend. He is not worth it." I could feel Lionel's muscles loosen slightly under my arms and released my grip. The warden turned and closed the cell door. He then exhaled a loud belch. When he was relieved, he spoke.

"You all can stay in here 'till you rot for all I care. However, I'm sure Commander Zant has special plans for you, and none of them are pleasant—you can be sure of that. Good day, prisoners," the greasy man said as he turned and left us in the darkness of our cell.

We were huddled together within the prison, with only the flame of the sconce outside our cell to provide a little bit of light. I made sure to address my concerns with Lionel before anything else. I wanted there to be no animosity towards me and the mission, so I cleared the air with the elder and apologized for not listening to his plan.

After hearing my apology, he immediately forgave me. He told me the strategy was sound and the best chance for success; he only needed a bit of time to process it and agree. Hearing his approval made me smile. Now that I communicated to Lionel, I turned my attention to the rest of my companions. We were trying to make the best of our situation when our fellowship was cut short.

The walls of the prison began to rumble and groan all around us. The iron bars of the cell began to vibrate within the stone. I watched as the flames from the sconces in the hall flickered and then went completely out, leaving us in absolute darkness.

I could not see my hand in front of my face as I lifted it. My mind began to play tricks on me, hoping there would be light to banish the darkness. However, we all sat in the pitch black, unseeing. It was unsettling. I could hear one of my companions chattering his teeth together. Merwin was beginning to groan, and I told him to silence the negative talk. He immediately obeyed, and the company was thrust once again into an uncomfortable silence.

Suddenly, a sound blasted through the ground into our small cell, taking our breath away. The roar was loud and powerful all at once with a tangible sound to it. You could feel it. As the breath passed through us, I noticed a smell of decay.

Then came the sound like a rattle. I can only describe it as two large stones being banged together repeatedly, an unholy rhythm to Baelor that sounded from somewhere within eternity. The rattle vibrated throughout the cell, a jarring staccato beat that made my heart pound within my chest. Each of us gripped the one next to us and braced ourselves for a terror that had not been experienced in Shalistar for thousands of years. Then there was silence. A deep breath of exhaustion left us as the unknown eternal beings above ground prepared for their life-long purpose and then, finally, the destruction of Shalistar began.

Within the darkness, we heard the nightmare above us, the sound of buildings exploding, and debris crashing to the ground. As the ceiling shook violently, we felt dust particles falling onto our faces. Mixed within the sounds of annihilation was a chorus of screaming. Even though we were hundreds of feet below ground, we could still hear voices crying out in desperation to escape the doom.

Our arms were around one another in a tight grip. Trapped within the pitch-black darkness, it was the only way we could know for sure each of us was still there. I asked my companions periodically to sound their voices, to reassure my wandering mind that we were all present. Loretta cried out in compassion to Aleph several times to have mercy on those whose lives were ending. The rest of us held on tightly, praying the roof above us would hold and not cave in. My mind went wild with thoughts of what was going on above us.

The Nephilim reached the city and were now destroying it one stone at a time, leaving no living being alive in their wake. Part of my mind wanted to see it; the leader in me needed to see it. I wanted to gaze upon this enemy and see what we were dealing with so I could strategize the best course of action for defeating it. But I also knew that was not wise. Aleph gave us the safety of an underground prison in which to wait.

So, wait we did. We sat together, huddled in the darkness, as the horrific scene played out in the world above us. Muffled screams from men and women could be heard as they pleaded with this ancient enemy for their lives. Their pleading was abruptly ended. It went on for hours—screaming, buildings crashing, and the endless rattle, for hours and hours, until the final voice was suppressed, and the last stone broken—until all was silent.

It was decided as a group to exit the prison. We didn't have any idea whether the Nephilim had moved on or not. They could be waiting for us on the other side of the prison door for all we knew. But each of us felt the same way and decided that instead of sitting in the darkness letting our minds drive us mad, we should follow the peace, open the door of the prison, and step out into the world to see the aftermath of destruction that came from the hand of an ancient enemy.

Shrouded in darkness, we moved toward the cell door. Upon a quick investigation, we noticed the tremors had knocked it loose from the stone. Lionel and Groth tried several times to remove it completely from the hard rock, but the iron bars would not budge. Then I felt a light tap from Merwin.

"Will this help?" he asked, handing me a thin metal object. I couldn't see anything in the pitch darkness, but it felt like a lockpick. My heart leaped within me!

"But...how did you...?" I asked in wonder.

"Don't ask." He quickly rebutted, ending that conversation.

"Was it in the staff?" I urged him.

"Don't worry about it," he replied quickly. I decided to drop the subject.

We agreed that Loretta would be the best one of us to pick the lock due to her nimble fingers. She began to complain that she had never picked a lock in her life, but with a little encouragement from the group, she was soon kneeling in front of the iron door.

Unsurprisingly, Loretta's lockpicking was swift. She worked quickly, speaking to herself aloud. When we tried to insert a direction or two, she would quiet us, letting us know that the only instruction she would receive was from her own mouth. We decided to step back and let the woman finish the job. I'd never heard someone say their own name in one sentence so many times. It was comical, especially when she knew she wasn't doing the right thing. After several rebukes and even more encouraging words, the lock clicked, and the iron door squeaked. However, the tremors shifted the door so that it wasn't sitting flush with the ceiling and floor. Loretta tried to move it further, but the door would not budge.

"Allow me," Lionel huffed as he moved Loretta out of the way. "Groth, I need your weight," the elder stated to the woman's husband. Together, with several well-placed kicks, he and Groth were able to open the iron door far enough that we could each squeeze through.

Once we all exited the cell, we moved down the hall to the next obstacle. The wooden door to the staircase felt solid to my touch. Again, Loretta was on one knee, fiddling with the contraption and speaking to herself. This time she added a soft whistle as she worked with the lock. Before long, we heard a metallic click as it was sprung. Two more swift kicks later and we were standing on the other side of the door.

I could only see a faint sliver of light above us, which must have been coming through the crack at the bottom of the iron door. The closer we got to the top of the staircase, the brighter it got. Once we were at the top of the stairs, the tiny sliver of light became blinding compared to the darkness of the prison below. Loretta once again was on one knee, ready to pick the lock. She reached out a hand and touched the plate of the door, when suddenly the iron door gave and swung open.

Light flooded into the dark staircase, temporarily blinding us. It took a moment for us to blink out the brilliance and recover our sight. If I had it my way, I would have stayed blind so that I wouldn't have to see the destruction. But that was not to be, and the images I was about to witness would haunt me for the rest of my life.

As we crossed the threshold, the first horrific thing we saw was the mangled body of the warden lying next to the door, with the key ring in his dead hand. He was trying to open the door and escape down the stairs when either a large rock fell, or a part of the building collapsed on top of him. The rest of the office was in complete shambles. The wall facing the compound was completely gone, with only the threshold of the outer door still standing.

We found our belongings and weapons in the chests along the wall. Thankfully, the debris had not crushed them, or we would be without our equipment. But as luck would have it, they were undamaged and in the same place we left them before descending into the prison. We took a moment to put on our cloaks and sheath our weapons. Loretta counted all her vials before putting on the utility belt. She also made sure to add the lockpick to a small pocket in the back. Cal picked up his hammer and held it close to his heart, silently thanking Aleph for keeping it safe.

Now that our belongings were recovered, we walked slowly into the compound to see more bodies crushed and destroyed by the hands of this unknown enemy. Large stone fragments littered the open courtyard. Sharp rock was buried in the ground, as if flung downward from above with great force. There was no wonder we could hear and feel the rumble above us while in the prison.

We were all engaged in the search for survivors in the courtyard, facing east, when Loretta turned around and let out a loud shriek. Seeing her with a hand over her mouth and a look of absolute horror on her face, I turned the same direction. All at once, I knew why Loretta reacted the way she did. I looked upon the most devastating scene I ever imagined. The once beautiful city of Northcrest, with its formidable spires and breathtaking skyline, was gone!

All that remained of the stronghold were piles of ash and rubble. The tall buildings that provided shade as we walked towards the eastside of the city had collapsed. How could an entire city be gone? What kind of being could bring so much destruction? How were we supposed to stand up to the immense power and rage these monsters possessed?

I turned around to face my companions and saw the terrifying fear in each of their eyes. Did we hear Aleph correctly? Were we going in the wrong direction? Several paths led to Hammerfist. Had we taken the wrong path? As doubt crept in, I collapsed to the ground. The burden I felt in my heart was too heavy to carry. I remained on the ground as I took a moment to try and gather my muddled thoughts. Like me, my companions were having a tough time standing. Several of them fell to the ground as well. An emotional bubble burst within us, and we wept. The tears poured out of us for the dead as well as for the world who would soon see the destroyer first-hand.

I screamed in frustration. What did Aleph expect us to do? How were we going to overcome this enemy? I pounded my fists into the ground and continued to scream. I kept at it until I felt a hand upon my shoulder. Turning to look up, I saw the tear-streaked eyes of my elder and friend, Lionel.

"There's nothing we could have done, Anlace," he said softly.

"But what about him?" I cried out. "What about Aleph? Why didn't He stop this?"

"You know as well as I do, that is beyond our understanding."

"Why does it have to be, Lionel? Can't Aleph give us a clear answer for a change? Why does it have to be so hard? Why does He have to take away the ones we love to get our attention? Why can't it be easy?"

"Don't do this to yourself," Lionel said. "You know you can't carry that burden. You gave it up, remember?"

"It's back! It always comes back! I will never be rid of it… or her!" Lionel took a step away as I rose from my position. My anger surfaced for all to see. My companions stared at me, pitifully. I continued to shout into the air. "Is this it? Is this what you have for me? A world in ruin? You can keep it! I don't want it!"

I stormed out of the compound and into the city. I could see my companions were keeping their distance from me as I walked through the midst of destruction. One block after another was a picture of horror. Bodies of the dead were everywhere, crushed under rubble. I was in shock as I absorbed the immensity of the devastation around me. I was in a ruinous maze, having to turn around frequently due to the streets being blocked by crushed buildings. Fires broke out in several parts of the city as well. As soon as I saw them, I turned around, afraid of breathing any more smoke.

I searched one area after another, but alas, I found not a lone survivor. I strained my ears, hopeful to catch the cry of a trapped individual, but all I could hear was silence and the flickering of flames from what remained of a building caught on fire.

I reached the front gate where we entered and noted the same destruction there. The walls had large, gaping holes where the Nephilim smashed their fists or foot into the stone, turning it to dust. Dead soldiers, including the leader who escorted us, were scattered around the front gate. I turned around to look back at the destroyed city and saw my companions huddled together a good distance from me. They were giving me space so I could process what was happening. I was thankful for it, but I still wanted to be closer to them. I called them over and we all wrapped our arms around one another and wept. The tears flowed from all of us, Lionel included, as we processed the aftermath of the destruction.

"It's going to be okay," Loretta encouraged us. "Aleph knows what He is doing." I heard her words, but the doubt in my heart was festering, and I was not entirely sure. My thoughts went to Iska. Did she know about any of this? What would she do if she were here now? Would she be having the same reaction as me?

We silently made our way back to where we stored our carts.

I held my breath hoping they were still there. In miraculous fashion, they were! The carts were undamaged, but even more than that, the horses were still harnessed! Upon further inspection, I could see signs of struggle on their heads as they tried desperately to get away. The rope and harness rubbed their snouts and bodies raw, leaving gruesome marks. Loretta scampered up beside me, giving a soft groan as she petted the animals and spoke soothing words to them.

"Shhhhh. It's going to be okay there, big guy. The monsters are gone now." She opened one of her vials and spread the ointment on one of the horse's cuts. The animal gave a soft neigh and nuzzled the short woman. "Yes, I know...you were scared, weren't you? Don't worry, big guy. This ointment will make the burns feel much better."

Loretta continued her treatment until the horses were tended to. When her ministry concluded, we took our place in the carts, including Lionel. His horse understandably ran off. He appeared distraught.

"I had that horse since he was a foal," he said, his head pointed to the ground.

"I understand," said Cal, coming up next to him. "I, too, have lost an animal that was precious to me. It's hard to imagine how attached you will become. But someone wise once told me, "Cal, they never live long enough. He was right."

Lionel looked at our new companion with his mouth slightly open. I was afraid he might do something stupid, like punch him, but what happened next was altogether shocking. Lionel buried his head into Cal's shoulder and wept. This day was bringing out the deep, pent-up emotions in all of us. As I sat there and watched my elder cry like a little child, feelings of inadequacy rose within me.

Could I really do this? This adventure had started off on the wrong foot, that's for sure! First, I led us into a cleric's trap. Then, I nearly died from inhaling the smoke of an unnatural destruction spell. Finally, I lost my temper in front of all my companions after seeing the aftermath of the Nephilim.

Was this journey going to be more than I could manage? Why was Aleph silent? He wasn't before. But now, I couldn't hear His voice. What did all this mean? Why was I questioning orders? I was caught within a battle in my mind. The same as I experienced long before, when questioning my orders from Zant on my way to the palace. I felt like my mind was a chasm. I was torn between following Aleph and leaving the mission altogether. It was an unsettling feeling, and I was having a challenging time keeping a thought in my head.

Was this my future? Was I to go from one wrecked city to another until I went insane? The barrage of negative thoughts continued to pummel me as we continued around the outskirts of the city, heading northeast. The walls of the city had fallen on all sides, the once solid sandstone demolished in the blink of an eye. Within hours, a band of eternal beings laid waste to the large city. Which direction did they go? Were we headed right into their hands?

I was spent. All the thoughts I mustered completely wore me out. I laid my head back and closed my eyes, hoping that some semblance of Aleph would be there to greet me...but there was only darkness. "Is this it?" I whispered to Aleph once more. "Is this what you have for me?" I waited, hoping that I would hear the still small voice inside, the one that spoke for the past twenty years. But all I heard within me was silence.

CHAPTER
8

Deciding to rest for the night, we made camp on the outskirts of the city. The beautiful skyline of Northcrest, once visible for miles, was no more. I sat further away from the fire than the rest of my companions. The effects of breathing in the smoke were still fresh in my mind. Wanting nothing to do with it, I sat in the dark, alone with my unhealthy thoughts.

Mentally, I went back to all the battles I fought for King Tark and the cities we overthrew. Nothing we did in a week's campaign came close to the destruction the Nephilim did in a matter of hours. The thought of all the people whose lives were mercilessly ended made me shiver. No quarter was offered or any option for the inhabitants of Northcrest other than death.

What did the Nephilim look like? Could they speak? The hardest part of my turmoil was the unknowing. I still hadn't seen my enemy; therefore, I didn't know what we were dealing with. It was all too much to manage.

I pulled the cowl of the white cloak over my head and silently asked Aleph to take the images away. I closed my eyes, thinking that the scene would vanish, but all I could see within the recesses of my mind were thousands of mangled bodies, crushed under the stone of a collapsed city.

We supped with the provisions that were left, dried pork and veggies. Groth was not impressed and held his nose as he spooned in the greens. Loretta patted his back as he swallowed. "You see there, it's not so bad now, is it?" Groth looked at his wife with his mouth full of the veggies, not wanting to swallow. Finally, he did so, but I wondered if he was going to get up and vomit. After settling down, he repeated the process until his plate was empty.

The dishes were cleared, and we all watched the last bit of the sun go down behind the peaks of the Ternion Mountains. The only sounds were the crackling of fire and the soft, nervous tapping of Cal's hammer against a small rock. Suddenly, we heard a sound from behind us and turned eastward, toward the desert. Walking toward us through the dark sands was the silhouette of a large figure in a long cloak, whipping in the wind. Lionel and Groth immediately jumped up, their hands on their scabbards. I strode several feet toward the approaching stranger.

"Hello there!" I shouted into the desert. The figure didn't respond but continued walking confidently toward us, as if we weren't even there. I tried again. "Please identify yourself!" I shouted, more fervently this time. Again, the stranger kept silent, coming ever closer. Finally, I drew my sword toward the approaching figure and shouted. "I won't ask you again. If you don't respond, we will be forced to attack."

The stranger ignored us and kept coming. Lionel and Groth joined me in a defensive stance, ready to move into an attack position if needed. As the large stranger came closer, the light from the fire behind us showed on his features. He was a large man, with a bushy black beard and glowing blue eyes. As his form was completely revealed, he finally opened his mouth and spoke, calmly and gently.

"Greetings, my friends. I bid you a warm welcome and bless you in the name of Aleph."

"Jeru!" I cried out, abandoning my brothers, and running into the arms of the guardian. "Is it really you?" I asked desperately.

"It is," he responded as he looked carefully into my eyes. "You have been through quite a bit."

"You have no idea what we've been through!" I shouted angrily, pushing him back as the emotion overtook me. "Where have you been? These people...this city!" I cried, gesturing to the devastation behind us. Jeru followed my hand and looked painfully at the aftermath. A look of care and compassion overcame him.

"I am truly sorry, Anlace," he stated.

"Did you know?" I asked fervently. Jeru nodded his head in response. "Why didn't you tell me?"

"Would it have mattered?" Jeru questioned me.

"You let them die!" I screamed into the face of the large guardian. Jeru gently positioned me, so we were looking at each other.

"Aleph's wisdom is not like..."

"Enough about Aleph!" I shouted, cutting him off. "Aleph has been silent for days now. When we needed Him most, He remained quiet!"

Jeru looked back at me sternly, and I could feel the hard look passing through me. Suddenly, an impressive fear overcame me, as though I were standing at the edge of a large building, looking down. The awful feeling of falling off was replaced by the sudden relief of taking a step back into safety, a sensation that invaded my mind and heart.

Jeru was still staring into me with a gentle smile on his face as he spoke. "I think it is time you and I spoke, alone." He then gestured with his hand for me to follow him away from the camp, into the desert. I looked fearfully at my companions. They looked back at me with great concern. "Please join me now." The way he said those words was not a request, but a command.

I grabbed a small lantern out of my pack and walked with Jeru in the cool desert for over an hour. The guardian patiently asked me questions about Iska and the pain I carried for the past twenty years. He applauded me for opening up to Daeric and Esgar by reading the chronicle I wrote about my past, but he also wanted to inform me that my path to healing had only begun. He told me the process was long and complicated but trusting in Aleph and His timing was the key. He also told me not everything happens at once, but those wounds must be continually cleansed and bandaged before they heal. I enjoyed listening to the guardian. He spoke to me in ways that I could understand and relate to, using allegory and parables to get his point across. It was a refreshing time away from my companions, and Aleph knew I needed it.

After an enjoyable time of ministry, we came back to the immediate issue at hand. Jeru looked down at me for several moments before he spoke.

"Why are you doubting Aleph's abilities?" The words cut my heart like a knife.

"I'm sorry. I can't help it." I tried to reason with him but failed miserably. "I see nothing but hopelessness in front of me. All we have is a group of six against thousands of black cloaked soldiers and clerics. Not to mention the power of the Nephilim. How are we supposed to stand up to that eternal force?"

Jeru stood before me with his arms crossed and a serious expression on his face. "It's funny how similar you humans are in your thinking. Please take a seat." Jeru commanded, gesturing to a nearby rock. When I was seated, he continued. "I'm going to ask you a question, and I want you to answer." Jeru came over and kneeled in front of me, placing his hand on my shoulder and looking me directly in the eyes. As I met his gaze, it felt like a hand was gripping my heart and holding it.

"Do you really think you are in control?" His question brought a heaviness that made me bow my head in shame. He quickly placed a finger under my chin and lifted it so he could continue to gaze into my soul. "Has Aleph not provided everything you need thus far? Hasn't His eye been ever watchful and His hand quick to lend support?"

Hearing these questions from the mouth of the guardian brought a flood of emotion that I could not contain. I bowed my head again and began to weep. He continued his examination. "Answer me if you dare! Did Aleph not provide healing for you in the infirmary after Lady Iska's prayer was heard? Did His soothing breath not fill the gaping wounds in your back? Did Aleph not come to your rescue during the trial with Balafas, giving you words to speak and stirring the heart of Lady Iska to intervene and take you out of there? Did Aleph not cover you and Tobin in the alley so Lucien could not see you? Has Aleph not provided protection from the vagaries of magic by having His guardians sew you a cloak to wrap you in His marvelous light?"

The rebukes from Jeru by this time put me on my knees. I was completely vulnerable, and my soul laid bare. I opened my mouth to utter a response, but Jeru continued.

"Answer me, Father Anlace! Did Aleph not show you how to lead a group of men, not as their captain, but as a father? Did He not take all the insecurity and anger of your past, wad it up like a piece of paper, and throw it over His shoulder? Has He not provided you every day with His breath, strength, and courage to not only survive another day but to be lifted on the wings of guardians and walk freely in peace and joy all the days of your life?"

Tears flooded me as each word entered my heart. My eyes were closed, and as Jeru spoke, his words manifested as pictures in my mind of the glorious personality of Aleph the creator. I was seeing Him in every circumstance that I briefly forgotten. His words were powerful and cut my heart like a knife, but they were also encouraging, bringing peace. I felt the fear that gripped its decrepit hand around me and the camp lift off us. Jeru knelt and leaned in so I alone could hear him. He placed his hand on my head and spoke above a whisper.

"He is laughing. Do you know that?" Jeru whispered. "He

is laughing at our enemies. He sees their end and knows when their time is up." I dared to look up at the guardian and through tear-soaked eyes asked a question.

"How long will this continue? How long must we suffer?" Jeru took my hand and lifted me from off the ground.

"As long as it takes. Your suffering is good, Anlace. Don't you see this?"

"I guess I don't."

"Suffering is what cleanses you. It shows you who you really are and the faults that you carry. Only in suffering do you realize how frail and weak you are. At this time, Aleph can come and remove the poison from your heart."

"I don't understand," I replied.

"I know. Which is why I am visiting you. Your adventure will continue soon enough and will be filled with trials and tribulation. Your road is not easy, and you will need refreshing and encouragement before you continue. That is why I am here. I have brought you a gift." The guardian reached into the confines of his flowing robes and brought out a familiar looking journal.

"Wait a minute… that looks like…."

"Yes. It is the same journal you bought for Esgar in Rivertown."

"But…how?"

"I will try my best to explain this so you will understand. What you do not know is that like you, Aleph has a collection of books. A library, to say the least. These books have been written throughout all the ages, from many men and women. They chronicle the vastness of creation and hold wonderful stories about Aleph and His goodness. The book I present to you comes off a shelf from His library."

Jeru handed me the brown tome. I was shaking as I opened the book and looked down at the first page. My heart stopped as I read the words several times, not believing what I was seeing. Written in a thick font were the words...

THE BOOK OF ESGAR

"She has written this?"

"Not yet." Jeru responded.

"But how..." I began to ask.

"Remember, my friend. Aleph is not beholden to time as we are. He exists outside of it and therefore can move ahead, into the future, or behind, into the past. It is all the same to Him."

"What is this?"

"A chronicle of Esgar's past. But more importantly, a message to you."

"What kind of message?"

"That I cannot say. Matters of the heart are Aleph's domain, and I am merely a servant coming to deliver His message."

"Have you read this?"

"I have not. But I have been told by Aleph that the message within is especially important. It will help you answer some questions you may have. Esgar has an intimate knowledge of Aleph, unlike anyone else. She has also walked through trials unnumbered, and this journal will be an encouragement to you in some way."

I looked down again at the book I was holding and said a silent prayer to Aleph. Reading my thoughts, Jeru continued. "He has not gone silent, Anlace. He is always speaking to us. Sometimes, we must quiet the busy-ness around us to hear. But His voice is constant." I looked up into the guardian's eyes.

"When should I read it?"

"Tonight. Do not delay. The message is powerful and will eventually be shared throughout the entire world. This book is precious, and soon Aleph will speak to Esgar and put the words within her to write it. This book will be an artifact that the enemy will pursue. They will want it destroyed!"

"Why?"

"Read, and you will know," Jeru concluded.

"Okay. What about them?" I asked, pointing to my companions.

"They will read it as well. But you are first. Aleph is going to speak to you in a unique way as you digest the pages of this tome. Don't rush it."

"What about the Nephilim?" I cried out, looking around me.

"They have moved south. But don't dwell on those thoughts, Anlace. Now is not a time for worry. Read the book and be blessed." Without another word, Jeru walked away from me. The soft wind blew by, and light wisps of sand rose into the air. The night was still and quiet as I positioned myself against the smooth face of a large rock. The sand was soft under me, and the rock provided a good bit of support. I moved the lantern closer and laid the book on my lap.

I looked up and could see Jeru in the distance, sitting with my companions around the fire. Several bellowing laughs erupted from the group, which made me smile. They were obviously safe within the company of the guardian. Surrendering my will, I took a deep breath and opened the book. My fingers caressed the paper as I moved them over the title. I turned to the first page and focused my eyes. That evening, in the cool of the day, and in the presence of Aleph's guardian, I began to read the words of Esgar, princess of Raithe.

PART II

CHAPTER
9

I am taking the time by Aleph's request to write this. He said it is part of my healing process. This is not something I want to do. In fact, I'm absolutely terrified to go back to this in my mind. The horrific images have haunted me. My pain is in the past, and I have chosen a new identity. My name is Esgar, and I will never go back. Even unto my death, there will be no return. I will take my life before I ever cast another spell. I have forever disconnected myself from the vagaries of magic.

This is not my whole story, but what I remember...

I was four years old and sound asleep in my warm bed, thinking about a memory of Grandpa, who recently died. Thinking about any good memories of him was making it easier for me to go to sleep. On the edge of peaceful dreams, my bedroom door burst open. Mother swooped into my room and grabbed me by the wrist, squeezing it tightly.

"We have been summoned, Kristina!" she stated in a panic.

"Please ma...I'm tired. Want to go to bed." I began to cry.

"You will do as you are told, child. Come to me at once. The magistrate has called us to the steps of the palace. We cannot be late!" Mother opened my dresser and began frantically grabbing whatever she could to make me look presentable. "Your father's sister has brought trouble on all of us." I heard Mother grit her teeth as she uttered the word "sister."

"What's happening?" I asked, concerned about Auntie Iska. Mother whirled around to face me, a look of fear in her eyes.

"She has formed a reb…" That was as far as Mother got. Tears formed as she cupped her hand to her mouth, stifling a cry. It was hard to see Mother this way. She was usually confident and carried herself with an air of grace. But to see her like this—she was fearful…out of control.

"Ma…what is it?" I asked again, hoping to see some shred of resolve come over her, but alas, it was not going to happen. Mother continued to silently weep. After several moments, she came to her right mind.

"Stop looking at me child and do as you're told!" she snapped. I decided it was best not to tangle with Mother's emotions and joined her next to the dresser.

It was bedtime, and I wasn't accustomed to putting on a dress so late in the evening. The garment felt uncomfortably large on my small body. The fabric itched as well. Mother made fast work tying all my bows and tightening the straps. After it was in order, she began combing my hair. As she pulled on the tangles, I let out a squeal, which made her pull harder on the stubborn curl.

"Stop your crying! It doesn't hurt at all," Mother exclaimed.

"Yes, it does," I replied in tears.

"Well, if you kept it combed daily, we wouldn't be having this issue now, would we?! Look at my hair? Do you see any tangles?" I turned, looked up, and investigated her head of beautiful auburn curls.

"No, ma," I politely replied.

"That's what I thought. You need to take better care of your hair, Kristina. If you don't, it will look dry and matted." She continued to work on the tangles. After several agonizing moments of pulling my long, dark hair, she slammed the brush down on the dresser and turned me around.

"Let me look at you." Mother inspected her work. "Good enough. Now, dry your tears and meet me in the hall. We are being escorted by soldiers this evening."

I stopped and looked longingly to Mother. "Ma, maybe we can go horseback riding tomorrow?"

"No, I don't think so." She said quickly, turning away from me and walking towards the door. I looked at her, hoping she would change her mind. "No more stalling, child."

I finished putting on my shoes and joined Mother, who was accompanied by several soldiers in the hall. As we walked down the long corridor of the palace, I heard the roar of a crowd resounding outside the walls. The noise got louder and more intense as we came closer to the front entrance. It was almost deafening as the doors to the palace swung open.

I saw Father with my two older brothers at his side. He looked ash white and was having a hard time standing. Rufus and Morgan were holding him by his arms and struggling under the weight, trying to keep him from collapsing. What happened to Father? Why did he look so weak? What could I do to help him?

My thoughts were interrupted as I felt the rough touch of Mother, grabbing my arm and pulling me along. As I took my place beside my family, I gazed upon a massive crowd in the plaza below. They looked angry and were shouting and shaking their fists. To the right were the temple and a large marble staircase that descended to the plaza. Standing at the top of the stairs was the magistrate Balafas, and another bearded man dressed in black. Behind them in the shadows was the Dark Man I saw with the magistrate often. As he looked at me and grinned, I felt a cold shudder pass through me. I didn't appreciate his look at all. He scared me. Removing his gaze, he stared out over the large crowd with a pleased look on his face.

Balafas began to speak loudly and dramatically to the audience. He mentioned a rebellion that tried to overthrow the throne. This angered the crowd and they shouted louder than before. As their voices rose, Balafas' posture changed. He said he was appalled at the rebellion's actions. He called them unthinkable. People began throwing spoiled food on the steps leading up to the palace. Balafas continued addressing the crowd, letting them know that the rebellion was stopped, the ambassadors were rescued, and the leader of the conspiracy was captured.

Suddenly, the doors behind me opened, with two soldiers standing on both sides of Auntie Iska. Her head was down, and her hands were chained painfully in front of her.

I couldn't take it anymore—my emotions erupted. "Auntie Iska!" I screamed, running towards her. Suddenly, I felt cold, mailed hands grab me, pulling me back. The strength of the soldier was intense. My body left the ground, and I continued to scream until the soldier cupped his hand over my mouth. The cold steel was painful and the rest of my sounds were muffled. The soldier set me back down next to my older brother Rufus, who calmly held me.

I felt his comfort instantly and began weeping even harder. Then I looked up and saw Auntie Iska looking over at me. She looked longingly at me and mouthed the words silently: "It's okay. I love you." I reached out my hand, longing to be held close by her and experience her loving-kindness, which was so foreign between me and my parents.

Mother wore a hateful look on her face. She turned her head, not wanting to even look at Auntie Iska. I saw Mother clench her fists and hold her breath until she passed by. In desperation, I looked to my other parent.

Father stood there with a dazed look on his face, as if he were sleepwalking, not even a part of reality. He was oblivious to what was going on. I reached out and pulled on his pant leg, trying desperately to snap him out of the daze, but he kept looking forward with the same blank look on his face. Auntie Iska was now at the top of the steps, standing next to Balafas. His speech intensified as he continued his monologue.

The memory of what happened next will forever be burned into my mind. Balafas' voice reached its height as he shouted out the word "GUILTY," and the crowd roared loudly. I covered my ears and felt a flurry of movement around me as soldiers surrounded Auntie Iska. I saw one of them carrying a bucket. As he passed, red liquid splashed over the sides. He stepped up to where my aunt was standing. The rest of the soldiers moved out of the way.

The last thing I remember hearing was that Auntie Iska

was to be executed immediately. The crowd's roar was deafening as they shouted. Balafas raised his hands and began walking down the steps towards the plaza, as if he were a deity receiving praise from his creation. The bearded man followed one step behind him, leaving Auntie Iska all alone on the top step with the dark man grinning behind her.

With her sentence pronounced, she gazed in horror as the soldier with the bucket slowly approached. He lifted it in both his hands and heaved it forward over her. The red-dyed liquid, which looked like blood, now covered her to the soles of her feet. Her garment and white cape were completely drenched in crimson, symbolizing she was found guilty, and the blood which was spilled was upon her.

My heart broke as I watched the strongest, loving woman I ever knew, be reduced to a guilty criminal in the blink of an eye. I looked desperately at Father.

"Please Da! Help!" I cried aloud. But he only stared back as if he weren't even aware of what was going on.

The soldiers moved Auntie Iska down the steps to the foot of the plaza. I looked over to where she stood moments ago. A large pool of red liquid flowed slowly over the edge of the steps. I followed the trail to the bottom and saw soldiers bringing in a marble block. They were struggling to carry it and set it down with great difficulty. The rest of the soldiers were intent on moving the crowd and were met with some resistance. I saw swords raised upon those who were giving them trouble.

I felt like Father at that moment. I was in a nightmare, losing my sense of reality. Somewhere in the real world, I saw a large soldier pass me wearing a black hooded mask, carrying a large axe. Suddenly, rough hands grabbed me, and I viciously reacted with a spasm of movement.

"Leave me alone!" I screamed.

"I will not. Kristina, stop this behavior at once!" Mother scolded me, but I didn't care. The nightmare was real, and screaming was a perfectly natural response. "I said, stop your tantrum now, child!" I closed my eyes and cupped my hands over my ears, trying to block out the roaring of the crowd, hoping it would end. From my place in the dark, I heard Mother calling someone over and apologizing.

"My Lord Lucien! I'm sorry. I don't know what has gotten into her," she apologized.

"It is fine, my queen. She obviously has been through some trauma," the cold voice replied.

"Is there anything you can do? I would be in your debt," Mother asked.

"Would you, now?" the voice responded. "I have just the thing to help." My eyes were still closed as I felt hands on my shoulders. "Hold her still, now. A calm spell is all that is required." Mother tightened her grip on me. I sensed what felt like a sharp, claw-like talon touch my forehead and instinctively opened my eyes. To my horror, I saw the Dark Man standing before me, grinning. His long black hair flowed to the sides of his pale face, held in place by a glowing red band. It was his index finger touching me, sending cold shivers through my body.

"Don't resist the magic, little one. Let it flow over you." The Dark Man said, staring into my eyes. My stomach heaved and felt like everything I ate that day was going to come up. I squirmed and tried to move but couldn't. Mother had me in a tight grip.

"Stop resisting, Kristina," Mother instructed. I continued to squirm. The Dark Man opened his mouth, speaking guttural arcane words. Suddenly, it felt as though a multitude of unseen hands were grabbing me. I screamed again.

Lucien spoke louder and placed the whole of his palm over the top of my head. I felt like I was being doused with freezing water. In desperation, I kicked out with my foot. It must have landed because his hand immediately left my head. He stumbled backward, holding his crotch and moaning.

Mother turned me around and looked me in the face. "Why did you do that?" I stared back with tears in my eyes, defiant. I heard the Dark Man curse behind me.

"Filthy little wretch! You will learn to submit! By Baelor, I swear it! One day you will surrender!" His voice became fainter as he walked off, slightly bent over and shaking.

"You should not have done that, Kristina! That is Lord Lucien!" she cried, with a fearful look in her eyes.

"I don't care! I want to go to bed!" I screamed back. Mother, not knowing how to solve this, called over a soldier.

"Take her to her room." She looked at me. "We will talk about this later. You have dishonored this family with your actions tonight. You are no better than your whore of an aunt!" Once again, I was grabbed by rough hands and pulled away. "You will learn the way of things, Kristina. You are a princess now."

The soldier carried me through the front doors of the palace. As they closed behind me, all the noise faded to a dull roar. I was completely exhausted. I felt the cold touch of the Dark Man all over my body. I stared stonily at the walls of the corridors as we passed.

Finally, we made it to my room. The soldier opened the door, dumped me onto my bed, and walked out without another word. I lay there in shock with my eyes open, surrounded by stone walls. The images of Auntie Iska drenched in red liquid would not leave my mind, and the voices of the crowd shouting kept replaying in my head. The torment continued until suddenly, I heard in my mind the soft voice of Auntie Iska. She was singing a lullaby, like she did so many nights at my bedside. Her voice was soothing and calm. The song she sang was one I knew well and hearing her voice in my head was a blessed improvement to my situation. I began to softly sing the words of her song. As I did, I felt something. It was like a soft wind moving in the room. The wind moved over the flames of the candles. I saw them flicker, disturbing their illumination. The wind was dancing and responding to my words.

The soft gust blew over me, and suddenly, the cold from Lucien's touch left the atmosphere. Instead of cold tremors, I felt comforting warmth. It wrapped around me like a soft blanket, and with it came peace. The last thing I remember before slipping into unconsciousness was a voice. It was the softest voice, like a whisper, speaking to me from the inside.

I am with you always, Kristina. Finally, I lost all consciousness as sleep overcame me.

CHAPTER
10

Four long and lonely years passed. Mother's disdain of me continued to increase. Any time we were in a room together, she seemed uncomfortable merely being around me. It was a miserable time in my life, as I grew up desperately seeking her affection, hoping the stone of her heart would shatter, and she would remember her love towards me. But alas, with every passing year, she grew colder.

As for our upbringing, my brothers and I had no freedom to go anywhere or say anything that was not given to us on a piece of paper from the magistrate ahead of time. Going into the plaza or common sector was forbidden. Mother said that our lives were too precious to risk, and that our safety was of the utmost importance. So, I stayed within the confines of the palace, which became my prison.

My studies were conducted on the premises by a tutor who came in to see us every morning. She was kind and patient, and I enjoyed receiving instruction from her. Some weeks, it felt like she was all the interaction I had. Mother and Father were always with the magistrate and his "advisor," as Lucien was called. My dealings with the Dark Man, since the execution of Auntie Iska, were rare. But every time I saw him, he would look at me with a grin that made me altogether uncomfortable.

On the evening of my eighth birthday, Mother filled the royal dining hall with guests from all over. None of them were people I knew. In fact, when I asked her if I could invite anyone, she looked at me in shock, as though I asked her an appalling question. I was under no delusion that this party was for me. It was in fact another opportunity for Mother and Father to flaunt their power and prestige.

My older brother Morgan and I were bored and decided to play a little game. It was innocent at first, but because Morgan was at the helm, it quickly turned to mischief. It involved a powder he concocted during science instruction made of pure lemon extract. He put a small amount in a glass of water and told me to try it. I took a sip and immediately spit it out.

Morgan laughed, holding his stomach. "How'd it taste?"

"Wow, that's thour!" I exclaimed. I was having a hard time forming sentences. My lips were all puckered, and my tongue was numb. It was hard to enunciate.

With the experiment in hand, we stealthily moved over to the royal table and poured a generous amount into Mother and Father's goblet. Because there was a good amount of powder left, we put some into the magistrate's goblet as well. With the deed done, we darted away into the shadows and waited.

When it was time for the ceremonial toast, everyone gathered as Father made a boring speech about peace and prosperity in Shalistar and the conquest of Zulkanda, far to the east, which had begun. There were cheers from all around and praises given to King Remus and his family, may we all reign forever. I looked at Mother, and her face was beaming as the applause was received by her and Father. After the speech was given, everyone tipped their glasses back and drank deeply.

Morgan and I watched from the shadows of the hall as looks of displeasure instantly came over Mother and Father. They spit out their drinks, to the surprise of all. The magistrate followed suit, having tasted the foul beverage as well. The tablecloth and food in front of them were drenched in backwashed liquid. They were appalled as realization of the situation struck them. Father opened his mouth and began to shout at a servant, asking for the meaning of what happened.

"Thith drink is dithgusthing!" he shouted, unable to form the words correctly. Several snickers of laughter erupted from the audience. Mother turned her head to those who laughed, looking at them in disgust.

"He ith your king! It ith disgrathful to laugh at him!" More laughter erupted as she spoke. The powder worked brilliantly! Their speech was completely broken!

The magistrate stepped up and spoke. "That ith enough! I command you to thop it!" Even more uproarious laughter erupted from the crowd until the entire room was filled with it.

Morgan and I were laughing so hard we didn't see the long shadow of the Dark Man standing over us. "I think I know what has happened here." As we heard his voice, we looked up. He was staring through us and searching us. Even though the laughter felt so good, it couldn't stave off the chill of fear. We knew we were in trouble. All eyes in the audience turned towards where we were huddled. As I saw the hateful face of Mother looking at me, I knew it was going to be a long night.

I awoke from my bed the next morning with a yawn. I sat up startled as I looked to my left and saw Mother sitting there beside me. She obviously snuck into my room in the early morning. She looked tired and nervous, like she hadn't slept all night. I rubbed the sleep out of my eyes and greeted her.

"Morning, Ma," I said with a smile. She stared back at me with fire in her eyes. After several moments of unbearable silence, I tried again. "Ma? Good morning." Again, she glared at me with a look of disgust. "Ma…"

She cut me off. "Last night's behavior will never be repeated, Kristina. Do you understand me?"

"But Ma…" I protested.

"No buts, child! You embarrassed our entire family with your actions towards your father and me. You and Morgan will apologize to him upon your first day of school."

"School?" I asked her, wondering what she meant.

"Yes. It is obvious that your free spirit has gotten the best of you. Your Father and I met with Lord Lucien after you were dismissed, and we have arranged for you and your brothers to attend a special school starting next week." As I heard Mother say those words, I felt the temperature in the room grow colder.

"What kind of school?" I asked nervously. Mother stood up and walked over to the window. "Ma, what kind of school?" She wouldn't answer. She stared blankly out the window. "Ma, please tell me," I pleaded with her.

She finally answered. "Kristina, you are special, but require discipline. You need help, and your father and I are not going to be available. Lord Lucien has a program that he and Balafas have designed over the last decade to help facilitate the growth of those who are special. There are several of these schools in the city, but the one you will attend is the most prestigious and overseen by Lord Lucien himself."

My heart pounded as she revealed her plan to me. I nervously grabbed my blanket and held it close, trying to hide myself. "He will help you discover your talents and teach you how to use them effectively."

The shock of this news was taking its toll on me. I began looking around the room, trying to find a way of escape. Then a thought hit me.

"Why does everyone I care about leave?! First Auntie Iska, then Abigail, and now my parents!" I exclaimed, hoping for some form of comfort. Mother whipped around and looked at me in anger.

"You are never to mention that name—do you understand me, Kristina?! Your aunt was a traitor to this family and this kingdom. Her name will forever be associated with her treachery. I will not hear of it again from you or anyone else. The memory of her is dead to this family. Do you understand me?!" My heart hurt, hearing the blistering comments from Mother.

"How can I not speak about the only person who loved

me? Auntie Iska is the only one who showed me any type of affection!"

As quick as a snake, Mother crossed over to me and lashed out with her hand, connecting it with my cheek. A spasm of pain erupted on the side of my face. I looked up at Mother in shock. A moment of silence followed. Mother had a look of awe on her face, thinking about what she had done.

"She is dead, Kristina, along with the memory of her. Don't mention her name again," Mother replied coldly. She crossed over to the door of my room, leaving me alone in my bed, holding my throbbing cheek. She turned the knob, and the door squeaked open. "School begins tomorrow," she concluded, not looking in my direction. Without another word, she crossed over the threshold and slammed the door, producing a loud crash which echoed throughout my room.

The next morning, a handmaiden entered, helping me get dressed for school. Rufus and Morgan were going to the same place as I, so this would be a new experience for them as well.

I examined the uniform laid out for me. The tunic was dark and ugly. A crest of a golden dragon was embroidered into the fabric on the left chest side. The pants were made of fabric that was stiff and itchy. A black cloak with a thick cowl completed the ensemble. Along the bottom of the cloak was a deep red trim. I tried it on and noticed it was a bit too large for me. The trim of the cloak touched the floor. The handmaiden shrieked when she saw this and grabbed it from me. I watched as she pulled out a sewing kit from her pouch and began hemming the fabric. She worked expertly, and within minutes, the bottom of the cloak was fixed. She threw it over me again and smiled at her work.

I asked the handmaiden her name, but she looked at me and shook her head, grunting and gesturing with her hands. I was confused and didn't know what she was trying to communicate. I asked her again. She looked at me and placed a hand over her mouth, shaking her head.

"You can't talk?" I questioned. The maiden nodded her head "yes."

"I'm sorry. That must be hard." The woman shrugged her shoulders and went back to work checking my clothing. Suddenly, the door to the room burst open, and Mother swooped in. As she approached us, I stood up straight.

"You may leave us," she commanded the maiden. With a bow, she exited, leaving me alone with Mother. I held my breath, waiting for scolding words to come out of her mouth. She tussled the clothing and checked all the lengths to make sure they fit. After a thorough inspection, she turned me towards the door. "Your brothers are heading this way now. You will meet them out in the hall."

"Ma...I don't want to go," I said pleadingly. "Don't make me go. I'll act better, I promise!"

"Kristina, you will do as you are told," Mother responded.

"But Mama..."

"Enough!" I could feel the power of her shout. "So much rebellion is in you! Hopefully, Lord Lucien can straighten you out. He has requested your presence in the quad when you get to school."

"What kind of school is this?" I asked curiously.

"You will go where you are told, and there is nothing more to be said," she said evasively.

"Will I get to come back?" I urged her.

"That is entirely up to you."

"I don't understand."

"If you behave and listen to your instructors, you will come home each weekend." The last word Mother spoke produced a cold chill that passed through me. I didn't like the way it sounded.

A brief time later, we stood at the front entrance to the palace, surrounded by a group of elite guards. Rufus and Morgan were excited to be going to this new school. They spoke of the opportunities that came with such a privilege. I was not convinced and stood behind them. Mother didn't give us any kind of goodbye; she simply dropped us off at the front door and left. No hug was given, and no sweet word of encouragement was heard—just a quick turn of her heel, and she was gone.

"That was nice of Ma to say goodbye, don't you think?" Morgan jested.

Rufus punched him on his shoulder. "Don't be such a pain. She was late for a meeting or something."

"Yeah, like for the last ten years, huh?" Morgan returned sourly.

I started to get emotional, and Rufus bent down to hold me. "It'll be okay, Lil' Sis. We are going to a special place. We will lack for no accommodations and be given the best education."

"I don't want to go. I'm scared."

"I understand. But school is a lot of fun. It's a place where you can make friends." That comment made me perk up. Having friends would be nice. Rufus continued encouraging me. "Being a princess will have its benefits—you'll see."

"Will we be together?" I asked hopefully.

"No, Lil' Sis. You are eight years old. I'm four years older than you and will be with the bigger kids. Morgan will be, too. You'll be with your own class. It's okay, though—we will be together on the weekends when we go home."

"You mean we have to stay there all week?"

"Yes. We work all week, and then on the evening of the fifth day, we're allowed to go home." The soldiers began to line up. Seeing them, Rufus stood up and brushed his straight dark hair out from in front of his emerald, green eyes. "Come now, Lil' Sis, be brave. It's time."

The doors to the palace opened, and the brilliance of the morning light flooded in, making my eyes water. The lead soldier shouted a command, and the escorts all around us began moving as one down the steps of the palace. I looked back one last time, hoping to see Mother standing there watching over us, but all I could see behind me, through the clanging black armor of the soldiers, were several servants moving up the grand staircase on an errand.

We moved in unison at a quick tempo to stay within the protective cluster of soldiers. As we began marching down the steps to the plaza, the horrific memory of my aunt in chains flooded me. Years ago, she walked these same steps to her death. The memory tugged at my heart and brought tears to my eyes. Morgan heard me sniffle and looked down at me. He must have shared the same thought because he took my hand and squeezed it, acknowledging my pain. It was a comfort to feel his touch.

As we reached the bottom of the steps and moved into the plaza, I looked down at the smooth stone under my feet. Slightly to my right was a faded brown stain. I closed my eyes, fighting the images that wanted to invade my mind, images of Auntie Iska's execution on this very spot. Morgan squeezed my hand three more times. I knew we were sharing the same emotion.

"It's going to be alright, Sis." Morgan calmly said as we passed.

"Why didn't they clean it?" I asked.

"It's a reminder. They want all the people to know what happens to traitors," he replied.

"They should have cleaned it," I returned to him.

"Yes, Sis. They should have," Morgan said to the air, ending the conversation.

We continued to march through the wide-open plaza, over the bridges towards the massive central landmark, the Guardian's Fountain. Citizens were already out, enjoying the tranquility of the sound of water endlessly flowing. I looked up at the image of the guardians holding the figure of Baelor. The face that was carved intricately into the marble was shocking.

"Remember." I heard a soft whisper and looked up at Morgan, who was still holding my hand.

"Remember what, brother?" I asked curiously. He looked down and cocked his head in confusion.

"What are you talking about, Sis?"

"You just told me...remember?"

"Remember? No...I didn't."

"Just now, Morgan. You said, remember."

"Not sure what game we're playing right now, Sis."

"You didn't tell me to remember?"

"No, you must be hearing things." Morgan let go of my hand and looked out into the plaza, leaving me alone with my thoughts.

We walked through the large gate that entered the prestige sector of the city. Looking up, I saw many black cloaked soldiers standing guard high upon the stone ramparts, some of them looking towards the plaza and others watching over the prestige sector. From that vantage, they had an unobstructed view and could spot trouble from far away.

It didn't shock me in the least to see we were moving into this part of the city. Mother would never allow us to attend a school in the common sector. She thought of those people as an infestation that needed to be dealt with. Like rats in the cupboard, they were pests. It made me sad because Abigail was a commoner. I enjoyed being around my handmaiden. She was kind and taught me to paint, even though I was never any good at it.

I remembered one day she was teaching me to mix primary colors, and having a bit of fun with it—a little too much fun because the paint got all over the room and my clothes. Mother came in and about blew her top. That day, she docked my handmaiden's pay to reimburse us for the damage. Abigail agreed with her head held high. She was not going to let Mother get to her.

"Look over there!" shouted Rufus with excitement, bringing me back to reality. "I think it's a cleric!" I turned my gaze to the west end of the street. In front of a tavern was a handful of citizens standing around a man wearing a black uniform with a dark cloak. His cowl was pulled back, and he wore an intense look on his face. Rufus, unable to contain his excitement, ran over to where the group was gathered. Several of the soldiers broke rank and went with him, calling out to him.

"Your Majesty! We have a schedule to keep. We cannot be gallivanting in the streets!" Rufus didn't hear him. He was enthralled at seeing a cleric and was not going to be deterred.

Rufus stopped several feet away from the front steps of the tavern. The cleric saw him approach and bowed slightly, then went back to his demonstration. I heard the word "illusion" being spoken and looked through the legs of the soldiers towards my older brother. The dark-cloaked man was speaking words to the small crowd around him. I could see Rufus expectantly waiting for something to happen. After several moments, the cleric crossed his hands in front of his chest and moved his lips. Suddenly, his entire form vanished! The crowd and Rufus let out a gasp, seeing the man disappear before their very eyes. They looked around, trying to find him, but couldn't see him anywhere. The suspense was maddening, until suddenly, he re-appeared on the top step of the tavern. I saw him bend down and take an object from the step, quickly putting it into his pocket.

The air was filled with applause, as the cleric bowed. Rufus ran up excitedly, shaking his hand, pumping it up and down. The cleric bent over and placed his hand on Rufus' head. He spoke several words, then tousled his dark hair and smiled. He raised his hands to the crowd, and through all the cheering I heard the words: "…gift of Baelor."

Several moments later, Rufus rejoined us. He spent the rest of our walk talking incessantly to Morgan about the gifts of Baelor and how he desired to receive them one day. Out of his mouth poured a list of terms that were foreign to me. I was too young to understand what they were speaking of, but Morgan wasn't. He was as excited as Rufus and began asking him one question after another.

After our brief stop in front of the tavern, we made several turns within the cosmopolitan labyrinth of the prestige sector until we found ourselves in an open area. The stone buildings on either side of us fanned out, revealing a large cul-de-sac. At the end of the wide circle was a clean building with a bell tower. As we approached the north face of the school, I saw it dressed in massive marble columns along the front—an impressive sight to behold.

A large stone staircase led upward to the entrance, which was hidden in shadows from the columns. At the foot of the stairs was the main promenade, which went all the way to the street. A handful of smaller walkways branched out from the main path, winding around the building. On the sides of these walkways were planted small trees that bloomed within the morning light. Students dressed in uniforms identical to our own scurried up the steps to the entrance, anxious to get the day started.

As I took in the sight before me, I noticed how the risen sun was now casting long shadows over the building, giving it an ominous appearance. I looked over at my brothers, who were oblivious to anything going on around them. They couldn't stop talking about the cleric's demonstration. Seeing them lost in their own world made me feel lonely. I turned my face downward toward the stony street and sighed deeply. This day was already proving to be long and strenuous.

The front doors opened, and we were escorted into the main hall. As we crossed the threshold, I could hear children of all ages on the other side of the doorway. Now that we were in the building, our escort of soldiers was reduced to only three. The main hall looked old and smelled funny. Before us was a large staircase. To the right and left of it were two long hallways, with many doors along each side.

As we came into the center of the hallway, I looked up and noticed that the staircase winded around in a square and ascended four floors. Students in black uniforms were hurrying up and down these stairs, while adults strategically guided the flow of traffic.

The soldiers told us we were expected in the quad and led us past the large staircase. We continued halfway down the hall until we came to a large wooden door on the right. As we walked through it, daylight invaded the dark hallway, making us squint. We found ourselves in a beautiful courtyard that rested in the middle of the school. As my sight came back, I looked around to see windows surrounding the courtyard on all sides. I now understood the layout of the school. The staircase in the main hall went up to four different floors with a main landing foyer, like the one we entered. There were two hallways: one to the right and one to the left of the stairway. At the end of those halls was a shorter hall that connected the two longer hallways. The entire school was built in the shape of a rectangle, with a large courtyard in the middle.

I was proud of myself for having put all the pieces together so quickly in my mind. I wasn't going to get lost, that was for sure. As we came into the center of the courtyard, I noticed three chairs arranged in front of a large tree. I saw the form of Balafas standing next to someone else under the leaves. He saw us enter and politely asked us to come in and have a seat.

As I sat in one of the three chairs, I investigated the shadows and felt my heart stop for the second time that day. Leaning casually against the trunk with his arms across his chest was the Dark Man, Lucien. The red band on his forehead was creating a dramatic glowing effect within the shadows of the tree. He saw me and bowed his head, brandishing his handsome grin. I instantly felt cold all over.

"Welcome! Welcome!" The magistrate greeted us. "I am so excited to be here today! Everyone knows I have an extensive line of cases awaiting trial at the palace, but I have decided to be here and welcome you to my alma mater!"

I raised my hand, and Balafas addressed me. "Yes, child? So polite of you to raise your hand. How old are you?"

"I'm eight. You were at my birthday party two days ago, remember?"

Balafas chuckled at my comment. "And so observant as well. Nothing gets past you, Princess Kristina. You will make the perfect addition to our alumni one day."

Rufus raised his hand next, and Balafas called on him. "Yes, good sir?"

"Why are we here? In this school? Mother said it was for our education. What did she mean by that?" Rufus inquired.

"Your mother has such good instincts—motherly instincts. After recent events, I have counseled your mother to have you moved to this school. Here you can be under the watchful eyes of my best guard and learn from the most experienced instructors in all of Shalistar." Balafas glanced over to the Dark Man and quickly back to us. "You will have "certain opportunities" to learn what other children cannot."

"Magic!" exclaimed Morgan. I noticed a hungry look on Lucien's face, like he walked into a room with a steaming roast on the table. He looked longingly at my brother in a way that made me entirely uncomfortable.

Balafas politely told my brother to remain quiet. "Our institution will afford you prestigious opportunities that cannot be found elsewhere. Since my graduation many years ago, I have always desired the opportunity to improve the structure here, which is why I accepted the position as head of the board. We have made changes over the past years to the curriculum and created a reward system."

Rufus raised his hand, and Balafas gestured to him. "What kind of reward system?"

"All in suitable time, Your Majesty. The reward system is earned on merit. As you continue your studies with the rest of the students, know that you will be observed. If you show promise, you will be conferred to the "elite congregation," a status reserved for only the most distinguished students, capable of receiving a higher level of education. You three are to be given every opportunity available for that honor."

I raised my hand, and Balafas called on me. "When do we get to go home?"

"Dear child…I know this is all new to you, and we will do our best to make you feel welcome. School will resume throughout the week, and if the next day is a school day, you are required to be here on campus. We have dormitories for both boys and girls, separated by age. They are located on the fourth floor. If you have no demerits, you will be allowed to go home."

Morgan raised his hand next, and Balafas called on him. "What are demerits?"

Balafas looked over to Lucien again before continuing. "I wouldn't even worry about demerits, young prince. They are reserved for children who are not willing to submit to authority. But just so we cover everything in this orientation, a demerit is a disciplinary mark that will result in arduous labor over the weekend. We have many tasks to be accomplished, and none of them are ever pleasant. But, come now… let us not think about that. This is your first day, and we want you to enjoy your new school."

Balafas spent the next hour going over the boring details of schedules, classes, and mealtimes. He answered several of Morgan's questions about the dormitories and the way they broke up sleeping arrangements by age. He and Rufus were in the same age group and would be roommates. I, however, would be alone with a group of girls I didn't know. The thought of being separated from my brothers made me nervous.

I looked over at Lucien, who was leaning casually against the tree, smiling. Up until now he hadn't said a word, but I noticed he kept looking at the three of us with that hungry look in his eyes. I don't think Rufus and Morgan even noticed it, but it made me uncomfortable.

After orientation concluded, I was immediately separated from my brothers. I cried out, in a trembling voice, "Rufus! Morgan!" They turned around together, smiling.

"It's going to be okay, Lil' Sis," Rufus said. "We will see each other in a couple of days. The weekend will be here before you know it." With those words, Rufus and Morgan exited the courtyard to the right, leaving me alone with my female escort.

"Princess Kristina," a darkly smooth voice resounded. "It is time for you to get to class." I turned around to see the Dark Man standing behind me and smiling. He bowed and gestured with a swoop of his hand towards the escort, bidding me to follow her. She was a larger woman with curly blonde hair and wore a black and white garb to denote her status in the school. She was not a teacher but a servant who was assigned to me and those in my age group. The assistant stretched out her hand for me to take it. I reluctantly did so.

"It's going to be okay, Princess," she tried to comfort me. "We will take good care of you here." We moved over to the left side of the courtyard and opened the door to the downstairs hall. I looked back one last time and saw Lucien, the Dark Man, staring at me. I quickly turned back to the assistant.

"What is your name?" I asked the lady.

"Beth," she replied quickly.

"Nice to meet you. My name is Kristina," I politely returned.

"It is an honor, my lady," Beth responded. "Right this way, Princess. Your class awaits."

We walked down the hallway toward the back of the school. With every step, I noticed a deep reverberating echo. The sounds filled the silence. Instruction had begun, so the halls were completely empty. I felt small in the dark hall with the escort leading me. The stone walls on either side were illuminated brightly by many sconces, and above me the occasional candelabra was hanging by a chain. Large paintings depicting historical moments in time gave the dark hall a bit of warmth. Seeing the artwork brought a smile to my face as it reminded me of my handmaiden, Abigail.

There were no windows in the halls but only large wooden doors going into the classrooms. I could faintly hear the teachers' instructions on the other side of the doors as we passed by, arithmetic behind one and a history lesson behind another.

Suddenly, I heard swords clanging, and it made me jump. Beth squeezed my hand. "Don't be startled—these students are learning the art of the sword," she explained. "We've received the instruction of Master Wynn, our renowned sword master, for the past fifty years. He has trained many older boys and girls. He even instructed the magistrate himself when he was a student here."

The clanging faded as we moved along. When we reached the end of the long hallway, I looked to my right and saw another corridor that connected to the parallel hall. Halfway down, a staircase climbed upward to the other floors of the school. "This way, Your Majesty," Beth said politely, guiding me to a door on the left.

We went through another corridor and down a flight of stairs. Shrouded in darkness, my hands clenched into fists. It was hard to see because the staircase was lit by several small sconces. I couldn't see the bottom. Was it my imagination, or was it getting darker and darker the further down we went? The silence in this part of the school was alarming. I heard nothing except the soft, rhythmic breathing of my escort as we descended.

Suddenly, the silence was broken with the faint voices of children, chanting in unison. Hearing the unknown words made me feel uneasy. I was trembling and stopped to catch my breath. As I came back up, I saw my escort turn around.

"This way, Your Majesty," she said again in a monotonous voice. I didn't want to follow her anymore. Something was wrong, and I could feel it. Beth reached out her hand and squeezed my shoulder with a good amount of force that made me let out a slight shriek. She looked at me again, right into my sapphire blue eyes. "This way, Your Majesty."

Against my will, I continued to the final step, in front of a wooden double door. It opened to a room with no windows or furniture, except for a large desk in the far back corner. Children of all ages were seated in a circle within the middle of the room. The only light came from a large candelabra hanging from the ceiling. I slowly entered, standing slightly behind Beth, not wanting anyone to see me. The children didn't seem to notice me and continued chanting arcane words that I didn't understand.

Then I heard a soft, yet authoritative voice calling my name. The owner of the voice was sitting in a chair behind the desk. "Come to me, my child. Let me have a look at you." Beth took me across the room and stood me in front of the desk. I could see a hunched figure wearing a cowl, but the person's face was not visible. From the sound of the voice, it was definitely a man. He continued speaking softly and smoothly.

"You are here, Kristina, because you have been chosen," he began.

"I don't want to be here, sir. I want to go home," I responded defiantly.

"My dear child…" he said, shaking his head. The sooner you realize the truth, the better it will be for all of us."

"What do you mean?" I asked.

"What I mean is that you are going to stay here, with me and your classmates." He gestured to the children around me. "You will not be going home. You will not be eating, and you will not be drinking until I say so."

"What is your name?" I asked curiously.

"Who I am is not important, my dilemma is. Just so formalities are out of the way, you may call me 'Master.'" The voice paused for a second, waiting for a revelation to register. "You see, child, we have lost four years of instruction with you, and Lord Lucien made it abundantly clear that you are a very special child."

"Me, special?"

"Yes. Your brothers will come along in time. But you, my dear, are far beyond their skill level and still only eight years old. We are going to accelerate your learning," the soft voice continued.

"Learning what?" I asked.

The voice gave a soft chuckle. "The gifts, my dear."

"Gifts? What gifts?"

"The gifts of Baelor!" As he pronounced those words, a cold shudder passed through me.

"What are those, Master?" I asked slowly.

"Special skills, reserved for only the worthiest," the voice spoke. "You, my daughter, will become a cleric one day, and according to Lord Lucien, you have the ability to be one of the most gifted of all time!"

"I don't understand," I said.

The figure rose and came around to the other side of the desk. He knelt, and for the first time I saw his face. The flames from the candles on the desk danced within his eyes, giving him an eerie presence. He placed a finger under my chin and raised my head up. "My child…you really don't know, do you?"

"Know what?" I asked softly.

"That you are a slave! That your whole family is imprisoned! Your father is under the control of the mighty Baelor!" I started to step back from Master with a look of shock on my face. "It's okay, my child. It was bound to happen soon or later."

"I don't believe you…" I took another step back from Master, looking behind me. The chanting from the circle stopped, and the children looked at the two of us.

"Of course, you don't. Why would you? You are not a true believer…not yet."

"I demand to be released from this school," I commanded.

Master chuckled at my comment. "You are so precious and naïve. Lord Lucien said you would be quite the project." The hooded man continued to move toward me. "Let's give up the charade, Princess. It is time you knew who is really in control."

I stood up straight and commanded again. "I said that I demand…"

"You demand nothing!" Master shouted, and my heart skipped a beat. I stumbled over my feet and fell onto my bottom on the hard stone floor. "You, Princess, have no rights or privileges except what I say you have! You will go only where I tell you to go, and you will do what I tell you to do! Any deviation from my commands will result in a demerit. Do you understand?! I am not here for your entertainment, girl! I AM YOUR MASTER, AND YOU WILL OBEY!"

I heard enough. I scampered to my feet and ran towards the door. Beth was standing in front of it, hindering my path. She put a hand outward and spoke.

"It would be best if you obeyed," she said calmly. With a grunt, I shoved her with all my might and threw open the doors. I ran as fast as I could up the long flight of stairs and opened the door to the main hallway. I turned right and ran towards the front entrance. Wooden doors flew by as I passed them. I was only several yards from the front door when I saw Lucien to my right, watching me and grinning as I ran by. I finally reached the front door and pulled it open. Natural light from the sun poured into the dark keep, blinding me. I took a step outside and ran right into the chest of a dark, uniformed figure. I stumbled back from the collision and looked up into the hooded pale face of Master.

I stared, aghast. "How did he get here so fast?" Thoughts rushed through my mind.

"Going somewhere?" Master asked softly. I turned around to run but saw the Dark Man standing right behind me, grinning.

"It seems to me, Princess, that we better keep a close eye on you," Lucien stated. There was nowhere to go. I was trapped. Lucien looked to Master and nodded. Master moved behind me and spoke several arcane words. Invisible arms wrapped around my body in a tight vice. I couldn't move at all; they were held in place by a magic spell. Fear overtook me instantly, and I opened my mouth to scream. Lucien stepped forward and quickly spoke a word in another dark language. Suddenly, I felt like my mouth was gagged by an unseen cloth. My screams were silent. The magical gag was shoved farther into my throat, causing me to choke.

"Screaming will only make it worse, my dear," Lucien said coldly. The more you scream, the further the gag will go down your throat." I stopped screaming and looked into the eyes of the Dark Man. The handsome, pale-faced man looked right back into my own. As he did so, the red band on his forehead glowed. "I told you, Princess...one day... you would submit. You do not fully understand the power of Baelor, but you will." Lucien reached out his hand and placed it on top of my head, speaking several more arcane words. A drowsiness overcame me. "You, my child, will be a great weapon one day!"

I was slipping into unconsciousness and fought with everything in me to stay awake. As I faded into darkness, I saw Lucien look back at Master. "She's all yours. Take her back to class."

"Yes, my Master," I heard him say, and then I slipped completely into a dark void.

CHAPTER
11

Two years passed in the blink of an eye. I was completely immersed in a system of control, unable to break free. My spirit was broken, and all that remained was a shell of an existence. Days and nights came and went as I learned the arcane arts from the underground room, shrouded in darkness. Regular educational subjects were interspersed throughout the school day, but I was not fooled. This was not a normal school. We were slaves of Baelor, to be used and trafficked in the world system. We were taught only what was needed to fulfill the system's agenda, nothing more and nothing less.

As we progressed in our mystical studies, we were promised opportunities to learn more powerful spells and become heroes of Shalistar as we took on the mantle of a cleric, but for most of us, these were empty contracts. It was like a carrot being dangled before the horse to get it to trot, a means to an end. But the saddest reality of it all was that I allowed it to happen. I believed the lies spoken to me by Master, that I was a slave who needed to work to gain freedom. It was a tragedy, to say the least. I was in a nightmare, one that I believed would never end. That is, until the day after my tenth birthday.

◇

"Kristina!" I heard a lovingly soft voice calling my name as I sat in a circle of the dark room. We were chanting, summoning Baelor all morning, awaiting his messenger. I looked over at my friend, wondering if she heard the same voice. She was still in a trance. This voice was different, yet familiar. Like a lullaby from long ago sung over me in times of trouble.

Master was at his desk scribbling in his black book, as he did so often. I asked him a year ago what he was writing. He told me it was no concern of mine and to get back to my studies. That is the way it was with Master. He was always harsh and drove us to the edge. If we didn't wake up at dawn and pursue Baelor's messenger, it was a demerit. A minimum of three hours each day was spent asking for and receiving power from Baelor. It came with a price though.

When the messenger did come, we promised seven days of life to it. Once the agreement was made, the messenger would place his hand on us, and we would receive a portion of power for the day—one day of power for seven days of life. It was an unfair ratio but a daily requirement to operate effectively in magic.

"Kristina!" The sweet voice whispered again. It was so otherworldly and far away yet felt like it was in the room with me the whole time. I looked again at my classmates, wondering if I was going crazy. They were all focused on summoning the messengers and took no notice of me. I closed my eyes again.

"Kristina, my daughter." The voice made my heartbeat faster. I moved my fingers over my outstretched palms—they felt

damp. What was this feeling? It was contrary to anything I felt before. The air was heavy, but not in a foreboding way. The room was dark, but for whatever reason, I could sense a brilliant light on the other side of my closed eyelids. The voice called me daughter, as though it knew me intimately as its own.

"My child! You have broken the circle with Baelor." I heard a darkly familiar voice erupt in my mind. I instantly opened my eyes, and to my horror, saw Master standing over me. "Where is your concentration today?"

I was unsure of how to answer. My concentration was always on my studies, be it mundane arithmetic or arcane sorcery. It didn't matter—I was the ideal student, and I usually had no problems focusing during summons. Other students would nod off due to the early hours, especially after cramming all night for a test in history. But not me—I was always up and ready to summon a messenger. But today was altogether different. I felt out of control. "I'm sorry Master."

He looked hard at me, trying to gauge my words. All my classmates continued to chant, but I could see that several of them had their eyes open, staring at us and the conversation we were having.

"This is unacceptable, child," Master berated me. "Baelor hasn't sent a messenger to us today, and we need power. We are going on a field trip in several hours and will need all the power we can muster for it. Teleportation through illusion is no parlor trick. This is not like opening a locked door, child!"

"Yes, Master. I'm sorry for my lack of concentration," I stammered.

"Are you, now? Well then, can we get back to it then?!"

Master asked coldly, turning his back to me. All my classmates were staring at me. Their look told me everything. They were exhausted and needed my assistance.

I apologized and closed my eyes again. The brilliant light was gone for now. I no longer heard the soft, gentle whisper. I could only sense the familiar darkness of the eternal void. Once again, I connected myself to the circle of sorcery and continued summoning the messenger of Baelor.

After several hours, we were back in our dorm room, packing our belongings for the trip. Viveka was busily filling a bag next to me. She was my friend, and I connected with her in many ways. She didn't treat me like a princess, like the rest of the class did, which was fine with me. I didn't ever feel like a princess anyway.

She stopped packing and gazed over at me with a concerned look on her face. "Where was your mind during summons? What happened?" she asked.

I was once again at a loss for words. Even though I trusted my friend, I was uneasy about sharing the experience with her. I did something I never thought I would do. I lied. "I was thinking about Father and Mother. It distracted me." She looked hard at me.

"Father and Mother?" she questioned. "That's all?"

"We had a fight last time I was at home and said some things we didn't mean. I was thinking about how I would apologize."

"Well...let me know if I can be of any help. This weekend, maybe we can set up some obstacles or go swimming?" Viveka asked and went back to her packing. It was spring break, and we were finally headed on our field trip. This was a prominent event at the school that allowed us to leave campus and assist the magistrate's army in the field. Only students ten years and above got to go. This would be my first trip, and I was nervous. We were broken up into groups by age. The older you were, the more dangerous the trip would be. Because we were the youngest, our trip would not be perilous at all.

Master told us we would be assisting an expedition that was searching for an artifact. I could care less what the cause was; the fact that I would get to leave school and be in the outside world was making me burst with excitement. Without any further hesitation, I finished gathering my necessities and ran out of my dormitory with my backpack swinging behind me.

As I leapt down the stairway, I ran into Rufus and Morgan. They were excitedly running down the stairs as well. Rufus met my gaze and shouted to me, "Lil' Sis!" I stopped and waited for them to come up to me. "Where do they have you going?" he asked loudly over the noise of the raucous of students.

"The Rift! We found out this morning! What about you?"

"We are going to Sorrelia! A skirmish has broken out."

"Will you be okay?" I asked nervously.

"Don't worry, Sis. We'll be fine. We're going to be stationed far from any danger. We are simply there for support. We're not fighting. That's what clerics do, remember?"

"Yes. But I…" Morgan's larger frame crashed into Rufus.

"Come on, brother! They're going to leave without us if

we don't hurry." He then looked at me. "Hey, Sis! We'll see you when we get back!" he said quickly and grabbed Rufus, pulling him down the stairs. I watched as my brothers rushed out with the crowd of students. I felt a stab of loneliness as I saw the backs of their heads and heard their laughter as they joked with their friends.

"Kristina?" I heard the voice of my friend Viveka sound out behind me and turned to see her smiling. "Are you ready? Master is waiting for us."

"Yes. I was saying goodbye to my brothers. We hardly see each other anymore. It's funny, 'because we are only a hall away from each other every day."

"Well…I'm here with you. Let's go, before Master has our heads!"

Master was awaiting us in the underground room. Viveka and I were the last to enter. "It's about time! You two were almost left behind."

"Sorry, Master," we both said together.

"Now that you have decided to grace us with your presence, can you please take your place?"

My friend and I stood in the circle with the rest of the class. Master stood in the center, garbed in his black cloak. He walked slowly looking each of us in the eyes and giving us specific instructions for the ceremony.

It really wasn't that big of a deal—an illusion spell that connected us to an artifact of intervention. It was like opening a door at one end of a hallway and walking to another door at the other end. Once we were connected to the artifact that was at the Rift, our destination, we focused all our power on being there. The hard part was already done during summons—knowing you had to give up seven days of life for the power to perform the spell. Every time I did, I felt empty and abandoned.

When the messenger came, he was not polite. He took what was his, gave me the portion I was afforded, and left. No words of encouragement or congratulations ever came. He was aptly named—a messenger—and the message he brought was always the same. I was a slave, and he was the master. I could only have what he gave, nothing more and nothing less.

We closed our eyes, and as a group, crossed our hands in front of our chests. In unison, we spoke the arcane words of a teleportation spell. As the words went into the void of darkness, a door was opened. Standing next to the door was an escort draped in shadow. We all connected our minds to the void and walked towards the door. Before we could pass through, we were forced to make a deposit of power into the outstretched hand of the escort. That's how teleportation worked. It was simply a deposit.

We did this many times in class, teleporting from one side of the room to the other, always making the deposit of power along the way, from within the void. As always, the emptiness filled me. There were no words of thanks from the escort, only silence. As I walked through the door, I was enveloped in darkness, and then suddenly the entire world came into full view around me.

The light of the sun was blinding as we stood before a

massive stone wall. Within the wall was a foreboding fortress, and behind it were the majestic tri-peaks of the Ternion Mountains. Behind me, I could see a multitude of tents scattered throughout an enormous valley. "The students are here!" I heard a shout from behind. "Baelor's gifts have arrived!"

A black-cloaked soldier grabbed me by the scruff of the neck, pulling me away from my fellow students. I was shocked by his abrupt movements. Master was organizing the rest of my classmates into groups. He rolled his eyes and looked irritated.

"Fine, take my best student! You better bring her back in one piece!" Master shouted as I hurried away. The officer was moving me with great haste through the camp and passed many other soldiers until we reached the last tent before the large wall. He opened it, and I heard a horrific cry of pain. I was standing inside a tent with beds laid out in rows, and upon them were men. The officer gave me a light shove, forcing me to walk within the rows. To my horror, I saw the bones of arms and legs pointing in unnatural directions. There were gaping wounds and a lot of blood!

I gasped and turned to leave the tent, but the officer grabbed me roughly and pushed me further inside. I looked desperately at him, asking him to let me go. He would not relent but continued to shove me towards the beds. "Go, child. Calm these men!"

"What happened?" I asked softly.

"They were not successful, nor did they reach the summit! Because of that, they are in critical condition. Curse Aleph for this!"

I looked curiously at the soldier. "They need more than a calm spell." The soldier looked at me and gritted his teeth in frustration.

"I know that child! But there is not enough medicine!"

"But that means…"

"Yes, child, many of these people are going to die! You have been brought here to calm them until then." The gravity of the situation overcame me as I looked at the beds in front of me. I didn't know how to respond. My heart broke for them because what I had to give was not what they needed. I continued to walk with the soldier down the line, trying not to look at the inhabitants.

"How long have they been here?" I asked.

"A week. They bring in around twenty or so every day. Nobody has been able to make it to the top of Shaddyia. Once they get to a specific point, they keep falling. Aleph has set his will against us! I curse his name." I turned around and looked at the soldier.

"Why?" I asked. The face of the soldier turned pale at my inquiry. I could tell nobody ever questioned him that way before.

"Why what?" he stammered.

"Why do you curse Aleph's name?" I could tell he was taken off guard. Without an answer, he simply walked away in a huff, grunting under his breath. I was left alone, surrounded by many beds. The people stared at me in desperation. They were all in a great amount of pain from different injuries they incurred. I decided it would be best not to wait any longer. I swallowed deeply and sat at the bedside of an elderly man with a broken foot.

He was having a challenging time sitting up and his eyes were closed. I wet a soft cloth that was beside his head and lightly tapped it on his forehead. As the cloth touched, he started and gave a loud groan. His eyes opened as he gazed dreamily at me. "Have you come here to heal me?" he asked, full of hope. My heart sank at the question. Healing was unknown to us.

"No, sir, I have come to calm you," I responded.

"Oh, I was hoping you would heal me."

"No, sir. Medicine is still days away from arriving. That is why we are here. I am going to calm you, and then once you are documented, they will take you to the fortress."

"We tried…" He began speaking deliriously. "We tried to climb the knees of Shaddyia. But He wouldn't let us. He blew us off the mountain! He won't let us have the sword!"

"Who won't let you?"

"Aleph. These expeditions are pointless! The magistrate is delusional! We are never going to make it to the top! Never! Alestor is not meant to be taken! It's a cursed mission I tell you!"

"Why is it cursed?" I asked curiously.

"Because it is for vanity! Aleph will never allow us to make it! The sword is not the goal!" Suddenly, two soldiers came up and grabbed the elderly man, pulling him out of his bed. I heard him scream as his broken foot hit the armor of his captor. He continued to proclaim loudly to the rest of the inhabitants in the tent: "This is for vanity! All will come to nothing! Aleph will not allow any but the chosen one to the top! The sword is not the goal!" The soldiers commanded him to be silent, but the man continued shouting until they were out of the tent. Then his voice became muffled until I could no longer hear him.

The elder's words had a profound effect on the rest of the inhabitants, and they began to weep. Several of them asked Aleph aloud for mercy. Before long, the entire room was weeping and calling out the name. I was in shock. I never experienced anything like this in all my life. I saw and heard the desperation of the cries, and my heart was touched. All these people wanted was Aleph. But then I remembered my history lessons. Aleph abandoned Shalistar long ago, leaving the world to humans after King Rian took the throne. Since that time, Aleph had been silent. Why were these people crying out to him? Then I heard a voice from inside me speaking softly. It was the same voice that interrupted summons this morning.

"I am here, Kristina." My heart pounded loudly in my chest as I heard that still, small voice. It carried such great power.

A response was on the edge of my tongue, and I opened my mouth to answer, when the tent flap opened, and Master came pouncing in. A look of disbelief was etched on his face. "Insolent child! Can't you do anything right!?" he shouted over the cries of the people. He came over to me, grabbed me by the wrist, and pulled me outside the tent. "Report, young one! Why are these people still awake!? You were sent in there to calm them!"

"I was about to...I sat with an old man, and he began shouting and before I knew it, the whole tent started in, and..."

"Your excuses are getting tiresome, Kristina! You now have one demerit!"

"But Master…"

"Make that two! Shall we go to three?!" One look at the stern face told me I needed to keep my mouth shut.

"No, Master."

"Good. Now, go back in there and do what you are supposed to do! Calm them…now!"

"Yes, Master," I replied with my head bowed. With reluctance, I opened the tent and moved over to the first bed. All the inhabitants were still crying out for Aleph. Master came in and took the bed next to me.

"Now…do as I do, child." I followed Master as he crossed his hands in front of him and closed his eyes. Within moments, the circle to the void was joined and the portion of power we had been given during summons by the messenger was accessible. Master chanted the words, and I followed suit. To disobey at this point would result in extreme consequences.

Before I could finish the spell, I saw a brilliant flash of light and felt a warmth fill my being. This power was nothing like what I felt when magic was given. This was completely different. Magic was constricting and narrow, with only one possibility and one outcome. But this…was free. I felt as if endless possibilities were before me.

The weeping stopped, and all was quiet. I opened my eyes to see the inhabitants in their beds, resting soundly. Was that us? Did we do that? Somehow, I already knew the answer. No. This was another, otherworldly power on display. I looked over at Master, and a look of awe was on his face as well. We walked up and down the lines of beds and investigated the people. All were sleeping soundly, without any regard for the pain in their bodies.

The occurrence at the Rift shook me to my core. I had a hard time concentrating over the next couple of weeks. Master was not pleased at my decline in performance and made sure my time spent on the weekends was doubly excruciating. Therefore, I was assigned to scrub the floors. I was to do the first and second floor the first weekend, followed by the third and fourth on the next. I couldn't remove the thought of the miracle from my mind. I knew I was being overly dramatic, but something inside me hoped for more.

I was scrubbing viciously at a quick pace. The brush in my hand was destroyed from the hardwood floor, and I was about to stand and get another when I heard a soft whisper sound in the quiet, empty hall.

"Kristina."

I stopped my chore and held my breath. A warmth entered my body and filled me completely. I closed my eyes and lay prostrate in the middle of the hall, hoping to hear the voice again.

"Kristina. My daughter."

The voice was gentle and kind but carried a great amount of authority—even more authority than grandfather had so long ago. I was afraid to answer back. I felt that if I did, I would realize the voice wasn't real and that I was in fact speaking to myself instead.

That was when I heard the voice begin to hum. It was a deep, reverberating sound that created vibrations all the way to my inward being. I felt a presence all over me, soft and light, like silk sheets running over my skin, but moving through me as well. I could feel it under my skin and within every nerve of my body. The presence was within me! Deciding it was time, I took a deep breath and whispered a question.

"What are you doing?"

"Removing the poison."

"What poison?"

"The poison of magic."

"Why would you do that?"

"Because…I am the enemy of magic." A deep biting cold began to leave my body. The cold was coming out of me and being replaced with warmth. It began in my toes and started moving up my legs. When it got to my chest, I felt an uncomfortable sting of pain. I squirmed and started to get up, but then the voice spoke again. *"Be still my daughter. I am removing this abomination from your heart."*

"It hurts!" I cried out.

"I know. But it cannot stay." With great difficulty, I began to obey the voice and allow the coldness to leave my heart. I tried my best to stay still, but the pain was heavy. Curling into a fetal position, I found myself resisting the voice in my mind.

"Do you want the pain to stop?" the voice calmly asked.

"Yes. It hurts."

"Good…then trust me."

The next moments were agonizing, to say the least. As the

cold left me, I was sapped of all my strength. I laid helplessly weeping as I felt the magic leave and the warmth come. It was unlike anything I ever felt before. As the blistering shivers left me, I would weep, and then as the soothing warmth flooded me, I felt a calm, not unlike what the victims of the disastrous expedition felt as the presence moved over them. After all the cold left me, I sat up slowly. The presence was still there, right beside me. A simple thought invaded my mind and would not go away. I needed to know, so I opened my mouth and asked the question.

"Who are you?" I asked curiously.

"A friend."

"What is your name?" There was a moment of quiet, as if the voice were contemplating what to say next. Then it responded.

"I will tell you. But you cannot speak of this to anyone yet."

"Why not?"

"You will endanger yourself." The response from the voice took me off guard. I wondered in my mind what danger was meant, but even more than that, I needed answers to more important questions bursting within me.

"What do you want?" I asked courageously. At my question, I heard the voice let out a sound of pleasure, like the sound I made when I stopped to smell a fragrant flower.

"My desire, Kristina, is that we get to know each other."

"Who are you?"

"I am the one who will set you free."

"Set me free from what?"

"The bondage you are in."

"Please...tell me your name?" There was silence all around me. "Hello? Are you still there?" The voice went quiet. There was nothing moving in the air, only stillness. I waited several more seconds and then slowly opened my eyes. I saw the hard floor from the ground level in my peripheral vision. The long, empty hall stretched out before me. I slowly stood and took a couple of steps in a circle to see if anyone was there.

Realizing I was all alone, fear took hold of my heart. The thought that this moment might have been made up crashed through my mind. Was I insane? Had I imagined the voice? Was this presence all a figment of my imagination? In desperation, I turned around in circles, shouting into the air. "Please! Tell me your name!" My voice reverberated through the empty halls, and then once again, there was silence.

Suddenly, from out of nowhere came a brilliant flash of light that exploded throughout the entire hallway! The radiance blinded me as I covered my eyes with my arm. The brilliance was still there on the other side of my eyelids, like the morning during summons when the voice first called to me. I fought against the blinding light, opening my eyes and gasping. I lost my footing and fell back onto my bottom. My waking eyes looked out over the walls around me and saw a multitude of scribblings etched into every stone. Words were written and glowed with a soft golden light. I read the words...

KING. MEDIATOR. ADVOCATE. REDEEMER. JUSTIFICATION. PROPITIATION. JUDGE. REPAIRER. GUARANTEE. HEALER. WISDOM. PROPHET. CREATOR. DOOR. TRUTH. LIGHT. ALEPH. TAV. KEEPER. FRIEND. BROTHER. COUNSELOR. LOVE.

I walked slowly up and down the halls, reading the glowing words repeatedly. I moved my fingers along the dips and bends of the beautiful handwriting. As I did so, I felt a finger moving inside me, doing the same, writing the words from the stone onto my heart. I spent hours walking the halls and memorizing the words written on the walls until I stopped at one word that was highlighted brighter than any of the other words. I spoke that word aloud.

"Aleph?"

"*Yes.*"

"Is that your name?"

"*The name you will call me by, yes.*" I said the name aloud and felt a soft tremor travel throughout my entire being. It was a unique feeling, as though the name itself were alive and had a presence that would manifest by simply calling it aloud. I repeated it over and over again, enjoying the wave of emotion that flooded me every time I said it. This continued for what seemed like hours until I was sitting cross-legged on the floor. At this point, I was simply whispering my new friend's name. Then a thought came to me, and I decided to continue my conversation with the eternal being.

"I heard your name being cursed the other day by the soldiers. Then there were those who fell off the mountain, crying out for you."

"*The victims of the expedition were in desperation. You will find that those who are hurting will call out for me.*"

"But what about the men who cursed you?"

"*They have been poisoned like you, Kristina. But they have not chosen to seek me and are blinded by selfishness and greed. They have surrendered to Baelor because he has promised them all they desire. I am always here to respond when they call to me."*

"Who are you!? I mean…what are you?"

"My child, that would take a long time to explain, and your mind could not unravel all its mysteries. Let me just say I am your creator and the creator of this world. I have chosen you, Kristina, for a task of the utmost importance. I will not reveal it to you yet, because if I did, you would become so excited and tell everyone you know. Baelor would discover my plans and try to thwart them. So, we will do this step by step."

"What do you mean by that? I asked curiously.

"I mean that you will continue school after the weekend is over and listen for me to speak to you."

"I don't want to go back to school! I want to stay here with you."

"Oh…my child. I want to be with you, too. But you must trust me."

"I'm afraid."

"I know. But you are not alone. I have been with you, always." The soothing words of my newfound friend were a great comfort to me, but there was so much I needed to know.

"What do you want me to do?" I asked boldly.

"I want you to continue your studies as you have before. Don't worry—they will not see me in you."

"But why do I have to stay?"

"It is important for you to be in this place and arouse no suspicion. You must continue as you were."

"I don't understand."

"And you won't. Not for a while. My thoughts are not like your thoughts, and my ways are not like your ways. I am moving on behalf of the entire world, and you, Kristina, will be a very important part of it. Your aunt knew this well and walked with me."

"You knew Auntie Iska!?"

"Yes. We walked side by side and fellowshipped for many years. She, too, had trials unnumbered..."

"Why did you let her die?!" My frustrations surfaced before I knew it. I felt small and embarrassed at my outburst. However, Aleph continued patiently.

"Interwoven within the fabric of eternity is a characteristic that has governed the worlds I create. This principle has determined the destinies of countless lives, eternal and mortal."

"And what is that characteristic?" I asked.

"Free will—the power to choose. Some creations of mine have been given the authority to do so and others have not. Because you are human, you have been given the authority to choose. Iska knew this and made her choices. It was her choice and the choices of those around her that led to the outcome of her life. To produce the highest and best ending for all of eternity, I decided not to intervene in your aunt's execution."

"And you let her die?"

"Yes," Aleph gently concluded.

That final word was spoken inside me, but I heard it echo throughout the empty hallway. Aleph's warmth filled me, and I curled into a ball, as though a thick warm blanket was wrapped around me. I felt small and helpless in His presence. I held my breath as the response came into my heart. I desired to please this unknown entity but was afraid to say the words. I felt my heart beating in my chest and could feel the light breaths I took exiting my mouth. Aleph was here. I could sense His presence in the room, waiting patiently for me. I continued to battle with my mind and all the possible outcomes of my choices until I was completely spent. I held my breath until finally, in the still silence, I resolved my feelings and spoke aloud the words that formed my destiny.

"Okay. I'll do it." I could feel Aleph close to me, whispering in my ear.

"Thank you, Kristina." he said softly, gently. *"Now…awaken!"*

My eyes slowly opened to see the hard, solid floor of the hallway pressed against my cheek. I slowly lifted my head from off the floor, it felt heavy. Standing to my feet, I staggered a little. The sensation was foreign to me. It was a feeling I hadn't experienced in years. I felt peace.

I walked back over to the bucket of soap and water and picked up a fresh scrubbing brush. The water in the bucket felt different. The dirty, soapy water tickled my skin. All my senses were heightened. This new feeling put a smile on my face. I knelt on the floor, humming a song to Aleph as I began scrubbing once again. As the joyful melody escaped me, I was instantly reminded of Auntie Iska and how she sung over me years ago, before I entered the nightmare of magic and sorcery. However, this evening, I found my secret place where nobody could find me, a place where only Aleph and I resided—a place where I could fellowship with my true Master.

CHAPTER
12

I awoke the next morning with Aleph's presence inside me. As I walked the halls and attended summons each morning, I could feel Him constantly. It was a secret I carried. Messengers could not see Him. When they placed their hands on me, Aleph took the magic before it entered my heart, never allowing me to experience the effects of it. When asked to perform a spell, I would do as I was taught, but out of my mouth came different words, not the ones required to perform the spell. It sounded like gibberish.

The result of this action was a LOT of demerits. Master was baffled at the steady downward spiral of my abilities but didn't know what to do. Lucien expressly forbade Master from expelling me, so I stayed. I went from being star pupil to class misfit overnight. I was incapable of performing magic! It was an awkward thing, because with it came persecution from my classmates. They made fun of me and jested at my sudden inability, but it didn't matter to me. Because when I was alone, I would learn from Aleph.

What he taught me was far greater than any spell or conjuration. He took time to reveal His gifts and fellowshipped with me in conversation when nobody else would. It was the best time in my life. However, the more I got to know Aleph, the more I wanted to tell people about Him. Aleph continually corrected me about revealing my experience. This specific dialogue went on until I was fourteen years old. Then, at the height of being a social outcast to my peers and family, I decided to tell Rufus the truth.

The weekend finally came. I miraculously kept myself from receiving any demerits for the first time in about eight weeks, so I was able to stay at home for the weekend. Mother was not happy to see me. In fact, she seemed more disdainful towards me than ever before. Word had gotten out a couple of years ago that the princess was unable to perform magic. I was an embarrassment to her within society, but I didn't care. Nothing she said would hurt me anymore. She was who she was and there was nothing I could do to change that. All I could do was control my own actions. So, I was polite and kind to her, which only angered her more.

The door opened to the palace, and Mother was there with a host of servants and soldiers around her. Seeing her filled me with joy, and I ran to give her a hug. She stepped back and swiped her arm towards me, stopping my momentum.

"This behavior is unacceptable, Kristina!" she shouted. I looked right into her dark eyes and smiled.

"That's okay if you don't want to receive my affection, Mother. I don't blame you. You never received any from your parents, either." Without a word, Mother's hand flashed out and struck me on the cheek. I winced as the blow hit me and covered it with my hand. All commotion stopped, as everyone looked at us in shock. I took a step back from Mother, never taking my eyes off her. "It's okay...I forgive you." I retreated another couple of paces and turned away from the group, heading towards my room.

We ate dinner that evening under the large glass dome in the royal dining hall. Father ceased his duties for the week and joined us as well. I ate in silence, listening to stories from Rufus and Morgan as they updated Father and Mother about their final semester in school. It was more a report about their progress in Baelor's gifts than anything else. Father listened with interest, but Mother sat uncharacteristically quiet, poking at her food, and not eating anything.

"Master Rupert told me I am going to be adept at alteration and illusion before the semester ends. You know what that means, right?"

"No, son, I can't say I do," Father responded.

"It means he'll have unsupervised field trips to the front lines for the final year," Morgan butted in. "He can now assist clerics. Not a big deal, really. It makes him an errand boy," Morgan grunted. "I've already been adept at enchantments for over a year now."

"Yeah, so what does that make you? A glorified seamstress?" Rufus retorted. Morgan jumped out of his chair with an angry look on his face, as though ready to pounce across the table and strangle our older brother.

"Not to mention, I'm also an expert of the long blade!" Morgan returned. "Don't test me, brother! An enchanted sword can damage your body as well as your ego!"

"Sit down, both of you!" Father shouted. "Can we please have one evening where the two of you are not trying to gain the lead over each other?! How about a peaceful meal for a change?" Rufus and Morgan, out of respect to Father, sat down begrudgingly.

"There, now. That's much better. I have brought us together to tell you a bit of good news…Actually, your mother and I have good news."

We looked over at Mother. She looked a bit green in the face and was staring in horror at the plate of food in front of her. We watched as she grunted and heaved, bringing her hand quickly to her mouth.

"What is it, Mother?" I asked with care. She looked at me with spite and was about to let me have it when her whole body heaved again. She quickly stood up. Without a word, she dismissed herself, holding her hand over her mouth and trying to keep herself from throwing up all over the dining room floor. A nearby servant took swift action, coming over with a small bucket. Placing a hand on Mother's back, the maid guided her through the door to the kitchen. Not seconds after the door closed, we all heard the gut-wrenching sound of Mother throwing up into the bucket.

We turned to Father for a response. He kept a small grin and continued his announcement. "Your mother is not feeling well. She has been sick for the past few weeks. We were baffled at first, but now we know the cause of the illness. Your mother is pregnant."

Our evening supper ended abruptly after the announcement. I was glad I didn't have to see Mother again. If I did, she would've scolded me in some way. Father took several minutes with us, walking us down the hall and telling us how proud he was of our studies before he dismissed us for the evening. Before I could take another step, Rufus touched my arm and asked that I join him in the sitting room.

We sat alone next to the fire, remaining silent for several minutes. The quiet was unnerving, as I looked at my brother. He continued to stare into the flames. I was about to speak when Rufus interrupted me. "I hear you have hit rock bottom in your studies," Rufus stated, with a hint of resentment in his voice.

"Master mentioned it the other day. You know magic has become difficult for me," I responded.

"It really frustrates me sometimes, Lil' Sis. I work so hard to grasp the power and harness Baelor's gifts. But with you, it's like you don't even care! I can't believe I'm saying this, but I envy you." Rufus dipped his head, looking away from me.

"You don't have to give into them." I said, placing my hand on his knee.

He quickly pulled his head up and gazed into my eyes. I could see anger in his pupils. "Is that right, Sis? You know as well as I that status and rank is everything at our school. Our masters demand perfection! I'm not like you! I can't be mediocre!"

He stood up, crossing the room to the window. "It's not fair! I work so hard at my studies and still find myself falling behind! Did you know we were in Zulkanda last week on a field trip? The natives pushed our battalion back into the jungle, and we were losing the skirmish. Master Rupert called on me to cast an illusion spell that would cloak a group in camouflage, allowing several clerics to sneak into the enemy camp." Rufus turned away from the window, looking directly at me. "I botched it! A simple illusion spell, and I screwed it up! In front of all my peers, Master Rupert shamed me and made me sit out the rest of the trip."

"I thought you said you were going to be adept…"

"I lied, Lil' Sis!"

I looked at my older brother in sympathy. "Why?"

"It's because our entire existence demands perfection. As an heir to the throne, the world looks at us to solve all their problems. Do you think it will be handed over to a bumbling idiot!? How can you sit there and tolerate mediocrity within yourself? But even worse, how can you be at peace with it!?"

Suddenly, thoughts of Aleph came to mind. Rufus continued his rant, pacing back and forth across the room, shouting about how Mother and Father expected perfection as well and the stress it was causing him. Thoughts of my encounters with Aleph were on the tip of my tongue. Should I tell him about the creator? Would he even believe me? Would this change things between us?

I turned my head to see Rufus looking directly at me and realized my thoughts had taken me far away from the conversation in the room. "Where did you go now, Lil' Sis?"

"I uh…" I stammered nervously, torn between sharing my deepest secret with my oldest brother and obeying Aleph's command not to tell anyone about our encounters. Rufus could see the battle in my thoughts.

"What is it? It looks like you have something you want to

tell me." I felt a knot in my throat as my older brother looked deeply into my eyes. "Did something happen?" My heart was split in two. All I wanted was for Rufus to understand and be a part of my experience, but I also heard the warning from Aleph not to tell anyone. It was agony, and I knew that if I didn't, I would be haunted by it every day until I did. I took a deep breath and made my decision.

"I've met someone," I said with my head bowed.

"What?" Rufus said with a quick chuckle. "You met someone? Do you mean a boy? Does my Lil' Sis fancy a boy?" he asked.

"No…it's not a boy," I returned, slightly frustrated.

"Okay, now I'm confused. Who did you meet?" There was no going back. It was already too late. All I could do now was tell him and hope he didn't think I was crazy.

"I…met…Aleph." Rufus looked at me perplexed, with his mouth slightly open.

"Aleph?" He asked.

"Yes."

"The Aleph?"

"Yes."

"The same Aleph who created Shalistar and left?"

"He's not gone."

"Obviously," Rufus stated with no lack of sarcasm.

"I'm not lying."

"I didn't say you were," he quickly responded, brushing the dark hair out of his eyes. "Where did you meet Aleph?"

"It was years ago. In the hallway during weekend break. I was scrubbing the floors for Master."

"So...you were serving a demerit and the creator of Shalistar appeared to you?"

"I know it's hard to believe."

"No...not at all, Sis," Rufus said with disdain.

"Why don't you believe me?" I asked desperately.

"Because it's hard to wrap my head around it. Why would the creator of Shalistar appear after so many years of silence, and to you, of all people? Listen to the words you're saying, Sis!"

"I understand it sounds crazy. But I'm telling you the truth."

"I've heard enough." Rufus cried, throwing his hands up.

"Please Rufus…"

"Enough!" His shout made me cower into the sitting chair. I could see anger in his features, coming to the surface. "It's bad enough that I bare my soul to you regarding my struggles in school. But now...you mock me with a story so impossible, only to confound me?

"That's not it at all…" I began to cry.

"How can you kick me while I'm down?"

"It's not all about you, Rufus! I'm trying to tell you something so incredible…"

"And unbelievable!"

"I know it's hard to comprehend."

"There you go again! You insult my intelligence now! When will it end?"

"I'm sorry. I didn't mean to…"

"This conversation is over." Rufus looked at me with pitiful eyes and began to storm out of the room.

"What's happened to you? You used to laugh! You were my friend! Where has all that gone now? We don't talk any more. It's like you are embarrassed to even be around me." My older brother stood in the shadows of the room with his head bowed. "Is it worth it, brother?! Is having the gifts of Baelor really worth it?"

Rufus pulled his head up and looked directly at me. The fire in his eyes was evident. "Watch your tongue, Sister. I would advise you to take the rest of the weekend and get your head on straight. These fanciful delusions of a dead god are obviously hindering your capacity to think rationally. It's why you haven't been able to perform Baelor's gifts."

I was speechless as I listened to the words coming out of his mouth. They were hate-filled and full of malice. I never thought my oldest brother, the one I looked up to my whole life, would say such things about me. He came close and took my hand. As he did, I was filled with a cold chill. He looked into my eyes. I could see the glaze over his pupils. It was Rufus who was not in his right mind! He was completely obsessed with sorcery, and all reasoning was gone from my brother. His unhealthy ambition to advance was overtaking him!

"Sister…you would do well to realize that your school and our society are counting on us. These dreams of yours are nothing but a distraction to your purpose. It is time to come back down to the ground. Aleph is gone! The magistrate made it noticeably clear that any mention of the name is forbidden. He turned his back on this world a long time ago. Because he abandoned us, Baelor has come and brought his generous gifts."

"But at what cost?" I whispered the question through tear-soaked eyes. Rufus and I were locked in a contest of wills. Neither of us would turn our gaze.

"I don't want you to mention that name again, Kristina. It is forbidden."

"You sound like Mother, you know that?" I said, not looking away.

"We will not discuss this again. Do you understand me?"

"You can't stop me."

Rufus reached out his hand and gently moved it through my long dark hair. "Oh…you are wrong on that, Sister. I can and I will."

"What has happened to you?" I whispered one last time in desperation. Rufus looked at me with an evil grin and patted my hand. He then stood up and left the room without any kind of response.

As the door slammed shut, I threw myself onto the pillows of the couch and wept bitterly. I didn't know what to do. I disobeyed my master by revealing my relationship with him. Did my betrayal upset Him? Could we ever go back to the way it was? I felt ashamed and hid myself from the creator, not responding when I heard his soft whisper. It was a dark place I was suddenly in, and I needed help, but couldn't bring myself to go before Aleph. I hurt Him, and I knew it.

I heard voices in my mind that were not my creator, voices

that soothingly beckoned me to return to the void. The voices promised me they had what I needed to get through this circumstance. As the voices continued to speak, I waited to hear a reply from Aleph, but alas, there was none. He was silent.

I began to shake and closed my eyes. With great trepidation, I joined myself with the circle and met the messenger, who was waiting for me. My heart felt hollow and empty as I traded seven days of life for a meager portion of power. The magic entered my heart, taking my breath away. It felt like someone was standing on my chest as I crossed my shaking hands in front of me. Without any effort at all, I flawlessly spoke the words to perform a simple calm spell. Within seconds, the effects came over me. I slumped onto the hard floor in front of the fire, falling into a deep trance. With my final waking breath, I softly cried out.

"Aleph…forgive me."

The next several weeks at school were awkward. Rufus would not interact with me at all. I knew he hadn't spoken a word of our conversation to Morgan or our parents, but he remained distant. Even when we were home on the weekends, he would find some excuse not to be in the same room as me. I was having a tough time with it. This was my brother who was shunning me, and it was not a comfortable feeling.

Being absent from Aleph's presence left an emptiness inside me that needed to be filled. I allowed Master to teach me once again and opened myself up to deeper magic. He was impressed that my abilities came back so suddenly. My classmates were impressed as well—everyone except Viveka.

My sudden return created a competitive nature within her. She was disdainful towards me and found every opportunity to sabotage my progress. It broke my heart to see a once good friend turn on me because of competition. When I was a misfit, she left me alone, letting everyone else pick on me, but now that I was a threat to her attainment of the highest order, I had become her nemesis.

Everything changed between Rufus and me one weekend during break. I smarted off to Master and once again found myself scrubbing the halls. It was quiet in the school because everyone was gone for holiday. I felt a deep loneliness without any of my classmates around me. I hadn't returned to Aleph since I disobeyed, and the halls felt emptier than ever.

Suddenly, the silence was broken as I heard a familiar voice crying out arcane words. It was coming from the second floor. I abandoned my soap bucket and walked to the back hall, turning right. When I reached the staircase, I climbed to the second floor. The chanting was coming from a door on the right. I was about to take a step in that direction when Aleph's voice sounded clearly from within me.

"Step quietly, Kristina. Sit beside the door and be silent." The words from Aleph were stern and commanding, bringing me to my knees. The fear that overcame me cannot be put into words. Aleph had been silent for months, but now hearing his voice, it sounded as if He was there the whole time! I understood immediately that his instruction needed to be followed precisely. I did as he requested and stayed low, creeping over to the right side of the door. With my back against the hard, stone wall, I heard the chanting again and lost my breath. The owner of the voice was undoubtedly my

older brother.

The arcane words of sorcery were being spoken with great exertion. He desperately cried out for the messenger to come, using the spidery language of Baelor. I felt a deep pity for my brother as he shouted into the void of Baelor's darkness. My heart broke, hearing my brother's pain, but I knew that disobeying Aleph by revealing my presence was not an option. So, I sat there, listening to my brother continue his summons.

Suddenly, a loud, magical noise erupted, followed by a smooth and silky voice. "Young one! You have called, and Baelor has answered." The owner of the voice was none other than the Dark Man!

"Master Lucien! I'm sorry. I was summoning without supervision."

"It is okay, child! Baelor has seen your ambition and has sent me to you." Lucien replied.

"But...I was hoping to summon a messenger."

"And you have..."

"You are a messenger?" Rufus asked incredulously.

"I am. Your cry has summoned the chief messenger of Baelor."

"Chief messenger? I don't understand."

"And you won't. You humans think in such temporal ways. All you need to know is that Baelor has incredible plans for you, Master Rufus!"

"Master? No, you are mistaken. I am no such thing. I can't even cast a simple illusion spell."

"It is true. But Baelor has seen your desperation and has sent me to offer you a deal."

"What kind of deal?"

"Advancement, young one. How would you like to be conferred to the highest order?"

"Is that possible?"

"Of course, child. Anything is possible with Baelor. What if…you possessed the power to control fire?" Suddenly, the sound of a flame erupted, startling me to the core. Lucien continued his monologue to my brother, speaking of different powers that were available. I was having a hard time listening to the Dark Man spewing this filth and was about to get up when Aleph spoke again.

"Stay still. Don't move."

"I've heard enough," I whispered aloud.

"Not yet."

"Please. He is my brother. I can't listen to this."

"I understand your pain, but you must endure. You need to know the enemy."

As I continued to reason with Aleph, Lucien resumed his speech. "So, you see, young one. The power I have to give is only for a select few. Baelor has offered this gift to you and so much more."

"What else is there?" Rufus asked curiously.

"Dominance! How would you like to sit upon the throne of Rian?"

"But Father…"

"Your father is weak! He is in my thrall and needs to be replaced with one who is strong and mighty! That could be you. All you have to do is bow your knee and kiss my hand, and all of this will be yours!"

I couldn't take it anymore. I stood to run and felt an invisible hand against my chest keeping me in place. "Please… Kristina. Stay still."

"I can't let him take my brother!"

"I'm sorry, daughter. Your brother has already made his choice."

Lucien's voice boomed from the other side of the wall. "I bestow upon you, Rufus, son of Remus the rank of cleric. You are now chosen to stand before Baelor himself and receive power to perform the duties he has called you to! Stand before him now."

"My brother is my enemy?"

"No child. Your battle is not against your brother, but the one whom he now serves."

"Please, Aleph! Make this stop."

"I will not. Your brother has chosen. His path has been laid."

Lucien's voice continued. "You will take the remainder of the weekend and rest. You will not need to attend class anymore. You now have a higher purpose, to serve the Master of Shalistar. However, it is important for this encounter to remain secret. Nobody knows about me and the words I have said. To say anything about my identity is strictly forbidden. Do you understand, cleric?"

"Yes, Master Lucien."

I felt alone. I was angry at Aleph for not intervening. I couldn't go to Morgan, that was for sure. He was just as obsessed as Rufus was with advancement, only he was learning the sword. I could turn to no one. Aleph made it clear He was not going to help my brother. I was frustrated and confused. Why was he silent concerning these matters? It didn't make sense to me! So, I decided to steep myself further in the false comfort of sorcery.

Day after day, I summoned messengers with my fellow students in the darkness of the underground room, with Master observing us from his desk in the corner. Every day I chanted words of abomination from my lips, giving up seven days of life as I received the power of magic. The secret place where Aleph sang to me, spoke to me, and strategized with me felt far away, like a long-forgotten dream.

However, in His mercy, at my darkest hour, He came to me in the secret place, as though he was there the whole time. In that space, He revealed to me a plan so horrific, I doubted whether it was really Him speaking to me. If I was afraid of the outcome of my older brother's pledge to serve Baelor, I was now confronted with a much greater level of fear.

"Not many days from now, Lucien will appear to you and make you an offer to join him as a cleric, not unlike the offer your brother received. I want you to take the deal." Aleph could sense my apprehension at the request. *"This is not a promotion but has always been a part of my plan."*

Seeing the doubt in my mind, Aleph corrected me again. *"The decision to remain distant from me was your choice. But regardless of the choice, my plans will be established."* This rebuke was difficult to hear. *"You must realize Kristina, regardless of your choices I am always with you. The door of this possibility has been opened, and now we shall walk through it together."*

It was a lot to take in. I sat there before Aleph's light and let His words seep into my heart. As they did, I found myself resisting the commands of my creator. I felt trapped. I had chosen magic as my comfort, creating a chasm between my creator and me. My choices created a prison. Aleph was not letting me out of this place. He wanted me to stay here, as His spy. "For how long?" I wondered. "When was this misery going to end?"

As sure as Aleph's words, Lucien came to me in the dead of night. I was in my sleeping gown, feeling awkward as he stood before me. I looked nervously at my roommates, who were sound asleep. Their condition was confirmed as I looked back to the Dark Man. His hands were crossed in front of him, softly chanting words of calm magic to keep my colleagues asleep. I sat up and pulled the blanket up to my chest, covering myself.

He stood there, staring into my eyes, not saying a word. He was waiting for me to begin the conversation. My stubborn self stared right back, unmoving, until I heard the voice within me. *"This is it. Be polite and receptive."*

Hearing Aleph's voice brought courage and strength. I could see the true machinations of evil before me. Lucien was on a string that his master was pulling to make him move. The power was not his own, but his master's. A quick thought bounced across my mind that I couldn't ignore, but

I decided to table it for now and revisit it later with Aleph in the secret place.

"Princess Kristina…" Lucien began his monologue. It was like the one I heard him give Rufus before. I found myself impressed at the fact that none of my roommates awakened during the demonstration—even when the fireball crashed into the wall, setting it ablaze, before Lucien doused the fire with a word of magic, snuffing it out completely. Even during the loud raucous of that demonstration, they continued to sleep.

After the long-winded sermon from the Dark Man, I obeyed the words of my true master, the one who sees me in secret, and knelt, taking the hand of the Dark Man. As my fingers closed around his, I felt a drastic drop in temperature. A cloak of coldness was draped over me, yet the place where my heart resided felt warm. I hadn't experienced the sensation of Aleph's protection in years. But there he was. His hand was on my heart. He once again made it a place where the cold could not go, the poison could not get in. I was in awe of how this was playing out. Lucien didn't know that Aleph was with me, keeping the darkness from overtaking me.

As Lucien continued, my physical ears listened, but the ears of my heart were tuned into another master as he was speaking to me at the same time, from the inside. *"It has begun. You will now be transferred to the fourth floor and will dwell in the company of clerics, including your brother. I am going to be quiet now because I want you to listen to what the enemy reveals."* I was nodding my head in agreement to Lucien, but in my mind, I asked Aleph a question.

"How many of me are there? You know, spies in the enemy camp?"

"*I have many. The number is not important, daughter. Remember this, though. The enemy is powerful and not to be underestimated. However, Kristina, no matter what happens, or how many times you disobey me, I am always with you. I will never leave you nor forsake you.*" Aleph's words made me begin to weep. Lucien bent down and took my arm, helping me to stand.

"It is a natural reaction to such a high honor, Princess. It's okay if you want to cry," Lucien stated. However, it was not his words that broke me, but the soothing, loving words of my true Master. The creator of Shalistar revealed to me he was not upset at my disobedience. I resolved that no matter what, I would never let my mind come between us again.

CHAPTER
13

It was a façade—another system to keep us imprisoned. Although Rufus and I were granted the rank of cleric, we had yet to cast a single destruction spell. We were puppets, as was our whole family, always on the move across the world from one battlefield to the next. We never faced any real danger but were kept under guard by the toughest soldiers Balafas could spare.

Our responsibility was to keep the morale of the soldiers in good standing. As mouthpieces of the kingdom, we were given a speech the morning before the soldiers went to battle, to rally them to the cause and give them hope. It was a fruitless campaign that was slowly becoming a cancer to my brother, the ultimate blow to Rufus' pride. Each day, he died a little more inside, and without the comfort of Aleph, it was a miserable time in his life.

Four years passed since Rufus, and I were called to the front lines of Balafas's army. Since then, we traveled all over the southern part of the continent. I witnessed the strong arm of the kingdom scorch the swamps of Amah, ravage the inhabitants of Lake Ravach, and plunder the cliff dwellers in Zulkanda. Rufus and I spent endless hours sitting within the comfort of the royal cart, surrounded by many soldiers. I saw vast landscapes go by and kept an ongoing conversation with Aleph about the splendor of his created world. Some questions He answered, and others He did not.

The rich and beautiful world fascinated me and was calling to me. A deep desire urged me to break the bonds I was in and run free in the wild open. Every time my heart would go there, I would hear the small voice inside me. *"It's not time yet,"* He would say comfortingly. I settled back into the cart and exhaled, knowing that Aleph understood my passions, and that in His timing, He would bring these things to pass.

"Wake up, my Lord and Lady!" An abrupt voice of a soldier called from outside our extravagant tent. "Commander Zant needs you on the front lines!" I looked over and saw that my brother had not stirred. His bulk continued to lay still.

"Rufus," I said as I stretched myself awake. "It's time."

"What's the point?" my brother responded, his face buried in the pillow.

"You know we have a responsibility to the kingdom." Suddenly, my brother shot up and stared at me angrily.

"Do we, now? What is that responsibility? To stand as a puppet on a string?"

"You know what happens if we don't," I said, remembering the horror of the day Morgan refused to obey. Lucien knew exactly what he was doing when he cast the spell that blinded our brother permanently. He knew the results of that day would put fear into each one of us, keeping us in check so the plans of Baelor could be accomplished without a hint of uprising. Father and Mother were helpless to stop it, bowing in obedience each day to the whims of Lucien, the true ruler of Shalistar.

"I wish I had the same courage he did." Brother said, interrupting my thoughts.

"It didn't do him any good. He ended up submitting."

"How has it gotten this bad? Father and Mother have done nothing!"

"What are they supposed to do, Rufus?"

"Something! Anything! The kingdom is being torn from them, one thread at a time!"

"I'm convinced it was never theirs to begin with."

"You are right, Lil' Sis. It was never any of ours." Rufus ended the conversation and got out of bed with a grunt.

We both went to our isolated areas within the royal tent to get ready for the day. I changed into my uniform and donned my black cloak, thinking about Brother and the misery he must be in. He believed the lies of Lucien and bowed his knee. From that day forth, he truly became a slave. Since then, magic and the promise of power were carrots on a stick being held out to Rufus. For a while, he believed one day he would receive his kingdom, that they would come to train him in the art of destruction. However, as he waited, the emptiness of Lucien's lies consumed him. He slowly became a shell of a man, until all that remained was a broken appearance.

We finished dressing and stood before one another, inspecting each other's attire. Brother aged dramatically in the past four years. All the youthful energy he once had was gone. His skin was stretched and pale, with bags under his eyes. His soft, dark hair already had wisps of gray on the sides. He looked much older than his twenty-two years.

I straightened his collar, looked into his green eyes, and smiled. Within me, I hoped that today would be the day Aleph would reveal His presence to my brother and restore the glory of his youth back to him. I hadn't spoken to Rufus about Him since the evening by the fire. Aleph told me on several occasions since then that I was to remain silent about Him, and I obeyed.

It was the hardest thing in the world to watch my brother suffer. I only needed to step aside from the cares of the world and Aleph would be there to comfort me and give me life. Rufus, however, had nobody. So, I did what I could each day, but the true healing he needed was not something I could provide.

We opened the tent and walked through the maze of an army encampment to the preparation area. Meeting us was a courier, who handed us a speech for the day. Rufus took the parchment and thanked the courier cordially. I watched as Rufus broke the seal and viewed the writing. His eyes crossed over the words as they did for years on end. After the letter was read, he bowed his head and gritted his teeth. In a moment of courage, he looked the courier in the eyes and dismissed him.

We spent several moments with Commander Zant going over the schedule for the day. This was always a one-sided conversation, more a briefing to us than anything else. Zant never asked permission to do anything, and Brother didn't argue. He was too scared of what would happen if he did.

A brief time later, Rufus and I stood side by side on a crudely erected stage before the large army. For the next half hour, we read what was on the piece of paper. I watched as Rufus snapped into character. Even though it was false sentiment, he performed brilliantly. His words echoed loudly, and the crowd was immediately drawn into what he said. Rufus moved his hands and body in unison, marching back and forth across the stage. He was a master orator, overflowing with personality. I stifled a cry as I watched him and spoke my thoughts silently to Aleph.

"Why must he suffer? He would make such a fantastic king!" There was no response except the roar of the stirred-up crowd of soldiers. I closed my eyes and cried silent tears for my brother. His speech continued with great exuberance, stirring the hearts of those he stood before. The black-armored soldiers held on to every word spoken by Brother until finally, his speech was done.

After the ceremony concluded, Rufus and I were being escorted through the crowd as soldiers came up from all sides, praising us for our words. I saw them bow the knee and swear allegiance to King Remus and his family line, may we all reign forever. Rufus graciously took time with each of them and spoke with them about their lives and where they came from. They excitedly responded with a story from back home. Rufus was attentive and patiently listened to them. After they finished, he smiled and embraced them.

I looked behind me towards the stage and saw Commander

Zant watching intently with one hand on his sword. He was waiting for any sign of uprising, ready to react swiftly if Brother stepped out of line. One look at Zant told me the truth. We were expendable. I quickly moved up behind Brother and placed my hand on his lower back, whispering in his ear.

"We are being watched. Conclude this meeting, now." Brother stiffened as I said these words. He turned around sadly; his character broken. I saw desperation in his eyes.

"Can't you just let me have this moment?" he whispered back.

"You know I can't."

"When will this end, Lil' Sis?" I had no response. Seeing my doubt, Brother nodded his head and turned back to the adoring soldiers. "It is my hope that you bring the throne a mighty victory! Go now, all of you, and fight with all your heart!" The soldiers erupted in a shout that shook the camp. I looked behind me again to see Zant coming off the stage. It wasn't long before his rough mailed hands grabbed Brother and me by the arm and escorted us back to our tent.

The ceremonies continued, month after month and year after year. Every performance took a little more life out of my brother. Our family was imprisoned within a system of magic and sorcery, unable to escape! We were being trafficked throughout the world at the pleasure of Baelor and his chief messenger. As the conquest expanded to the corners of our continent, people of all ages were forced into the system of control. I watched as children were taken from their parents and sent to schools all over Shalistar. Like countless others, they were to be trained in the gifts of Baelor and turned into weapons of war.

Even I was falling into a pit of mundane hopelessness. The light within me was once again going dim, as I believed the lies. No matter how many times I heard Aleph's voice, I still found myself doubting. Nothing changed—my life was still a miserable existence! I was on the edge of losing it all when suddenly, like a thief in the night, Aleph appeared to my brother and me in a mysterious way.

CHAPTER
14

We were in Corsonia. Rufus and I finished our speech and were on stage behind Commander Zant. He was walking back and forth, staring into the eyes of the soldiers, weighing each of them and their level of fear, as he always did before a skirmish.

"The Order is here!" His deep voice echoed throughout the camp, stirring a commotion at the mention of the enemy. Zant held up a hand, and the soldiers went silent. "Their white cloaks were spotted going into "The Blistering Boar" only an hour ago. There were two of them, loading food and supplies. The traitors are in the building on the second floor. I have confronted the order before and need to warn you. Do not rely upon your skills alone to overtake them.

"These warriors in white are crafty and quick on their feet. They dance around defensively, parrying your blows until you tire, and then they strike. They have mastered the blade and are experts at the wielding of it. I will repeat myself: do not engage this enemy alone. Is that understood!?"

"Yessir!" The black cloaked soldiers resounded together.

"The Order of the Elect has eluded us for years. They have stayed hidden since their banishment eighteen years ago.

Their sanctuaries have been shrouded from us. Only recently, we were able to capture one of them. He is a member of the sanctuary of Shelbye. Through skillful torture and manipulation, he has revealed information leading us here." I looked over at Rufus. The black cowl resting over his head completely covered his face in shadow, but I could still see his eyes scanning the surroundings, searching for the enemy.

"The order comes here several times a month and brings supplies to the people. It is our job today to shut down this distribution ring and bring these members of the order before Lord Lucien. He is interested in their well-being for now."

As I continued to listen to Zant speak, my thoughts drifted. We spent years imprisoned within this army. From one field of battle to the next, I stood beside my brother giving speeches of empty promises. These words fell short and hollow as countless lives were lost in pursuit of protecting Father and his throne. Since we were only mouthpieces, we were not allowed to be an active part of any battle. We were told that our lives were too valuable. However, we knew in our hearts this was a lie. Like every other piece in Lucien's kingdom, we could be tossed aside at any moment and replaced. I wondered how long it would be for me and my family before our value ran out.

Later that day, a cry resounded from within the ranks. Rufus and I exited our tent to see a group of soldiers moving through the crowd. The shouts and hollers were deafening, and I ran to see what the commotion was all about.

Before the entrance to the leader's tent was a group of

soldiers I never saw before. One of them was wearing a crimson cape. This brute was not a member of the king's army but looked like a mercenary. Not knowing we were royalty; he pushed Brother out of the way and stood next to Zant. Removing his helmet revealed a crusty blonde mane that fell to the sides of his face. His cheeks were full of matching golden hair as well. He stepped forward and spoke loudly. His voice was raspy and course.

"I found this dog cowering in a corner," he said to Zant, pointing to his prisoner. As the crowd parted, I saw whom he was discussing. There was a pitiful man at his feet, covered in a white cloak with red trim on the bottom. The white of the cloak was almost unrecognizable, being covered in mud and dirt.

"How many of you did it take to bring him down?" Zant asked.

"Not sure, sir. When I found him, he was already spent. His leg is broken, as you can see."

"So, you did not engage him in combat?"

"No, we didn't."

"Lucky for you," Zant said with a smile as he patted the mercenary's arm. "I congratulate you on the capture, even though he was wounded. I need more leaders in the direction of Sommerset. What is your name, soldier?"

"Agus Tull, my Lord."

"Allow me some time to get the paperwork in order. But your bravery has been on display, and you will be rewarded for it. I will make you a captain in the magistrate's army!"

"Thank you, my Lord."

Zant looked down at the figure in white. He kicked his foot softly into his side. The body moved painfully, grabbing his broken leg. Zant grunted and turned to the soldiers around him. "They are finally being revealed to us. Our enemy will not be hiding much longer. Baelor is shining his light upon them. Like cockroaches, they will scurry, and we will squash them! Blessed Baelor!"

All of us at once shouted in unison. "Blessed Baelor!"

He looked directly at Rufus and me. "It's time to get you both to safety. Agus Tull and his soldiers will escort you by cart, back to Lord Lucien. We don't have any time to lose, and all the artifacts of intervention are currently in use." He turned to Agus Tull. "If the prisoner tries to escape, you know what to do. Don't kill him, though. He is valuable alive. Do you understand me?"

"Yes, Lord Zant!" Agus sounded.

"Good. You will be given further instructions after you have deposited this filth before our Lord." Zant huddled close to the man. "You really thought you could hide from us? Your dead god cannot save you now. Lord Lucien will get what he wants, and the rest of your brothers will meet their fate. It won't be long now, monk!" Zant finished his taunting by spitting on the body of the prisoner and standing to his feet.

"Take this mistake away from me, now."

With a flurry of movements, Agus Tull and his fellow soldiers picked up the prisoner and stood him on his feet. They tore the white cloak from his body and threw it on the ground. As the cloak hit the dirt, a cloud of dust rose into the air, blinding a soldier who was standing over it. Annoyed, he rubbed his watering eyes. Without another word, the member of the order was loaded onto the cart, screaming from the pain in his broken leg. As we were leaving to mount our horses, Zant produced further instructions.

"You two will sit with the prisoner in the cart. Make sure he doesn't try anything funny. If he escapes, I will be holding the two of you responsible. Is that clear?"

"Yessir!" we shouted in unison. As Zant left, I watched Rufus grit his teeth, submitting to the orders. Without another word, we climbed into the cart and sat across from the prisoner. Several minutes later, we were off and heading south towards Raithe.

In the dead of night, we passed through the outskirts of Swaltayer. At this hour only soldiers and a couple of misfits were in the streets. I watched from an elevated position as the troublemakers were being rounded up for being out past curfew. I heard a grunt from the prisoner across from me and turned my attention back to him. He was staring at me with a steady gaze.

His hands and feet were tied, so there was no conceivable way for him to try any kind of attack. I sensed that was the furthest thing from his mind. Rufus sat next to me with his head down, cowled in his dark cloak. He was not speaking to me but seemed frustrated with the situation.

I met the gaze of the man across from me and felt a sensation I hadn't experienced in years overcome me. I was breathless as I stared into his eyes. There were cuts all over his dirtied face, and blood dried into his short brown beard. Several of his teeth were missing, undoubtedly from blows rained down upon him by the magistrate's soldiers. He was a dirty, disgusting mess; however, the eyes that stared into me from across the cart were soft and knowing. Looking into them brought familiar sensations. My mind went immediately back to the years spent with Aleph and the way we walked and talked together before I disobeyed.

My mind flooded with thoughts of impurity. The deaths of all the people I witnessed these past years overwhelmed me, and I began to cry. I turned my gaze from the stranger's eyes, unable to look at him. It was altogether too painful. I winced and drew myself inward, not wanting to even be on the cart. I wanted to jump off and run as far away from this man as I could. I took the cowl of my cloak and drew it over my head, removing as much of the prisoner from my peripheral as possible.

"He's not mad at you." A soft voice came from the man across from me—a voice so soft, yet authoritative. I knew he was speaking to me and not my brother beside me.

"We don't need to hear anything from you, traitor!" I looked up slowly from my concealed position and turned to Rufus.

"Leave him alone, Brother."

"Don't listen to him, Lil' Sis. His words will corrupt you." It was hard to listen to Brother. All I could think about was the pain in my heart. My tears continued to silently flow as I drew further inward.

The man continued to speak. "He's not done with you, Kristina." My breath was caught in my throat. I couldn't speak. Rufus stood up and leaned over the man.

"How do you know her name, dog? Tell me at once!" Rufus shouted, slapping the head of the man. He looked up at

Brother and responded with a smile.

"The same way I know your name, Rufus, son of Remus." My brother didn't appreciate the response and slapped the man harder.

"I command you to tell me how you knew our names… or else." Rufus threatened, moving his hand to the scabbard at his side. Immediately, the man turned his attention completely upon my brother.

"Was it worth it, young man? Is this the reward you have chosen?" he replied, his tied hands pointing towards the soldiers around us. "Aleph has so much more to offer you than Baelor." Rufus, hearing those words, struck the man again across the mouth.

"How dare you mention the name of the dead god to me? I curse the name of Aleph! He abandoned us! He left us all alone in a world of war and suffering!"

"Not true, young one," the soft voice retorted.

"How can you say that?"

"Why do you think he abandoned you? Is that what you know? Or is that what you have been taught?" Rufus took a step back, speechless. He lost his balance and was about to fall off the cart. Suddenly, the man stood to full height, grabbing him before he could go overboard. The ropes that bound the prisoner were severed as easily as butter. I stared in shock as he held my brother in his arms, keeping him from a nasty fall. Brother was shocked at what had just happened. He looked behind him over the side at the hard road below and back into the eyes of the stranger.

"Why did you do that, man? You could have let me fall."

"It was in Aleph's interest to keep you on the cart, free of harm."

"Who are you?" Brother asked curiously.

"I am a steward of the words of Aleph. I have a message for your master." Rufus took a minute to process what the stranger spoke. He gently helped the man back down to the floor of the cart. As the prisoner hit the rattling wood planks, he reached down to his broken leg and grimaced in pain.

Rufus sat carefully next to me, drawing his cowl back. He looked into the stranger's eyes. "How did you stand on your feet?"

"You know, young man...I'm not sure about that. It feels like fire right now. Quite painful it is."

"But...your ropes broke. You stood up on a broken leg. I would have fallen."

"Yes. You've been falling for a while now. It was time someone caught you." Rufus looked at me, desperate for answers. The look I saw, I will never forget. It was a look of sorrow and longing.

"Don't worry, young man. Aleph isn't mad at you, either," the prisoner said with a sigh, as he settled back into the cart.

I awoke the next morning as we were edging along the Elder Woods, heading southwest towards Raithe. I stretched out my muscles, looking behind where I sat. I could see the expanse of the massive forest, far in the distance. A pack of foxes emerged and were chasing several smaller animals close to the battalion of soldiers that escorted us. Looking across from me, I saw the prisoner sitting next to my brother.

Rufus' head was not cowled, and I could clearly see the battle of emotions on the surface of his face, like he was wrestling intensely with his thoughts. As I stretched, I heard him speak.

"Good morning, Lil' Sis," he said, his head still bowed.

"Good morning, my lady," said the prisoner politely. Without a word, I nodded to them both, unsure of what to say. My thoughts were out of control in my mind. Here was my brother sitting next to a member of what must be the Order of the Elect, obviously in turmoil regarding his thoughts. What did this man say to him? Why was my brother sitting next to him? What happened while I slept? In response to my unspoken questions, the prisoner leaned forward and answered.

"Your brother and I have had quite a chat."

"About what?" I asked curiously.

"The past," the prisoner responded. I looked over to Rufus, who still had his head bowed, not looking at me.

"Rufus… are you okay, Brother?" He slowly raised his head, and I could see the puffiness under his eyes. He was crying.

"I'm sorry, Lil' Sis. I'm sorry I never believed you."

"What changed?" I questioned.

"Everything," he shared quietly. I looked outside the cart at our escorts.

"What about them?" I asked, pointing to the soldiers in front and behind us.

"They don't care. Their minds are on whatever they want. We've had little interruption. In case we were, I tied his hands together, to keep up appearances."

"Are you okay, Brother?" I asked, in desperation.

"I am now, Lil' Sis." I looked over to the stranger.

"Thank you." I said softly.

The prisoner looked back at me and smiled. "It is my pleasure, Esgar." Hearing that name made my heart skip a beat. It sounded foreign, but also familiar, as if I knew it my whole life.

"I don't understand. Why would you call me that?"

"Because it is who you are. It is who He has chosen you to be."

"Do you mean Aleph?" I asked longingly.

"Yes. He is near to you and soon will lead you into a new season."

"How do you know this?"

"Aleph has shown me. You two are part of my mission in this world," the man stated, pointing to Brother and me.

Rufus butted in. "We have to get you out of here."

"That will not be happening, young sir. I have a message for the magistrate and the one called Lucien."

"Please, sir," I pleaded with him. "You don't know who you are dealing with. Lord Lucien is not who he seems."

The prisoner reached his hands out and placed them around mine, looking directly into my eyes. "I know very well who it is we are dealing with, and I am not afraid of my end. Aleph is moving mightily and aligning the remnant. You, Esgar, are part of that remnant."

"You speak in mysteries, sir."

"Don't worry, Princess. You will know His plans soon enough. You bear the mark." He pointed to the star upon my forearm that was there since birth. "Since your beginning, he has marked you for greatness." Rufus leaned in, interrupting the conversation.

"You made sure you were captured! You wanted to go before Lord Lucien, didn't you?" asked Rufus with wide eyes.

"Yes, young sir. However, it was not my intention to break my leg in the process. But yes…Aleph has prepared me for this moment. It is what He has requested."

"What are you going to say?" Rufus asked again. I watched as the stranger looked up into the sky. He kept his gaze there contemplating his next response. As if receiving an answer, he spoke.

"I'm sorry, young prince. But that is not your concern at this time."

For the next day, the prisoner sat across from Rufus and me on the cart as we made our way closer to Raithe. Even though it was surely to be the stranger's death when we reached the city, he showed no fear of any kind. He did experience tremors of pain from time to time due to his broken leg, but that was all.

When we stopped for a break in the mid-afternoon, Rufus and I decided to find a sturdy branch we could use to fashion a splint for our friend. As we jumped off the cart, the burly soldier in a crimson cape came riding up with several men behind him, stopping us abruptly.

"Now where are you two going?" Agus Tull asked with a

snarl.

"We thought it would be a clever idea to make a splint for the prisoner's broken leg." Rufus explained confidently. "He will need to walk if he is summoned to appear before the magistrate."

"He can be dragged through the streets, screaming in agony for all I care." Agus responded viciously.

"Now look here…" Brother began.

"No…you look here." Agus interrupted. You may be a cleric, but concerning the transport of this prisoner, I am in charge. Papers are already on their way to the desk of the magistrate promoting me to captain, so if I were you, I'd start getting used to the fact that you will be taking orders from me." Brother straightened his posture to show his obedience. "Good, now ask me again."

Brother looked over at me and then back at Agus Tull. "Captain, do we have permission to create a splint for the prisoner's leg?"

"Not on your life, cleric!" I heard enough from this foul creature and drew back my cowl so the captain could see my face. I pulled the sleeve of my tunic, revealing my forearm and the mark upon it.

"Do you even know whom you are addressing, captain?! I, Kristina, daughter of Remus and Princess of Raithe, command you in the name of the King, to stand down!" All the color immediately drained from his face as he stared down from his horse.

"Uh…then…I." Agus stuttered as the realization struck him. "Then he must be." He said pointing to brother.

"That's right, captain. He is Rufus, son of Remus and heir to the throne of Rian." Rufus looked from me to Agus Tull and a smirk crawled across his face.

"Your Majesty…I apologize." Agus said with great difficulty.

"Good…now with that out of the way. My sister and I will be taking a moment to ourselves. When we get back, I expect this caravan to be off. We must make it to Raithe by evening, am I understood captain!?"

"Yes, Your Majesty." Agus said through gritted teeth.

When Rufus and I were out of earshot from the caravan, we spoke about what the prisoner said to Rufus. "He knew everything about me. The good and the bad. He knew it all, as if Aleph were allowing him to see through me. I never had anyone speak to me that way, Lil' Sis. It was impressive but scary at the same time."

"I can understand that. When Aleph appeared to me it was the same way."

"Wait a minute…Aleph came to you?"

"Yes."

"You saw him?"

"Yes, but he has been quiet these past couple of years," I stated sadly. "I haven't heard him much at all. I know he is still here with me, but I can't hear his voice anymore. Isn't that strange?"

"After the events of today, I'm open to strange."

"So…what do we do now?" I asked Brother curiously.

"I'm going to talk with Father. He will want to hear of this and will know what to do. After the trial, let's go together and tell him everything. I think he will understand."

"What about Mother and Morgan?"

"One step at a time, Lil' Sis. Let's start with Father, and then I think afterwards, we will know how to proceed."

We returned to the cart, climbing in with a sturdy branch in hand. I looked over to Agus Tull waiting impatiently by the cart for us to return. After we were seated, I nodded to him and gave the command to continue. He nodded back with an annoyed look on his face and gave the signal for the men to march. The cart continued moving along the road.

Rufus began to splint the prisoner's leg, and after several failed attempts, he got it into the correct position. I cut the ropes from around his hands and used it to keep the splint in place. Although his leg was still throbbing, the splint helped, and he sat back with a look of relief.

"Thank you, my lord," he said with a bow.

"You are welcome," Rufus replied.

The prisoner looked quickly to both sides of him and to the front of the cart, where our driver sat. Up until this point, the driver hadn't heard nor been concerned with our dealings in the back. He couldn't hear because of the horses. Either way, the prisoner seemed satisfied and leaned closer to me.

"I know you are confused. It's okay. Aleph has gone silent in my relationship with him, too." My eyes grew bigger as the stranger continued to speak aloud the thoughts of my heart. "The reason for his silence is not usually known but is always necessary." I looked over at Rufus and saw him leaning in, not wanting to miss a bit of this dialogue. "My words to you are either sound wisdom from Aleph or the ramblings of a crazy man. It will be up to you to decide which."

"What does Aleph want with me?" I asked desperately.

"A monumental task that is to be done by your hands will shake the foundations of Shalistar and bring the world to its knees. You will stand within the waters of life and remember the words of your creator." Suddenly, the prisoner's eyes glowed with a small flame of light. He took my hand. The sensation was powerful and comforting all at once. "Don't be afraid, Esgar. Aleph is here with you now!"

The evening fully set as we entered Raithe. The tall structures loomed all around us as we made our way swiftly through the main roads towards the palace. Agus Tull was shouting for people to move along the busy streets as we came by, even ordering the soldiers in his command to remove people forcefully, if they were slow to obey.

Until this moment, Rufus and I sat in silence, letting the words the prisoner spoke settle in our hearts. Brother gazed out into the city, with a blank look on his face. I gently reached out and touched his knee, startling him back to reality. "What is it, Brother?" I asked carefully.

"It all looks so temporary."

"What does?"

"The buildings. The market. The stone of the streets. The people. All of it."

The prisoner looked to my brother and smiled, patting him on the other knee, gesturing to him that he was right, and his thoughts were correct. "Now that you know, young sir, you will have to decide the best course of action with the time you have left."

"How will I know if the voice I hear is Aleph's or my own?"

"Matters of the heart are complicated, and often the voice of Aleph can be mistaken for our own. Like anything else in life, it takes time and pursuit. However, once you experience His presence, you will be changed."

The massive gate to the sector opened before us. We rode up the steep main road to the top of the impossible cliffs, where the palace sat. The road wound upward around the edge of the city. Backward and forward it zagged, carved into the western side of the cliffs. Looking out, we could see many ships on the calm waters of the sea coming into the wharf, finishing their errands for the day. I never took this route before, but then I was never an escort for a prisoner either.

I noticed how the road at several points forked into another direction, allowing us into other parts of the city. The cart and our escorts stayed straight, climbing until we reached a tall stone wall at the top. Agus Tull halted the caravan before a large door carved into the rock.

Moments later, the prisoner was pulled off the cart. He grabbed his leg and cried out in pain as his foot hit the hard stone surface of the road. "Leave him be!" I shouted at the soldiers. They immediately released him, and he fell to the ground in a heap. Rufus and I jumped off the cart and gently picked up our companion. Wrapping our arms around his frail body, we held him steady.

"We will escort the prisoner ourselves!" Rufus commanded.

Agus Tull's voice boomed from the top of his horse.

"I would not suggest that Your Majesty. This dog is crafty and may take advantage of…"

"I said, we will take the prisoner to the throne room and before the magistrate," Rufus instructed, interrupting Agus. "This gentleman has requested an audience in the presence of the king. What this prisoner will confess needs to be heard by all. Please send for our father and mother." Agus stared at my brother through his helmet with his mouth slightly open. "This is what I have commanded, and my orders will be followed!" The brute was contemplating what my brother requested, and his posture on top of the horse showed that he was not enthused. I thought he was going to disobey.

After a moment of thought, he responded. "I will do as you have asked, Your Majesty." Agus bowed his head and barked several orders to his subordinates. They were off on an errand to request the presence of Father and Mother.

The prisoner, still leaning heavily on us, whispered to Rufus. "You have done well, young one. What I have to say will need to be heard and witnessed by all."

The passageway from the prison to the throne room was dark and dirty, involving many winding steps. This made our escorting of the prisoner doubly hard. We worked together to keep from falling over at several points. We passed many cells wrought with iron bars and rooms with large wooden doors, with only a small slot to peek in.

Voices of men and women cried out from within the cells, begging us to help them. My heart broke, hearing their cries as we passed. What had they done to deserve such punishment?

I was sure that not all of them were guilty. Many of them were strategically placed here by the magistrate to keep them out of the way.

After numerous tight corridors and one final staircase, we came to a large wooden door. Above the top of the door was crudely painted in a deep crimson color the word "GUILTY." I took a deep breath and steadied myself. A soldier came before us and pulled the door. As it opened inward toward us, a soft glow entered the dark hallway, blinding us. We blinked several times, adjusting our eyes to the light on the other side of the door.

"Have courage, young ones," the prisoner stated softly. "This is all by design." Rufus and I looked at each other and nodded. Taking a tight hold of our prisoner between us, we walked through the "Door of Guilt" and into the royal throne room of the palace.

CHAPTER

15

The door closed and filled the hall with a loud reverberating echo. I was startled and instinctively turned around to find a soldier positioned behind us, standing at attention. All eyes were on the three of us as we made our way slowly from the shadows into the center of the throne room.

My breath caught as I saw the magistrate rustling several documents while sitting at a large wooden table at the foot of the upper dais. Standing behind him with his arms across his chest was Lucien, the Dark Man and chief messenger of Baelor. Our eyes met and an evil grin spread across his face, causing my brother's grip to tighten upon the prisoner's body. I could only guess the feelings coursing through him right now as he battled the thoughts in his mind.

I moved my eyes up the dais to the two thrones at the top, where Father and Mother sat. Standing beside Father with his hand upon the side of the throne was Morgan. His eyes were covered with an ornate black mask, concealing the scars Lucien gave him years ago. Next to Mother was my youngest brother, Devon. All four of them looked down at us in puzzlement, not knowing why they were summoned. The truth was, none of us knew, except that our companion requested it.

Brother and I moved over to a smaller table in front of Balafas and placed the prisoner down carefully. He groaned in relief as he sat in the padded chair. After he was released, Rufus and I moved to the side and stood at ease, observing the trial.

The magistrate continued busily scanning several documents at his desk. The entire throne room was eerily silent. The only sound was the turning of pages. I looked up at Father again and felt pity for him. Mother sat there, looking bored. This was a nuisance to her, and it was perfectly clear by her posture that she didn't want to be here.

After endless silence, Balafas stood before the prisoner, staring into his eyes, and looking for the most incriminating evidence of guilt—fear. The defendant stared back, unflinching. After several intense seconds of standoff, Balafas began the trial.

"Hear now the instructions of this court. You will not speak unless you are spoken to and will only give information that is relevant to this case. I will not tolerate any deviations from the truth in any way, shape, or form. I hold you under oath before the supreme authority of His Majesty, Remus I, ruler of the realm of Shalistar and all its inhabitants. Do I make myself perfectly clear?"

The prisoner leaned forward and responded politely. "Yes, Your Grace."

"Good. Now please state your name for the record." Several moments passed, but the prisoner did not respond. I watched as a small grin flashed across our companion's face. Balafas leaned forward again. "Did you not hear me, accused? I asked for your name, and you will give it to me now."

His smile brightened as he spoke. "I have gone by many names. But you may call me...Glynn." The Dark Man was not amused. He looked at this stranger seated before him with a searching gaze, trying to figure out the secrets this man was keeping from him.

"I guess that will do for now, Glynn. So, where are you from?" Balafas asked.

The dirty prisoner leaned forward, across the entire table, and softly asked a question. "Can we skip the charade, Your Grace? I'm sure we are all busy and have other pressing matters to address. You will find that I am going to be most accommodating regarding your questions."

Balafas was struck with awe at the boldness of this stranger but didn't know how to proceed. Glynn continued speaking. "In response to your thoughts, Magistrate...yes. I am aware that my death is imminent, and no, I am not afraid of my outcome. I have come here for a specific purpose. Aleph has given me the task of revealing the locations of the hidden sanctuaries in Shalistar."

Awe overtook Balafas when he looked at his master. Lucien was just as baffled. It was a comical scene to behold as Balafas stumbled, rising out of his chair. "You amaze me, accused. You come in here and throw all the protocols out the window. Then you speak the blasphemous name of the enemy as though you are best friends. Now you mock me by telling me you will willingly give up the location of all your brothers? Quite a show, to say the least. Why should I believe you?"

"Because, Magistrate, you know that what I say is true,"

the prisoner continued. "You are part of Aleph's plan, too, an important part, indeed. It will be you who gives the order to destroy the sanctuaries, and this act will be the catalyst that will scatter the brothers to the four corners of Shalistar. Only then can they truly fulfill their purpose. The sanctuaries were necessary for a time, but now they must be removed."

Balafas stood there staring at the stranger with his mouth slightly open, unable to speak. The next voice to be heard resounded from the top of the dais.

"How do you know such things?" asked Father.

Glynn bowed deeply before responding. "May I stand?"

Father investigated the stranger with a perplexed look on his face. "Can you?"

Glynn nodded and slowly stood up out of his chair. Everyone in the hall gave a gasp as the man with a broken leg walked to the edge of the dais. Balafas moved away from the prisoner, running into Lucien. The Dark Man gave an annoyed grunt and shoved the magistrate aside. Glynn ignored the two and addressed my father, mother, and two brothers. "As you can see, Your Majesty, the leg which was broken has been mended before your very eyes. This has been done as a sign to you today."

"A sign for what?" Father asked in bewilderment.

"To show you that Aleph has not left you alone. He has been here the entire time." Balafas stumbled back over to the prisoner, interrupting him.

"I demand to know the locations of the sanctuaries, now!" Glynn whirled around, facing the magistrate. He gave a soft chuckle and answered.

"The sanctuary of Shelbye can be found in the wide open past the western wall on top of the cliffs, overlooking the sea. Near to the royal cabin, I might add. The sanctuary of Chisenhall is past the eastern wall of the city overlooking the waters as well, and the sanctuary of Sommerset is located at the crossroads, again in the wide open."

"In the wide open?" Balafas stammered. "But how?"

"Aleph would never allow you to see them until he wanted you to, Magistrate." Glynn quickly responded. "Now may I please continue my response to His Majesty?" Balafas nodded his approval and sat at the table, beginning to make some notes. Lucien started to take a step forward toward the prisoner.

"You stop right there, foul spirit!" shouted Glynn. As if he hit a wall, Lucien stopped dead in his tracks.

"I demand that you tell me who you are!" Lucien shouted.

"Silence, fiend!" exclaimed Glynn with boldness. The Dark Man was frozen in place, grunting and gasping, unable to speak! His voice was removed! Satisfied with the outcome, Glynn turned and looked at Father. "I apologize for the interruptions, Your Majesty. You may now ask me your questions, freely."

Father, with wide eyes, looked at the stranger and spoke. "Who are you? What is your name?" Glynn took a step back and looked over at Rufus and me. My heart pounded in my chest as a large grin spread across the stranger's face.

Suddenly, the dirty man at the foot of the dais began to glow as if light were shooting outward from the inside of his body. The light exploded into the shadowed areas of the room, temporarily blinding all of us. The radiance caused

Rufus and me to squat and wrap our black cloaks around each other. The beams of light continued to shoot out, one after another. Balafas was on the floor, his hands covering his eyes, whimpering. Lucien stood there, transfixed, as the light passed through him, unable to look away and not able to speak due to the last command of the stranger. Father, Mother, and my brothers cowered as well.

As I slowly opened my eyes, everything became brilliant. I could no longer see a prisoner standing before us, only a ball of light. Then the light began to dissipate, and the figure was once again revealed. Glynn was gone. Standing before us was a huge man with a bushy black beard. He was clothed in bright armor and wearing a white cloak with red, blue, and green trim at the bottom. He walked over to where Rufus and I were. The large man reached out his gloved hand and helped us to stand. Turning back to the center of the room, the stranger addressed my father.

"As I stated before Your Majesty, I have been known by many names. But you may call me Jeru. I am your guardian, sent from Aleph the most high. It is an honor," Jeru stated, bowing deeply.

"Deceiver!" shouted Lucien, breaking free from the silence. "How dare you come into my kingdom without authority?"

"Silence!" Jeru boomed; his voice shook the pillars that held the high ceiling into place. Lucien immediately closed his mouth. The guardian walked over to the Dark Man and spoke softly. "You know the next step, Adversary. What you must do, do it quickly!"

"Has the time come? Is the shift upon us?" Lucien asked the guardian.

"It is—now, go!" At his command, a magical sound resonated, and Lucien vanished before our eyes. The guardian named Jeru turned back to Father. "Your Majesty."

"Why are you here?" Father asked in awe.

"My purpose is two-fold. The first part was to deliver the sanctuaries and the second is to bring you a message from Aleph, Himself."

"What is the message you bring, Guardian?"

"Aleph is not angry with you. The deception you and your family have experienced has been an attack of the enemy. This deception took the form of a dark cloud which hovered over your family for a long time, affecting many generations. The path you have before you is not going to be easy, and you will need fellowship with Aleph as the end approaches."

"The end? What are you talking about?" Father asked.

"I cannot say any more, Your Majesty," Jeru replied.

"I command you, as the King of Shalistar, to tell me," Father proclaimed with an authoritative voice.

"With all due respect, Your Majesty, I must decline." Father's bluff was called, and Jeru stood defiantly. The guardian looked at all of us and smiled. Raising his hands above his head, he shouted in a language I never heard before. As his voice boomed, the ground under us shook. A beam of radiance shot forth from Jeru into the center of Father's throne, wrapping all of us in light. My body was stretching, growing larger. All over my skin, I could feel tiny pulses of electric current. I wanted to scratch my arms from the sensation.

"Make it stop! Make this sorcery stop!" I heard Mother

screaming from her seat atop the dais. Devon was draped over her as the brilliant light passed through them both. "Baelor, save me from this wickedness!" I heard her cry once more. As if in response to her desperate plea, all the light suddenly vanished.

Jeru was nowhere to be seen. How long were we with Aleph? Time obviously passed because the soldiers were gone. The only one left in the room was Balafas. He sat at the table, scribbling notes furiously, breathing deeply and gritting his teeth. It was several moments before he realized the light was gone. Seeing us, he jumped out of his chair and bowed.

"Your Majesty...I uh..."

"There is nothing to be said, Balafas," Father said dreamily. What happened here today was ministered to us by the hand of Aleph, Himself!"

"But Your Majesty, the decree!" the magistrate cried.

"Overruled! From this moment forth, the name of Aleph will be thought of in the highest regard! His name will be spoken from the capital city of Raithe to the frozen wastes of Kvistad.

"Perhaps...Your Majesty needs some time to reflect on the events of today?"

"I do not need any more time, Balafas! I have reflected enough my entire life! I sat by and let this kingdom be ruled by everyone around me. All I have done is move my pen over papers and shown up to deliver speeches that were already written for me. It is time for me to finally awaken and become the leader this world needs."

"You have spoken truly, Your Majesty. The world needs you. Which is why I suggest a short holiday with your family. Your kingdom will be here when you return. I mean, there is nothing more important than family, am I right?" Father looked to Mother, silently asking for her thoughts on the situation. She was in another place, consumed by her thoughts in an almost trance-like state. Not receiving any help from Mother, Father leaned forward and responded.

"My friend, since you put it that way...you may be right. My family and I should rest. It has been so long since we have spent time together. I think we will go on a holiday. Is the waterfront cabin ready in Shelbye?"

"Yes, Your Majesty. It is in perfect condition for you."

"Excellent. We will leave at first light. When I return, I will meet with you and Lord Lucien as well. I will have questions for both of you."

"I understand, my King. I hope you all rest well, and I look forward to your return," he said as he turned away from us, but not before I could see the evil grin stamped across his face.

CHAPTER
16

The windows opened to a breathtaking seaside vista. For the first time ever, we were on holiday at our royal cabin, right off the western coast of Shelbye. Our large cedar homestead lay on top of a high cliff overlooking the massive expanse of the Western Sea. I could smell the salt in the air and hear the crash of waves upon the rocks hundreds of feet below.

As I strained my ears, all I could hear was the sound of nature—no raucous soldiers were shouting in an army camp or classmates scrambling down the halls. My ears welcomed the solitary sounds of blessed nature. As I took it all in, I exhaled, daring myself a moment of peace. Aleph created a scene outside my second-story window that was beyond imagination. The early afternoon sun was at its peak, creating immaculate warmth that stretched out upon the surface of the water. The animals played harmoniously together around the cliff. Far along the horizon, birds dove into the water, catching fish that swam closely to the surface. It was a perfect afternoon, one that I never wanted to end.

The serenity was interrupted by a light tap on the door to my room, followed by the sound of Mother's voice. "Kristina?" she called.

"I'm here, Mother." I circled around as the door swung open. The woman standing on the threshold had a glazed look in her eyes. Something was different. I noticed immediately she hadn't stormed into my room.

"I wanted you to know we are joining for dinner after sunset. Your Father would like to address all of us at once." The words she spoke were automated, with no emotion at all. It was hard for me to wrap my head around the change within my mother. She looked hypnotized, taking me completely off guard.

She continued to stand there, nervously twitching her hands together in front of her. I looked at her and waited. "Mother? What is it?" She looked up at me emerging from the trance, disoriented with her surroundings. "What is it, Mother?" I asked carefully. Several more seconds of silence passed before she finally spoke.

"I…will see you this evening." She resolved to leave her thoughts unspoken, and without another word, closed the door to my room. I was left alone, undone by what just happened. Suddenly, there was a soft knock at the door. My heart stopped again. Did she come back to speak her thoughts aloud?

"Lil' Sis?" It was Rufus' voice this time. "Can I come in?"

"Sure," I responded, disappointed. The door opened, and my older brother crossed the threshold.

"What's wrong with Mother? It looked like she swallowed a frog as she passed me in the hall," he said with a chuckle. I turned away from him and looked out the window, deep in thought. He came further into the room. "Are you okay Lil' Sis?" I didn't respond but shook my head to the sides.

"Did she say something?" Again, I shook my head, silently. Rufus stepped up softly beside me and placed a hand upon my shoulder. "Are you okay?"

I smiled at him and turned back to the vista out my window. "It's beautiful up here," I said evasively. "Why have we never come before…as a family?"

"Our life has never been normal, Sis, and our parents more concerned with power and prestige, than the well-being of their family."

"It's sad, Rufus. Mother…something is wrong."

"What's that, Sis?" Rufus questioned.

"Mother…she seemed so empty, and her words sounded hollow. In the throne room, within the light…I heard her. She cried out for Baelor!"

"Baelor? Are you sure?" he asked with great concern.

I crossed over to the door. "I love you Brother. But can you please leave? I need some time to myself."

"I don't understand," he responded, crossing over to me. He placed his hand gently upon my shoulder and looked me in the eyes. "Are you sure?"

"Yes. I need to sort out my thoughts."

"Very well. If you need anything, I'm right next door." He opened the door and left me alone.

I crossed back over to a chair next to the window. I couldn't feel Aleph near me, even when I closed my eyes. I began to panic, so I simply breathed and allowed myself a moment to relax. I let my head rest back into the soft pillow at the top of the chair, and before I knew it, was weeping silent tears.

"Where are you?" I cried, hoping desperately for an answer.

◇

That evening, we gathered downstairs around a large oaken table, enjoying each other's presence for the first time in a long while. In fact, this was the first time since Devon was born six years ago that we all supped together. It was an odd feeling, very unlike the times my older brothers would try to gain an advantage over each other to impress Father. So much happened since then.

I looked across the table at Morgan. My beloved older brother wore an ornate mask over his pupils and would never see again. Lucien's cruelty was a mark that would forever be stamped upon my brother's face. I got choked up and was about to cry when Morgan spoke.

"Don't worry about me, sister. It's not as bad as you would think," he said, looking directly at me. Morgan poked the food with his fork. I didn't know how to respond—none of us did. So, we continued eating in awkward silence.

Shortly after the meal was cleared, Father and Rufus enjoyed a port wine for dessert. Father was fighting an inward battle and could no longer contain what was within him. He lightly tapped his knuckles on the table, gaining our undivided attention.

"My family. I uh…don't know how to say this. I never had to apologize for anything in my life before. It is undeniable that our creator is still with us. Aleph has not left us alone. I'm not sure what to believe about anything I have been taught. I feel completely vulnerable and exposed." I looked over at Mother and saw her blank, hypnotic stare. Was she listening? Could she even hear these genuine words?

"I guess what I'm trying to say is…I'm so sorry, for everything. I have failed each of you as a father, and I am deeply convicted for it. I will try…"

That was as far as Father got. Suddenly, we heard loud cries from our royal guard at the front of the keep. "We're under attack!" The shout was followed by a loud clanging bell that signaled danger. We all sat motionless, in disbelief, listening to swords clanging, followed by the sound of painful screams outside our front door.

Then came the unmistakable sound of destruction spells flying through the air. The house shook as fireballs crashed into the side. The impact knocked us off our feet. We were slowly regaining our bearings when a soldier ran into the dining room from the left side.

"Your Majesty, we must get you out of here! There are too many of them!" he shouted. As soon as his sentence ended, he gasped and grabbed his chest. A sword tip protruded slightly from his torso. He looked down and tried to grip the tip of the blade but simply fell forward. Standing behind him was the shape of a muscled, burly soldier wearing a crimson cape and a golden helm.

He leaned down to the fallen soldier and quickly retrieved his sword from the body. Father stood in front of us with his hands stretched outward. He stood up as straight as he could and addressed the menacing captain.

"I demand to know at once the meaning of this intrusion!" Father shouted authoritatively to Agus Tull.

"Maybe you should be addressing him?" Agus returned, gesturing to the other side of the room. We followed the sweep of his hand. Standing in the front doorway, silhouetted against the bright fires behind him, was Lucien, the Dark Man.

"My Lord and King." He bowed his head slightly and stepped into the room.

"Lord Lucien." This time it was Mother who came to stand in front of Father. "Please spare my children. They are innocent!" Father looked at Mother in shock. "He is the one you want," she said, pointing to her husband.

"Jessilyn...what are you doing?" Father asked quietly. Mother turned to him.

"Isn't it obvious, Remus? Your time is up," she said coldly. Mother looked back to Lucien, who was taking in all the fear manifested in the room.

"Well-spoken, my Lady," Lucien taunted. Mother took one more step towards the Dark Man, bowing her head.

"It is my pleasure, my Lord," she said. "However, I would request that my Lord spare the children for now. They are truly innocent and have no..." Mother stopped speaking as she felt the stare of the Dark Man upon her. Lucien continued to gaze at the woman, pleased at the sight of her groveling.

"Jessilyn," he spoke cruelly. "Wasn't it you who confided in me that you wished to be rid of your children?" We all turned toward Mother, looking at her in shock. "Wasn't it you who traded their very lives to me in return for the power and prestige of the kingdom? Deals made before Baelor are binding and have no expiration!"

"You cannot take my children," she stated defiantly, taking another hesitant step toward the Dark Man. Lucien chuckled.

"Decrepit woman! The Shift is upon us, and the royal family must be removed—including you and your children!" Without any further hesitation, Lucien spoke a familiar string of arcane words and stomped his foot down hard upon the wooden planks under him. Suddenly, Mother gasped, reaching to her mouth. She tried to speak, but all that came out were muffled, soft screams.

Lucien looked directly at me, and the recollection of my first day of school flooded me. I could see in my mind the terrifying moment when Lucien and Master gagged me. "You might tell your mother to keep quiet," he said mercilessly.

Reluctantly, I helped my fearful mother back to the rest of the family. The look on her face told the entire story. Her plan backfired, and she was afraid. Father spoke next. "Why Lucien? Why are you doing this?" Father cried desperately.

"Foolish king!" Lucien snarled. "Do you ask a dog why it barks? Or a fish why it swims? No! They do it because they were created to do it! I am the adversary of Aleph, and it is my purpose to destroy this world. One way or another, I will do it, and you and your feeble mind will not stop me!" Lucien took a step back from Father. He spoke an arcane word, and from out of nowhere appeared several black-cloaked individuals.

The next moments were a blur. Somewhere in time, we were escorted by the clerics and given filthy rags to change into. Once dressed, we stood out front of the blazing house. Before us was a battalion of soldiers, led by Agus Tull and a cart led by horses. My heart stopped beating in my chest as I saw our transportation. Only days before, Rufus and I were on the same cart, leading the prisoner Glynn to Raithe. Now, it was our turn. I saw Father resisting the hands of the soldiers that held him.

"Please! I am your king! You don't have to do this!" He pleaded with them. "Release us now, and this insubordination will be forgotten!" None of the soldiers moved to help. "I said…I command…" Suddenly Father gasped and grabbed his throat, like Mother did earlier. Lucien walked up next to him, inspecting the spell he cast.

"Silence," the Dark Man commanded. Father stared back into the Dark Man's ambitious eyes, unable to speak due to the magical gag. Lucien spoke several more arcane words, and I felt the terrifying feeling of a gag in my mouth. My brothers gasped beside me as the spell overtook them as well. We stood there huddled together, looking on at our captors, fighting the fear that wanted so badly to overtake us. Several soldiers appeared with sacks and stood behind us, awaiting the order.

"We cannot take the risk of them being discovered or recognized," Lucien continued. "Put the sackcloth over their heads!" At that command, my entire world went black. All I could see was dark material, and all I could smell was the dirt inside an old sackcloth that held food or grain from long ago.

"Now that nobody can see their faces…" Lucien spoke the spidery language of sorcery and a tickling sensation overcame me. It lasted for several minutes and then was gone.

Applause erupted from the soldiers, praising Lucien and Baelor for the gift of illusion. They continued to marvel excitedly. "How did he do that? They all look younger! The little prince looks like he's three!"

"You have seen the power of Baelor!" Lucien shouted over the battalion of warriors. "Let us rid ourselves of this weak royal family and usher in the greatest time in the age of Shalistar! Blessed Baelor!"

The entire company shouted in unison. "BLESSED BAELOR!" Our hands and feet were tied in front of us, as we were placed onto the cart. I began to cry from within the hood, my heart pounding in my chest. I could sense the fear in the rest of my family. It was thick and tangible.

"Get them safely to Raithe, Captain." Lucien commanded. I heard a magical noise that signaled Lucien's teleportation, followed by Agus Tull shouting to the battalion.

"We will go through the strait of Corsonia, across to Sommerset! Move swiftly, men!" As the cart began to move, one thought crashed through me repeatedly. I couldn't speak it audibly, so I kept it in the front of my mind, thinking it over and over again.

"Aleph, come quickly. Come quickly to our aid!"

CHAPTER
17

I opened my eyes to see familiar dark fabric inside the sackcloth. The cart stopped moving. I heard faint commotion behind me. "Why are we stopped, soldier? We must make it to Raithe by tomorrow evening. It is imperative. We cannot be late!" Devon wiggled violently beside me.

"I can move! I can speak!" Devon whispered to me. In the next moment, I felt little feet running along the cart. Did he break free of his bonds? Then I heard a scream and what sounded like a thud as Devon fell off the back of the cart. Several muffled sounds followed and another voice from the same direction, speaking to Agus Tull.

"Sir, if I may," the voice said.

"If you do, then I'll beat you till you bleed." The foot of one of my family members was tapping my toes, trying to get my attention. I assume we were all thinking the same thing. We began to grunt and scream, embracing the agonizing pain of the gag going deeper into our throats, choking us in the process. I hoped desperately that the voice would hear us and recognize us.

"What could this boy possibly have done wrong to deserve such a permanent fate?" I heard another thud and grunt. It sounded like Agus Tull put an end to the conversation. I stopped screaming. The gag loosened its painful grip in my throat, and I was able to think clearly again.

There was another voice, an older voice than the first. "That is my boy! You had no right!"

"You better teach him the order of authority in Shalistar. I don't have to explain myself to him!" The next string of dialogue between the man and the captain was intense. We sat there on the cart, listening to the exchange. The captain issued threats and taunts, insulting Aleph, and calling him a dead god. At one point, I thought there was going to be more bloodshed, but the other voice remained calm and collected throughout the entire conversation. Then the man said something that got my attention.

"The king would not approve," the older voice stated.

"He's not here now, is he?" I heard Father, screaming into the gag at the top of his lungs. He rocked violently against his bonds. Hearing and feeling the vibration of Father's desperation made me cry. Our situation was out of control! Why was Aleph not helping us? Were we abandoned for good?

"If the lad comes off the cart again, I swear by Baelor he will suffer greatly before his execution." The finality of the word "execution" took my breath away. Agus Tull announced the warning aloud to put us in fear and send us a message that conspiracy would not be tolerated.

"Farewell Father, for now." He ended his conversation with the man, and after several moments, we were off and moving along the road. Not too much time passed before I heard another conversation behind me between two of the soldiers.

"Why didn't we attack? They looked vulnerable to me," the first soldier said.

"I'm not sure. The captain had strict orders not to engage."

"Are we coming back?"

"I'm sure. I mean, the sanctuary is sitting there in the wide open. How have we not seen this before now?" The two soldiers moved on ahead of the cart. I could no longer hear the rest of their conversation. I sat back and rested my tired head against the wood planks of the cart. The thoughts of Mother's betrayal crashed repeatedly into my mind as I fearfully cried myself to sleep.

"Stand your ground, dogs!" I awoke to the sound of Agus Tull's raspy voice. How long were we out? It felt like minutes, but somehow, I knew it was longer than that. I heard shouts from soldiers all around me.

"The fog is thick, sir! We can't see anything in this darkness!" Agus spat curses and bucked his horse away from the cart. My mind raced with thoughts as to our whereabouts, when suddenly, the bonds loosened around my hands. Then a finger touched my throat, and a warmth spread throughout. The pain and pressure of the gag released. I took several deep, heaving breaths of fresh air and continued to take the sackcloth off my head.

The disorientation only lasted a few moments before I got my bearings. It was hard to see anything. Not only was it night, but the area was blanketed in an unnatural fog. I could barely see the torches of soldiers in the distance. All around me were the trunks of large oak trees.

I looked down and noticed the illusion spell affecting the appearance of my age was broken. I was back to my normal self. I heard Rufus breathe deeply, as Lucien's silence spell was suddenly released from his throat as well. He took a couple of moments to get himself together and whispered hoarsely, "Lil' Sis. Are you okay?" I quickly tore the sackcloth from him and kissed his cheek.

"Yes. I'm going to get us out of here." I untied the bonds from Brother's hands and feet. He struggled to a crouching position within the cart.

"What about the rest of them?" he said, pointing to our family. I heard them all desperately crying against the gag.

"Untie them as well," I said. I bent down, working on Father's bonds when suddenly I heard a soldier cry out.

"HALT! How did you get loose?" Rufus didn't hesitate. He dove headfirst from the cart into the body of the soldier on top of the horse. His weight hit the soldier, knocking him from the saddle. The two of them fell into the thick fog, out of sight. I heard several more grunts and screams from the soldier, crying for help. Then I saw Brother appear from out of the fog with a sword at his side. He held out his hand for me to take it.

"It's now or never, Lil' Sis. Come on!" I looked back one last time at my family.

"We can't leave them," I replied, in tears.

"Sis, if you don't move now, you will die!" he said loudly. I heard an incoherent gasp from Mother beside me. Gritting my teeth, I took hold of Rufus' hand and swung myself over the cart, hitting the ground with a thud. Hand in hand, we ran into the blanket of fog, leaving Father, Mother, Morgan, and Devon to their fate.

As we tore through the brush, we heard soldiers not far behind us. "They went that way! Don't let them escape!" We ran harder and faster through the thick fog. All around us were massive trees. The sticks and thorns of the brush cut through our legs as we went along. The dead leaves crunched as our bare feet traveled over them. Regardless of the pain, we kept moving. The shouts of soldiers behind us drove us to increase our speed.

"Where do you think we are?" I cried as we ran.

"Elder Woods," Rufus shouted back. "Based on the course from Sommerset, it would be the most logical."

"What do we do now?"

"We get out here and then we find…" Suddenly, I heard a scream come from Brother as his hand released mine, and we both fell forward with great intensity. The hard floor of the woods took the breath out of me as I collided with it. I saw Brother close to me, crying out in pain and grabbing his side. Scraping myself off the filthy ground, I moved slowly and dizzily through the fog until I found myself beside him. He was keeled over and shaking.

"Rufus! You must get up. The soldiers are behind us," I shouted hysterically. "What is it? What's wrong!?" Rufus picked up a stick and stuck it between his teeth, biting down on it to conceal his painful squeals. Through gritted teeth, he pointed to his side. I looked down to my horror and saw the source of his torment. The shaft of a long arrow protruded from his side.

"They got me! The coward shot me!" he cried painfully.

"We have to keep moving!" I commanded. Rufus, with great difficulty heaved himself up, distributing all his weight onto me. It was more than I could bear, and I was having a tough time keeping him upright. I was able to distribute the weight evenly and began moving off to the right side of a large oak. The ground beside it opened into a gully. The oak's roots traveled down into the chasm, providing cover from watchful eyes. We ducked under the large root on the slope of the gully and waited silently.

I heard the frustrated voices of soldiers as they came through the area. "I got one of them. He's bleeding out like a stuck pig! They couldn't have gone far."

"We'll find them. Keep checking the perimeter," The other soldier replied. We sat still as they passed by. Rufus muffled his scream by biting down on the stick in his mouth.

After they moved away from us. He took the stick out and turned to me. "Are you okay, Lil' Sis?" he asked painfully, wiping beads of sweat from his forehead.

"I'm fine," I said as I turned my gaze to my brother's side. "They got you," I cried.

"Yeah," he said painfully. I touched the fletch of the arrow, and my brother squirmed. "Please stop, Sis," he said desperately.

"We have to pull it out," I prodded.

"No. If we do then they will know where we are. No stick is going to stifle that scream. There is no way I could be quiet while you are doing that."

"But Brother, we have to get out of here."

"It's not happening," he said bluntly. "I'm not going anywhere."

The realization struck me. "No, Rufus. I'm not going to leave you."

"Yes, you are."

"I won't do it," I said defiantly.

"Listen to me, Kristina," Rufus winced. "You can and you will."

"No. Please don't make me go alone."

"You are not alone, Lil' Sis. Aleph is with you."

"Please don't mention that name," I said, shaking my head. "You are coming with me."

"It's not my path." He exhaled deeply, fighting against the pain.

"How can you say that? How can you know that?"

"It's not important. Now listen to me. The soldiers are coming back this way. When I tell you to run, you go. Don't look back…just run." The emotion was too much to bear. I thought for a moment that I would stay here and disobey. However, knowing that was not an outcome he would accept, I wrapped my arms around my brother and hugged him with all the strength I had. Then I looked into his eyes.

"I'm sorry, Rufus," I cried. "I'm so sorry. I was going to save you."

He took my hand gently, looked directly into my eyes and smiled. "You already have, Sis."

I didn't know how to reply. Nothing was adequate at this moment, but I had to say something. "Tell everyone I love them. Even Mother."

"I will," Rufus said and shoved me painfully away. "Go now. Run!" He turned away from me, scanning the soldiers in the distance. I stood there defiantly, not moving. He turned back to me. "For the first time in your life, obey! Run now!" He screamed and stood to his feet, staggering, and holding his bleeding side. He jumped up and shouted at the top of his lungs, running to the bottom of the gully to intercept the soldiers. I watched in horror as my brother jumped onto one of them, knocking him over in the process. I saw Rufus pull the sword from his scabbard and stand in a defensive position.

Other soldiers were running towards the fight. I heard Brother sound a war cry as the rest of the soldiers came into view. The sound of swords clanging echoed through the wood as my brother held them off. With great reluctance, I stood to my feet and quietly climbed over the edge of the gully. Behind me were the cries of my brother as the soldiers overwhelmed him with their swords.

"That's enough!" one soldier commanded. "He is to meet his end on the chopping block! Captain made it clear! Take him back to the cart!"

There was nothing I could do to stop it! I decided it was time to obey my brother's words, and with great reluctance, I slowly turned away from the oak tree. Without looking back, I ran as fast as I could into the deep fog of the Elder Woods.

I was shivering from head to toe as I made my way through the endless fog, not because I was cold, but because of the horrific thoughts that were repeated in my mind. My heart was torn, and there was not going to be any resolution for a long time. The wound I felt was deep. My brother sacrificed himself so I could get away, and I allowed him to do it. I was not only lost in a deep dark forest, but also within the scenes of my past.

I trudged through the fog with trees all around me, not knowing at all where I was going. I heard terrible sounds of wild animals. Menacing growls belonged to some hideous beast I could not see. The possessor of the snarl saw me as a snack, wanting to tear me limb from limb. But for whatever reason, they never attacked. Some unseen hand kept them away from me, and I was able to continue through the darkness.

When I reached a place of safety, far enough away from the soldiers, I collapsed. All my strength left me, and I was unable to rise. My throat was completely parched and desperate for a drink of water. I crawled slowly to a large tree trunk that was hollow from the inside. It was wide enough for me to fit into. Still on my hands and knees, I made my way inside the trunk. Before I rested my head against the interior, I saw the thick fog dissipate outside. I sat there, weeping for my family left on the cart, weeping for Rufus and his bold sacrifice, weeping for everything else in my miserable life. Tears fell until there was no more strength to even be awake. Then, with one final heave, I cried myself to sleep.

I opened my eyes in the morning and rain was falling. Right outside the entrance of the trunk was a large piece of bark that was hollowed out in the shape of a bowl. Some of the rain was gathered in a small pool of water within the piece of bark. I gently picked it up and brought the bowl to my lips. Before I knew it, I finished the meager amount of water, desperately wanting more. The rain was coming down hard, so I sat the bark outside the entrance and waited until it was full. I repeated the process several more times until I satisfied my thirst.

I sat there for another hour within the trunk, contemplating my next move. I knew I couldn't stay here forever, so I decided to follow the sun and direct my path north. As I traveled through the Elder Woods, the sun wasn't easily recognizable through the leaves of green overhead. The tall oaks camouflaged the sky from view in most places; however, several times the canopy broke, allowing me to see the direction of the sun.

The floor of the forest was not entirely comfortable, but I had tough feet and was not bothered too much by the surface scratching my soles. I walked carefully until I reached the edge of the forest. Luckily, we hadn't traveled far when the fog came, which made my journey to the edge of the wood brief. Before long, I broke from the cover of trees and found the North Road. I followed it, going in the direction of the Ternion Mountains.

That evening, I came to a hill that boasted a quaint inn with a thatched roof and a small stable beside it. Several travelers were stopped and resting there for the evening. I stealthily moved in the shadows to where their cart was stowed within the barn. Keeping an eye out for any kind of disturbance, I climbed into the back. Resting against the side were several trunks.

I looked around one more time and then opened the first

trunk. Within was a collection of soft garments. To my great luck, buried at the bottom was a pair of leather shoes that were my size. Without a thought, I grabbed the shoes and a brown travel cloak. I inspected the tunic and pants within the trunk as well, but they were quite large for my smaller frame. I would have to make do with the tattered, filthy rags I wore for now. I was starting to put on the shoes when suddenly, I heard the barn door open and quickly ducked into the shadows of the cart.

A stable boy came in, finishing his evening side work before calling it a night. I sat still as he passed me several times, putting away his tools. He performed one last circle of the barn, and then left. As I heard the latch click, I breathed deeply. He hadn't seen me.

I quickly put on the leather shoes and sighed in relief. I put on the travel cloak and clasped it. Even though it was summer, nights could be cool, and if it rained, the warmth of the material would be instantly felt. With great stealth, I opened the door to the barn and ran off as fast as could, heading north.

After several days of grueling travel, I stood on a rolling green hill overlooking the old town of Sommerset. The tall, stacked buildings didn't give me the warm, inviting feeling as before. I was now a fugitive, and danger loomed around every corner. I needed to be cautious of soldiers because they were looking for me. On top of that, I was starving. The rain was plentiful on the way up, so I was able to stay hydrated, but food was scarce. I settled for a handful of berries, which made me throw up shortly after. My stomach was signaling me, telling me it would not be ignored any longer. I needed to find sustenance, and fast!

I pulled the cowl of the travel cloak I "borrowed" over my head to keep my face hidden as much as possible. Even from here, I could see a cluster of soldiers at the bridge over the Parulin River. They were undoubtedly searching for me and stopping travelers, inspecting them as they came into town.

I stayed as far as I could away from them and walked around the outer walls until I came to the northwestern part of town. Soldiers were stationed there at the bridge as well. I lowered myself into a thick bush, camouflaging myself from view. Watching the soldiers through the leaves, I thought to myself how easy it would be to walk up to them and turn myself in. The torment inside gave me no rest and surrendering would put my misery to an end.

"I let them die," I continually said to myself as I sat there. The scene of my brother being overrun by the soldiers played itself repeatedly in my head. I did nothing. I hid and let them take Rufus down. My cowardice led to his destruction!

Then I was struck with a thought. "All I need to do is cast a calm spell. My nerves were shot, and I felt nauseous. All I needed was a simple incantation to put me out. Then I wouldn't have to think about all the memories, at least for a little while. Huddled within the cover of brush, I sat curled in a ball with my cloak around me. Within the dark cowl, I closed my eyes and joined myself with the void. Immediately, as if it were waiting the whole time, the messenger appeared. Shaking uncontrollably, and in utter desperation, I gave it another seven days of my life in exchange for a small portion of power.

The magic entered me, filling my being. It was all so familiar.

As the tingling sensation passed through me, I cried.

"Why has it come to this!?" My heart ached deeply for someone else, but that being was far away and silent for years. Baelor, on the other hand, had a messenger waiting for me when I joined the circle of the void.

"Where are you?" I cried out quietly. I waited, hoping the still small voice would respond. All I could hear were the ambient sounds of Sommerset all around me. There was no voice.

As tears fell from my face, I closed my eyes again and spoke the arcane words of sorcery, casting a calm spell. "What did it matter, anyway?" He wasn't coming for me. I made Him mad, and this was my end. I was all alone, without a family, without a home or a place to rest my head.

All the worry and pain vanished as I fell into a magical slumber, far away from any guilt or harm from others around me. There was nothing, and I felt nothing. I went completely numb as the power of the spell overtook me. I lay down within the brush, my eyes gazing skyward. There...was... nothing and I...felt...nothing.

As darkness fell, the spell lost its power, and I came out of hiding. Most of the soldiers only stayed until the day was over. But once the people went to their homes for the evening, they moved into town and sat at the tavern for a night of drunken revelry.

The streets were still busy, so I was able to steal the food I needed from vendors' stalls as they looked the other way. The years I spent at the school taught me how to be silent on my feet, so I stole an apple and some bread before the vendors knew anything.

I was darting around a corner when I saw a large brute with a crimson cape stumbling out of a building on the right. I ducked back behind a near empty textile stand and watched the unmistakable form of Agus Tull stagger past me. He was shouting words to his soldiers down the street.

"Hey! You guys had not forget why we're here! "He stuttered drunkenly. "Somewhere in here this town is a runaway princess! I juss know it! You better have stay on your guard! Let don't the booze keep you from finding her!" He finished by falling into a stand directly across the street from me. I watched Agus Tull awkwardly get up, spilling all the wares into the street. The vendor tried to help him but was clubbed across the skull as the soldiers came to their captain's aid.

"Iss okay! I'm fine!" he stammered to them. "Take me to the Hog! I need a drink!" The soldiers braced him on both sides as he stood. The piggish oaf then took two steps and fell to his knees, vomiting every bit of alcohol he consumed that evening out onto the hard stone road beneath him. It was sickening to watch. People passed by, groaning, and covered their noses at the smell.

After several disgusting bouts of relief, he stood up again and, with the help of his soldiers, staggered back down the streets towards the Swarthy Hog. With my wares in hand, I moved in the opposite direction, heading back towards the river. I walked along the edge of town until I found myself in front of a barn. As before, I made sure I was unseen before ducking within the barn. It smelled old and dusty inside but was kept and clean. I looked up and saw several stories of wooden rafters. In the far back corner was an area covered in shadows. It was used for storage, with large barrels and instruments for farming. I cleared a space and laid down some hay to soften the hard floor. It was vastly different from the softness of my palace bed, or even the dorm room bed for that matter, but it would do.

I sat down and ate my apple and bread hungrily. They were gone in minutes. Without any errands left and in the quiet of the shadows, I sat in silence. What I heard in my mind was beyond imagination. As the thoughts pummeled me again, I placed my hands on the sides of my face cupping my ears, hoping the voices in my head would stop. They kept coming. Along with that I saw in my mind vivid pictures of my family sitting in prison awaiting their execution. It was too much to bear. I wept bitterly, begging Aleph to take away the pain. Once again, there was nothing.

As I sat there shaking, I closed my eyes and joined myself with the circle of the void. Once again, Baelor's messenger was there, waiting for me. I made my deposit of seven days of life and received the portion of magic I needed to get me through this night. I didn't even wait for the messenger to leave. I started speaking the words of the spell, and the soothing calm overcame me once again, drowning out the sorrow and pain of my past, until once again…there was nothing.

I was startled awake by the touch of a hand on my shoulder. "I don't have any life to give!" I shouted as I shot out of the nightmare. Disorientation flooded me as I looked up into the face of a large farm boy with curly red hair.

"Are you okay?" He asked gently.

"Leave me alone." I cried, jerking away from his touch, and cowering into the dark corner.

"It's okay." He replied, showing me his hands. "I heard you from outside. You were having a nightmare."

"You heard me?!" I asked fearfully, thinking of the soldiers.

"Yes. Are you in trouble?" He asked carefully. I looked into the eyes of the farm boy and saw genuine concern for me. I couldn't hold back the emotion I was feeling. The emptiness that consumed me was overwhelming and I began weeping softly. "It's okay." He came closer to me, and I cowered even further into the corner, like a frightened dog.

"Don't worry. I'm not going to hurt you. My old man always said doing honorable deeds is like breathing. Can't live life without it!" His reply cut a fissure through the dark atmosphere I was trapped in. "You can stay in the barn if you like. Don't worry about Mum and Da. This will be our little secret."

I simply nodded my head from within the darkness of the cowl. "Thank you." I replied softly.

"What is your name?" I shook my head signaling I wasn't going to tell him. "Don't want to tell me?" I shook my head again. "I understand, but what am I supposed to call you?" He made a valid point and I decided to acknowledge the question.

"Esgar." I replied.

"Your name is Esgar?"

"Yes."

"Nice to meet you, Esgar. My name is Wil." He reached out his hand for me to shake it. As I did, he smiled. "Have you met anyone else around here?" I shook my head. "Well then, let me be the first to welcome you to Sommerset."

CHAPTER
18

The week passed slowly for me. Despite the kindness shown to me by my new friend Wil, I continued to fall deeper into a chasm of depression. The food and water he brought could not bring me out of the dark hole I was in. Every day, I stayed within the confines of the shadowed barn. Each morning, I awoke and summoned the messenger, like I was trained to do for so many years. After receiving my portion of power, I would slip myself into an unnatural calm spell. I didn't want to deal with the pain of losing my family, and magic was the easiest cure.

Wil would come in with a tray of food and water several times a day and see me laid out in a trance. He was gracious enough and left me alone. He didn't ask me to leave but let me continue in my selfishness. The spells were not permanent, only providing relief for a fleeting period of time, and when they broke, I felt a little emptier than the time before. I would come out of a trance and ache all over, wanting to stay within the calm spell for a little longer. I became an addict, always needing more, but never finding peace or satisfaction.

So, for the next week, my days followed the same pattern. I would calm myself as much as possible during the daytime, and then after the sun set and the soldiers were in their revelry at the tavern, I would sneak out of the barn and roam the streets, staying in shadows and observing the town as much as I could. It kept my mind off the pain—that is, until I was back inside the barn.

As the silence of night set in, my mind would go back to the thoughts of my family. Because my power ran out, I would go back to the void and meet the messenger to start the process all over. This was my existence. I was barely hanging on to the thread of life, until the day I let it all go.

I awoke with a scream as I came out of a nightmare and clapped a hand to my mouth to stifle the scream. "Has anyone heard me?" I thought. "What was I doing screaming like that?" I washed myself as best I could with a bucket of water Wil provided. After getting cleaned up, I sat myself in the dark corner and closed my eyes, connecting to the void. Today, something was different. There were no messengers to be found. Before, they were always there, ready to take my deposit. For some reason, today they were not.

I groaned in frustration and committed myself to summons, like a ten-year-old child who spent hours of time creating a connection to the void and summoning a demon. Hours passed, and no messengers came. I opened my eyes and wiped the sweat from my head. I looked down near my area and saw two trays of food and water. How long was I within the void? From the looks of it, I missed two meals. I walked over to a large crack in the side of the barn and looked through it. I could see the fields of the valley rolling westward, and the sun was moving into the horizon. I guess I tried summoning all day because the evening was coming quickly. The sky was tinted red as the sun positioned itself for a glorious setting.

I watched in utter astonishment as dark, oppressive clouds moved within my peripheral view from out of nowhere. The bright sky instantly turned to dark gray, streaked with red— horrific to look at. The sun was completely lost within the clouds. What just happened? A loud wind blew, and the planks of the barn shook. I moved away from the walls and backstepped until I was in the middle of the structure. The shaking became violent. I thought the planks were going to be ripped out of place all around me. This was not a safe place to be, so I made a bold decision to open the door to the barn and step out.

Everyone had taken to the streets, looking at the skies. The oppressive clouds stretched in all directions. Within the wind, I could hear moaning and crying that took my breath away. I collapsed to my knees, holding my heart. I closed my eyes, begging Aleph to tell me I was wrong. But somehow, I knew I wasn't.

Wil came running from around the corner and collapsed next to me, taking deep breaths as he spoke. "Everyone has been asked to meet at the square. A delegate from the magistrate has appeared."

As we made our way through the streets, I looked around me at the faces of the people. They all looked concerned. Something wasn't right, and I silently prayed that the premonition within my heart was wrong. A large crowd was already gathered at the square. I stood in the back, cowled in my cloak as I heard the announcement from the delegate.

He was hollow and empty as he spoke to the crowd, as

though his errand was an annoyance to him. His words brought my fears into reality, my cries were silent within my broken heart. Thoughts of my family and memories we shared passed through my mind. It was too much to take in or accept. Any hope left was now gone. I was alone, the last of my family line.

Then a realization struck me. I was in greater danger now than ever before. Lucien and the magistrate murdered my family in cold blood, and this was nothing but a show of strength, a secret message telling me they would stop at nothing to hunt me down and kill me too. Nobody around me was safe.

Wil turned around and looked at me with tears in his eyes. The news from the delegate, announcing to Sommerset the execution of the royal family, hit him hard. Then I heard a moan erupt from the entire crowd. They mourned the loss of their king and his family with groans and wailing. The delegate raised his hand for order, but the crowd would not relent. Several townsmen roared and tried to attack a nearby soldier. They were cut down before they knew what hit them. As their bodies fell, more screaming came from people nearby, and more rebellion ensued.

What followed were several attempts to overthrow the soldiers. They were no more successful than the first, and then like a tidal wave, the entire square was in an uproar, shouting and shaking their fists. The crowd was on the verge of a riot.

Hearing the chorus of despair from the people was making me lose my mind. I needed to get out of there, immediately. I turned and ran right into a large soldier standing unknowingly behind me. He staggered a bit and then looked down at me in rage. I was frozen in fear as he grabbed my arm.

"Watch where yer goin', wench! I oughtta skin yah for that!" He looked down at the arm he was holding. His eyes locked onto the exposed star on my forearm, the symbol that revealed my royal identity. His mouth opened wide and shouted for his comrades to come to his side. By that time, a riot had begun, and the groaning and wailing was loud, he could not be heard. I knew that if I didn't react quickly, I was dead. So, I kicked my foot out as hard as I could. It connected in the right spot because his grip immediately released. I watched the soldier groan and keel over in pain, holding his crotch.

I ran out of the square as fast as I could. The sound of violence was a dull roar behind me. I cut through alleys and back streets between the tall stone buildings, not stopping for a second until I was back at the barn. I huddled in the corner and rocked myself back and forth, moaning in pain as thoughts of my family plagued my mind.

I closed my eyes and thought of Aleph. I begged him to come to me. I was so scared and out of options. I listened as the moaning winds died out and were replaced by the sound of a violent mob trying to overthrow the soldiers. The clang of swords and occasional screams could be heard in the distance.

When I thought it couldn't get any worse, I heard soldiers assembling on the other side of the barn door. I investigated the rafters high above. Could I climb up there and hide? The thought of falling from that height was not a pleasant one, but I really didn't have a choice. I quickly climbed on top of the barrels to the high window on the western wall. The sill was large enough for me to stand on. I steadied myself and jumped out to a large beam that functioned as the main joist, stretching out over the entire barn. I was able to pull myself up. The soldiers were continuing to argue about coming in. I was running out of time.

Stepping carefully with my arms outstretched, I walked one step at a time over to the opposite side of the barn to a small catwalk that was used to reach the upper beams. I took the catwalk all the way up. The construction was sturdy at the top, with plenty of wood beams to walk on and cross. I was safely hidden high in the dark when the barn door opened.

Two soldiers stepped into my makeshift home with torches in their hands. I was not worried. Even with the torch, I was so high up in the shadows, they would not be able to see me. I crouched in the corner, above my straw mattress, holding on to the cross beams. The soldiers staggered as they patrolled the barn, complaining about the orders they were given.

"She wouldn't corner herself like this. We need to be looking somewhere else!" grumbled one soldier.

"Like where? The tavern?" the second soldier countered.

"Good idea!

"Captain said we better find her, or it would be our heads!"

"Captain, eh? Always drunk, that one is."

"And you're not?"

"I didn't say that now, did I?"

"Have you searched enough? She's not here. Can we move along before she makes it to the northern continent? We do have a riot on our hands."

"Yeah, this barn is clean."

The soldiers made one last search within and exited through the front, closing the barn door behind them. I sat there, huddled in the darkness, listening to their footsteps go away. I was shaken at the realization of my family's demise. I could hear the announcement from the cleric playing itself over in my head on an endless loop.

I couldn't move. I was frozen in fear. I held onto the rafter tightly, feeling the blood flow from my fingers. As I looked down from my location at the top of the barn, an idea came to me. What would happen if I threw myself off this rafter? This high up, it would kill me. The torment would cease, and I would be free. All it would take is two steps, and then it would be over. Unable to stop myself, I stood up to my full height and lifted one foot, placing it out over the expanse. I closed my eyes and was about to take another step when from within me I heard a whisper.

"Kristina." My heart melted as I heard the voice.

"Aleph?" I asked, hoping desperately for a response.

"Yes," he gently replied. I closed my eyes and shook my head.

"No. You left me all alone. You abandoned me," I cried.

"No, my daughter. I have been here the whole time."

"LIAR!" I screamed aloud, not caring about whether guards would flood the barn. "You let me suffer! You let my family die!"

"Yes. But we are not done yet. I am sending you help. They will be here soon. Please wait for them."

I was spent and had no emotion left. "I'm done with you,

Aleph! I can't do this anymore. Can't you let me die!"

"I cannot."

"Why?"

"Because I love you." The gentleness and sincerity of His words pierced my heart, and I began to weep again. He did not say another word to me that night. I was shaking for hours as I felt the tremors of Aleph's voice within me. There was no denying His power and authority, but why was He silent for so long? Why did He let me suffer the way He did? Regardless of the pain and emotion I felt, the second my head hit the hay, I was sound asleep.

I shot out of bed the next day as I heard my friend's scream echo throughout the barn. "Why did you do that, sir?! The boy was unarmed!" I heard a soldier ask the question from the other side of the barn door.

"You need to understand who is in charge," Agus Tull barked. "I have heard from several people who spotted a cloaked woman coming out of this barn! I will not be lied to again!"

"You are drunk, sir. The boy was innocent, and you killed him."

Hearing those words made my heart break all over again. My only friend in the world was mercilessly killed while protecting me. The all-too-familiar feeling of despair overwhelmed me.

"Boris and I searched the barn the other day. There was nobody here, nor any evidence to lead us to believe he was harboring a fugitive. Check your facts next time, sir."

"How dare you speak to me in that manner, dog! I will have your head!" Agus threatened. A scuffle and the sound of swords clanging was followed by the sounds of more soldiers separating the two men.

"That's enough, the both of you!" the third soldier shouted. "Let's go have a drink and cool off." The suggestion was met with grumblings and groans, then agreement from both parties. Several minutes later, it was silent.

The sun was setting as I slowly got up and made my way to the barn door. I noticed a red liquid flowing through the crack at the bottom. I slowly opened the door and looked down in horror to see the slain body of my friend Wil. He was lying face down in a pool of blood. The soldiers left to go to the tavern, and only a few stragglers were passing by. They stared at me fearfully as I held the body close to me. Offering no assistance, the people continued on their way.

First my family, and now, Wil. The depth of sorrow gripping me was beyond my ability to control. The emptiness that consumed me was a deep, dark hole I could not get out of. Aleph's words the other day meant nothing at this point. He said he was sending someone to bring me out, but I didn't care anymore. The burden was too great.

I dropped the heavy body and went back into the barn. I closed the door behind me and huddled myself into the corner, rocking back and forth. I looked up at the instruments hanging on the wall to my left and eyed a sharp dagger, used for cutting the flesh of pigs. I slowly got up and walked over to the instruments. Without another thought, I grabbed the dagger and went back into my corner. I continued to rock, weeping uncontrollably as I thought of all the pain in my life.

Like Master spoke over me so many years ago, I was a slave to a system of magic and sorcery, trafficked all over the world and delivering a message of false hope, while being promised power and prestige. In the end, the trap was sprung, and my family was murdered. Turning to familiar remedies, I drowned my sorrows with magic, only to create more emptiness. Finally, here I was. At the end of all hope, I sat in the corner, with a dagger to my wrist, preparing to cut myself.

"One good stroke," I thought. "A quick stab of pain, and it'll all be over." I stared down at my wrist. I held the blade tightly in my hand and placed it only inches from my main artery.

"Don't do it, Kristina," Aleph spoke from within me.

"I have nothing left to give," I responded. "Everyone I love is dead. I am a danger to everyone around me."

"Yes, but the prison door will soon be opened, and you will come out of the darkness you are in."

"And then what…"

"You will find me."

"Where?"

"At the top of my mountain. You and I will be together, and you will learn from me. Face to face."

"I can't."

"Yes, you can. Put the dagger down."

"I can't. There is too much pain."

"I know. This pain you were not meant to bear alone. It is now time for you to hand it over to me. You don't have to carry this

burden anymore."

"I don't know how."

"Simply lie down, and let me remove the poison from within you, once again."

Unexpectedly, the memory of me with Aleph in the halls of the school came back to me. I remember being a little girl and lying in His presence for hours, letting Him remove the poison of magic from my heart. He spoke to me in ways that nobody here could understand because Aleph saw me for who I really was. He knew who I was created to be.

Rocking back and forth, I gave Aleph permission to do what only He could do. His warmth surrounded me as His spirit coursed through the depth of my being. I gasped as His hand found the poison that seeped into my heart over the years. I could feel the venom being removed and started to squirm.

For what seemed like several hours, I laid with Aleph, letting Him remove it all: magic, sorcery, depression, hate, guilt, and fear. It was the most painful experience in my life, but when it was finally over, I sat up and looked around the barn. I saw everything clearly and heard the soft patter of bugs along the floor. Unfortunately, the moment was short lived. As I heard a loud, ear-splitting screech, I clapped my hands over my ears to muffle the volume. The screech was followed by screams from all around. I curled up into a ball and rocked back and forth.

"What is that?" I asked Aleph.

"The Shift. It has begun."

I sat in the corner, listening to the screams all around me. Sometimes they sounded so close, I thought they might be inside the barn with me. As if from nowhere, a loud, magical noise erupted in the atmosphere, and there appeared before me the familiar shape of a messenger. I blinked my eyes in awe at what I was seeing. How was this possible? This was not the void yet standing before me was one of Baelor's minions.

"It is time to choose whom you will serve, Princess!" the raspy voice of the messenger croaked. I cowered away with my hand outstretched.

"I don't understand…"

"Silence, mortal!" the messenger screeched. "The shift is upon us, and all that was secret is now made known. You must now choose whom you will serve! Will it be Aleph or Baelor?"

"Choose? Why do I have to…?"

"This is your final chance, Princess," the messenger said threateningly as it pulled a long black dagger from its robes. "You will now choose. Either power or death!"

Courage exploded within me, and I stood to full height in the presence of the messenger. I investigated the pale hooded face and spoke. "I choose life! Life with the creator! I choose Aleph!" The messenger screeched and grabbed my wrist. The touch was icy cold and filled me with dread.

"Baelor has a gift to bestow to all who follow and are surrendered to his will…You will not thwart his plans!"

Suddenly, the large door was kicked in, and two men entered carrying torches in their hands. The older man stepped forward and shouted, "Release her, foul spirit! She is Aleph's child!"

"I think not, monk!" screeched the messenger. "Baelor has laid claim to her soul!"

"Baelor claims nothing because her soul cannot be owned by another!" the man retorted. I was yanked by my hair back into a standing position. The messenger shoved me between the man and itself, brandishing a dagger and placing it at my throat.

"Wise words indeed, monk! I think we will steal her soul, then!" he taunted. The cold steel began to move. I closed my eyes, ready for the end of my life. Suddenly, a violent wind blew through the barn. My captor was thrown against the back wall. A brilliant light, like the one I experienced in the throne room weeks before, shot out in all directions. I turned away covering my eyes.

As the light dissipated, there stood the familiar form of a guardian, dressed completely in light. As the guardian moved closer to the messenger, I heard another ear-piercing screech as it cowered away. The guardian raised his finger and spoke.

"Go!" At that command, the messenger disappeared, along with the demonic presence that saturated the barn. I collapsed to my knees, shaking uncontrollably. I bowed my head, unable to look the guardian directly in the face. Strong hands lifted me up, and instantly, the warmth of the embrace filled my being. He placed his hand on my forehead and spoke.

"Child...have no fear. The torment has ceased. Aleph has heard your cry." I recognized the voice and looked up bravely to confirm my suspicion. As I stared into the eyes of the stranger, I remembered the glowing eyes of Glynn as he sat across from me in the cart on our way to Raithe. He whispered to me in a voice that nobody could hear. "Yes, Esgar. It is me. Aleph has sent me to rescue you."

"I'm so sorry." I wept in his arms. "I'm so sorry for everything!"

"That is in the past. But you must listen to me now. You are in great danger. These men will take you to safety, and you must follow them." The guardian turned to my rescuers, giving them instructions before leaving. Before I knew it, he was gone, and I was left alone in the care of the two strangers.

We stealthily left the barn and made our way through the town, avoiding all human contact. Screaming was heard everywhere as the people of Sommerset were forced to make a choice. As we passed the square, we saw a group of clerics giving a demonstration of power. I watched in horror as they practiced their dark magic on townspeople who did not side with the enemy.

Before long we made it to where their cart was stowed. The older man was struggling with the horses, and I decided to help. He looked over at me and spoke. "I see you have experience with horses."

Not wanting to have any kind of conversation with this stranger, I kept my answer short. "A little."

After several minutes, we were on our way, traveling southeast. I looked back at the town of Sommerset, and a pang of sorrow overcame me, followed by a feeling of peace. I had escaped! For the first time in a long while, I had hope.

The time of torment in my life finally ceased. The chapter of magic and sorcery is written, and the evil exposed for what it truly is: a prison. In this place, the enemy kept me locked away, my attention distracted by temporal things. But within the darkness, a light shone brightly, and a voice called to me, asking me to trust Him and step out into the unknown. I decided to take a chance and follow the voice.

As I sat within the cart, staring across at the handsome young man named Daeric, I knew in my heart my adventure had only begun. All the pain and suffering could be left in the past because Aleph was leading me to a new place where I could learn how to live freely, without prison walls. I took a deep breath and leaned my head back against the rickety wood planks, deciding to let the adventure take me wherever my creator wanted me to go—a place where I would abide in Aleph and learn who I was truly created to be.

PART III

CHAPTER
19

I closed the tome with a breath of relief. My heart was full, and the immensity of Aleph's presence was tangible. Tremendous peace overcame me as I laid my head back against the rock. I exhaled deeply, letting Esgar's words flood over me again. The harsh reality of what she conquered was overwhelming! She embraced suffering as a part of her life! Thinking back over my own existence, I realized we had a lot in common. I understood why Aleph wanted me to read her book.

The evening was quiet. I looked over at my companions and saw them all laid out, sound asleep. Jeru departed sometime in the night, without saying goodbye. The guardian's quiet dismissal might have bothered me before, but now that I was with Aleph, I didn't mind. The swirl of poisonous thoughts dissolved. I could feel the stillness of the cool desert night as I gently bowed my head, whispering to my creator.

"I'm sorry," I said in a hushed voice, waiting to see if He would respond. In the stillness, I let Esgar's words comfort me. Aleph's silence didn't mean he had gone away. The truth is He never stopped speaking. I came to terms with the fact that it was me who put Him in a box, thinking it could only be one way. The reality was that Aleph had countless ways of communicating with me.

"Anlace." My thoughts were interrupted by the sweet voice of my creator, whispering from within.

"Your servant is listening," I replied, my head still bowed.

"This part of the journey will require you to hear my voice clearly. I will now speak plainly with you."

"Why has it taken this long?" I asked boldly.

"To put it simply, you were not ready."

"But...I am your general and master of the order."

"Titles are for the prideful. Like Esgar, all you need to know is that you are loved." The heaviness of Aleph's presence fell on me, crushing my frail human form in a weight of glory. The tangible feeling penetrated my outward being and went straight to my heart. I heard humming beside me and turned my head to see who was there. All I could see for miles was the empty desert. There was a soft laugh, and the humming began again, this time from the other side. I jerked my head in that direction, looking for the source, but saw nothing.

"Is that you?" I asked Aleph excitedly.

"Yes," the amused voice replied.

"I can hear you now. Not from within like before, but right here."

"Yes, you can. The vanity within you has been revealed and the walls of your heart have crashed. Not unlike the city behind you." I turned and looked at the desolation of Northcrest, trying to understand the meaning of his words. *"Let me heal you, Anlace, and we will continue the journey."*

"Where are we going?"

"Hammerfist. There are people in bondage who need to hear my words of hope. A dark presence sits upon the throne and is keeping my children from coming to me. The darkness needs to be removed from the place of power. You and your companions will help me with that task."

"And then what?" I pressed the creator, hoping for further revelation.

"One task at a time. Your brothers are doing the same as you. They are following my voice and being led across Shalistar, to the place I need them to be."

I had a picture in my mind of a game Halsey, and I played within the palace. We spent many nights improving our skill. It was a game of strategy that involved placing pieces upon a board, all the while considering the counter moves of the opponent. Once my strategy was accomplished, I struck, taking the opponent's defenses down.

"Yes, Anlace. Your thoughts are correct," Aleph said, interrupting the pictures in my mind. *"I am placing my people strategically all over the world."*

"For what purpose?" I asked curiously.

"Not yet," He replied quickly. *"You don't need to be burdened with the future. Keep your attention on the present. When it is time, you will know. But come, now; it has been a long day, and you need a bit of rest before sunrise. Your companions will be ready to leave at first light."*

I rested until the sweet voice of Loretta whispered in my ear. "Time to get up, sleepyhead. We have an exciting day in the desert ahead of us." I strained to sit up and saw the entire camp broken down. Everything was packed on the carts, and my companions were all staring at me, ready to go. Had they intentionally packed silently, allowing me a bit more time to rest? Regardless, I was thankful. The little sleep I got was blessed by Aleph. I stood on my feet, completely refreshed.

Soon we were off, moving slowly along the hard, dry road towards a cropping of colorful cliffs. Cal sat with me up front in the cart while Merwin stayed in the back, resting his leg. He was completely healed, but Loretta was stubborn with her patient and made him stay off it for another day.

The road took us through a valley within a series of high cliffs. The face was carved of vibrant red rock streaked with gray and white boulders. It was sheer and made me nervous as I looked up. Easy place for an ambush, I thought to myself. I could see a path ahead of us that forked off the main highway and went upward to the top of the cliffs. I asked my companions if we should go in that direction. It was agreed that being at the top of the cliffs would fare better than the valley.

We followed the narrow path for hours, as it went up the rock face. The road carved into the steep cliff was wide enough for the cart and horses. The wheels went over the side, but luckily, the horses felt it and adjusted their direction the opposite way, keeping us from becoming unbalanced and going over the edge.

Looking down, we were about a hundred feet up. Rocks and dirt slid down the steep side until all that remained was air. Small boulders crashed as they hit the road far below us. The balancing act continued until we finally reached the top of the cliffs. As the surface became flat, we beheld a large tree, full of leaves and tasty looking fruit. I blinked my eyes thinking the tree was a trick of the mind. But as I approached and touched the sturdy trunk, I knew it was real. Aleph, in His infinite wisdom planted a tree long ago to protect us from the wrath of the sun while providing comfort before our dangerous journey into the sand dunes.

The canopy provided a generous amount of shade, and we quickly moved our cart and horses under it, taking a deep breath of exhaustion. It was late afternoon, and we were all spent. Our muscles ached from the steep climb we made. We decided it would be a promising idea to rest under the leaves of the tree until tomorrow morning.

The horses greedily drank from a bucket Groth held out to them, neighing their protest of the desert heat, and sidestepping each other to get a better angle. Loretta moved to the edge of the cliff with the spyglass, exploring the sand dunes below. She moved her head slowly, taking in the light brown landscape that taunted the weary traveler. Suddenly, Loretta stopped moving. I realized something caught her eye as she pointed into the distance.

"What is it?" I asked curiously.

"Hammerfist," she stated boldly.

"Where?"

"There. You can barely see it—on the other side of the desert."

"You know what they say about Virym, right?" I asked as I moved up next to her.

"Yes, I remember my geography lessons. It's a cruel stretch of land—a wide-open sandbox of dunes. Hammerfist lies on the eastern side, standing tall and cruel, mocking the traveler because the distance is further than one would think." She turned my way, brushing her short dark hair from her eyes. "Anlace, how do we travel over sand dunes with a cart?"

I let the question from my short companion remain unanswered for now and started unpacking what we needed to make camp. The cool of the shade was a blessing to us all. We were able to cook a bountiful meal with the provisions we brought and tuck into our tents for a full night's sleep.

At dawn, the heat was already bearing down on us. Even under the leaves of the massive tree, we could feel the intense desert temperatures. As we broke down our tents, Loretta sidled up to me.

"Anlace, you didn't answer me earlier. How do we travel over sand dunes with a cart?"

"We don't."

"But all my remedies…" she responded anxiously.

"Take only what is necessary."

"Were leaving the carts?" Merwin asked.

"Yes. How is your leg?"

"It's okay."

"Good. You will be riding with Cal," I directed. "Loretta, you and Groth can share a horse. Lionel and I will ride stag. Be sure to pack as much water as you can. I'm not completely concerned about food. We can live without that for days, but water is a necessity."

My companions removed important items from off the

cart, with some mild bickering about what was important. I reminded them to make room for tents. A corporate groan followed, telling me nobody thought of that one. After a good amount of rummaging, we hefted our heavy backpacks onto the horses and tied them as best we could.

On top of the cliffs, out from under the leaves of the tree, the temperature was hot and dry. The Ternion Mountains, far northwest, observed our slow descent into the Desert of Virym. The snow-covered caps looked impossibly far away. As we descended into the rough sands, my mind considered the cold that Daeric and Esgar traveled through to reach the top of Shaddyia. Would they have preferred the blazing inferno of the desert or the sub-zero temperature of the heights? The thought made me laugh.

Lionel looked over at me, annoyed. "Don't tell me you're going crazy again? We just got into the dunes. Better not stray on me now."

"I'm fine. I had a funny thought is all." I shared it with the elder, and he joined me in my analysis of our opposite circumstances.

Side by side, we rode. The horses were steady as we went up and down the sand dunes. We decided to strategically halt at the top of every dune and let the animals rest, giving them a meager supply of water before moving on. We tried the same strategy for our water consumption as well. I kept my eyes out for whatever plant and animal life I could.

In the distance, I saw a massive desert buffalo running freely. The animal gave no indication of needing rest. It was majestic to watch the beast gallop through the sand across the horizon. Aleph created an animal that could thrive within the barren wasteland and go a long time without water. I wish I were created like the desert buffalo. We would be at our destination by now and not sloughing through miserably thick sand.

Water conservation was important in the Desert of Virym. We needed to make sure there was enough to get us to the plateau on the other side. If we could make it to that point, we stood a chance to find another water source. Before then, we needed to be careful. Selfishness would not be tolerated, so I decided to put Lionel in charge of distributing the canteens. His stubborn character was exactly what we needed. Merwin tried to take an extra sip of water, and I heard a loud slap, followed by a curse from Merwin's mouth. After that, nobody tested Lionel's authority.

We moved slowly through the dunes in silence. The blazing sun above us scorched our bodies as we climbed upward. Everyone but Cal decided to use their cloaks as a face covering to block out harmful rays from the giant flaming mass. Our lips were cracked and bleeding. Every breath we took was like inhaling steam over a hot stove.

The day was miserable. I kept checking the direction of the sun in the cloudless sky to see if we were on course. The skyline of Hammerfist looked no closer now than it did hours ago when we started our trek into Virym. The stories were true about this place. There was nothing but light-brown sand all around. The heat of the sun consumed every bit of stamina and morale from us the further we went.

Several times I redirected my companions. Loretta called out to us that she could see a cropping of tropical trees on the horizon and started to steer her horse in that direction. I knew it was a trick of the mind and sidled up next to her and Groth. I saw a desperate, glazed look in their eyes as they focused on the false vision. After several calm words of encouragement, I was able to convince them that what they were seeing was a trick of the mind.

Shortly later, Cal jumped off his horse and fell face down into the sand, crying out for us to leave him. I stopped and knelt near my new friend, taking a moment to console him. I reminded myself of the trauma the man recently experienced with the loss of his family. Everything that was once a solid reality had turned to shifting sand beneath him. The sun brought out all the pent-up emotion of the dire circumstances. He needed to vent, so I let him.

We sat there as Cal processed everything that happened to him. I let him shout at the top of his lungs. I let him scream for us to leave him there and go on without him. When he ran out of breath and collapsed into the sand, I gently helped him take a drink of water. Then I held him close, telling him it was going to be okay. After several moments, he was restored to his right mind. At that time, I opened my pack and took the final package from within.

Cal received it, opening it curiously. He was speechless as he held the ugly brown fabric in his hands. Amid the sands of Virym, I placed a hand on our new companion and performed the initiation ceremony. Placing the cloak over his shoulders, I welcomed him into the order. As he stood, the rest of my companions shouted and cheered. He gave me another tight hug, and we mounted our horses.

◇

No shelter from the heat could be found anywhere. Scattered throughout the sand were large stones of architecture. Were they dwellings from an age long ago? Regardless of their place in time, they cast no shadow nor gave relief from the dry nightmare around us. All we could see were the Ternion Mountains behind and the gloomy skyline of Hammerfist before us, resting upon a high plateau.

We carefully traveled all day until we finally reached the final rise that took us to the top of a high cliff overlooking the deadlands. Breathing deeply from the steep climb, we stood together, donned in our cloaks, with our arms around one another. We took small drinks of water as we beheld in adoration the sunset in the west. The sky was painted with brilliant colors of orange and purple, creating a masterpiece of color. The dense clouds in the sky, created an illusion of distance that stretched into the heavens, a breathtaking end to a grueling day.

The heat from the afternoon was dissipating and cool air began to blow wafts of sand into the air. We stayed there watching the wind blow through the dunes we traversed. It was hypnotic. Unexpectedly, my trance was broken by a magical noise from behind us, followed by a sinister female voice.

"Master was right. You are predictable." I whirled around and saw the face of the young woman Viveka staring hatefully back at me. Her hands were raised, and the flames of a spell were sparked on the edge of her fingers. I stood fearfully before the young woman and ushered my cloaked companions to stand behind me. Then I took a fateful step towards the cleric with my hands out in front of me.

"Please, Viveka. You don't understand. There is a greater enemy..."

"I will not listen to your poisonous words, dog!" She spoke an arcane word and there appeared all around us ten more clerics clothed in black. Destruction spells were on the edge of their fingers. "So sad, monk! You traversed through the dunes, an impressive task, I must say. Most don't make it an hour within the endless sand, but you...somehow have made it this far."

"Viveka." I spoke calmly to the young cleric. "I'm sorry for your pain. I know what Master has done to you. You and Kristina were subjected to mental torture from which there was no escape." The young woman's face contorted as I said the name of her friend from long ago.

"How...do you know about Kristina?"

Ignoring her question, I continued. "You believe to have given up years of life to Baelor in exchange for the power you wield." Again, Viveka's face showed a flush of emotion. The pain she was trained to bury deep inside was coming to the surface.

"Shall we dispatch them?" shouted one of the clerics. A moment of hesitation followed.

"Keep him alive," she said, pointing at me. "Kill the rest!"

The quiet evening was broken by sounds of clerics releasing magical spells all around us. Immediately, we huddled low to the ground. Our white cloaks kept the effects from harming us but with every spell that hit, the circle of clerics moved closer. If this kept up, they soon would be within striking distance. It would be impossible for us to raise our defenses if several of them commenced a melee assault. I breathed deeply as the spells continued to hit us. With every magical explosion, the clerics came closer.

Suddenly, to my right, Loretta stood up and removed herself from the group. Viveka saw it, too, and commanded her clerics to take her out. I watched, helplessly, from my huddled position as the short, quick-footed woman began to move her body in grand gestures. Her arms moved above her head in a graceful pattern. Her legs shifted with her arms in a beautiful way.

I couldn't believe what I was seeing. She was dancing—dancing in circles while the wicked magic pummeled her on all sides! Undeterred by the assault, she added her voice to the elegant movement of her body. She sang in a language reminiscent of my darling, Iska, the way she prayed while caring for my broken body in the infirmary many years ago.

And now...the way Loretta was moving before us was something unknown in this world. The movement and gestures were coming to her from eternity. I looked again to make sure it was my companion in front of me. The clerics around us stopped casting spells and stared open-mouthed at this woman who was unafraid of the power they wielded. The lovely dance continued as her singing got louder. Viveka took a step back, baffled by the woman's actions. She looked around at her fellow clerics and shouted. "End her life, now!"

The clerics lifted their hands and were about to shout another chorus of unholy spells, when suddenly, there was a brilliant flash of light. Out of eternity appeared ten large guardians clothed in radiant white robes and glowing armor. They stood between the clerics and my dancing companion.

The clerics, unsure of what this new arrival meant, backed up several steps. Fear was etched into Viveka's face. In desperation, she shouted to her team to destroy them as well.

The clerics, as one, cast their spells. All the guardians raised a single hand and shouted. "Enough!" Their voices echoed throughout the Desert of Virym with a mighty sound. The vibration sent a tremor through the ring of clerics, knocking them off their feet.

Intense silence followed for several moments. The clerics tried to rise from the dry ground but could not move from their position. What followed was a loud, ear-splitting shriek, and from within the darkness a magical noise erupted. There appeared upon the top of the plateau ten of Baelor's messengers, draped in black cloaks and dark hoods. They all appeared to be human-like but with pale faces, and their eyes glowed an eerie red color.

A guardian turned to Loretta, bestowing a gesture of respect. My companion saw his recognition and ended her dance with a polite bow. He leaned down and took her hand, helping her rise. "Thank you for the dance. Aleph is most pleased and has sent us to aid you." I saw the look on her face. She was dazed, as if she awakened from a dream. Loretta, in awe, stared into the face of the large guardian. He whispered another word to her and guided her back to us. Groth gave an outburst of excitement and grabbed his wife, holding her tightly. Loretta continued to stare at the guardian as he took his place in front of his enemy—a magnificent sight to behold. A dark ring of messengers stood where the clerics were only moments before. Shadowed faces contorted into a look of rage and disgust as they faced off against the brilliant light of Aleph's guardians.

One of the messengers spoke, and his ghastly voice echoed into the night. "How dare you interfere with the hour given to us! This is our time, and we have all authority to be here!"

"Quiet!" returned the guardian. "You have invaded Aleph's path! The chosen ones must fulfill their purpose until the revealing!"

"You are mistaken. There is no treachery here." The messenger replied deceptively.

"You lie! Like your master! Your minions were given orders to destroy this group, and that is strictly forbidden! You will be judged."

"Try it, slave!" the messenger cackled. "We have waited a long time for this! Raise your swords and prepare for Baelor's fury!" In unison, the messengers drew dark blades from within their robes and stood battle ready.

In response, the guardians drew their swords and raised them above their heads. The blades caught fire, glowing a vibrant orange against the backdrop of the dying light. "This is your last chance. Leave this world now. Find a hollow place to cower in the darkness. If you stay, you will be vanquished and sent back into the void from which you came!"

The messengers, full of resentment, shrieked loudly. "We are already sentenced to damnation! It will be a pleasure to remove you and your pitiful humans from this plane of existence as well!" In a flash of light, the messengers and guardians flew into the skies. We watched in awe as the Eternals of Shalistar battled within the atmosphere above.

The messengers and guardians abandoned their human form as we witnessed massive glowing bodies clashing with hideous, foul creatures. Fluttering wings were cut off a dark messenger's body. In the distance, it fell to the ground. As the body crashed into a large dune, an explosion of sand and dust followed. A guardian flew down next to the wingless being. With a shout, the guardian raised his flaming sword and brought it down powerfully into the chest of the dark messenger. The defeated being let out a shriek as the final blow was given.

I saw a stir of movement out of my peripheral vision and turned my attention back to the clerics around us. The effect of the vibration ended, and the clerics were gathering themselves. I looked at my companions and nodded. At once, we shouted and charged the stunned enemy. Knowing their spells would not stop us, they drew their swords and met us in combat.

I stayed close to Loretta and Groth and parried the swings of several clerics. I was impressed by their skill and remembered Esgar's written past. A master swordsman trained them, and it showed. Their attacks were calculated and precise. They attacked two at a time, to try and wear us down. However, Lionel, Merwin, and I practiced for years in the art of outnumbered strategy. We were ready for them.

Our blades met again, and we parried the blows with ease. I launched myself into the air over their heads, taking the two I fought completely off guard. They barely had enough time to parry, throwing themselves off balance. Another feint and then a quick stab ended one of my foes. Another joined him to try and tire me out, but it didn't work.

Groth helped me dispatch the newcomer by slashing with all his might. The big man had no technique, but his brute strength, coupled with my mastery, tired him out quickly. I ended him with a swipe of the blade across his skull. The final cleric tried to come at me from the side. I quickly sidestepped and let his momentum do the rest. He went right past me and impaled himself upon Lionel's blade, which was outstretched and ready.

"What took you so long?" the elder howled. I looked over and saw that my brother and Cal dispatched three clerics.

Before I could respond, I heard a scream and saw Viveka lashing out at me with her sword. I swatted it away easily, holding my weapon in a defensive position. The girl was a wreck, her face dirty and bleeding. Her eyes flamed with hatred for me and my companions. I decided I would try to talk some sense into the young woman. She charged again, and I swiped her blade away.

"Stop this, now!" I shouted to her.

She looked back at me, in tears. "You don't understand, monk. I can't!"

"Yes, you can! Kristina did, and so can you."

"She was a traitor! Lord Lucien removed her whole family from power, permanently!"

"Your master is lying to you…" Suddenly I looked up and saw Lionel moving into an attack position. "No! Leave her alone!" I commanded my brother. He looked at me hesitantly and then relaxed his stance. I gazed back at Viveka. "Look above you, child." She hesitated. "Don't worry. If I wanted you dead, you would be."

I watched as the young woman slowly looked into the skies. "Did your master ever mention this?" Her face instantly turned to shock and awe. I stole a moment to look up myself and see the battle continue between the guardians and messengers.

Streaks of light were mesmerizing as flaming swords clashed against dark metal. Shrieks echoed from messengers as they impaled a guardian. I saw the brilliant light fall into the desert.

"That's right! We are only a small part of this story. Lucien cares nothing for you. The war he is in is much greater than we can imagine. It goes back a long way. He is using you! He has always been using you! The life you have given him is not his to take. It is all a lie! A method of control! Kristina knew this. She found a better way, and you can too!"

"And what's that? A dog of Aleph?" We looked up to see another flash of light as more guardians joined the battle.

"You don't know the power you are standing against. You will not win." Viveka looked back at me and wiped the tears from her eyes.

"I don't want to win. I want out! I don't want any of it! Not you! Not Baelor! Not Aleph! None of it!" Viveka turned and assumed an attack posture.

"Don't do it, please."

"It's too late."

"No, it's not. Please don't do this."

"If I stay, they will find me and kill me. If I go back again, empty handed, Master will kill me. There's no way out."

"It doesn't have to be this way," I pleaded one last time. I saw Viveka relax her grip and stance for a moment. I looked over to Lionel. He had a pitiful look on his face, shaking his head.

"Yes, it does," Viveka said calmly. Her shout erupted as she continued a thrusting attack. I parried the blow and countered with one of my own. As my blade extended, she lifted her defense and leaned into my sword. Seeing her deception, I tried to stop the momentum, but it was too late. I screamed as the blade went through her.

She gave a gasp, dropping her sword and collapsing into my arms. "Why did you do that? Why?" I shouted as she stared back at me.

"Thank you," she said quietly.

"That was stupid, do you know that?"

"I'm sorry," she whimpered as death approached. Finally, she locked eyes with me and whispered softly. "I'm so sorry. I was deceived." She let out her final breath and then died in my arms. I held her close, unable to hold a thought in my head. Above me, the battle was ending. Somewhere along the horizon the final messenger was falling into the dunes below. I stared into the unseeing eyes of the young woman. Baelor tormented her to the point where she believed there was no escape. She used me to end her suffering. It was too much to bear.

Lionel came up and put a hand on my shoulder. "It's what she wanted, Anlace. It's not your fault." I was battling a stir of emotions within. Why did I care so much for this girl when I dispatched the rest of the clerics without a thought in my mind? Was it the words of Esgar describing her friend that knit my heart to hers? Did I have a personal stake in seeing her redeemed? I let many unhealthy thoughts go through my mind as we cleared the top of the plateau of bodies and set up our camp site. Dinner was quiet that night as we ate together. When everything was cleared, and we were all stretched out in our sleeping mats, I closed my eyes to go to sleep. My final words that day were spoken to my companions.

"It's been a long day. Tomorrow will have trials of its own. I can't do this without you, and I'm so grateful for your company. See you in the morning."

CHAPTER
20

I left camp and sat on the edge of a cliff facing east as the sun rose before me. The rays from its brilliance begin to form along the wasteland, scorching the surface of dry rock. I finished writing everything down as best as I could.

My heart is crushed by the loss of Viveka, and I'm having a tough time making sense of all that happened. The rage of the Nephilim and the catastrophic outcome of their power is beyond description. Seeing the buildings destroyed is one thing, but their merciless mission of destruction, making sure nobody is left alive, that is truly a horrific sight to behold. Every time I close my eyes, I see vague images of massive arms plowing into the stone structures, turning the architecture into dust—one building after another until the entire city is in ruins. The horror is unstoppable and the worst part about it, I don't even know what "It" looks like. The image I have in my mind is merely my imagination at work.

Aleph made sure I was up at sunrise before the rest of my companions awakened. There was a lot to discuss about everything that happened earlier. We made it out of the Desolate Plains of Virym, barely hanging onto the thread of life. A pack of clerics tried to take us out, but we successfully dispatched them. Our goal lay miles away, with nothing left between us and Hammerfist except a large stretch of thirsty, lifeless ground. I spent the morning studying the outside walls of the hard stone fortress before me.

The city lay on top of a large rock peninsula overlooking the barren wasteland to the southwest. I saw a sharp, uneven skyline of buildings from miles away. They were carved out of the hardest sandstone and matched the desolate, dull brown color of the rock all around it. Hammerfist was a brutal joke for travelers from Northcrest. Once they reached the desert plains, the skyline appeared and hope would rise; however, as you traveled into the dunes, the exhaustion of countless rises and crests in the sand would overcome you, and the city would seem further away, never getting closer and always out of reach, taunting you. Once you finally made it to the last valley, you were treated with another impossible obstacle.

The sheer rock face seemed to mold itself into the foundation of the city and provided no footholds, making it impregnable from three directions. The only way into the city was from the east, allowing the defenses to reign fury on any approaching army. As I took in the scenery, I chuckled to myself. Aleph never made it easy.

"Have I humored you, Anlace?" I heard Aleph softly whisper.

"I thought we were supposed to be hidden. Wasn't this going to be an infiltration?

"It is."

"How do you figure that?" I replied. "The city is fortified on three sides. There is only one way in."

"That would seem to be the case... from your point of view."

"What do you mean?" I asked my Creator.

"There are hidden roads, older than the city. Look past the surface of this problem, Anlace. All you see is the precipice, but where I need your attention is beneath the surface," Aleph rebuked me.

"I don't understand."

"It's okay. I am here to help you. What you do not see is hidden from you because your eyes are on the massive fortress looming in front of you. It's a stronghold for sure, and one that must come down. The only way to infiltrate this type of enemy encampment is to soften your viewing perspective and allow yourself to take in all that is around you, as when you fight an enemy with the sword. Close your eyes."

I followed Aleph's instructions. *"Now, I am going to breathe on you, and when you feel the soft wind blow across your face, I want you to open your eyes and look out again. This time, take your eyes off the stronghold and observe the whole picture. I have already provided the answer, and it is now time for you to see it."*

It was quiet. All I could hear was my steady breathing. The cool of the morning air was still and silent. Suddenly, I felt a soft wisp of air blow right past the tip of my nose. If I were not still, I never would've felt it, but it was there. In obedience, I opened my eyes and looked out once more into the horizon. My mind immediately wanted to go to the massive hulking structures sitting on top of the rocky peninsula, but I willed myself to divert my attention from the sandstone city.

I looked to the north and saw nothing but dry wasteland as far as the eye could see. I peered into the distance and drew slowly back to the walls of the city, looking for the answer Aleph was giving me. There was nothing. I tried again, this time looking out as far south as I could until my eyes began to water. I slowly came back until my gaze was at the southern walls. Again, nothing stood out. I was getting frustrated but decided to continue.

I stood up from my sitting position and leaned over the side of the cliff I was sitting on. I looked as far down as I could without losing balance and falling over the side. I held my gaze steady for several seconds. Again, I felt the wisp of Aleph's breath on the tip of my nose. I slowly moved my eyes along the floor of the valley. As I scanned the horizon below me, I saw streams of wind moving through the sand and blowing clouds of dust into the air. I reached into my bag and pulled out the spyglass given to me by Merwin before the Battle of the Rift. I brought it up to my eye and magnified my gaze. I continued moving it towards the base of the sheer western cliff—and then I saw it.

There was a small sliver in the wall of rock. The fissure was camouflaged in the morning by shadow and would be cooked by the brilliance of the sun in the afternoon. Travelers, or any person for that matter, could easily miss it, but it was there, hidden from all. I observed as the dusty streams of wind blew past the crack in the rock. Suddenly, I noticed the stream split, and dust was carried into the fissure. Upon further investigation, I guessed the crack might be able to accommodate a human body, but only one at a time. Excitement rippled through me as I lowered and stowed the spyglass. Aleph had shown me the way! A hidden path within the foundation of rock led to the city from underneath. It was time to awaken the others.

As I entered camp, the tantalizing aroma of sausage and eggs filled the atmosphere. I smiled, seeing the familiar shape of our resident herbalist hunched over a pan, adding a pinch of grill spice. According to her, it was the extra kick of flavor that all delicious food deserved. She moved quickly from the pan to another pot, checking the temperature of its contents, moving with purpose, and not wasting a beat.

Loretta looked up and greeted me with a dramatic wave of her hand, speaking at the same speed as her movements. "Morning, sir! You look as fine as fiddlesticks! Did you figure out a way into the city?" I looked curiously over at Loretta. "Oh, don't worry, after a long road trip with you and climbing a mountain with your son, I pretty much figured out both your mannerisms. He takes after you in many ways—always needing to get away and solve problems out in his mind. Always early in the morning, I might add. Then when he comes back, he's right as rain."

"I am truly impressed with your observance."

"Groth always said it's my best attribute."

"Only beside your cooking!" Groth boomed as he came out of his tent. "Good morning, Anlace. What's on the agenda for today? Are we going to infiltrate a heavily defended enemy city?"

"That seems to be the plan, yes."

"Please tell me we are going to do it after breakfast. I'm starving! My stomach is gnawing on my backbone!" Suddenly, a groan erupted from the tent to the right.

"You three couldn't let an old man sleep in a bit now, could you?" growled Lionel as he threw open the flap to his tent. "You pups could do with some manners. The elderly have brittle bones and need an hour or two more of sleep if we are going to be productive."

"Maybe we would if you weren't snoring all night!" Merwin exclaimed as he came into view with several bundles of dry sticks in his hands.

"Where in Aleph's keep did you find kindle in this forsaken place?" asked Lionel.

"You don't want to know," Merwin replied with a grin.

Lionel decided the answer was sufficient and huffed over beside the fire, continuing to grumble under his breath. Loretta skipped over with a cup of morning drink and placed it in Lionel's hand, giving him a pat on the shoulder.

"Breakfast will be ready soon," she stated and skipped away.

Lionel stared at the cup that so quickly appeared. He took a quick sniff of the contents and was overcome with the aroma. It made him smile, and he softly replied with a thank you before he went back to sipping the drink.

"Where's Cal?" I asked Merwin as he stood beside me, handing me a crisp red apple.

"He was up as early as you. He went to search for a water source. Not much out here, and I can't imagine finding one. He is persistent, I'll give him that."

"Somebody has to be!" Cal exclaimed, as he came into view, carrying a large water sack.

"Where did you find that?" I asked him.

"Aleph and some weird plant," he replied shortly. We all looked around and shrugged in agreement.

With everyone gathered, we shared the bountiful breakfast Loretta prepared. When the meal was finished and the dishes cleared, we sat together in a circle to begin our discussion of the infiltration that was about to occur. I looked around me at this small group of warriors and smiled. Aleph really went above and beyond this time. Only weeks before, we were amid thousands, and now we were a group of six—hand selected by Aleph to infiltrate an enemy city to bring about change. I could not begin to imagine how He was going to do this.

We set off after our meeting concluded. This part of the journey was going to require sure footing down narrow paths, so we needed to leave the horses behind. With only a pack on our backs, we began the steady descent down the plateau and into the dry rock valley below. The morning air blew into our faces, bringing the heat with it. Halfway down the plateau, we stopped for a drink of water.

It seemed like one false step would result in severe injury. The dirt under us was loose, and many times we held onto the red rock to keep from slipping. It was a slow decline, but soon we were standing on the solid ground in the arid wasteland.

Before us was a wide-open stretch of cracked and jagged terrain. The little rain that this land received was no benefit to the fallow soil. There was no life here at all, only terrifying dust storms. But when it came to our adventure, the chances of anyone patrolling this place would be slim, which gave me hope for our infiltration.

We traveled slowly and carefully over the rises and crests of the unforgiving wasteland. The barren rock was a mixture of grays and browns, providing a dull and sad landscape that stretched to the horizon. The morning sun did little to soften the hard surfaces beneath us, which were in stark contrast to the skies above. A blanket of gray clouds streaked with brilliant orange made the sky look like a blazing inferno. It was ominous, foreboding, and beautiful all at once.

The darkness fought to drown out the radiant orange but could not keep the colorful masterpiece fully hidden. With Aleph's majesty on full display above us, we kept our heads up as we traveled, looking to the terrifying beauty of the skies instead of the depressing land around us.

Nothing about this part of our journey was enjoyable. The uneven ground was hard on the soles of our feet. Even our thick leather boots provided little comfort. As a dust storm passed, little pebbles would find their way into our boots and burrow into the soles of our feet. Our tattered white cloaks, however, protected us from the sting of weary winds as they gusted by.

Hammerfist sat above us, always out of reach. Even as we passed through the gully and began to steadily move up the steep cliff face towards the rock peninsula, the city seemed so far away. We decided the best way to stay in good spirits was to break often. We used Aleph's water provision sparingly and took time to rest. We were not going to let these lands get the best of us.

◇

We pushed onward, coming ever closer to the cleft in the rock Aleph showed me earlier. As we neared the shadows of the peninsula around lunchtime, I strained my eyes but had a challenging time finding it. Because of the sun's location, the fissure was perfectly hidden in the shadows and difficult to locate. Several times, my companions asked me if I saw a desert vision. I repeatedly affirmed them that I was not going crazy, and that Aleph showed me a secret way.

Tensions rose as we got closer and still were not able to discover the cleft. However, before everything got out of hand, we were treated to another small dust storm on the horizon. As wisps of sand and dirt rose into the air, I commanded my team to focus on the base of rock in a specific direction. Several moments later, I heard Cal shout.

"I see it! It's there, hidden in the shadows. You can see the windstream part where the sand goes inside!" He asked for the spyglass from Merwin and took some time with each of us, pointing out a landmark on the cliff. He had us move the spyglass slightly to the right of it. One by one, we gave a shout of excitement. Now that we knew where we were going, we headed straight toward the small cleft.

The fissure was not big at all. Loretta would have no trouble fitting inside, but the rest of us would have to squeeze. Groth studied the opening, and I saw a look of concern.

"I'm not going to be able to fit," the large man stated glumly.

"Of course, you are!" Loretta quickly returned. "I've already thought about that. Cal is a smith and I've seen him pull out that trusty hammer several times. All that rock needs are a couple good poundings, and we can create a bigger hole."

Cal spoke up, "I'm not sure my hammer will be able to break through the rock."

"It's sandstone, silly. With enough strength behind it, I'm sure it could."

"My hammer is made of the finest metal," he said, removing it from his pack and handing the object to Loretta. She took it and turned it over several times, adoring its fine craftsmanship. "The hammer is nearly indestructible, a family heirloom passed down from my father's father."

"It's kind of small for a smith's hammer," Loretta observed.

"It's not used for crafting weapons. I have other tools for that. It is more of a symbol of status, like a magistrate's gavel. I have kept it with me for years."

Groth held out his hand. "Can I see it?"

Cal nodded to Loretta, and she passed it to Groth. The hammer was made completely of iron, about a foot and a half long with a sturdy head at the top of the shaft. Seeing the hammer in Groth's massive hands, it almost looked like a child's toy.

"Can I use it?" Groth politely asked Cal. After several moments of intense contemplation, Cal agreed.

Groth and Lionel approached the fissure and spent time studying the gap. After some clever calculations, Groth swung the hammer in a specific place. His brute strength was impressive. As the hammer connected with the rock, a chunk broke off. We encouraged our large friend as he continued his job. The hammer swung and more pieces of rock exploded. He continued tirelessly for about an hour, until the fissure was the right size to fit his massive body through.

Upon completion, Groth handed the hammer back to Cal. Our new companion took the hammer from the sweating brute and nodded in a gesture of respect. "I have a job for you after we get through this adventure. I could always use a man of great strength in the occupation of smithing." Groth wiped the sweat off his head and smiled with a flush of embarrassment. He went over to stand next to his petite wife.

"You've done good today, sweetheart. I'm proud of you," Loretta stated, giving the large man a hug and a pat. "Oh, but aren't you all sweaty and gross now," the short woman exclaimed, shoving him away.

Now that the fissure was adjusted to where Groth could pass through, I removed the small lantern from my pack. "It's going to be dark in there," I told the group. We won't be able to see a whole lot. Are you all going to be, okay?"

I received a nod from all my companions except Groth. He looked like a small child who was afraid to go to bed because of the long shadows in their room at night. Loretta was taking some time to encourage her husband and remind him of their trip to the caves of Vardel and how everything turned out okay. She ended the dialogue by telling him she loved him and wouldn't force him to do this if he didn't want to. I immediately saw courage fill the large man as he heard these words. He arose with a new-found confidence.

One last piece of business needed to be addressed. We inspected our cloaks and agreed that the magic spells last night had burned a lot of the outer garment away from the pure white material underneath. The cloaks were now compromised, so we took them off and stowed them in our packs. Our disguise, once we entered the city, would have to come without the cloaks on our bodies. I prayed to Aleph for no more run-ins with clerics and a successful infiltration.

With my lantern in hand, I squeezed through the tight fissure in the side of the cliff. As I passed through the rock, all sunlight from the exterior was snuffed out, and I was immersed into a deep darkness, with only a small circle of light protruding from the flame. I looked around and realized, to my horror, that the lantern would not produce enough light. I understood that if any clerics awaited us within the catacombs of this dark underground labyrinth, we would not see them coming…until it was too late.

CHAPTER
21

Groth's pitiful form was last to enter through the fissure of the cliff. His body completely collapsed into the darkness, forcing us to bend down and lift him off the ground. His teeth were chattering, and his body shaking. This part of the adventure was going to be terrifying for the brute. I thought for a moment he should stay behind, but instantly put the thought away. Splitting up the team would weaken us, and if he were left behind, Loretta would stay as well.

I leaned close to the man and whispered some encouraging words, which got him to a standing position. I handed him the lantern, telling him he could hold it. That seemed to help a little. It worked out well because he was tall and able to keep the flame above all our heads, providing the best direction of light. It was still hard to see anything. I could barely make out an archway to the left.

We huddled together, trying to solve the puzzle of the dark. Loretta searched her utility belt and pulled out one of her precious vials. She popped the small cork off the top, and a unique sound echoed throughout the cavern. I heard a loud tearing echo to my left and saw Lionel ripping a generous part of his inner tunic. He handed the cloth strip to Cal, who wrapped it tightly around the head of his iron hammer. Loretta poured the contents of her vial out upon the strip of cloth. Cal asked Groth for the lantern, which he nervously gave over. Cal touched the flame to the strip of cloth, and another "whooshing" sound filled the dark space.

What followed was a generous sized flame that engulfed the head of the hammer. Loretta encouraged us, saying the contents of the vial would hold the flame for a long time. Cal passed a brilliantly lit torch over to Groth in exchange for the lantern. The smile on Groth's face was priceless as he accepted the object. He was filled with elation as he lifted the makeshift torch. Immediately, the light invaded a portion of darkness. It was not a perfect solution by any means but was far better than before.

The chamber was illuminated, enabling us to see through the darkness. The room was part of an ancient system of catacombs. The walls were made of smooth sandstone, with sporadic carvings of primitive markings. Aleph only knew how long these corridors had been here. We walked slowly but surely from one room to the next. The torch kept us from tripping several times on collapsed floors.

I waited for a monster to jump out and challenge us, like in the stories I heard as a kid. But I knew the truth about matters like that. Monsters existed, but they were not in the form of a vicious beast ready to devour me for turning into a dead end within a dark maze. The monster that haunted us was challenging the creator of this world. Its messengers were real. The Nephilim were real. The images in my head about lurking horrors were just my imagination.

I took a deep breath and said a silent prayer to Aleph. Abruptly, from within the darkness, a rush of wind filled the entire chamber. We huddled together as the wind moved through us, bringing with it warmth and comfort. I heard the gentle sighs of my companions as they experienced the same feelings as I. Out of nowhere, a small flame appeared out of thin air and rested upon the top of Merwin's head, illuminating more of the darkness. I gasped and gestured for my brother to look up. As his eyes lifted, he moved his hands through the flame. He let out a cry of surprise because his hand remained unharmed.

Shortly later, another flame appeared and then another, until all of us were crowned with little flames above our heads. With this amount of light, the entire room was illuminated. We were in a chamber that functioned as a subterranean crossroads with four archways to choose from. Nobody remembered which direction we entered from. Before fear could take hold, I saw the flame above Merwin's head shoot out towards the archway to our left. A sconce on the wall, next to the doorway, was ignited. Seconds later, the flame came to rest back on top of Merwin's head.

"Look!" I cried. "The sconce is lit! Aleph is showing us the way." We followed His lead. Using the flames above our head, He lit a sconce next to the correct doorway, guiding us through the maze. As we went along, Aleph would highlight specific walls, showing us unique carvings along the way. As we viewed the inscriptions, we discussed the mysterious meaning of them.

"I wish Marec and Artour were here. They would know what these mean." I said as I puzzled over the glyphs. We continued through many rooms and chambers and walked safely down long corridors that turned sharply right and left until we finally came to an open area.

As we entered the space, the darkness dissipated within the center revealing an ancient temple. The ornate stone furniture was covered in dust and spiders that measured as large as my hand. I shivered as they crawled over the stone. How could anything survive down here in this decrepit place?

The feeling I got was cold and foreboding, like some ancient evil was lurking nearby. Lionel called me over. He was examining what looked like a primeval altar with carvings etched into the stone. As I ran my fingers over the solid surface, I felt a chill course through my body.

"What is this place?" I asked aloud.

"Looks like a temple," Cal responded.

"What kind of temple?" Loretta whispered.

As if in response, Aleph's wind blew throughout the chamber. Dust clouds billowed up from the ground around us. "Come together, now!" I shouted to my companions. We quickly joined in the middle of the room. As soon as we were together, the flames above our heads began to rise. Suddenly, wisps of fire shot out in every direction, bouncing off the walls and ceiling. We ducked as the flames crossed each other directly above us. One flame struck with a popping sound, directly into a darkened sconce. The torch was lit, bringing light to the wall along that side of the room. The next flame followed suit, crashing into a sconce along the adjacent wall.

The marvelous demonstration continued until all the flames connected with the unlit sconces around us. Once again, by Aleph's divine power, the entire room was lit. The chamber was larger than we realized with an odd shape to it. There were five walls of equal length instead of the usual four. Every wall had its own door except for one, which was immediately to the right of the wall through which we entered. The awe of seeing Aleph's fire was quickly replaced with fear. The torchlight revealed jagged, terrifying murals painted on the walls. Without light, they were shrouded in darkness, but now we could see and fully examine them. We walked over to get a closer look.

The first mural was to the left of our entrance. It was a depiction of time long ago. Humans bowed before a dark beast, offering sacrifices upon an altar that looked like the one in this room. Moving to the left, the mural continued to the next wall. The ancient deco revealed an army of messengers standing before a cluster of humans. The messenger's hands were outstretched as a command was being given and the humans were receiving an orb of light as a gift.

The following wall revealed several humans with light around their heads, enlightened to a new idea. The paintings were life-size so that the circles of light were at eye level. The effect in the dancing torchlight was eerie. The next image showed a separation of humans in the form of a large chasm. Above the fissure was the dark beast. On one side was a group of humans with light around their heads, and on the other, a group reaching out in desperation towards the beast that was elevated above the chasm. This group of humans possessed no ring of light around them.

The final picture was on the wall through which we entered. It showed a large beast, fully armored, with an army of humans behind and in front of it. Around the beast on all sides was a depiction of fire. All the humans within the army were adorned with rings of light around their heads. The army was shown charging into a group of normal humans.

After viewing the last picture, I took a step away and breathed deeply. Lionel moved back towards the altar. "Hits kind of close to home, don't you think?" he asked compassionately.

"Yes," I gasped. "Closer than I would like."

"How long ago were these drawn?" Merwin asked.

"Ages ago, from the looks of it."

Lionel leaned over the altar again, examining it closer than before. "Aleph has answered our question," he said, nodding his head in confirmation. "This was a chamber used to worship Baelor." The words hung in the air. "It was long ago when life was primitive. Long before the days of King Rian. Regardless, Baelor was preparing the minds of the people and tainting the bloodlines even then."

Groth and Loretta stood away from the final picture, holding each other tightly. They both looked shaken by the graphic images on the walls. "I've seen enough Anlace. Can we go?" Loretta pleaded from within her husband's embrace.

In agreement, I asked Aleph once again which direction we should proceed. As soon as my voice connected with the atmosphere, the flames left the sconces, plunging the outer walls in darkness. The flames bounced across the room and illuminated a single sconce next to one of the doorways. Without another thought, we all scurried through the threshold.

Our journey through the subterranean labyrinth continued for hours. Aleph led us from one room to another. There were many turns, and the way seemed completely lost. We trudged in silence, hearing only the echo of our footsteps along the solid surface below.

My mind was playing tricks on me. Were we going in circles? Was Aleph assessing our stamina and fortitude? When would this dark nightmare end? In response to many questions was another series of rooms followed by a long corridor. It seemed to go on forever, until we stopped.

Hindering our path was a large, iron door. Unlike the rest of the catacombs, the door was not ancient but more modern looking. It had an ornate lock with iron hinges in the jamb. Without a word, Loretta moved in front of the pack with a lockpick in hand. I enjoyed seeing her excitement at the prospect of picking another lock. She diligently moved the pick around until she heard a metallic click as the door squeaked open.

On the other side was an open expanse. I moved into the cavern-like room and beheld a stone staircase rising into the darkness. Absent a railing on either side, it looked as if the staircase were floating on air with no end in sight. It was curious and terrifying to see.

I told my friends to stay close and follow me single file. As I took the first step up the staircase, the flame above me went out. I turned around to see the same happen to the rest of my companions. All we had was the lantern to light our way. The steps were solid and sturdy under our feet. I couldn't help but think who or what built this staircase, let alone the catacombs through which we traveled. The amount of architecture and planning must have taken decades to complete. I was thankful that the craftsmanship was sound as I climbed.

Around an hour later, we stopped to catch our breath. Each of us took a step and carefully lowered ourselves down to sit. As we hit the stone, a deep exhaustion overcame us. All I wanted to do was sleep, but my mind was fighting to stay awake. I looked down at my companions on the steps below me. They were all asleep! My mind was racing at this point, trying to understand Aleph's intent.

"Relax, Anlace. It is time to rest."

"What are you doing?"

"Giving my beloved sleep."

"For what purpose? We must be close to the top."

"You are. Remarkably close, indeed. But you don't need to come out from underground yet. Sleep and be patient. Rest and be refreshed. You will awaken when it is time." Aleph's hand came over me, accompanied by a heaviness of warmth and a deep burden to sleep. Struggling to keep my eyes open, I rubbed the burn in them. Then I felt Aleph's wind blow throughout the cavern and abandoned myself to slumber.

There was no way of knowing how long we slept. The tiny light from Groth's lantern was the only source of illumination in the large cavern. As my eyes opened, I felt supernaturally refreshed, like I was stretched out in a large bed for the night. I carefully sat up and gently whispered to my companions that it was time. Hearing my voice, they looked around, confused.

"Aleph wanted us to have sleep before continuing," I reassured them.

"Could he have picked a stranger location?" Lionel barked.

"I didn't mind it. What about you my dear?" Loretta asked her husband.

"Could've used a pillow, but other than that, it was fine," Groth returned.

We all got to our feet, stretched the last bit of sleep out of our limbs, and continued climbing the floating staircase to the top. After a nice rest, we were energized. The steps were no problem for us. We moved at a nice pace, climbing higher and higher.

I continued to strain my eyesight to see if I could spot the top of the stairs. Aleph said we were remarkably close, and if I had to guess… Suddenly my thoughts were interrupted. I held up a hand to stop our ascent. Together, we froze dead in our tracks. I leaned my ear into the darkness. Was it my imagination, or was I about to slam right into the gravity of my mission? I turned around and asked my companions a question, hoping I was wrong.

"Do you hear that?" I asked with a quiver in my voice.

"Hear what?" Merwin asked, straining his ears.

"In the air. I hear voices," Loretta said softly.

"I hear them too," Cal said. "They are very faint. But it sounds like…"

"Chanting," I gasped. We stood, still as statues. I reasoned in my mind, if we didn't move, the sound might go away. However, I knew what we heard was real. The situation we found ourselves in was eerily similar. A dark staircase with slivers of light. The only difference is that we were ascending and not descending. As we continued upward, the chanting got louder, more pronounced. With every step our suspicions were confirmed. Somewhere close by was a room of children in the middle of summons.

CHAPTER
22

My heart pounded. I thought it might leave my body and fall on the floor. Aleph led us secretly into a school that was housing children on the verge of summoning messengers! What were we supposed to do when we broke the surface? The arcane chanting brought a cold chill into the atmosphere. It continued to play over and over, getting louder and louder, until we finally reached the summit.

An odd contraption appeared at the top of the landing—a pulley system with a basket and an incredibly long coil of rope. Next to the pulley system was a small wooden door. It was ordinary and dull, with only a round knob on it. My companions were on edge as the voices commenced. It sounded like they were in a room right next to us.

I looked back to my companions and placed a finger to my lips, signaling them to be silent. I slowly reached out my other hand and closed it around the knob. Turning it, I heard a metallic click and the door swung open toward us. Light flooded into the darkness, making us adjust our eyes to the brilliance. On the other side was a source of light coming from a sconce on the wall. We crept into the room and began our investigation.

It was a large closet, with supplies on both sides, featuring black cloaks and uniforms hung neatly in rows. Remembering Esgar's description of the uniform she wore, I looked at the stitching, and sure enough, there it was: the emblem of the golden dragon on the left side of the tunic. Larger cloaks hung towards the back, which must be replacements for teachers. My mind was racing with thoughts, so I instructed my companions to go back into the stairwell. When the door was closed and we were shrouded once again in darkness, I began my briefing.

"I'm not entirely sure what our immediate future will bring. However, I know Aleph does everything for a purpose. He wanted me to read Esgar's book so I would be prepared for what we are going to see. I can't go into all the details but believe me when I say it is an abomination. These children are being deceived."

"So, what do you think we should do?" Lionel asked.

"Subterfuge. Your favorite strategy, am I correct?" I replied to the elder.

"You are. So, who do you think should go?"

"Only me for now. It's too dangerous for all of us. I need to find out exactly where we are and what this place is. After I gather some information, I will return, and we can strategize the plan further."

The companions agreed, and I turned the knob, entering the supply closet once more. This time, I put on the instructor's uniform. The first thing I noticed was how stiff and itchy it felt. Esgar couldn't have been more correct in her description. The uniform was uncomfortable, and I couldn't wait to be rid of it. I pulled the large black cloak around me and clasped it in the front. The garment felt bulky and awkward, nothing at all like the free-flowing guardians' cloak that was a second layer of skin to me.

I slowly exhaled my breath, asking Aleph to protect me. I was undoubtedly in the middle of a school that was dedicated to the instruction of Baelor's gifts. Without my guardian's cloak, I was unarmed and exposed to the effects of magic. I had to be on my toes and look around every corner because a single destruction spell could mean the end of my life.

I stepped into the first floor of the building. The corridor was long and dark, with no windows to produce any natural light. The interior was crafted of obscure sandstone and illuminated by sconces along the walls. Hanging from the ceiling were large candelabras. Heavy wooden doors were on either side of the hall, leading to classrooms. To my immediate right, children were in the midst of summons. Their chanting was altogether uncomfortable to hear, so I walked quietly to the left. I figured if this building were a replica of the school Esgar described, there would be an adjoining hall to the back which led to a staircase in the middle.

My assumption was correct. The staircase was exactly as she described. I ascended to the fourth floor, not taking any time to explore. As I reached the landing, I looked over and saw another door to my immediate right. It was small with a distinctive look to it. I tried to turn the knob, but it wouldn't budge. I was about to turn and head back down the stairs, when suddenly, I heard a polite voice from behind me.

"Good morning," the gentleman announced. I stood frozen in my tracks. What was I supposed to do? I was discovered!

"Stay calm. Your name is Keely," I heard Aleph say from within me.

"Good morning," I returned, still facing the door.

"You must be one of the transfers?" Footsteps were approaching.

"Yes," I said haltingly. "My name is…Keely."

"Really?" The voice replied excitedly. "Master Keely from Terradell?" The disguise was working, and the enemy had taken the bait. I took a deep breath and turned around to face the one who stopped me. He was an elderly man with short graying hair, dressed in the same uniform as I and garbed in a black cloak. The instructor was only several feet from me and extended his hand. "It is truly an honor!"

Without hesitation, I immersed myself in the role I was playing. Taking the stranger's hand, I pumped it up and down several times. "I didn't catch your name?" I asked the instructor.

"My name is Liam. I teach arithmetic. Nothing quite as exciting as what you bring to our school. Your skill and mastery are renowned! All the students have been looking forward to your arrival for quite some time. We have been without a master of the blade since before the term began. Your presence is welcome, Master." Liam gave a slight bow. I was baffled at what transpired. The teacher looked at me with a curious grin. "Were you trying to reach the bell tower?" he asked, gesturing to the door behind me.

"Yes, I was. I heard the view from the top is breathtaking."

"Well, I don't know about all that. I mean it's not the Western Sea at sunset, but it's nice to gaze out at various parts of the city from time to time." He reached into his robes and pulled out a key. "Allow me?" I stepped to the side, letting the instructor unlock the door. "It's a suitable place to have a pipe. Don't let the headmaster catch you. He can be extremely unforgiving."

"I'll remember that." I returned a bow and turned to go through the door. I quickly turned back around, asking another question. "What time is breakfast?"

"It will be after summons are over. Our students must be fully prepared for the day before any other activities, including arithmetic, can commence. It's when I take my leisurely walk through the school, when it's quiet, and I have my thoughts to myself."

"I understand. Well, it was nice speaking with you, Master Liam."

"No sir. I am no Master. Liam will be fine."

"Well then, Liam. Thank you for your help."

"Absolutely. Anything for a master swordsman," the teacher concluded with a smile, exiting the fourth-floor hallway.

The door led to a narrow winding staircase, climbing steeply upward. No wonder this area was under lock and key. A misstep could lead to a severe injury. A bit of natural light seeped into the stairwell from above. I took my time, making sure I didn't trip over my cloak. The climb took longer than expected, but soon I opened a trap door and was standing a hundred feet above the roof of the school.

Looking out, the city all around me was surrounded by desert that stretched into the horizon. I could see a good bit of distance in every direction; my view was only blocked by several buildings that were taller than the bell tower I stood in. Shimmering heat blurred my vision the further out I tried to gaze. Sitting on top of the cap rock peninsula, I was able to look west and see the journey we made through the sand dunes and wasteland.

Hammerfist was similar in appearance to Northcrest; however, the buildings were constructed of a darker rock, giving the city a more intimidating feel. Tall spires rose across the horizon, stretching high into the sky. It was an imposing sight, to say the least. The city was a stronghold that could withstand many assaults. Even the Nephilim might have a challenging time destroying its formidable walls. I could barely see the city we escaped, far away. I am sure there was a corporate outcry at the missing skyline, and panic had seized the natives, but I couldn't tell from where I stood.

Below me the day was started, and hundreds of people were scurrying along on daily errands, occupying the many horses and carts in the city streets. The constant ambient sound of busy city life filled the atmosphere. The people were awake and bustling.

I spent many days in Raithe, in service of Princess Iska, patrolling the streets. I recognized the smells and sounds of city life. I had no doubt about my current location. The school resided within the middle of the prestige sector.

I allowed myself several minutes to take in the infrastructure around me. I scanned rooftops above and narrow alleyways below, going through escape scenarios in my mind if we were compromised. As my eyes traveled along the rooftops, an impressive building stood out, close to my vantage point. It was a large bulking structure with twin spires reaching up to the heavens.

"*That is your destination,*" I heard Aleph speak.

"Should I get the others?"

"*Yes. Brief them on the layout of the city, then at nightfall you will leave the school.*" I scanned the exquisite structure. Many soldiers were standing guard out front and upon the rooftop. It looked as though infiltration was going to be tricky.

"Is this the palace?"

"*Yes…a place where honor was once celebrated. Kings sat upon the throne and fellowshipped with me from within its halls. They would lead by serving the people. Now it is a place of desecration, a throne used to enslave and conduct the will of Baelor. You have heard with your own ears, the students at this school summoning messengers. This institution, and many others like it, are being used to traffic young men and women. It is an extension of Lucien's power. Like Viveka, they are being prepared for war and used for their abilities. It is an abomination that must be stopped. The source of wickedness is there, in that building.*"

I returned to the supply closet without incident, rejoining my companions. They were visibly startled as I came through the hidden door into the staircase. I sat them down and briefed them on what I discovered, not missing any details regarding the palace nearby. The next hours were agony to wait. We decided to move further down the stairs in case the door opened.

Our strategy paid off. We settled into the shadows as the storage room door burst open. From the shadows, we overheard a heated conversation between master and student.

"This is the last time you will break your connection with the void!"

"But Master, it's not my fault," protested the little boy.

"I don't want to hear your pathetic excuses. An hour in the basket will set you straight!"

"No, Master!"

"Get in now! I won't ask you again. Do you want to swing for an hour or a day?"

"Please Master..." The boy began to sob.

"Your tears are pathetic, child. A servant of Baelor will not be allowed the comfort of crying. You must be strong and vigilant! This is to help remind you of that."

"I won't do it again!"

"Enough of this! Either you get in the basket, or you will swing for an entire day and receive a demerit for weekend work!" The child continued to sob. "STOP CRYING... NOW!"

As the exchange of harsh words continued above us, I could feel Lionel moving close to me. "Let me go end that monster's life, Anlace. He's not worth the fodder within a hog's trough."

"Stay put, my friend. I don't like this any more than you do. But this must play out." Lionel grunted and moved several steps away from me, surrendering to my command.

Hidden in the shadows, we heard commotion as the child sat within the basket. The Master moved over to the pulley and turned the crank, lowering the basket into the open space beside the staircase. The weeping child had no idea there was an end to the abyss, even though it was thousands of feet below. All he could imagine was an endless chasm. So, this was a method for administering control? What monsters these clerics were!

The master slammed the door shut, leaving the child suspended within the pitch-black darkness. The rope tightened as it softly swung the child back and forth. I whispered to Aleph, asking him what to do.

"You must remain hidden. Even though your intentions are good, you will cause the child to be alarmed, and he will reveal your presence to his masters."

"This is wrong."

"Yes. Baelor's methods are cruel and the closer we get to the end; the intensity will increase."

"What do we do?"

"You are doing it…even now. Be silent. Don't allow yourselves to be seen."

I quietly went to each of my companions within the darkness, whispering Aleph's words to me. Reluctantly, we all agreed to obey. It was agony to wait. Hearing the whimpering of the child was like hearing fingernails scratching on a chalkboard. He cried out apologies for the first half hour, promising he would behave if they came and rescued him from the basket. When the child was spent, he got quiet and whimpered miserably.

The supply room door finally opened, and the child shouted his apologies with great exuberance, promising not to break concentration with the void again. The master seemed pleased at this excited response and turned the crank, raising the basket back up to the safety of the landing. When the child was on the top step, he threw himself into the master's arms, begging for forgiveness. The master smothered the child with platitudes of comfort, leading him back through the supply room door.

We were baffled by the scene that took place. Loretta finally broke the silence. "Poor thing. He must have been terrified!"

"We must stop this. These children…" Merwin exclaimed.

"I agree…" I then shared Aleph's instructions with my companions. To stay hidden, we decided to rest and meditate until nightfall and then escape into the city.

Aleph signaled us by manifesting a flame within our midst. We grabbed our packs, quietly climbed the stairs, and opened the supply closet door. There were enough uniforms and cloaks for us, including an oversized one for Groth! Once dressed, we opened the door to the hallway. The corridor this evening was silent. These schools were built the same all over Shalistar. So, remembering Esgar's description, I directed us to the right, quickly following the hall toward the front.

Groth opened the large oak door, exiting the premises as quickly as he could. We were close on his heels, darting across a large courtyard full of walkways and benches until we hit the streets. When we were safely away from school grounds, I turned back to look at the front. It was a large sandstone building with impressive columns along the front. I looked up and saw the bell tower I stood upon earlier, rising into the sky. I said a silent prayer for the children trapped within and vowed that somehow, I would return to make it right. Aleph, in response to my prayer, blew a soft wind right past the tip of my nose.

It was agreed to lay low until morning and find a tavern nearby. If I were correct, masters of the school would be held in high regard, so we stayed garbed in the black cloaks. The streets were near-empty this evening, considering the cool weather and cloudless sky. Looking up through the surrounding buildings, the heavens were bursting with beautiful stars. I wished I were back at the top of the bell tower with an unobstructed view, so I could bask in the breathtaking scenery painted above, but that was not going to happen. We needed to pull up to a table and discuss our mission.

The citizens left after the Night of Shadows were awkward and fearful, roaming the streets without purpose. They were not useful for Baelor's purposes, so he cast them aside. It was pitiful to witness. Seeing our cloaks brought horrific memories to them of that fateful night. I felt sorry for them. They bowed their knee to Baelor's messenger out of fear for their lives.

We located a beggar close to the school. Looking into his eyes, I saw the same thing I had seen in Northcrest: emptiness. These people were devoid of life. We humbly asked him for directions to a friendly tavern. The man stuttered as he gave us his recommendation, a place called "Halvern's Tavern," near to where we were standing. We thanked him and made our way quickly towards the lively establishment.

My companions and I sat around a table in the corner of a

building that was overflowing with colorful woven tapestries. The decorations were highly impressive, and I found myself lost in the intricate patterns around me. None of us took a sip of our beverages because we were busy staring in amazement at all the beautiful artwork.

My companions and I were roused from our stupor by a commotion nearby. The men were belligerently drunk, a demonstration of anger and hostility I hadn't witnessed since my days of being in King Tark's army. The spirit in this place was one of hopelessness and depression. I told my companions they needed to watch every single step they took—not because of danger, but because I didn't want us to upset the population and risk blowing our cover.

We watched the regulars empty their glasses and continue in debauchery. How anyone could have any level of amusement in this place, I couldn't imagine. It was hard to watch. There was no joy or silliness to the party, a stark contrast to the vibrant tapestries that hung on the walls. These people bowed their knee to Baelor and were lost. The only hope they had was at the bottom of their glass. They simply wanted to forget their problems and stay alive another day while doing it.

Another round of fighting broke out in front of us. I quickly told my companions to lift their mugs. My instincts were correct. Suddenly, the body of a brawler came crashing into our table. The wood splintered and split as the table was broken by the unconscious drunkard. We sat awkwardly holding our mugs without a table to set them down on. Looking at each other, we shrugged. It seemed like a good moment, so we saluted our creator and took a large gulp of the beer.

It was nowhere near the satisfying flavor of the pint I shared with Daeric at the "Swarthy Hog" in Sommerset. As the liquid went down my throat, there was a foul aftertaste. Cal made a disgusted noise and spit the liquid out of his mouth. I didn't go that far myself, but the beer was definitely not my favorite. We all stood up, moving away from the unconscious body that ruined the table. The brawler who sent him flying was in the throes of starting another fight. This time, we moved ourselves out of the way of the miscreants by taking the stairs near the entrance, leading to a nice balcony that overlooked the entire tavern. We sat at a table against the railing and exhaled. It was much quieter up here, and we were able to talk without having to shout or dodge a fight.

We tipped our mugs until they were empty—all of us except Cal. He refused to take another swig of what he called "horse urine." After the first round was finished, he asked permission to buy the next. We graciously accepted, and Cal dismissed himself to go back to the barkeep.

He returned shortly later, accompanied by an elegantly dressed man next to him. They were both carrying glasses of wine. "Please set them in front of my companions," Cal instructed.

"Yes, Master. We will serve only the finest drink to you and your people. I am humbled that you are here with us. My name is Halvern, and I own this establishment." The proprietor bowed before our group. "I apologize for the troublesome folk around here. As you probably have guessed, it has gotten worse since..." His voice trailed off and his head bowed. Loretta stood up and moved over to him quickly placing a hand on his shoulder.

"We understand, good sir," she stated sympathetically. "My

fellow masters and I would like to have a moment alone. Can you please see to it we are not disturbed any further? Except, of course, when we need a refill."

"Why yes, master. I will personally guarantee that." The owner bowed again deeply. "If you need anything, simply raise a finger and we will come to serve you. No need to get up again. My best bartender will be watching and have drinks headed your way immediately."

"What about food?" Groth asked excitedly. "What's on the menu?"

"I'm glad you asked. We have roasted desert buffalo, paired with red potatoes, onions, and carrots. It is a crowd favorite and absolutely delicious."

Groth immediately raised six fingers and nodded his head enthusiastically. "We will take it!" Halvern looked pleased at my large companion's outburst and bowed deeply before dismissing himself. I turned my attention back to the table and my friends. In front of each of us was a large glass of wine. Remembering the instructions of Marec, I swirled the glass, letting the liquid splash the sides. Cal watched me, impressed at my understanding of etiquette.

"I see you have experience in wine?" Cal asked.

"Yes. A great man taught me quite a bit," I responded with a smile.

"Well, then, you will already know this is a fine selection." Cal addressed the rest of our group. "I apologize for my behavior earlier. But I could not bear to drink such foul beverage. I care more about each of you than that. So, I took it upon myself to serve you an exquisite wine. I hope that is, okay?"

"Fine by me, lad. It all goes down the same way in my book," Lionel stated.

"I appreciate your generosity. A good man will always upgrade a beverage. Here's to a good man!" exclaimed Merwin, raising his glass. We all followed suit and touched our glasses together. "It's been an honor adventuring with all of you. May Aleph guide our steps and illuminate our path!" Merwin concluded.

"Aye!" We agreed and tipped our glasses. I watched as several of my friends drank the entire serving in one gulp. I stifled a laugh at their cavalier reception of the wine glass. However, I sympathized with them because there was a time, before I met Marec and sat at Lady Iska's table, when I would have done the same.

I took a moment and quietly prayed for Seth and Marec before taking the first sip from my glass. The flavor of wine exploded in my palette as I breathed in the aroma through my nostrils. This was an excellent wine, indeed! Marec would have given his seal of approval for sure. I nodded to Cal, giving him my thanks. He smiled back at me, pleased at my reception.

It was difficult to discuss any part of our mission. We were having such a wonderful time atop the balcony in "Halvern's Tavern." It's what we all needed—a moment to unwind and let the stress of our responsibilities melt away. Even though it was dangerous, and the odds of blowing our cover were high, I didn't feel any hesitation within me to stop the revelry.

Lionel was tasked with keeping an eye on the front door and alerting us if anything interesting came about. My elder brother was focused like a hawk. Nobody entered the tavern without him knowing it. He had the entire place memorized in no time, including a way out if we needed a quick escape. With our bases covered, we continued celebrating late into the night.

Contrary to Halvern's words, we were not left alone. Our table was full of smiles and merriment, drawing many characters into our midst. We were careful with our words but generous with our joy. We didn't keep anyone away and met all kinds of people. The delight we shared, transferred from one table to another. The fighting had stopped, and people were laughing. It was tangible. What we carried was so valuable to these people who had lost all hope. They needed love and fellowship, and we were not hesitant to share it. Just when I thought the night would never end, a group of soldiers entered the building with a cleric in their midst.

They occupied a table close to the barkeep. My companions and I held our breath, waiting for them to discover us. We were frozen in place, unable to move. Lionel leaned in close and spoke with me.

"We can't leave this building without them seeing us. They are perfectly positioned to spot our departure."

"What about the second floor?" I asked desperately, glancing behind me.

"No. The only exits are on the first floor. We're trapped. This was a bad idea coming here, Anlace." Hearing the elder's report, I exhaled slowly, trying to gather my muddled thoughts. Across the table, my companions shared the same anxious look.

What was happening to me? Why couldn't I keep a clear thought in my head? Suddenly, the cleric rose from his seat and turned his face directly toward us. I investigated the pale face driven by ambition and fear. His look confirmed everything I suspected. They knew we were here!

The cleric opened his mouth and shouted several arcane words towards the balcony where we sat. Without the protection of our cloaks, the spell hit me like a ton of bricks. I was expecting fire or electric currents to course through me, but instead my entire body went numb.

"Anlace?" I turned to Loretta to see an expression of dread on her face. "I can't feel my body. What is happening?" The arcane words from the cleric became louder, the spell capturing all of us in our seats. We couldn't move!

Accompanied by the numbness, all my thoughts were muddled. Nothing made sense, except one thing; the entire atmosphere was calm and silent. I heard the steps of the cleric's leather boots as he climbed the stairs to where we were sitting. His voice became louder and more distinct as he approached our table.

Even though I knew he was human, he reminded me of Lucien. His hypnotic words in the arcane language were smooth and without hesitancy. He was confident in his approach. By this time, the spell rendered us speechless. My face was numb. We sat there dumbly, looking up at the dark cloaked figure before us with our mouths wide open. He continued speaking words of dark magic until we were rendered helpless. I heard a chair scrape along the wood floor until it was positioned at our table. The cleric adjusted his black cloak and sat down, placing his leather gloved hands upon the solid wood. He looked right at me and spoke.

"You must be Anlace." Hearing my name brought a shiver of fear. "I have been told by my master that you would come, and sure enough, he was right. I am shocked that you fell into our trap so easily." We tried to respond, but all that came out was an incoherent grunt.

"No need to trouble yourself with words. I am simply the escort for you this evening. My master has desired to meet with you for quite some time." I stared back dumbly, trying to make sense of everything. "Don't worry, Anlace. All will be revealed shortly." He then stood up and walked to the edge of the balcony, addressing the soldiers below. "You may take them now."

A line of clerics stood in front of the tavern, chanting words of magic under their breath. I looked to the side and saw another cleric placing a large coin bag into the hands of the beggar who gave us directions to the tavern. Behind the line of clerics was a cart with several soldiers standing guard beside it. It was obvious this was a conspiracy against us. How long had they known we were in the city? What gave us away?

Because our legs were numb from the spell, we had to be dragged out of the building. The guards worked together to pull each of us onto the cart. When we were all assembled, the command was given, and the cart moved along the city streets. I couldn't bear to look at my companions. They trusted me as their leader, and once again, I led them into the hands of danger. I closed my eyes, bowing my head in shame.

My foolishness was going to get us all killed.

The cart rolled to an abrupt stop at the foot of a massive marble staircase. Soldiers were stationed everywhere, which helped me recognize our destination. We were at the palace. The face of the building was exquisite. No other structure came close to its beauty. The brilliant night sky radiated with countless stars that shone a soft glare, making the palace gently glow. The sandstone had numerous carvings and intricate patterns, depicting everything from kings to guardians. Tall white columns lined the front of the building, giving the structure an impressive appearance. However, my investigation of the beautiful building was cut short.

The master's spell had taken full effect and we were completely numb, forcing the soldiers to carry us by our arms and feet up the steps of the palace. It took the strength of four guards to heft Groth's body along. As I was carried like a piece of furniture up the stairs, I looked into the beautiful night sky above me and thought to myself, "how low had I become?" I was being carried into the palace to meet an unknown enemy. I couldn't even walk myself into the master's presence. I had to be carried! How pathetic! I couldn't bring myself to turn my head and look at my companions. I was too ashamed. It was my fault we were here. I was the leader, and I was going to carry the blame.

The doors to the throne room opened. I saw two rows of ten clerics, standing parallel to each other, leading up to the dais. Sitting upon the throne was a black hooded figure. He sat with his leg draped over the arm of the throne, reading a familiar looking book. As the soldiers laid us down at the foot of the throne, he quickly closed and concealed it. His head was turned towards the left, keeping me from seeing his face.

Several words of magic erupted from the throne. Suddenly, I felt my hands and feet as blood came coursing through my entire body. I could move my legs! My companions were still lying helpless on the ground, so I surmised the dark figure on the throne only released me from the spell. I slowly sat up, trying to position myself to see the face of the mysterious figure, but the cowl of the cloak overshadowed him. Silence was broken as the figure addressed me.

"You are a pathetic sight to behold, Anlace." There was something familiar about the voice. I tried to assemble the vocal cords in my brain. The effects of the spell were released, but I was still groggy and overcome with symptoms of heavy drinking. The figure continued to speak.

"You killed one of my best students. When Viveka did not return from Virym, it was obvious that you were close." The voice was from a long, dark past. As he continued to speak, the pieces fell into place. As if knowing my thoughts, the dark figure turned his head towards me.

"Yes, Anlace. You recognize my voice, don't you?" The hooded cleric placed a hand to the side of his cowl and pulled it back. As the face was revealed, my heart skipped a beat. "I know we have aged a bit since the last time we met…" I stared into the hateful dark eyes of the man who sat upon the throne. His black hair was pulled back and held tightly in a ponytail. The beard upon his face was the same color as his hair but speckled with spots of white.

I hoped I was wrong, and this was a cruel nightmare from which I would awaken. But alas, it was not. The room was real. The dark figure before me was neither my imagination, nor the effects of drunken revelry. Sitting upon the throne was the murderer of Daeric's father, back to torment me within this plane of existence, until my final breath. I gasped, and an echo filled the entire hall as I said aloud the name of my enemy, solidifying within my mind the reality of my present circumstance.

"Roderick?"

"Yes Anlace…it's me."

CHAPTER
23

I spent a lot of time over the years rehearsing what I would say if I ever met Roderick again. None of my preparation mattered. I had no desire to converse with him on any level. His curiosity about my life was discomforting. I could tell he was enjoying it. Like a viper squeezing prey, he could devour me at any second. Knowing that the thrill would be over quickly, he poked and prodded me with open ended questions about my life. I didn't give him the satisfaction of a response. The pleasantries were merely a charade to keep me off balance, until turning his attention to more serious matters. When his voice and posture changed, I was careful with my answers.

"What are you doing in my city, Anlace? Have you come to avenge the traitorous whore? Did you really think you could sneak up on me and put a knife in my back? It is obvious you are uneducated in the gifts of Baelor. We can see you; do you know that? We can see everything."

I remained silent, allowing my enemy to speak. "How did the cloaks fit? I wanted to be sure everyone had a perfect match to their size. Especially the behemoth," he said, pointing to Groth. I turned away, trying to assemble my thoughts.

"I knew it!" my enemy shouted excitedly, keeping me on edge. "It is shocking how well I know you! Of course, you would try to sneak in through the catacombs! Of course, you would don a disguise!"

I felt a soft wind blow across the tip of my nose. I turned back to see if Roderick felt it. He was oblivious, reveling in his victory. Aleph was with me, even in this room. Embracing the revelation, I interrupted my enemy.

"We're here to warn you," Roderick stopped his laughter and cocked his head. His smile vanished and was replaced with the look of a desperate man. I knew I hit a nerve and continued. "Do you understand? I said we are…"

"Stop!" The cloaked man shouted. "I don't want to hear another word from your lying tongue."

"You haven't seen what we have," I pressed my enemy.

"I said to shut your mouth," Roderick replied coldly.

"You would do well to listen!" I raised my voice. "You obviously have no idea what is coming your way." I saw Roderick's eyelids flicker as I continued to challenge him. "The Nephilim have been released by your cowardly master and are destroying this world. They will start with the cities and the people. Once they have turned every block of stone, they will continue to ravage nature until there is nothing left but devastation. The mighty walls of this city cannot stop the destroyer." Roderick swirled a wine glass and took a long drink.

"You are so weak and naïve. Of course, the Nephilim are coming. I am counting on it. Only with their entrance can the Revealing occur." Roderick raised his glass in a toast. I gave way to a look of doubt and unbelief. Roderick saw it and immediately took advantage. "What's that? Has your dead god not told you about the Revealing? Has he truly left out the most critical piece of the puzzle? Do you not know about the deal He and Baelor made?" Roderick gave an evil laugh at the revelation and finished the last of his wine.

"Now isn't that like Aleph? Always leaving his people in the dark and speaking in cryptic words!"

"What is the Revealing?" I asked curiously.

"Let your dead god tell you." he replied cruelly.

"Please, Roderick. I need to know."

"Grovel some more, Anlace. I think it's working!" my nemesis said sarcastically.

"I know you have no reason to grant me this request, but please." I asked desperately. Roderick stared at me for several moments. A smile spread across his lips.

"It won't do you any good. You won't be alive to see it." The words he spoke hung in the air like a rotting cadaver swinging from a noose. This was not a threat. My enemy meant every word. I looked over at my companions who were still caught in the spell. I couldn't do anything to free us. If I tried to attack Roderick, he would dispatch me in seconds. If by some miracle I were to survive my futile attempt, the other twenty clerics in the room would turn me into a pile of ash.

Suddenly, a door opened, and a cleric entered the throne room, carrying a bundle of cloth. As he approached, I could see a pile of dirty brown cloaks with gaping holes in the fabric, revealing a brilliant white hue underneath. He was carrying our guardian's cloaks! Without a word, he dropped the pile at the feet of Roderick and turned away.

To the right of the throne, was a bronze laver with a cloud of smoke pouring from it. The glowing embers within the basin illuminated the dais. Looking back at Roderick, I saw an evil grin on his face. I shook my head, pleading silently with my nemesis. He looked back at me, rolling his eyes. "You bore me, Anlace. Is this what you have become? An errand boy? A lap dog? Where is the fight? Where is your strength?" He picked up the cloaks and walked over to the laver.

"Don't do it, Roderick! We can help you!" Roderick looked back at me. I saw a glimmer of fear come over his face. He stared down at the bundles in his arms and hesitated. I thought maybe my words were getting through to him. He looked back at me and shook his head.

"No…sadly, you cannot." Without further hesitation, he threw the bundle into the fire. I watched helplessly as the flames coughed slightly. There was a loud "whoosh" as the material was set ablaze. I stared into the flames, watching the symbol of our order burn. I bowed my head and softly spoke Aleph's name.

"He's not going to help you, Anlace. Don't you know the destruction of this world is the path of Aleph? That is why we are necessary. We are the abeyance that is keeping Aleph from destroying this world! We are the only ones who can stand up to Him and keep it from happening." A heavy weight fell on me. I was nauseous as Roderick's words flooded my mind. I turned away from the throne. I couldn't look at the man. The most devastating part of this revelation was that Roderick's words made sense.

"I will give you one chance." His hypnotic words coursed through me. The courage I felt earlier was quickly waning. "Join us and help us fight the Nephilim. If we combine our strengths, then we have a chance to win. You and your companions will not be harmed and will be given a rank of honor in my army. I will send word to Raithe, letting the magistrate know that all your crimes have been forgiven. You will not have to run anymore. You will not have to hide. Everything I have, all the power I possess that was given to me by the mighty Baelor from his chief messenger, will be yours. Simply reach out, take my hand, and it will all be over."

I looked up at Roderick with tear-soaked eyes and reached out my shaking hand. A smile spread across his lips. His grip was cold, but solid and firm. It felt rough and heavy. My companions saw what I was doing, and a muffled scream escaped their lips.

"Say it…" Roderick whispered into my ear. "Say it out loud." This was it. I reached my end. I knew there was no way I was coming out of this the same way I entered. I was changed. Taking a deep breath, I spoke.

"I surrender…" Quick as a viper, I took Roderick's hand and pushed it with all my force in an unnatural direction. I heard the snap of bones as my nemesis buckled over, screaming in pain. He fell back, cupping the injury close to his chest. Sweat beaded down his forehead as he shouted in rage to his clerics.

"Take him down! No spells! I want him alive!" I stood there, defiantly staring up at my nemesis. "That was a mistake!" he shouted, wincing in pain. I braced myself as the clerics overcame me. I withstood many punches and kicks before collapsing to the floor. How long they continued their assault, I wasn't sure. A final kick to my forehead sent my world spinning. Then, everything went black.

I awoke with a start. Once again, the room was spinning, and my head was throbbing. As I sat up, I felt a painful jolt in my side and reached to hold it. Loretta was next to me, softly moving her fingers over the bruised area.

"Don't move, sir. I'm not a physician, but I think you might have a cracked rib or two."

"You are free?" I responded painfully.

"Yes, the spell wore off of us about an hour ago."

"Where are we?"

"Prison," announced Lionel, coming into view. "Seems to be the common factor this time around." I heard a pop as Loretta carefully took a small cork off the vial in her hand.

"They didn't take your utility belt?" I asked.

"Yes. But I always keep a vial hidden away from my belt for only the most extreme circumstances. Now, quit talking and let me do my thing." I obeyed the diligent woman and let her work. Looking through the bars, I saw what little light we had coming from a sconce on the wall. Cal and Groth were sitting against the iron door. Wishing he had his hammer; the smith began fidgeting with whatever he could find. Settling for a couple of small rocks, he continued his nervous habit. Groth watched his wife tend to me with a look of concern etched on his face. He tore a piece of cloth from his tunic and dipped it in a bit of liquid that was flowing down the walls. Groth placed the damp cloth on my forehead. It felt cool but smelled terrible. I had to strain from gagging.

"They sure did a number on you." Loretta stated, full of concern as she examined my ribs. I felt her fingers press into my side and a stab of pain shot through me. I gasped and moved my hand to cover it. Loretta hushed me and placed her hand on the damp cloth. "I know it's painful, but please lay still." I reluctantly obeyed. "Now, when I apply the balm, you may feel a tickling sensation that you want to itch. Not a clever idea, sir. The balm needs to do its work, and interrupting the process is not proper. Balms are like us in a lot of ways—they like to do their job effectively and don't like anyone looking over their shoulder to see if the job is getting done."

"Oddly, you make sense," I whispered. Loretta's fingers circled my side. I immediately felt a warm and tickly sensation as she gently spread the balm. The lady was right! All I wanted to do was scratch where the balm was applied. I moved to do so and felt a rough hand grab me.

Lionel leaned in closer. "She knows what she is doing," I grunted and moved spastically to try and position myself for an itch, but the elder held my hand tightly. All I could do was grunt as the agony passed. After several minutes, I was calm again. The balm was doing its job. My side didn't hurt quite as much. I asked Loretta for something to help with my pounding headache, and she told me she couldn't spare any more, but not to worry, she tended to the more serious injuries.

I knew Roderick had specific plans for us because we were

still alive. We sat together in our small cell, all six of us, awaiting our fate. With nothing but time, we circled and began discussing the recent events. Allowing everyone to speak gave me all the information I needed to come to an accurate conclusion—we fell into a deadly trap!

It was sprung when Viveka returned to give Roderick the news of our existence. After our second encounter at the top of the plateau, Roderick knew we were close. He removed any opposition from within the catacombs, allowing us safe passage. With Aleph's help, we were able to make it secretly into the city—or so we thought.

Roderick instructed his people to place disguises in the supply closet. When I encountered the arithmetic teacher and told him my name was Keely, the final part of the plan was in play. The enemy waited until we donned uniforms and snuck out of the school. Several well-placed beggars were given detailed instructions and a bag of gold in their pocket. It was a full-proof plan. We were lured into the tavern, like hogs to the slaughter. Once inside, Roderick dispatched a group of clerics to surround the building, speaking incantations, muddling our thoughts, and keeping us focused on revelry. Once we were deep into our cups, he sent a master to deliver the final spell. With our cloaks left behind, there was no defense against the magic, rendering us helpless.

The enemy was crafty, allowing us time to make our mistakes. They were patient and willing to outlast us, which made me nervous. Hearing our discussion made me realize our weakness. Without the cloaks, we needed to be careful, our movements calculated. We would take no unnecessary risks, and every step forward would be discussed openly amongst the group.

Suddenly, Cal and I were pulled out of our cell and marched down the hall to a room with an iron door. Standing next to it was a large soldier. When the door opened, I saw my nemesis sitting at a wooden table next to a weapons rack. Beads of sweat were dripping down his forehead. His skin was pale, and a fever had taken over his body. The hand I broke earlier was bandaged and held tightly against his chest. It gave me great satisfaction knowing that my enemy was incapable of healing spells and was sitting in front of me, shuddering in agonizing pain.

Roderick stared at me in hatred. His straight black hair was disheveled. His tight ponytail was loose, allowing clumps of his long dark hair to fall from the sides of his head.

"Leave him outside," he said, pointing to Cal. "I want a word alone with this one." My companion gave a worried expression. I nodded my head, letting him know it was okay. Our escorting soldiers turned the smith around and moved him out of the room. When the iron door closed loudly, Roderick leaned forward and pointed to the chair across from him.

"Sit down, Anlace." I slowly seated myself, not taking my eyes off him. The nemesis waited, allowing tension in the room to reach its peak. Roderick stared into my eyes, searching my soul. I could feel cold tremors coursing through me as he tried reading my mind. I held my ground and stared back, trying not to show any emotion. When he realized he was not going to gain any ground using that strategy, he leaned back and nodded. Reaching into his black cloak, he revealed the familiar book he was reading earlier. He set it down, opened it up to a random page, and began reading.

"Interwoven within the fabric of eternity is a characteristic that has governed the worlds I create. This principle has determined the destinies of countless lives, eternal and mortal."

"And what is that characteristic?" I asked.

"Free will—the power to choose. Some creations of mine have been given the authority to do so and others have not. Because you are human, you have been given the authority to choose."

Roderick closed the book and placed it on the table in front of me. He pointed at it with his uninjured finger. "This is a remarkably interesting chronicle. Touching, to say the least." Roderick leaned back and scratched his short dark beard with his fingers. "So, Princess Kristina is alive? I wouldn't have guessed it. I was under the impression the entire royal family was sentenced to death. Interesting, indeed." He tapped the cover of the book. "The world is not ready for these words, Anlace. They will only stoke a flame that has been burning for years. Is that your master's plan? What makes you think the world will even believe these mad ramblings?"

"If He wills it, then there will be nothing you can do to stop it!" I returned boldly.

Roderick spoke a word of magic, and a small flame protruded from his index finger. He moved the tip of the flame closer to the book. "Really? Another word from me, and this fantasy will become history."

"You are naïve," I stated harshly. "Do you think your parlor tricks can stop the will of Aleph? He has thousands of copies in His collection. You will not quench this word." A look of desperation flashed across my enemy's face, coupled with a look of fear.

My enemy was afraid. But of what? He knew something and wasn't saying it. I placed my arms across my chest, not budging. Roderick gave a sigh and stood up. He leaned over the table and spoke menacingly.

"You are harboring a fugitive and will be held responsible if she is not returned. Tell me, Anlace, where is Princess Kristina?"

"Why didn't you ask me about her earlier?" I challenged.

"I was going to…until you rudely broke my hand!"

"She's gone. Far beyond your reach," I responded confidently. Roderick gave a soft chuckle, shaking his head.

"Anlace, you don't have a princess here to save you. It's you and me now. I am your magistrate and can make the last part of your life easy or painful. The choice is yours."

I leaned forward until my nose was only inches from Roderick's. "I am telling you the truth. I don't know where she is. And if I did, I still wouldn't tell you."

My nemesis kept his gaze and grinned. He was about to speak and abandoned his words, nodding his head. He moved to the iron door and opened it. "Bring him in," he called into the hall.

I heard the scuffle of feet, followed by the form of my new friend Cal being roughly handled by two soldiers. Two additional guards walked in behind them and slammed the door shut. Roderick moved over to a weapons rack along the side of the room and selected a large, gleaming saber. He took a step back and swung it through the air, filling the atmosphere with an unpleasant sound. My stomach turned, and I began to sweat.

Cal looked at me with a horrified look on his face. Roderick moved the blade slowly in front of my companion's chest. "Here is what is about to happen. I will ask you a question, and if you do not tell me the correct answer, I will begin removing your friend's limbs from his body. We will start with his right hand." Roderick stopped in front of Cal and addressed him coldly. "A smith is useless without a hand. Am I right?"

"Tell him nothing, Anlace!" Cal shouted bravely. I gritted my teeth, took a deep breath, and jumped up from my chair in the direction of the weapons rack. Before I could leave my seat, rough mailed hands of the soldiers grabbed my arms, pulling them painfully behind me.

"Don't try it, hero!" the soldier mocked. "Another move out of you, and we break your arms!" Roderick was pleased with the situation and gestured to the other soldiers. They shoved Cal onto the wooden table, forcing his right arm out in front of him. One soldier put all his weight on my friend's limb, securing it in place. Roderick positioned himself along the back of the table. He slowly placed the gleaming edge of the sword several inches from the wrist above Cal's right hand.

"Don't do it, Anlace!" Cal screamed. Roderick lifted the blade high, poised to strike.

"Where is Princess Kristina?"

"Tell him nothing!" Cal screamed. Roderick looked at Cal in disgust and spoke an arcane word. Suddenly, my friend's outbursts became muffled screams.

"Last chance! Where is the princess?" Roderick turned his head towards me. His eyes were on fire. I could not negotiate with him—I had no choice but to tell him the truth.

"She is with Aleph."

"You better make sense quickly!"

"Princess Kristina has walked through the doors of Aleph's temple at the top of Shaddyia. She is with our creator now, far beyond your reach."

"Impossible! Nobody has been able to climb to the top. You are lying!"

"I am not! She has made it safely to the top. Not even your fallen master could prevent the will of Aleph from coming forth." I could see the gears of Roderick's mind turning. The blade in his hand was coming down slowly until it rested at his side. "If what you say is true, we have no time to waste." Roderick put the blade back on the weapons rack and addressed his soldiers. "Take the prisoners and prepare them for public execution. Gather all the inhabitants to the steps of the palace. They will witness the punishment for treason."

A slight look of ease came over my friend as the soldiers pulled him up from the wooden table. I guess death would be a better alternative than the loss of his hand. The soldiers pulled me up as well. I jerked away and spoke my peace.

"You can't stop this, Roderick. Aleph has made his move, and his wrath will be swift. Removing me and my companions from Shalistar will not hinder His plans." Roderick's brow wrinkled as he heard my words.

"You are right. I can't stop Aleph. But I can have peace as this world ends knowing that you are no longer a part of it!" He lifted his broken hand painfully and pointed one of his shriveled fingers at me. "Take this traitor and his friends! Prepare them for death!"

CHAPTER
24

The doors flung open, flooding the keep with light. Our armored escort stayed close to our side as we took our place at the top of the palace steps. Above us, ominous clouds hung low in the sky with streaks of brilliant orange. The atmosphere was unnerving. It looked like fire was erupting within the gray shadows above. I sensed something was stirring and looked over to my companions to see if they felt the same.

Assembled on the marble staircase were two rows of clerics standing across from each other. Their pale faces gazed up at us, shrouded within their black cloaks. The look of hatred upon their face clearly revealed what they thought of us. They were masters of the school and Roderick's closest followers. Each of them possessed an unlimited supply of Baelor's power and wouldn't hesitate to release it in the form of a hideous spell if any of us tried to escape.

The people of Hammerfist were assembled in the plaza below, being treated to a liar's monologue from the lips of their leader Roderick. They grasped at every false word he spoke. Within the crowd, students in black cloaks spoke nervously to their friends beside them. Halvern and the beggar who duped us were in attendance as well. As I met their gaze, they quickly turned away, not wanting to make eye contact with me. It was quite a turnout for such a brief period of time.

As we descended the marble steps, the crowd cursed us, throwing whatever spoiled food they possessed. Turning away, I saw an apple hit Loretta in the head, taking her to the ground. Groth cried out, shoving his captors aside. Before he could reach his wife, he was detained by a handful of soldiers. I heard curses coming from the brute's mouth as they got him back in line.

Loretta struggled to get up, not receiving any help from the soldiers. My heart broke to see my friend brought so low. If it was just me, fine. I would die, and it would be over. But to see them in pain was agony. I softly prayed that Aleph would quickly ease our suffering.

Roderick continued to speak words of hatred about the order and the great enemy, Aleph. He asserted that it was Aleph's will to destroy this world and Baelor had chosen the clerics to make a stand. The crowd hung onto every word of this hateful speech, adding their rage to the burning fire.

My companions and I stood upon the edge of the final staircase that led into the plaza below. Six blocks of marble were brought and placed at the foot of the steps amid the crowd. I was reminded once again of the horrific day in Raithe when Iska's life was taken from her. There were many similarities here today.

In response to my thoughts, I looked over and saw six soldiers carrying large buckets. They slowly approached until they were only a few feet away from us. One soldier shouted a command to the rest. In unison they heaved their buckets in our direction. My breath left me as the red liquid drenched me from the top of my head down to the soles of my feet. I lifted my hands and looked at my palms. Was it blood? I heard Loretta shriek next to me as she examined her stained garments, as well. I closed my eyes, begging Aleph to end this nightmare for all of us. I held my breath, hoping for an answer. But alas, there was only silence.

Was this it? Were we to be martyrs? For what end? Why would Aleph lead us all this way only for us to be executed? I was brought back to reality as I saw rough hands grab Loretta and move her down the stairs. I cried out to Roderick, begging him to stop this insanity and spare her life. Either he was ignoring me or couldn't hear me over the roar of the crowd. Regardless, Loretta continued moving towards the marble block.

What cruelty! How evil could one man be? Why didn't he execute all of us together and be done with it? Was he going to make us watch as we were killed one at a time? Suddenly, I felt the breath of my nemesis upon my ear, whispering to me.

"I told you, Anlace, I would make it my life's mission to take away everything from you. Your friends will die, and you will be witness to it all!"

"Damn you, coward!" I screamed and gritted my teeth.

"No. I damn you," Roderick concluded. Turning his attention back to the bottom of the steps, he shouted, "Put her into position!" The crowd's roar was deafening. Groth screamed and tried to move but was pinned to the ground by four soldiers. He reached out his hand, screaming his wife's name.

Loretta looked up at her large husband and spoke, "It's okay, big guy. It'll be over soon enough. Don't cry any more, okay?" She was cut off as the soldiers pushed her down onto her knees in front of the block. The soldiers were large, forceful brutes, compared to her small-framed body. A hand was on top of Loretta's head pushing it down until it rested on top of the marble block. The indention in the block made it so the head was hanging off the edge, giving the executioner plenty of space to make a clean cut.

The roar of the crowd ceased as Roderick raised his hand. Only Groth's muffled curses were heard. My nemesis stood before the crowd and spoke. "You have been found guilty of treason and are sentenced to death by beheading!" Roderick turned to the executioner and nodded. The hooded soldier moved into place above Loretta's small body. In cowardice, I closed my eyes.

Within the darkness, I heard a cry from the mouth of the executioner and heard the axe coming down through the air. Suddenly, a loud clang echoed into the atmosphere, as if the weapon had struck metal. I heard a corporate gasp and opened my eyes to investigate.

Loretta was there, leaning over the block, her head still a part of her body. Slightly above her, was a glimmer of golden light. Suddenly, there was a flash, and a shining blade appeared from out of nowhere. It was floating in midair above my companion's head. The blade of the axe was stopped and crossed with the blade of the floating sword. The executioner, perplexed, tried to raise the axe but was unable to do so. He was frozen in place.

"Enough!" A loud booming voice erupted, splitting the atmosphere. The word sent pulses of energy into the crowd. Everyone was thrown backward from the force of the voice.

There was another flash, as the wielder of the sword was revealed. It was a large man wearing shining silver armor and draped in a white cloak with red, green, and blue trim along the bottom. Upon his face was a full, bushy black beard. My heart stopped as I saw the form of our guardian, Jeru.

Roderick motioned to the clerics along the marble steps and a magical noise filled the air. The dark cloaked figures vanished. Satisfied with their departure, Roderick moved towards Loretta. Jeru, sensing the deception, whipped around, quick as lightning, his blade cutting through the air. Before my nemesis could move, Jeru was facing him, his sword at Roderick's throat. "You have done enough for one day," the guardian spoke. I saw a look of horror overcome my enemy as he looked down at the glowing blade. Jeru nodded and moved back over to where Loretta was still positioned. He leaned down and gently lifted her shaking body to a standing position, whispering encouraging words in her ear.

In fury, Roderick extended his hand and spoke a word of magic. Out of his finger came a ball of fire. Jeru moved in front of Loretta and held up his hand. "Silence!" he shouted. All at once, the flaming mass stopped in midair, its motion ceased. The guardian breathed onto the flaming mass, making the element vanish! He looked intensely into the face of my nemesis.

"Do not do that again!" Jeru commanded Roderick. Suddenly, I saw my enemy collapse to the floor, shaking miserably in fear. Placing his hands to his temples, he rocked back and forth, begging Loretta's rescuer to have mercy on him. The guardian took a knee next to the trembling body and reached into his dark robes. He carefully removed *The Book of Esgar* and tucked it into his large belt. Jeru stood and looked at the soldiers near us. "Release them now and return their equipment!" Without hesitation, the soldiers took their hands off us and retreated to recover our belongings.

Jeru turned back to the nervous audience. "Here me now!" He raised a hand, and the crowd immediately ceased its commotion, focusing all their attention on the guardian. "Your cry of suffering has been heard. Aleph understands the pain you have gone through. Had you known the creator, you would have escaped or given your life freely. Because you did not, you fell prey to an unmerciful master. You became a slave, to be trafficked in this world at the pleasure of Baelor. I am here today to show you a more excellent way.

"Do not be fearful. Your creator knows how this is going to play out and has made provision even at the end." Jeru gestured toward us with his large hand. "Aleph has provided leaders who will care for you and protect you. They will not abuse you or sell you out for profit or ambition. They have been tried and tested, walking through the flames of tribulation. Have no fear in following them. Aleph has shown you a sign of his goodness by sparing the life of this young lady." He pointed to Loretta.

"Remember it well, for this world will undergo devastation that has not been seen in thousands of years. The fallen ones have been released. Our world is ending." Suddenly, the city began to shake around us. I saw sandstone buildings and spires across the landscape begin to crack and splinter. Jeru looked into the dark-clouded skies, searching for an answer. The atmosphere split as a horrifying roar sounded. Within the unholy discharge, I could hear the unmistakable sound of a deafening rattle.

CHAPTER
25

I stood above a desperate crowd that earlier cursed my companions and I to a gloomy death. It was ironic that we were now standing before them as their leaders. Panic seized the people, but they were frozen in place, unable to move from the fear that gripped them. They stared at me hoping for an answer. Instead of smothering them with false encouragement, I spoke the sobering truth.

"We are not safe. The sounds you hear are the Nephilim. These creatures are responsible for the destruction of Northcrest." A moan escaped from several members in the crowd. I raised a hand, asking for silence. "The only chance we have for survival is underground."

Merwin and Cal finished loading our recovered backpacks from the guards and stepped forward, lending their support. "If you want to live, you will follow these men. They will take you into the catacombs far beneath the city. If you choose to go your own way, you will die. This enemy will not accept surrender nor offer any quarter. They are tasked with your complete annihilation. We are now headed in the direction of refuge. Please, don't go home to pack anything. Stay with us, and we will get you to safety."

◇

As my brief speech concluded, I watched the entirety of the crowd surge behind Merwin and Cal, headed in the direction of the school. The clerics who were on the upper steps of the palace vanished the second Jeru appeared. I made a mental note to track down every one of those cursed devices that I could.

I gathered Loretta, Groth, and Lionel over to where Jeru and I were standing. Lionel looked behind him and pointed to the shaking body of Roderick. "What about this pile of buffalo dung?"

"He stays with us. I don't want him out of our sight."

"We ought to throw him off the outer wall," Lionel growled.

"Don't harm him. We need to source information from him." I looked over at Jeru, and he gave me an approving nod. "If you see anyone in the streets, beware. They may be clerics. Even though their ranks have been shaken, I don't think they are going to willingly surrender. Be wary of the soldiers as well. They seem to have fared better, but we still cannot trust them."

"You are right about that," Roderick spoke up from the ground. "This city is a prized possession of Baelor. We will die defending it!"

"You're going to die all right!" Groth moved to strangle Roderick. Jeru placed a hand on the brute's shoulder. Immediately, Groth ceased.

"Don't worry, my friend. I promise you; he will have his day." Groth looked down at the cowering body of Roderick and relented.

"It can't come soon enough!" Groth snapped, moving away from the nemesis.

Lionel tied Roderick and threw him onto the cart along with all our recovered equipment. I didn't want to give Groth a chance to murder the fiend when we weren't looking, so I made him ride a horse next to me. We weren't in the saddle for more than a second, when we felt another massive tremor under us. It was so heavy; the street began to crack.

Wasting no time, Cal whipped the reins from the front seat of the cart, and we were off. I looked above us to see a brilliant wisp of light against the darkened skies. Jeru was with us. Moving with haste down the stone streets, we dodged fissures as they appeared. The roaring and tremors were coming on stronger, with fewer intervals of silence between the contractions.

People were scurrying in terror all over the streets. We shouted for them to move out of the way as we hurried down the road. Our most straightforward path was blocked by debris from the quakes, forcing us to turn around and go another direction. We made our way down a narrow alley until we were stopped in our tracks by another obstruction. This time, it was an overturned cart blocking the way. I was about to instruct Groth to remove it when I saw five clerics come out from cover.

I heard Roderick shout from behind me. "Destroy them!" Words of magic were spoken. Fire and ice erupted from the cleric's hands. One fireball exploded to my right, causing my horse to panic. The animal neighed and bucked, throwing me off in the process. I hit the street, and pain shot into my side, as I landed on the injured half of my body. I lay there, awaiting another fireball to burn me alive.

"He's exposed! Finish him!" I heard Roderick scream from behind me. Within my peripheral vision, I saw a cleric separate himself, speaking a word of magic. I tucked myself into a ball and awaited my death.

Suddenly, I heard another sound, like a rushing wind coming from above. I saw a pillar of light crashing into the alley from the sky. The entire congregation of clerics were crushed under the weight of the light. As it dissipated, all that remained was a deep crater and the form of a guardian. The opposition was obliterated. Jeru pointed at me.

"Enough stalling. We need to get to the school, fast! They're coming!"

We were in a race against time. I was unsure of what Aleph wanted us to do when we got to the school, but I decided not to dwell on it. He needed us for a purpose, and that was good enough for me. Thinking was only going to slow me down. After another sharp turn, we passed Halvern's tavern. It was not much further from here.

When we pulled up to the school grounds, we were met with resistance. Cal and Merwin were halted in the street with a massive crowd behind them. About fifty soldiers and the group of clerics from our execution were on the front steps, hiding behind the massive columns. There was a good enough distance between us to dodge destruction spells, but they were keeping us from our goal, and that was not good. Every time we tried to take a step towards the school, the clerics would fire an attack.

Fear took ahold of the crowd around me, and several of them tried to rush the front door. The clerics made an example out of them, showing they would attack anyone who came near, including students! I jumped into the back of the cart, grabbing Roderick by the cloak.

"Tell them to stand down," I commanded.

"No," he replied with a cool smile.

"You would let these people die? If they stay out here, they don't stand a chance!"

"Not my problem!"

"You are a coward," I said incredulously. "You are nothing but a frightened weasel who thinks only of himself!" Lionel came to my rescue, pulling me off the man.

I jumped off the cart and looked in awe at the clerics. They left a trail of bodies all the way to the street. The people were huddled together, nervously murmuring their doubt. The students were cowering in fear, wondering what to do. I felt terrible for them. They had been deceived and now saw the truth. Their masters cared nothing for the people, and the trail of dead bodies clearly showed it. I met the eyes of students, begging me to help. My heart flooded with compassion. All I wanted to do was protect them and provide a way out.

In frustration, I looked skyward. Where had Jeru gone? Before the question could settle in my brain, I saw something falling from the sky. It floated down like a feather being whipped in the wind. As the object got closer, my heart leapt. It was a white cloak with green trim at the bottom! As it neared, I jumped up and grabbed it with my hands. The familiar fabric was soft and smooth. I didn't hesitate to put it around me. Suddenly, I heard several more sounds and looked up again. A multitude of the same white material was falling from the heavens, creating a stark contrast to the dismal skies.

As the cloaks fell within the crowd, I heard a clamor of confusion. Merwin jumped onto the cart and addressed everyone. "Have no fear! Put the cloaks on!" He led by example, wrapping himself in the protective material. "You see. Put it on like this." Before he could utter another word, he was hit directly by an electrical current that sent him flying off the cart. I screamed and ran over to see the still body of my brother in the street. Concerned citizens gathered around him as well. All was quiet.

Suddenly, Merwin jumped up and smiled. The crowd gave a sound of elation as they saw him whole and complete. "You see! These cloaks are a gift from Aleph! If you wear them, you will be safe from magic!" I heard a murmur as the crowd registered the information. They began moving around, grabbing the cloaks. I watched as the citizens, students, and several soldiers put them on. I leaned down and grabbed one, throwing it into Cal's hands. I didn't really care if Roderick got one. If he got hit by a rogue fireball, that was his problem.

In unison, we turned in the direction of the school. I looked around me at the people. There was fire in their eyes. The deception they were once under had passed, and they were ready for retribution. A loud war cry erupted from within the masses, and we charged the front doors of the school.

CHAPTER
26

As we clashed with the soldiers, we relied on our quick movements in hand-to-hand combat. I stayed close to Merwin and Lionel, because together we were a violent storm. Several soldiers charged us with their blades drawn. As one, we moved and dodged their attack. With a quick sweep of the leg, my enemy was on his back. I followed up with a vicious throat attack, using my knee. The soldier gasped as I cut off his air supply.

I took his sword and continued the battle. Merwin and Lionel took the same strategy as I. We were now armed with swords and moving through the battlefield, strategically heading toward the columns. The soldiers tried to waylay us with an assault from the sides, but we were too quick. We moved gracefully, parrying their attacks, and responding with our own. The soldiers were soon disarmed, unconscious, or dead.

We made short work of any soldiers trying to take advantage of the unarmed citizens. Before long, the soldiers understood the gravity of the situation. They gathered and met us in the middle of the school courtyard. There were ten against three. This time, the clerics assisted by blasting the ground with magic spells, hoping to cause a diversion and weaken our defenses. It was a sound strategy that nearly took us out. However, we worked together and were able to lay our enemy down. When the last body hit the sand, blowing up a dust cloud, I saw Cal bringing Roderick towards me.

His eyes as were full of hatred as he scanned the battlefield. His final effort to overcome us failed. "It's over, Roderick. Tell your clerics to surrender."

"Why would I do that?"

"Save the last bit of humanity you have for your men! Tell them to stand down. I give you my word, they will not be harmed." Roderick took a moment to look into my eyes and moved slowly toward the school. He lifted his hands and addressed his clerics.

"Don't be afraid. They will not harm us. They gave me their word that if we surrender, all will be well. I ask you to listen and obey me." Roderick turned around and nodded his head towards me. "Men...I command you...to unleash hell!!!" Suddenly, Roderick ducked and rolled towards the school. The clerics came out and shouted arcane words in unison. An eruption accompanied the spells that emerged from their hands. They kept it up until Roderick was behind the safety of the columns. I heard a commotion from the enemy followed by a ringing sound, as if a metal object was dropped on the ground. Realization struck—they were trying to escape!

"Don't let them leave!" I shouted to my companions. Together, we charged the front doors of the school. As we hit the steps, I heard chaotic voices crying out words of magic. There was a loud, mystical noise, and all but one of the clerics vanished! The final cleric screamed in panic as we approached, trying to cast one last spell. Before it could be released, Lionel ran the cleric through with his sword.

The battle out front of the school ended, but the roar of the Nephilim continued relentlessly. Everyone was shaken and afraid, so we gathered the people into groups before entering the school. With a little organization, the crowd was calm enough for us to safely move inside.

I was the first to enter and immediately greeted by several teachers. Liam stood at the front and came to shake my hand.

"I don't know who you are, but I want you to know we have no respect for magic and couldn't care less if..." I cut Liam off mid-sentence.

"We will have time for discussion later, my good sir. For now, we must get to safety. Please help me usher the people through the supply closet door." The elderly teacher gathered the faculty, giving them instructions. They fanned out down the hall, keeping the crowd in a nice, orderly line.

By the time we safely escorted them through the door and onto the massive staircase, the roar and tremors were constant. The sounds were coming from all around us, making the sandstone walls shake with vibration. We were running out of time, so I asked Groth, Loretta, and Cal to stay with the people. They reluctantly agreed and blessed us before we made our way back inside.

We went through the school without hesitation, climbing the back stairwell to the fourth floor and taking a quick left through the door leading to the bell tower. As we came through the trapdoor, into view of the city, I could see fiery clouds above us. A deep looming shadow covered the entire city.

"What do we do now?" I heard Merwin cry out.

"I have no idea," I responded.

Looking into the horizon, I saw a massive sandstorm begin to form outside the city walls. As minutes passed, the storm grew larger, stretching itself in all directions. The entire city was surrounded by an unnatural cloud of sand. Looking below, I saw a handful of people scurrying about. Thankfully, most of the city's inhabitants were safely underground. All that remained were deviants and soldiers upon the formidable walls. They were now tasked with defending the city against a force that was undefeatable. None of them would survive this day.

The roaring stopped, and then there was silence. The air was still, and nothing moved. I placed my red dyed hands on the sandstone railing and waited nervously for what was going to happen next. Suddenly, a rattle ripped through the silence, an unnerving staccato beat. The rhythm was contrary to the pounding in my heart, making my head split with pain. Struggling to stand, I forced myself to look out. I felt a tap on my shoulder as Merwin handed me a spyglass.

"Snagged it from a toppled cart in the street. Thought we might need it." I nodded my thanks and put the piece up to my eye.

Marching through a wall of dust and sand, I saw a monstrous form. The being stood at least a hundred feet tall. Its lumbering gait made the earth shake with every step. In appearance, the giant was something out of a nightmare. Its head was swollen with painful-looking horns protruding from the top of its forehead at random angles. The horns were surrounded by a mane of dirty, shaggy hair that fell from the edges of its skull. The texture of its skin was dry and coarse like the surface of the desert wasteland we recently traversed. Its flesh was black as pitch and seemed to repel the light. Cracks and fissures ran the length of its arms and legs, glowing like hot magma rock.

Within its massive hands, it held the bones of a creature long extinct. The Fallen One was banging the bones together without any type of rhythm, creating the jarring rattle that haunted me for the past week. Even at this distance, I could feel it in my chest.

The Nephilim came closer, with eyes glowing red, like the one who summoned it—Lucien. Unlike the confident gaze of the chief messenger, its eyes were drawn and withered, like it was sad and confused. When I investigated them, my mind became cloudy. All I could see was the darkness of the eternal void.

The legs of the being were almost human, carrying it along in a shuffling, measured pace. Its feet seemed not to feel the ground at all, crushing boulders into dust while claws at the end of its toes scored deep, hideous gashes in the earth. Its chest and torso were a chaotic mess, with numerous scars glowing dull orange under its thick, black skin. The creature wore no clothing save for an iron garment of some type it wore around its waist for modesty's sake.

I put the spyglass down, taking in the surroundings from my natural viewpoint. I lost my breath as I counted not one, but fifty Nephilim heading towards the city from all directions. In an unholy, synchronous motion, they moved toward Hammerfist. I quickly put the spyglass back up, focusing my attention on the fallen beings. As I did so, all the Nephilim stopped. I kept my gaze on the creature and waited, holding my breath. I saw the being turn its head and look directly at me with its somber eyes. It could see me! It knew I was here! My heart felt a spasm of inward pain as I met the eyes of the creature. Suddenly, the entire world around me vanished!

I was falling through an endless abyss of darkness. I was alone, and there was nobody—nothing but emptiness. My heart pounded as I realized I couldn't feel Aleph. He was not here. This place was absent from Him, absent from His light. The pain I felt was too much for words. I felt unmade, uncreated. I felt separated. I felt...lost.

Within the void, I heard a voice echo. "I'm sorry." The words were simple and primitive, sounding like a child who disobeyed his father. "I'm sorry." The voice sounded again. A wave of emotion flooded me. I felt remorse for something I did. I told a secret I wasn't supposed to tell. I was ashamed of my actions and wanted to apologize, but I couldn't. I was alone. There was nobody to apologize to. There was nothing except the eternal void.

Suddenly, the chaotic world swirled back into focus. I gasped as my brothers grabbed me, keeping me from falling off the bell tower. I heard the spyglass drop and shatter underneath my feet. Slowly, I turned and saw my brothers looking at me in curiosity. All I could do was shake my head and gasp. They held me close and comforted me, telling me it was okay.

Abruptly, the booming voice of Jeru sounded from behind. We turned in unison and gave our full attention to the guardian. "The Nephilim will forever be without knowledge. They are separated from the presence of Aleph. They have no memory of his goodness. The only thing they know is the shame of their actions. There will never be forgiveness and absent from the comfort of Aleph, they have been filled with Baelor's rage."

I looked back to the horizon and saw the Nephilim continue to approach. "You have seen their turmoil. Aleph has given you a glimpse of their suffering. They have been trapped for a long time and are here now to destroy this world."

"How do we stop it? How can we stop them?"

"You cannot. Only the audible voice of Aleph can stop the destruction."

"Why doesn't he return?" Why does he allow this to happen?" I saw Jeru's face cloud over with thought. "Tell me!"

"The veil has not been lifted."

"Stop talking in riddles. Please, speak plainly!" I commanded the guardian.

"We don't have time for this, Anlace. There is more at stake than you can imagine."

Suddenly, there appeared in the skies above us thousands of dark creatures with wings and hideous bodies. An ear-piercing screech emitted from the creatures, forcing us to clamp our hands over our ears. After the sound passed, I looked dazedly into the eyes of the guardian.

"You don't understand the gravity of the war we are in." Jeru stated quickly. "Daeric has opened the door and released another adversary."

There was a brilliant flash of light, and above us appeared thousands of cloaked guardians. A battle had begun in the skies above. "I promise you, Anlace, I will tell you more at another time. The Revealing has begun. Eternals are battling openly in the sight of humans now. Nothing is hidden, and soon all will be revealed, including the physical presence of Aleph and Baelor! I must go to battle now. Do not move from this spot! You will be safe here!"

My brothers and I watched as the guardians and messengers waged war. I heard otherworldly shrieks and screams as both guardians and messengers were slain, falling from the sky. It was difficult to keep up with the amount of activity above me, so I turned my attention to the Nephilim.

They reached the perimeter and began pounding the stone with their hands and feet. The walls fell like castles made of sand. It didn't take them long to make their way into the city. I shrieked as I heard the cries of people and soldiers who had not taken precautions. I was turning in all directions, watching as one building after another was pounded and stomped flat until all that remained was a pile of rubble. The Nephilim went from one building to the next, fanning out, making sure not to miss any structure. The city of Hammerfist in all its beautiful glory was suffering the relentless power of the Fallen Ones. Dust and sand rose as buildings fell. The Nephilim roared and beat the structures with their ancient bones until there was nothing left.

Foolishly, I asked Lionel and Merwin what we should do. The elder responded with a resounding slap across my face. "How long must I suffer your lack of belief? Trust Aleph! His guardian said to wait here." I rubbed my jaw and looked at Merwin.

"I trust Aleph. No matter what, I'm staying here, sir." I took a step back from my brothers and continued to witness the carnage all around me. Looking up we watched the battle in the sky. Guardians and messengers were everywhere, fighting with an intensity not seen in this world, until now.

I was in a daze. The sound of war was everywhere, the entire city had been destroyed. The only building left was the one we stood upon. The Nephilim had us surrounded. As they stepped toward us, I looked one last time into their gloomy eyes, feeling a deep pity for the fallen beings. A roar exploded into the atmosphere as a creature raised its fist, preparing to pound it into the side of the building.

CHAPTER
27

The Nephilim were unwavering in their purpose. I shouted to Lionel and Merwin to move away from the edge. The monsters stood fifty feet from our location. They were pummeling the rooftop and walls of the school, desperate to see it fall, but for a mysterious reason, the stone held. Aleph placed his protection over the building, and there was nothing they could do to bring it down.

Their frustrated roars echoed throughout the land. They pounded harder, sending us off our feet. Merwin fell back over the edge of the bell tower. In desperation, he lashed out and wrapped his hand around the railing. Lionel and I stumbled over, grabbing his arms. Merwin hung helplessly over several of the monstrous forms. Their hands reached up to grasp his legs and pull him apart; however, they were several feet away from getting a firm grip. They cried out with a frantic roar. I looked down at their distracted faces, and my heart felt a stab of pain. I felt sorry for these poor creatures. They were completely lost, with no hope of redemption.

Lionel shouted to me, and I returned once again to the chaos. Merwin was screaming at us to help him. Lionel and I got a solid grip around my brother's arm and pulled.

After several good tugs, Merwin was standing next to us, until a tremor knocked us off our feet again. I knew Aleph's protection was over the building, but I wasn't sure how much more my frail body could take of the constant pounding. My legs felt like jelly, and my balance was shaken. The barrage continued. One creature hammered the building, roaring until the frustration was too much. Exhausted, it slunk away from the school and retreated to let another have a turn.

Suddenly, a horn sounded, drawing my attention away from the nightmare in front of me. A group of guardians flew full speed in our direction. They slowed their approach, drawing their swords as they came within striking distance of the hulking enemy. In a flurry of combat, the entire company of guardians attacked the Nephilim.

Sounds of chaos erupted as the fallen creatures lashed out with their arms and feet, trying to destroy the guardians. The size of the Nephilim dwarfed the guardians, making it look as though they were trying to swat flies. All at once, a brilliant flash of light leveled the playing field as a group of guardians magnified in size until they were standing toe to toe, looking the monstrous creatures in the eyes. The battle continued as several of the massive guardians surrounded the Nephilim and struck with flaming swords, releasing a bellowing cry of pain as they cut into Nephilim flesh. Instead of continuing the fight, the Nephilim roared and ran away like children crying about an injury and needing comfort from a parent. After an intense display of combat, the guardians ejected the fallen ones from the city.

Seeing that the battle was now hopeless, the creatures left, fleeing in all directions. We watched in curiosity, hoping they wouldn't turn back for another attempt at the guardians.

The battle above us continued, and our rescuers dismissed themselves, returning to assist their company against the messengers.

My brothers and I were anxious to leave the bell tower but decided we would stay until the fight was over. Aleph's protection kept us from being destroyed. The school was the only building in the entire city that stood. It was hard to tell who was winning the battle above us. Guardians and messengers fell out of the sky as both sides suffered loss. This war was not going to end today. When both sides lost too many to continue, the sounds of battle finally ceased.

We sat in silence, observing the shifting weather. The afternoon sun broke through the ominous gray clouds and brought warm light that radiated the stone of the bell tower, the only building in the city left standing. We peaked over the edge of the railing to observe the bodies of guardians and messengers left behind, but to our amazement, they were gone! There was no evidence of an eternal battle that was fought above the city. All that remained were piles of rubble and destroyed buildings as far as the eye could see.

My brothers looked at me and shook their heads in disbelief. There were no words that could describe the emotions pouring through us. Without another thought, Lionel leaned down to open the trap door. We followed his lead and quickly moved into the school's interior.

Everyone was safe. Hundreds of feet below the surface, Loretta, Groth and Cal did an admirable job keeping everyone calm. They reported lots of panic and even an occasional vomit as the vibrations took hold of the citizens. However, everyone was sound. Once we debriefed the citizens of Hammerfist about the situation, bracing them for the destruction they were about to experience, we exited the school through the front door.

As we emerged from darkness, into the light of the afternoon, a loud groan escaped the mouths of the people. I could sympathize. Everything they owned was now lost. It would have to be a fresh start for them—for all of us. We would have to somehow rebuild our lives that suddenly came crashing down.

My companions and I sat within the courtyard of the school under a large tree and met with the people. They came asking questions and begging for help. We took time with each family and encouraged them to seek Aleph in their trouble and lay all their hurts and pains down before him. For the students and those who were trapped in sorcery, they were separated and being held on the fourth floor.

A group of soldiers who left Baelor's service to join us, were useful for keeping them under strict watch. The last thing I wanted to do was give the students any sense of imprisonment, but they needed redemption from years of torment. They were slaves in a system of control. Healing was not going to come overnight. But thankfully, Aleph had a vast amount to give. He would be patient and kind in His service to those students, and in time, they would be redeemed from the deception of Baelor. Regardless, my companions and I agreed never to remove our protective cloaks and to sleep with one eye open. We would be vigilant and not fall into complacency.

◇

It was a long day, the first of many. I was in the headmaster's room resting my feet and preparing to lie down for a short nap. As I placed my head on the pillow, I saw a large form sitting away from me, in a chair across the room. I bolted upright, reaching for my scabbard. Before I could draw, I heard the voice of my friend and guardian.

"Blessings, Father Anlace. I bid you favor and a warm welcome from Aleph, the most high!"

I jumped out of bed and ran over to the guardian. He rose and met me with a warm embrace. "You're alive!"

"Yes. Indeed, I am!"

"I was afraid I would never see you again."

"And here I am."

"I don't know what to do, Jeru. The people are looking to me for answers, and I have none to give."

"It's okay for you to feel this way. The world is being shaken to its core, and the only answers for a hopeless world are found in Aleph. Remember the vision, Anlace. He has placed you upon His throne. The battlefield represents the world. The piles of rubble are the cities. Aleph is allowing this world to be shaken to rubble. Within this destroyed world, He has chosen His leaders. They are His and for this purpose He has placed you upon a throne and given you His mantle of authority. You will now lead these people during the darkest of days.

"Hammerfist is only one of many cities that will undergo the same fate. From the ashes of this war will rise a leader for each of these cities. You are not alone, Anlace. Take comfort in knowing that. Aleph has many leaders He is raising up. You have now seen the enemy and the extent of this eternal battle. Take this knowledge and lead your people. Rule Hammerfist, and await the return of Aleph."

"What about Daeric and Esgar?"

"They will be with Him when He returns. Only a human can bring the physical form of Aleph into our world. It has been written this way since the beginning of time. It has only happened once before when Rian walked back through the door of Aleph's temple. It will happen again, and we will see the creator face to face."

"What about Baelor?" I saw Jeru's face cloud over with a shadow as I mentioned the name of the enemy.

"When Aleph returns, so will Baelor." I let that word sink into my heart. It would keep me sober as I walked through many trials in the years ahead.

"What do I do now?"

"Rest, my friend, and as Aleph leads you, write down everything you have experienced. The recollection of these events will cleanse you and help you understand in a greater depth what Aleph is trying to speak. Remember, Anlace. Aleph is never silent and is always nearby. He is the one who sees and his every thought about you is love."

I said goodbye as we stood on a balcony overlooking the open courtyard. I gave the guardian the best hug I could and bid him farewell. In the wisps of brilliant light, he shot into the sky. I took a deep breath and walked back into my quarters. I sat down at my desk in the headmaster's room, next to the fireplace.

Lying neatly on top of the writing table was a familiar looking book. I carefully opened the first page and saw the distinct handwriting of Esgar. I smiled and began to turn the pages until I made it all the way to the end. With a gentle exhale, I opened a drawer to my right and tucked the princess's chronicle safely away, next to my own personal testimony of Iska. Opening the drawer on my left revealed an empty journal towards the back. As light began to fade outside, I moved my pen over the first page. Before I could finish a sentence, Loretta bounced in and addressed me.

"Evening, sir." Seeing her intrusion, she covered her hand over her mouth. "So sorry...did I interrupt you?" I looked at her with my mouth slightly open. "Anyway, I wanted to get your opinion on dinner this evening. Groth and Cal were able to kill a bunch of desert buffalo, and I wasn't quite sure the best way to prepare the meal. Did you want it over the open fire, or on the grill? Should I use some spice or keep it normal for those with a soft palate? Should we tenderize it for the kids or let them chew until it disintegrates?" I sat back, closed my eyes, and smiled.

"Thank you," I said softly to Aleph and then turned my attention back to my friend. "Why don't we go ask everyone and figure it out together?"

"Oh, great idea, sir!" she replied. Without another word, I closed the tome I was writing in and focused my attention where I was needed. Aleph gave me the gift of a new family, and I wasn't going to take it for granted another day in my life.

The End of Book II

Daeric and Esgar will return in

Eternals of Shalistar
THE VEIL OF ALEPH

ABOUT THE AUTHOR

Stephen Early is an enthusiastic entertainer who has spent a lifetime honing his creative skills in writing, voice acting, presentations and theater arts. He has been a lifelong fan of the science fiction/fantasy genre and grew up reading the classics like The Lord of the Rings, The Chronicles of Narnia, Treasure Island, The Adventures of Tom Sawyer and many more. As a humble servant, Stephen's deepest passion is showing youth and children alike how to dream in a world full of adventure. He lives in Texas with his beautiful wife Esther and their four lovely daughters. For more information on this book series, go to eternalsofshalistar. com. You can also follow us on Facebook or on Instagram at #eternalsofshalistar.

Made in United States
Orlando, FL
27 August 2022